GET A
LIFE,
CHLOE
BROWN

GET A
LIFE,
CHLOE
BROWN

A Novel

TALIA HIBBERT

A V O N

An Imprint of HarperCollinsPublishers

GET A LIFE, CHLOE BROWN. Copyright © 2019 by Talia Hibbert. All rights reserved. Printed in the United States of America. No part of this book may be used or reproduced in any manner whatsoever without written permission except in the case of brief quotations embodied in critical articles and reviews. For information, address HarperCollins Publishers, 195 Broadway, New York, NY 10007.

Designed by Diahann Sturge

ISBN 978-0-06-294120-6

This is for my mother, who did whatever it took.

ACKNOWLEDGMENTS

There are so many people I have to thank for this book. I'm about to sound like an overenthusiastic starlet accepting her first Oscar, and I don't even care, because this was truly a team effort. Some of the people I want to thank probably don't realize they were on my team—but you were, guys. You shared your loveliness with the world, and I absorbed it like sunlight, which means you're part of the team. Surprise!

So, where to begin? At the beginning, I suppose. Thank you, Frances Annie Nixon. I wish you had lived long enough to see your name in my book. Sometimes I imagine you recommending this story to your uptight friends, then cackling when they complain about the sex. I miss you.

Mum: thank you for reading to me, even when people told you not to bother. As always, everyone was wrong and you were right. Now you have it in writing. Please don't abuse this power.

Truly, my tiny troublemaker: you're the only one who doesn't judge when I talk to imaginary people. I appreciate you.

Thank you to Sam for picking up whenever I called, answering whatever random, contextless question I asked, and not being offended when I hung up without saying good-bye.

To Dr. Griffiths, who looked me in the eye and said, "First things first: I believe you." I can't explain what you did for me that day. Thank you.

KJ Charles, without you and your never-ending well of kindness and support, I probably wouldn't be in this position—so thank you, thank you, thank you. Courtney Miller-Callihan, my wonderful agent, thank you for believing in me and for handling my constant social awkwardness. Thank you, Nicole Fischer, for turning my sorta-kinda story into an actual, honest-to-god, decent book. And thank you, Ainslie Paton, Therese Beharrie, Em Ali, Charlotte Stein, and all the other authors and friends who ever put my mind to rest.

Orla, Divya, Michal, Maz, and Laila: whenever I'm stressed, you guys appear like tiny sunshines, as if you have some kind of sixth sense. Thank you for making me smile. Thank you to Mrs. Smith, Mrs. Marriott, Mr. Marriott (no relation!), and Mr. Cleveley—and no, I can't use any of your first names. It's not allowed.

Thank you to Avon for being all, "Hey, yeah, you can write this book for us." I almost passed out, but still, much appreciated.

Finally, thank you to everyone who told me that I'd never succeed. You guys make me feel like a triumphant R & B songstress, and the closer I can get to Beyoncé, the better.

AUTHOR'S NOTE

This story touches on the process of healing after an abusive relationship. If this is a topic that you're sensitive to, please be aware. I hope I have treated the issue, my characters, and you, the reader, gently.

PROLOGUE

Once upon a time, Chloe Brown died.

Nearly.

It happened on a Tuesday afternoon, of course. Disturbing things always seemed to happen on Tuesdays. Chloe suspected that day of the week was cursed, but thus far, she'd only shared her suspicions via certain internet forums—and with Dani, the weirdest of her two very weird little sisters. Dani had told Chloe that she was cracked, and that she should try positive affirmations to rid herself of her negative weekday energy.

So when Chloe heard shouts and the screech of tires, and looked to her right, and found a shiny, white Range Rover heading straight for her, her first ridiculous thought was: *I'll die on a Tuesday, and Dani will have to admit that I was right all along.*

But in the end, Chloe didn't actually die. She wasn't even horribly injured—which was a relief, because she spent enough time in hospitals as it was. Instead, the Range Rover flew past her and slammed into the side of a coffee shop. The drunk driver's head-on collision with a brick wall missed being a head-on collision with a flesh-and-blood Chloe by approximately three feet. Metal crunched like paper. The middle-aged lady in the driver's seat slumped against an airbag, her crisp, blond bob swinging. Bystanders swarmed and there were shouts to call an ambulance.

Chloe stared, and stared, and stared.

People buzzed by her, and time ticked on, but she barely noticed. Her mind flooded with irrelevant data, as if her head were a trash folder. She wondered how much the repairs to the coffee shop would cost. She wondered if insurance would cover it, or if the driver would have to. She wondered who had cut the lady's hair, because it was a beautiful job. It remained relatively sleek and stylish, even when she was hauled out of her car and onto a gurney.

Eventually, a man touched Chloe's shoulder and asked, "Are you okay, my darling?"

She turned and saw a paramedic with a kind, lined face and a black turban. "I believe I'm in shock," she said. "Could I have some chocolate? Green and Black's. Sea salt is my favorite, but the eighty-five percent dark probably has greater medicinal properties."

The paramedic chuckled, put a blanket around her shoulders, and said, "Would a cuppa do, Your Maj?"

"Oh, yes please." Chloe followed him to the back of his ambulance. Somewhere along the way, she realized she was shaking so hard that it was a struggle to walk. With a skill borne of years of living in her highly temperamental body, she gritted her teeth and forced one foot in front of the other.

When they finally reached the ambulance, she sat down carefully because it wouldn't do to collapse. If she did, the paramedic would start asking questions. Then he might want to check her over. *Then* she'd have to tell him about all her little irregularities, and why they were nothing to worry about, and they'd both be here all day. Adopting her firmest I-am-very-healthy-and-in-control tone, she asked briskly, "Will the lady be all right?"

"The driver? She'll be fine, love. Don't you worry about that."

Muscles she hadn't realized were tense suddenly relaxed.

In the end, after two cups of tea and some questions from the police, Chloe was permitted to finish her Tuesday-afternoon walk. No further near-death experiences occurred, which was excellent, because if they had, she'd probably have done something embarrassing, like cry.

She entered her family home via the north wing and skulked to the kitchen in search of fortifying snacks. Instead, she found her grandmother Gigi clearly waiting for her. Gigi whirled around with a swish of her floor-length, violet robe—the one Chloe had given her a few months ago on Gigi's fourth (or was it fifth?) seventieth birthday.

"Darling," she gasped, her sparkling, kitten-heeled mules clacking against the tiles. "You look so . . . peaky." From Gigi, who was both a concerned grandparent and a painfully beautiful ragtime legend, this was a grave statement indeed. "Where *were* you? You've been ages, and you wouldn't answer your phone. I was quite worried."

"Oh, God, I'm so sorry." Chloe had left hours ago for the latest of her irregularly scheduled walks—*scheduled* because her physiotherapist insisted she take them, *irregular* because her chronically ill body often vetoed things. She was usually back within thirty minutes, so it was no wonder Gigi had panicked. "You didn't call my parents, did you?"

"Of course not. I presumed, if you'd had a wobble, that you'd collect yourself shortly and command a passing stranger to find you a taxi home."

A *wobble* was the delicate phrase Gigi used for the times when Chloe's body simply gave up on life. "I didn't have a wobble. I'm feeling quite well, actually." *Now, anyway.* "But there was . . . a car accident."

Gigi managed to stiffen and gracefully take a seat at the marble kitchen island simultaneously. "You weren't hurt?"

"No. A lady crashed her car right in front of me. It was all very dramatic. I've been drinking tea from Styrofoam cups."

Gigi peered at Chloe with the feline eyes that lesser mortals tended to fall into. "Would you like some Xanax, darling?"

"Oh, I couldn't. I don't know how it would react with my medication."

"Of course, of course. Ah! I know. I'll call Jeremy and tell him it's an emergency." Jeremy was Gigi's therapist. Gigi didn't strictly *need* therapy, but she was fond of Jeremy and believed in preventive measures.

Chloe blinked. "I don't think that's necessary."

"I quite disagree," Gigi said. "Therapy is always necessary." She pulled out her phone and made the call, sashaying to the other side of the kitchen. Her mules clicked against the tiles again as she purred, "Jeremy, darling! How *are* you? How is Cassandra?"

These were all perfectly ordinary noises. And yet, without warning, they triggered something catastrophic in Chloe's head.

Gigi's *click, click, click* merged with the *tick, tick, tick* of the vast clock on the kitchen wall. The sounds grew impossibly loud, oddly chaotic, until it seemed like a tumble of boulders had fallen inside Chloe's head. She squeezed her eyes shut—wait, what did her eyes have to do with her hearing?—and, in the darkness she'd created, a memory arose: that crisp, blond bob swinging. The way it remained so smooth and glossy against the black leather of the gurney.

Drunk, the nice paramedic had said, sotto voce. That's what they suspected. The lady had been drunk in the middle of the afternoon, had mounted a pavement and plowed into a building, and Chloe . . .

Chloe had been standing right there. Because she walked at the same time of day, so as not to interrupt her work routine. Because she always took the same route, for efficiency's sake. Chloe had been standing *right there.*

She was too hot, sweating. Dizzy. Had to sit down, right now, so she wouldn't fall and crack her head like an egg against the marble tiles. From out of nowhere she remembered her mother saying, *We should change the floors. These fainting spells are getting out of hand. She'll hurt herself.*

But Chloe had insisted there was no need. She'd promised to be careful, and by God, she'd kept her promise. Slowly, slowly, she sank to the ground. Put her clammy palms against the cool tiles. Breathed in. Breathed out. Breathed in.

Breathed out, her whisper like cracking glass, "If I had died today, what would my eulogy say?"

This mind-blowing bore had zero friends, hadn't traveled in a decade despite plenty of opportunity, liked to code on the weekends, and never did anything that wasn't scheduled in her planner. Don't cry for her; she's in a better place now. Even Heaven can't be that dull.

That's what the eulogy would say. Perhaps someone especially cutting and awful, like Piers Morgan, would read it out on the radio.

"Chloe?" Gigi called. "Where have you—? Oh, there you are. Is everything all right?"

Lying bodily on the floor and gulping air like a dying fish, Chloe said brightly, "Fine, thank you."

"Hmm," Gigi murmured, slightly dubious, but not overly concerned. "Perhaps I'll have Jeremy call us back. Jeremy, my dear, could you possibly . . . ?" Her voice faded as she wandered away.

Chloe rested her hot cheek against the cold tiles and tried not to add more insults to her own imaginary eulogy. If she were in a twee sort of musical—the kind her youngest sister, Eve, adored—this would be her rock-bottom moment. She'd be a few scenes away from an epiphany and an uplifting song about determination and self-belief. Perhaps she should take a leaf from those musicals' collective book.

"Excuse me, universe," she whispered to the kitchen floor. "When you almost murdered me today—which was rather brutal, by the way, but I can respect that—were you trying to tell me something?"

The universe, very enigmatically, did not respond.

Someone else, unfortunately, did.

"*Chloe!*" her mother all but shrieked from the doorway. "What are you doing on the floor?! Are you ill? Garnet, get off the phone and get over here! Your granddaughter is *unwell!*"

Oh dear. Her moment of communion with the universe rudely interrupted, Chloe hauled herself into a sitting position. Strangely, she was now feeling much better. Perhaps because she had recognized and accepted the universe's message.

It was time, clearly, to get a life.

"No, no, my darling, don't move." Joy Matalon-Brown's fine-boned face was tight with panic as she issued the nervous order, her tawny skin pale. It was a familiar sight. Chloe's mother ran a successful law firm with her twin sister, Mary, lived her life with almost as much logic and care as Chloe, and had spent years learning her daughter's symptoms and coping mechanisms. Yet she was still thrust into full-blown panic by the slightest hint of sickness or discomfort. It was, quite frankly, exhausting.

"Don't fuss over her, Joy, you know she can't stand it."

"So I should ignore the fact that she was lying on the floor like a corpse?!"

Ouch.

As her mother and grandmother bickered over her head, Chloe decided the first universe-mandated change in her life would be her living quarters.

The mammoth family home was suddenly feeling rather snug.

CHAPTER ONE

Two Months Later

Oh, you are a gem, Red."

Redford Morgan attempted a cheerful grin, which wasn't easy when he was elbow deep in an octogenarian's toilet bowl. "Just doing my job, Mrs. Conrad."

"You're the best superintendent we've ever had," she cooed from the bathroom doorway, clasping one wrinkled hand to her bony chest. Her shock of white hair fairly quivered with emotion. Bit of a drama queen, she was, bless her.

"Thanks, Mrs. C," he said easily. "You're a doll." *Now, if you'd just stop shoving bollocks down your loo, we'd be best mates.* This was the third time in a month he'd been called to flat 3E for plumbing issues, and frankly, he was getting tired of Mrs. Conrad's shit. Or rather, of her grandsons'.

Red's rubber-gloved hand finally emerged from the toilet's depths, clutching a soaking-wet clump of paper towel. He unwrapped the little parcel to reveal . . . "This your vegetable cas-serole, Mrs. C?"

She blinked owlishly at him, then squinted. "Well, I'm sure I've no idea. Where *are* my spectacles?" She turned as if to hunt them down.

"No, don't bother," he sighed. He knew full well it was vegeta-ble casserole, just like it had been last time, and the time before that. As he disposed of the clump and peeled off his gloves, he said gently, "You need to have a word with those lads of yours. They're flushing their dinner."

"*What?*" she gasped, clearly affronted. "Noooo. No, no, no. Not my Felix and Joseph. They never would! They aren't waste-ful boys, and they love my dinners."

"I bet they do," he said slowly, "but . . . well, Mrs. C, every time I come over here, I find a little parcel of broccoli and mushrooms clogging your pipes."

There was a beat of silence as Mrs. Conrad grappled with that information. "Oh," she whispered. He'd never heard so much dejection in a single word. She blinked rapidly, her thin lips pursing, and Red's heart lurched as he realized she was trying not to cry. Holy fucking hell. He couldn't deal with crying women. If she dropped a single tear, he'd be here all night, eating bowls of vegetable casserole with enthusiasm and sparkling compliments.

Please don't cry. I get off in ten minutes and I really fucking hate broccoli. Please don't cry. Please don't—

She turned away just as the first sob wracked her thin shoulders.

Sigh.

"Come on, Mrs. C, don't be upset." Awkwardly, he peeled off his gloves and went to the sink to wash his hands. "They're just kids. Everyone knows kids have as much sense as the average goat."

Mrs. Conrad let out a little burble of laughter and turned to face him again, dabbing at her eyes with a hankie. Old people always had hankies. They hid them on their bodies like ninjas with throwing stars. "You're right, of course. It's just . . . Well, I thought that casserole was their favorite." She sniffled and shook her head. "But it doesn't matter."

Judging by the wobble in her voice, it really did.

"I bet it's a damned good casserole," he said, because he had the biggest fucking mouth on planet earth.

"Do you think so?"

"I know so. You have the look of a woman who knows her way around the kitchen." He had no idea what that meant, but it sounded good.

And clearly, Mrs. Conrad liked it, because her cheeks flushed and she made a high, tinkling sound that might have been a giggle. "Oh, Red. Do you know, I happen to have some on the go right now."

Of *course* she did. "Is that right?"

"Yes! Would you like to try some? After all your hard work, the least I can do is feed you."

Say no. Say you have Friday-night plans. Say you ate five beefsteaks for lunch. "I'd love to," he said, and smiled. "Just let me go home and get cleaned up."

It took him thirty minutes to shower and change in his own flat, down on the ground floor. Came with the job. Since he led a life of daring excitement these days, he swapped his charcoal overalls for—*drumroll, please*—his navy blue overalls, fresh out the washer. Truth be told, he had no idea what he was supposed to wear for dinner with an old lady, but his usual shit-kicker boots and old leathers didn't seem quite right.

It was only as he locked his front door that it occurred to Red—this whole situation might not be quite right. Was he supposed to have dinner with tenants? Was that allowed? He didn't see the harm in it, but he was fairly new to this superintendent lark, and he wasn't exactly qualified. Just to be sure, he pulled out his phone and fired off a text to Vik, the landlord—and the mate who'd given him this job.

Can I have dinner with the nice old lady in 3E?

Vik's reply came fast as ever.

Whatever gets you going, mate. I don't judge.

Red huffed out a laugh, rolling his eyes as he put his phone away. And then, out of nowhere, he heard it.

Or rather, *her.*

Chloe Brown.

". . . see you for brunch, if I can," she was saying. Her voice was sharp and expensive, like someone had taught a diamond how to speak. The sound scrambled his mind, her crisp accent reminding him of people and places he'd rather forget. Of a different time and a different woman, one who'd clutched her silver spoon in one manicured hand and squeezed his heart tight in the other.

Chloe's husky timbre and the memories it triggered were the only warnings he received before rounding a corner and coming face-to-face with the woman herself. Or rather, face-to-throat. As in, she was right fucking there, and they collided, and, *somehow*, her face slammed into his throat.

Which hurt. A lot.

The impact also did something terrible to his airflow. He sucked in a breath, choked on it, and reached for her at the same time. That last part was an automatic reflex: he'd bumped into someone, so now it was his job to hold that someone steady. Except, of course, this wasn't just *anyone*. It was Chloe whose waist was soft under his hands. Chloe who smelled like a garden after a spring shower. Chloe who was now shoving him away like he had a communicable disease and spluttering, "Oh, my—what—? Get off!"

Cute as a button, but her tone cut like a knife. He released her before she had an embolism, wincing when his callused hands caught on the pastel wool of her cardigan. She stumbled back as if he might attack at any moment, watching him with flinty suspicion. She always looked at him like that—as if he was thirty seconds away from murdering her and wearing her skin. She'd treated him like some kind of wild animal ever since the day they'd met, when he'd shown her around the flat he never believed she'd lease.

She'd moved in a week later and had been disturbing his peace with her ice-queen routine ever since.

"I—I have no idea how that happened," she said, as if he'd secretly orchestrated the whole thing just for a chance to grab her.

Gritting his teeth, he tried to assure her that this wasn't a mugging or a botched kidnapping attempt—that, despite his tats and his accent and all the other things that made classy women like her judge guys like him, he wasn't *actually* a dangerous criminal. But all that came out of his mouth was a useless wheezing noise, so he gave up and focused on breathing instead. The pain in his throat faded from a poisonous yellow to a faint, lemon twinge.

He didn't even notice her sisters until they started talking.

"Oh, Chloe," said the shortest sister, Eve. "Look what you've done! The poor man's coughing up his garters."

The other sister—Dani, they called her—rolled her eyes and said, "Do you mean *guts*, darling?"

"No. Should we do something? Go on, Dani, do something."

"And what should I do? Do I look like a nurse to you?"

"Well, we can't let him choke to death," Eve said reasonably. "What a waste of a gorgeous—"

Chloe's voice carved through the bickering like a blade. "Oh, be quiet, both of you. Weren't you just leaving?"

"We can't leave *now*. Our favorite superintendent is in crisis."

See, while Chloe had hated Red from the moment they'd met, her sisters, Dani and Eve, seemed to love him. They shared her cut-glass accent, but not her apparent classism. He thought of Dani as the elegant one, with her shaved head and her floaty, black outfits. She had a smile so pretty it should be illegal, and she flashed it like a lightbulb whenever their paths crossed. Eve, meanwhile, was the fun one, the baby sister with long, pastel-colored braids and an air of frantic energy that crackled around her like lightning. She liked to flirt. She also liked to wear polka-dot outfits and clashing shoes that offended his artistic sensibilities.

If either of *them* had taken flat 1D five weeks ago, that would've been just fine. But no—it had to be Chloe. Had to be the sister who made him feel like a rough, scary monster. Had to be the uptight princess who'd decided he was dangerous simply because of where he came from. Why she even lived here, in a cheerfully middle-class block of flats, was a fucking mystery; she was obviously loaded. After Pippa, he could spot the gloss of a wealthy woman from miles away.

But he wouldn't think about Pippa. Nothing good ever came of it.

"I'm fine," he choked out, blinking his watery eyes.

"See?" Chloe said quickly. "He's fine. Let's be off."

God, she irritated him. The woman had just cut off his fucking oxygen and she still couldn't show him common courtesy. Absolutely unbelievable. "Nice to see you're still sweetness and light," he muttered. "Teach those manners at finishing school, do they?"

He regretted the words as soon as they came out of his mouth. She was a tenant. He was the superintendent, by the grace of God and his best mate. He was supposed to be polite to her no matter what. But he'd figured out weeks ago that his good nature, his filters, and his common sense all disappeared around Chloe Brown. Honestly, he was shocked she hadn't reported him already.

That was the weirdest thing about her, actually. She snapped at him, she sneered down her nose at him, but she never, ever reported him. He wasn't quite sure what that meant.

Right now, her heavy-lidded eyes flashed midnight fire, narrowing behind her bright blue glasses. He enjoyed the sight on an aesthetic level and hated himself for it, just a little bit. High up on the list of annoying things about Chloe Brown was her beautiful bloody face. She had the kind of brilliant, decadent, Rococo beauty that made his fingers itch to grab a pencil or a paintbrush. It was ridiculously over the top: gleaming brown skin, winged eyebrows with a slightly sarcastic tilt, a mouth you could sink into like a feather bed. She had no business looking like that. None at all.

But he knew he'd mix a million earth shades to paint her and add a splash of ultramarine for the square frames of her glasses. The thick, chestnut hair piled on top of her head? He'd take that down. Sometimes, he stared at nothing and thought about the way it would frame her face. Most times, he thought about how he shouldn't be thinking about her. Ever. At all.

Each word deliberate as a gunshot, she told him, "I'm so awfully sorry, Redford." She sounded about as sorry as a wasp did for stinging. As always, her lips and tongue said one thing, but her eyes said murder. He was generally considered an easygoing guy, but Red knew his eyes were saying murder right back.

"No worries," he lied. "My fault."

She gave a one-shouldered shrug that he knew from experi-ence was rich-people speak for *Whatever.* Then she left without another word, because their verbal battles were never actually that verbal, beyond the first few passive-aggressive jabs.

He watched her spin away, her poofy skirt swishing around her calves. He saw her sisters follow, and waved a hand when they sent him concerned, backward glances. He heard their footsteps fade, and he pulled himself together, and he went to Mrs. Conrad's flat and ate her awful casserole.

But he didn't think about Chloe Brown again. Not once. Not at all.

Some people might say that writing a list of items to change one's life after a brush with death was ludicrous—but those people, Chloe had decided, simply lacked the necessary imagination and commitment to planning. She gave a sigh of pure content-ment as she settled deeper into her mountain of sofa cushions.

It was Saturday night, and she was glad to be alone. Her back pain was as excruciating today as it had been yesterday, her legs were numb and aching, but even those issues couldn't ruin this peace. When she'd put pen to paper in her quest to get a life, finding her own home had been the first entry she'd written. She'd met that goal, and—unnerving superintendents aside—she had nothing but good to show for it.

Through the slight gap in her living room window's cur-tains, she caught a glimpse of the September sun's evening rays. That warm, orange glow rose above the hulking shadow of her apartment building's west side, making the courtyard nestled at the center of the building all shadowy and peaceful, its blooming autumnal shades rich as earth and blood. Her flat was similarly soothing to the nerves: cool and silent, but for the gentle whirr of her laptop and the steady tap of her fingers against the keyboard.

Happiness, independence, true solitude. Sweeter than oxygen. She breathed it in. This was, in a word, bliss.

It was also the moment her phone blared to life, shattering her calm like glass.

"Oh, for heaven's sake." Chloe allowed herself precisely three seconds to wallow in exasperation before grabbing her phone and checking the display. *Eve.* Her little sister. Which meant that she couldn't simply switch off the ringer and shove her mobile into a drawer.

Drat.

She hit Accept. "I'm working."

"Well, that simply won't do," Eve said cheerfully. "Thank goodness I called."

Chloe enjoyed being irritated—grumpiness was high on her list of hobbies—but she also enjoyed everything about her silly youngest sister. Fighting the curve of her own lips, she asked, "What do you want, Evie-Bean?"

"Oh, I'm so glad you asked."

Fudge. Chloe knew that tone, and it never boded well for her. "You know, every time I answer your calls, I quickly find myself regretting it." She hit Speaker and put her phone on the sofa arm, her hands returning to the laptop balanced on her knees.

"What rubbish. You adore me. I am catatonically adorable."

"Do you mean *categorically,* darling?"

"No," Eve said. "Now, listen closely. I am about to give you a series of instructions. Don't think, don't argue, just obey."

This ought to be good.

"Karaoke night begins in one hour down at the Hockley bar—no, Chloe, stop groaning. Don't think, don't argue, just obey, remember? I want you to get up, put on some lipstick—"

"Too late," Chloe interrupted dryly. "My pajamas are on. I'm finished for the night."

"At half-past eight?" Eve's enthusiasm faltered, replaced by hesitant concern. "You're not having a spell, are you?"

Chloe softened at the question. "No, love."

Most people had trouble accepting the fact that Chloe was ill. Fibromyalgia and chronic pain were invisible afflictions, so they were easy to dismiss. Eve was healthy, so she would never feel Chloe's bone-deep exhaustion, her agonizing headaches or the shooting pains in her joints, the fevers and confusion, the countless side effects that came from countless medications. But Eve didn't need to feel all of that to have empathy. She didn't need to see Chloe's tears or pain to believe her sister struggled sometimes. Neither, for that matter, did Dani. They understood.

"You're sure?" Eve asked, suspicion in her tone. "Because you were awfully rude to Red yesterday, and that usually means—"

"It was nothing," Chloe cut in sharply, her cheeks burning.

Redford Morgan: Mr. Congeniality, beloved superintendent, the man who liked *everyone* but didn't like her. Then again, people usually didn't. She shoved all thoughts of him neatly back into their cage. "I'm fine. I promise." It wasn't a lie, not today. But she would have lied if necessary. Sometimes familial concern was its own mind-numbing symptom.

"Good. In that case, you can definitely join me for karaoke. The theme is duets, and I have been stood up by my so-called best friend. I require a big sisterly substitute as a matter of urgency."

"Unfortunately, my schedule is full." With a few flicks of her fingertips, Chloe minimized one window, maximized another, and scanned her client questionnaire for the section on testimonial slide shows. She couldn't quite remember if—

"*Schedule?*" Eve grumbled. "I thought you were abandoning schedules. I thought you had a new lease on life!"

"I do," Chloe said mildly. "I also have a job." *Aha.* She found the info she needed and tucked it away in her mind, hoping brain fog wouldn't turn the data to mist within the next thirty seconds. She hadn't taken much medication today, so her short-term memory should be reasonably reliable.

Should be.

"It's Saturday night," Eve was tutting. "You work for *yourself.* From *home.*"

"Which is precisely why I have to be disciplined. Call Dani."

"Dani sings like a howler monkey."

"But she has stage presence," Chloe said reasonably.

"Stage presence can't hide everything. She's not Madonna, for Christ's sake. I don't think you are grasping the gravity of this situation, Chlo; this isn't just a karaoke night. There is a competition."

"Oh, joy."

"Guess what the prize is?"

"I couldn't possibly," Chloe murmured.

"Go on. Guess!"

"Just tell me. I am bursting with excitement."

"The prize," Eve said dramatically, "is . . . tickets to Mariah Carey's Christmas tour!"

"Tickets to—?" Oh, for goodness sake. "You don't need to *win* those, Eve. Have Gigi arrange it."

"That's really not the point. This is for fun! You remember, *fun*—that thing you never have?"

"This may come as a shock to you, darling, but most people don't consider karaoke exciting."

"All right," Eve relented, sounding rather glum. But, as always, she brightened quickly. "Speaking of fun . . . how is that list of yours developing?"

Chloe sighed and let her head fall back against the cushions. Heaven protect her from little sisters. She should never have told either of them about her list, the one she'd written after her near-death experience and subsequent resolution. They always made fun of her itemized plans.

Well, more fool them, because planning was the key to success. It was thanks to the list, after all, that Chloe's imaginary eulogy was now looking much more positive. Today, she could proudly claim that if she died, the papers would say something like this:

At the grand old age of thirty-one, Chloe moved out of her family home and rented a poky little flat, just like an ordinary person. She also wrote an impressive seven-point list detailing her plans to get a life. While she failed to fully complete said list before her death, its existence proves that she was in a better, less boring, place. We salute you, Chloe Brown. Clearly, you listened to the universe.

Satisfactory, if not ideal. She had not yet transformed her life, but she was in the process of doing so. She was a caterpillar tucked into a universe-endorsed chrysalis. Someday soon, she would emerge as a beautiful butterfly who did cool and fabulous things all the time, regardless of whether or not said things had been previously scheduled. All she had to do was follow the list.

Unfortunately, Eve didn't share her patience or her positive outlook. "Well?" she nudged, when Chloe didn't respond. "Have you crossed anything off yet?"

"I moved out."

"Yes, I had noticed that," Eve snorted. "Do you know, I'm the last Brown sister living at home now?"

"Really? I had no idea. I thought there were several more of us roaming the halls."

"Oh, shut up."

"Perhaps you should move out soon, too."

"Not yet. I'm still saving my monthly stipend," Eve said vaguely. God only knew what for. Chloe was afraid to ask, in case the answer was something like *A diamond-encrusted violin, of course.* "But you moved out weeks ago, Chlo. There's all sorts of things on that list of yours. What else have you done?"

When in doubt, remain silent—that was Chloe's motto.

"I knew it," Eve sniffed eventually. "You are letting me down."

"Letting *you* down?"

"Yes. Dani bet me fifty pounds that you'd abandon your list by the end of the year, but *I*—"

"She bet you *what*?"

"*I* supported you like a good and loyal sister—"

"What on earth is the matter with the pair of you?"

"And this is how you repay me! With apathy! And to top it all, you won't help me win Mariah Carey tickets."

"Will you shut up about the karaoke?" Chloe snapped. She ran a hand over her face, suddenly exhausted. "Darling, I can't talk anymore. I really am working."

"Fine," Eve sighed. "But this isn't the last you've heard of me, Chloe Sophia."

"Stop that."

"I won't rest until you're no longer such a boring—"

Chloe put the phone down.

A second later, a notification flashed up on her screen.

EVE: ☺

Chloe shook her head in fond irritation and got back to work. The SEO of local restaurants, hair salons, and the other small businesses on her roster wouldn't maintain itself. She sank into the familiar mental rhythm of research and updates . . . or rather, she tried to. But her focus was shattered. After five minutes, she paused to mutter indignantly at the empty room, "Dani bet fifty pounds that I would abandon the list? Ridiculous."

After ten, she drummed her fingers against the sofa and said, "She simply doesn't understand the fine art of list-based goal setting." The fact that Dani was a Ph.D. student was neither here nor there. She was too rebellious to grasp the importance of a good, solid plan.

Although . . . Chloe supposed it *had* been a while since she'd taken stock. Maybe she was due a check-in. Before she knew it, her laptop was closed and abandoned in the living room while she strode off to find the blue sparkly notebook hidden in her bedside drawer.

Chloe had many notebooks, because Chloe wrote many lists. Her brain, typically fogged by pain or painkillers (or, on truly exciting days, both), was a cloudy, lackadaisical thing that could not be trusted, so she relied on neatly organized reminders.

Daily to-do lists, weekly to-do lists, monthly to-do lists, medication lists, shopping lists, Enemies I Will Destroy lists (that one was rather old and more of a morale boost than anything else), client lists, birthday lists, and, her personal favorite, wish lists. If a thing could be organized, categorized, scheduled, and written neatly into a color-coded section of a notebook, the chances were, Chloe had already done so. If she didn't, you see, she would soon find herself in what Mum called "a wretched kerfuffle." Chloe did not have the time for kerfuffles.

But the single list contained in the notebook she now held was not like all the others. She opened the book to the very first page and ran her finger over the stark block lettering within. There were no cheerful doodles or colorful squiggles here, because, when she'd designed this particular page, Chloe had meant business. She *still* meant business.

This was her Get a Life list. She took it rather seriously.

Which begged the question—why were its check boxes so woefully unticked?

Her questing finger moved to trace the very first task. This one, at least, she had accomplished: *1. Move out.* She'd been living independently—*really* independently, budgeting and food shopping and all sorts—for five weeks now, and she had yet to spontaneously combust. Her parents were astonished, her sisters were delighted, Gigi was yodeling "I told you so!" to all and sundry, et cetera. It was very satisfying.

Less satisfying were the five unachieved tasks written beneath it.

2. Enjoy a drunken night out.
3. Ride a motorbike.
4. Go camping.
5. Have meaningless but thoroughly enjoyable sex.
6. Travel the world with nothing but hand luggage.

And then there was the very last task, one she'd checked off with alarming swiftness.

7. *Do something bad.*

Oh, she'd done something bad, all right. Not that she could ever tell her sisters about *that.* Just the thought made her cheeks heat. But when she took her notebook back into the living room, guilty memories dragged her gaze, kicking and screaming, toward the window. The forbidden portal to her *something bad.* The curtains were still closed, the way she'd left them ever since her last transgression—but there was that little gap of light trickling through.

Perhaps she should go and pull the curtains tighter, cut off that gap completely, just to make sure. Yes. Definitely. She crept over to the wide living room window, raising a hand to do just that . . . but some sort of malfunction occurred, and before she knew it, she was twitching the curtain to the side, widening the gap instead of closing it. A faint shard of light stretched toward her across the courtyard's patio, merging with the last gasps of the dying sun, and she thought to herself, *Don't. Don't. This is horribly invasive and more than a little creepy and you're just making everything worse—*

But her eyes kept on looking anyway, staring across the narrow courtyard, through a not-so-distant window to the figure limned within.

Redford Morgan was hard at work.

Call me Red, he'd told her, months ago. She hadn't. *Couldn't.*

The word, like everything else about him, was too much for her to handle. Chloe didn't do well around people like him; confident people, beautiful people, those who smiled easily and were liked by everyone and felt comfortable in their own skin. They reminded her of all the things she wasn't and all the loved ones who'd left her behind. They made her feel prickly and silly and frosty and foolish, twisting her insides into knots, until all she could do was snap or stammer.

She usually chose to snap.

The problem with Redford was, he always seemed to catch her at her worst. Take the time when some yummy mummy had cornered Chloe in the courtyard to ask, "Is that a wig?"

Chloe, perplexed, had patted her usual plain, brown bun, wondering if she'd slapped on one of Dani's platinum blond lace fronts that morning by mistake. ". . . No?"

The yummy mummy hadn't been impressed with Chloe's lack of conviction and had therefore taken matters into her own hands. Which, in this case, had involved grabbing Chloe's hair as if it were a creature at a petting zoo.

But had Redford witnessed *that* disaster? Of course not. Nor had he heard the woman's chocolate-smeared child call Chloe a "mean, ugly lady" for defending herself. Nooo; he'd swept onto the scene like a knight in tattooed armor just in time to hear *Chloe* call the woman a "vapid disgrace to humanity," and the child a "nasty little snot ball," both of which were clearly true statements.

Redford had glared at her as if she were Cruella de Vil and let the yummy mummy cry on his shoulder.

And then there'd been that unfortunate incident in the post room. Was it Chloe's fault that some bonkers old lady named *Charlotte* Brown lived directly above her in 2D? Or that said bonkers old lady, sans spectacles, had mistakenly broken into Chloe's post box and opened the letters within? No. No, it was not. It also wasn't Chloe's fault that she, incensed by the *literal crime* committed against her, had reacted in the heat of the moment by finding the old lady's post box and pouring her morning thermos of tea through the slot. How was she to know that Charlotte Brown had been awaiting seventieth birthday cards from her grandchildren in the United States? She *wasn't* to know, of course. She wasn't psychic, for heaven's sake.

She'd attempted to explain all of that to Redford, but he'd been glowering so very hard, and then he'd said something awfully cutting—he was good at that, the wretch—and Chloe had given up. Superior silence was much easier to pull off, especially around him. He turned her into a complete disaster, and so, by day, she avoided his company like the bubonic plague.

But at night, sometimes, she watched him paint.

He was standing in front of his window, shirtless, which she supposed made her a pervert as well as a spy. But this wasn't a sexual exercise. He was *barely* even attractive in her eyes. She didn't see him as an object, or anything like that. From a distance, in the dark, with that sharp tongue of his tucked away, she saw him as poetry. He had this visceral quality, even when he was glaring at her, but especially when he painted. There was an honesty, a vulnerability about him that captivated her.

Chloe knew she was flesh and blood and bone, just like him. But she wasn't alive like he was. Not even close.

He was in profile, focused on the canvas in front of him. Sometimes he painted haltingly, almost cautiously; other times, he would stare at the canvas more than he touched it. But tonight, he was a living storm, dabbing and daubing with quick, fluid movements. She couldn't see what he was working on, and she didn't want to. What mattered was the subtle rise and fall of his ribs as his breathing sped up, and the rapid, minute movements of his head, birdlike and fascinating. What mattered was *him*.

His long hair hung over his face, a copper-caramel curtain with shreds of firelight throughout. That hair, she knew, hid a strong brow, probably furrowed in concentration; a harsh, jutting nose; a fine mouth that lived on the edge of smiling, surrounded by sandy stubble. She liked to see the fierce concentration on his face when he painted, but she knew it was for the best when his wild hair covered all. If she couldn't see him, he wouldn't see her. And anyway, she didn't need to see his face to drown in his vitality. The spill of copper strands over those broad shoulders; the ink trapped beneath his pale skin; that was enough.

If someone asked her what his tattoos looked like, she wouldn't be able to describe the images they displayed or the words they spelled out. She'd speak about the dense blackness, and the pops of color. The faded ones that seemed ever so slightly raised, and the ones that flooded him like ink spilled into water. She'd speak about how strange it was to choose to bleed for something, simply because you wanted to. She'd speak about how it made her feel and how she wanted to want something that much, and on a regular enough basis, to build her own equivalent of his countless tattoos.

But no one would ever ask her, because she wasn't supposed to know.

The first time she'd stumbled across this view, she'd turned away instantly, squeezing her eyes shut while her heart tried to break free of its cage. And she'd shut her curtains. Hard. But the image had stayed with her, and curiosity had built. She'd spent days wondering—*Was he naked? Naked in front of his window? And what had been in his hand? What was he doing in there?*

She'd lasted three weeks before looking again.

The second time, she'd been hesitant, shocked by her own audacity, creeping toward the window in the dark and hiding behind almost-closed curtains. She'd peeked just long enough to answer her own questions: he was wearing jeans and not much else; he was holding a paintbrush; he was, of course, painting. Then she'd stared even longer, hypnotized by the sight. Afterward, she'd crossed *Do something bad* off her list and tried to feel good instead of guilty. It hadn't worked.

And this time? The third time? *The last time,* she told herself firmly. What was her excuse now?

There was none. Clearly, she was a reprehensible human being.

He stopped, straightened, stepped back. She watched as he put down his paintbrush, stretched out his fingers in a way that meant he'd been working for hours. She was jealous of how far he could push himself, how long he could stand in one place without his body complaining, or suffering. Or punishing him. She twitched the curtain wider, her envious hands moving of their own accord, a little more light spilling into her shadowed guilt.

Red turned suddenly. He looked out of his window.

Right at her.

But she wasn't there anymore; she had dropped the curtain back into place, spun away, slammed herself against the living room wall. Her pulse pounded so hard and so fast that it was almost painful at her throat. Her breaths were ragged gasps, as if she'd run a mile.

He hadn't seen her. He hadn't. He *hadn't*.

Yet she couldn't help but wonder—what might he do, if he had?

CHAPTER TWO

Why would a woman who all but hated Red spend her evening watching him through a window?

He couldn't say. There was no good reason. There were bad reasons, reasons involving fetishes and class lines and the shit certain people considered degrading, but he didn't think those applied to Chloe Brown. Not because she was above lusting after a man she looked down on, but because she didn't seem the type to lust at all. Lust couldn't exist without vulnerability. Chloe, beneath her pretty exterior, was about as vulnerable as a bloody shark.

So maybe his eyes had deceived him. Maybe she hadn't been watching him at all. But he knew what he'd seen, didn't he? Thick, dark hair pulled into a soft bun; the sky-bright glint of those blue glasses; a lush figure in pink pin-striped pajamas with buttons marching up the front. Cute as a button, neat as a button, always dressed in buttons. He knew exactly who lived in the flat that faced his across the courtyard, and he knew—he *knew*—that he'd seen her last night. But why?

"Red," his mum barked. "Stop *slicing* so loud. You're ruining my nerves, you are."

The distraction, ridiculous or not, came as a relief. He was sick of his own repetitive thoughts, a murky, khaki color in his mind. He turned to face his mother, who was perched at the table wedged into one corner of her tiny kitchen, right beside the window. "You want to complain about my chopping, woman? When I'm over here to make *you* lunch?"

"Don't get cheeky," she said, giving him the death stare. She was legally blind in one eye, but lack of sight didn't stop her irises from stabbing him.

He tried to look innocent. She huffed grandly and turned back to the window, twitching the net curtains aside. She ruled her cul-de-sac with an iron fist and spent most of her time waiting for supplicants to arrive.

This time, the supplicant was Shameeka Israel, a doctor at the Queen's Medical Center. When she came for Sunday lunch with the great-aunt who lived three doors down, Dr. Israel became Our Meeka, or alternatively, Little Gap. She arrived at the window with a pot of oxtail curry and said, "Here, Ms. Morgan. Auntie made you some for the cold."

Mum's glower softened at the sound of the doctor's voice. "Gap. You're a good girl. When are you going to marry my Redford?"

"Soon, Ms. Morgan. All right, Red?"

He winked at her through the window. "It's a date."

She grinned, flashing her gap teeth, then put the oxtail inside the windowsill and said her good-byes. As soon as her Lexus pulled out of the car park, Red whisked the pot away from his mother's grasping hands. She'd already lifted the lid, stuck a finger into the curry, and sucked.

"Oi," he scolded. "You'll spoil your lunch. I'm making you pistou soup."

"What in God's name is that?"

"The balls off a badger. Steamed."

She snorted, screwing her angular face into an expression of disgust. "Sounds about right." Mrs. Conrad wasn't the only drama queen in Red's life. Add his mum and Vik to the mix, and he was practically drowning in them.

He was just about to tell her the actual ingredients of pistou soup when she leaned toward the window, her voice rising to the level of a low-flying airplane. "Oi, Mike! I can see you, you scumbag! Get over here."

Mike was, essentially, Mum's good-for-nothing boyfriend. This was how they flirted. Red took himself to the stove and stirred his pistou soup, pointedly ignoring the things Mike shouted back. The guy was in his seventies, drank like a fish, and was round the bookies every afternoon like clockwork. Red did not approve.

It wasn't as if he could say anything about it, though. Not when Mum had warned *him* about his last girlfriend, Pippa, and he'd merrily ignored her to the bitter, bloody end. He wasn't exactly Mr. Relationship Expert. But he wouldn't think about Pippa, or London, or his countless mistakes, because it only pissed him off, and Red hated feeling pissed off. Chill and cheerful was more his speed.

He was just regaining his equilibrium, clearing the dishes after a decent lunch, when Mum approached his most sensitive subject with all the delicacy of a rampaging rhino.

"Back to selling any paintings yet?"

Ah, his favorite topic. "Not yet," Red said calmly. A little too calmly, but Mum didn't seem to notice.

"Gee up, babe. You've been messing about for years now."

Years? "It's only been eighteen months."

"Don't correct your mother."

He really didn't get enough credit for his boundless patience. Maybe he should make himself an award. *To the Much-Put-Upon Redford Thomas Morgan, in Recognition of Endurance in the Face of Pointless Questions About Art.* Something like that.

"You can't let that nasty little rich girl destroy your career," Mum went on.

Too late. Red squirted a liberal amount of washing-up liquid into the bowl.

"Don't give me the silent treatment, Redford. Answer me. What've you been up to? You *are* working, aren't you?"

"Yes," he sighed, because if he didn't tell her something she'd nag until his ears bled. "Mainly freelance illustration. Building my portfolio." *Again.* "I just finished these pen-and-ink drawings of a brain and a bottle of port."

Mum looked at him as if his head had fallen off.

"Lifestyle magazine," he explained. "An article on erectile dysfunction."

She huffed and turned fully away from the window, spearing him with her still-seeing eye. It glinted suspiciously from behind her amber-tinted glasses. "You've been drawing pictures for magazines since you were a boy. What are you waiting for? Sell some bloody paintings again. You have done some, haven't you?"

Oh, yeah, he'd done some. He'd been painting as obsessively as always, and some of it was even half decent. But it was *different*. It was different, and he was different, and the things he knew were different, and after all the bad decisions he'd made . . .

Well. Red had plenty of work to sell. But thus far, he didn't have the balls to show it to a single soul. Every time he considered it, a familiar, cut-glass accent reminded him of a few things. *You try so hard, Red, and it's pathetic. Accept what you are, sweetie. You were nothing before me, and you'll be nothing after me.*

Chloe Brown's bladelike enunciation had nothing on Pippa Aimes-Baxter's.

And why the fuck was he thinking about Chloe again?

"You gonna be a landlord forever?" Mum demanded.

He shook his head sharply, like a dog, brushing off the unwanted memories. "Vik's the landlord, Mum. I'm his superintendent."

"You should take a leaf out of Vikram's book, in my opinion. Who could stop that boy? No one. Nothing."

True. Vik Anand, aside from being Red's best mate, was a minor property mogul who'd given Red the superintendent job after . . . well. After Pippa. Red was only vaguely qualified, but he hadn't fucked anything up yet, and he was a decent plumber. Decent electrician. Excellent decorator. Damned hardworking.

Shit at the admin, but he did his best.

Aaaand, he was making excuses.

"You're right," he said, scrubbing out a saucepan, squinting when his hair fell into his eyes. It was like seeing the world through tall, dead grass at sunset. His fingers were turning red in the almost-boiling, bubbly water, the tattoo of MUM across his knuckles as bold as ever, each letter sitting just above his granddad's silver rings. That tattoo hadn't been his brightest teenage decision, but the sentiment remained: he loved the hell out of his mother. So he looked over at her and repeated, "You are absolutely right. Tomorrow morning, I'll get on it properly. Start planning. Think about a new website."

She nodded, turned back to her window, and changed the subject. Started gossiping about Mrs. Poplin's witless nephew who'd gone and knocked up the girl from the corner shop who had a missing front tooth, could you believe?

Red Hmmm'd in all the right places and thought about how to make Kirsty Morgan proud. He ended his visit with a kiss to both of her cheeks and a promise to pop in during the week, when he could. Then he put on his helmet and leathers, got on his bike, and sped home to the apartment building that was his blessing and his excuse.

He was not prepared for the spectacle he found outside.

CHAPTER THREE

Walking improved heart health, significantly reduced one's chances of breast cancer, and qualified as a relatively low-impact sport. Despite this last fact, and despite the New Balance walking trainers Chloe had bought especially, her knees were bloody killing her.

"You," she muttered to the pavement beneath her feet, "are a first-class scoundrel."

The pavement refused to respond, which struck her as rather petty. If it was bold enough to jar her bones with every step, it should be bold enough to defend its reprehensible solidity.

Then again, Chloe's current predicament *could* be her own fault. She'd skipped her painkillers this morning because she was feeling lively—so she probably shouldn't have spent the last twenty-seven minutes messing around outdoors, gulping down the crisp autumn air and pushing herself just a bit harder than usual. Hindsight was 20/20, and all that.

She could feel familiar tendrils of soreness burrowing into her body's weak points, could see the dull gray of exhaustion at the edges of her mind. But she was nearly home now. Chloe wandered across the little park opposite her building—*Grass! Thank Christ*—and planned to reward herself with some lovely drugs, fluffy pajamas, and several dark-chocolate-chip cookies. Dark chocolate, obviously, was an extremely healthy choice. The antioxidants canceled out the sugar almost entirely.

Oh—there was a cat in a tree.

She stopped short, her thoughts scattered. A cat. In a tree. Had she stumbled into the pages of a children's book? To her right stood the oak tree that dominated most of this random green area, and in the highest, spindly branches of that oak sat a cat. It was both a familiar concept and a completely baffling sight. For all that she'd heard of cats in trees, she'd never actually come across one.

She folded her arms, squinted against the too-bright, too-pale sky, and listened to the creature's plaintive *miaow*s.

After a moment, she called, "You sound as though you're stuck."

The cat screeched its affirmative like a miniature murder victim. It was small, but wonderfully fat, with fur so gray as to seem almost black, and piercing eyes that said, *Surely you won't leave me here?*

Chloe sighed. "Are you sure you can't get down? I don't mean to be rude, but you know how this goes. Some gullible, bleeding-heart type clambers into a tree after a cat, only for said cat to leap mischievously down at the last second—"

Another shriek, this one blatantly indignant.

"Fair point," Chloe conceded. "Just because you appear well, doesn't mean you don't require help. I, above all, should know that. I will call the fire brigade for you."

The cat miaowed some more and glared down at her, a skeptical smudge against the sky. She was now quite certain that it was saying something like, *The fire brigade, you wasteful cow? Don't you realize we are in an era of austerity? Would you take much-needed public services away from children trapped in bathrooms and old ladies who've left the iron on? For shame.*

This cat, like most of its species, seemed rather judgmental. Chloe didn't mind; she appreciated bluntness in a beastly companion. And . . . well, it had a point. Why should she bother the fire-type people when she had a semifunctional body of her own? Fetching this cat might not be the cleverest way to end her walk, but then, staid, sensible Chloe Brown was dead. *New* Chloe was a reckless, exciting sort of woman who, in moments of crisis, didn't wait for the assistance of trained professionals.

The thought plucked at her like a harpist plucked at strings. She vibrated with ill-advised intent. She would dominate this tree.

A decent hand- and foothold were required to begin; she knew that from watching a young Dani scamper up and down these things for years. The oak's trunk was both soft and hard under Chloe's hands, its bark crumbly and damp, its core immovable. She liked the contrast, even if it scratched at her palms and threatened to snag on her leggings. Her waterproof jacket made an odd, slithery noise as she reached up toward the first branch. Then her fingers closed around a sturdy bough, and she

heaved herself up as her feet pushed off the trunk, and everything felt utterly free.

Her muscles were still weary and her joints still ached; the
only difference was, she no longer gave a damn. There was a
nasty little voice in her head that warned her she'd pay for
this, that her body would demand retribution. She had been
practicing telling that voice to eff off, and she did so now.
The cat's whining spiked as she climbed, and Chloe chose to
interpret that as enthusiastic cheerleading. *Well done, human!*
miaowed the cat. *You're a total badass! You should definitely add
this to your Get a Life list so that you can cross it off immediately
and feel extra accomplished!*

Chloe considered, then discarded, the cat's generous
suggestion. The Get a Life list was an historical document that
she couldn't bring herself to alter.

"Thank you, though," she panted, and then worried about the
fact that she was panting. Her lungs were working overtime and
every breath felt like the edge of a saw. She had a metallic taste at
the back of her mouth that reminded her, unpleasantly, of blood,
and also of the days when she'd had to run laps in PE. Apparently, this climb was wearing her out—but she'd been taking irregular walks for years, damn it. Surely she should be a semipro
athlete by now? Apparently not. The human body was an inconvenient and unreasonable thing.

She kept climbing, anyway, and developed a system. She'd
drag herself onto a sturdy branch, shuffle along on her bottom—
rather undignified, but it couldn't be helped—reach for the next

branch, drag herself up . . . and so on. It worked like a charm and took forever, probably due to her frequent rest breaks. And then, all of a sudden, she got so high that the branches thinned out.

Oh dear.

Chloe was not petite. She was on the taller side, big boned, and well insulated for the winter. Like a rabbit. Except the insulation lasted all year round. Her size wasn't something she often thought about, but as she reached a particularly slender branch, she could suddenly think of nothing but. She eyed the branch suspiciously. Could it take approximately fifteen stone of woman? She doubted it.

"Cat," she said, or rather, wheezed. "You might need to come down just a bit. Throw yourself into my arms, perhaps." She released her death grip on the branch, clenched her core to ensure her balance, and held up encouraging hands. "Come on, then. Leap of faith and all that."

The cat did not look impressed.

"I won't drop you," she said. "Promise. I'm an excellent catch. I played netball for the county team, you know."

The cat gave her a hard stare.

She sighed. "Yes, it was over a decade ago. Which is mean of you to point out, by the way."

Perhaps the cat appreciated her honesty, because it extended one delicate paw and seemed to consider a path of descent.

"That's the spirit, darling. Down you pop."

With alarming agility, the cat did indeed come down. Chloe was surprised, all things considered, that it didn't leap comfortably out of the tree and leave her behind. Judging by its suddenly silky movements, it must've been able to. And yet, instead of making its escape, it hopped from one branch to the next until it came to rest on her lap, precisely as directed.

She stared at the bundle of smoky fur currently nuzzling her stomach. After a moment of astonishment, she choked out, "You can't actually understand me, can you? Because if so, don't worry. I'll protect your secret to the death."

From beneath her, a rough voice punched through the Sunday quiet. "So will I."

She almost fell out of the tree.

After that heart-jolting moment, Chloe clutched a nearby bough for balance and blinked down at the source of the words. She found Redford Morgan squinting up at her, his hands in his pockets, his fine mouth curved into what must be a smirk.

Oh, no. Oh, no, no, no, no, no. She became uncomfortably aware of the cool, prickly sweat coating her skin, the strands of frizzy hair that had escaped her bun, and . . . oh, yes, the fact that she was sitting in a tree, talking nonsense to a cat. Ridiculous. Absolutely ridiculous. Embarrassment leaked past her most stalwart defenses to flood her cheeks with unwanted heat. She searched for something appropriately cutting to say and discovered that every intelligent thought in her head had evaporated.

Gigi's voice came to her like a divine message. *Keep calm, Chloe, dear. And whatever you bloody do, don't fall.*

Sound advice from Imaginary Gigi.

"Hello, Mr. Morgan," she croaked, then kicked herself. *Mr. Morgan?!* She'd regressed. *Redford* had been bad enough. At this rate, she wouldn't call him "Red" until 2056.

His strange little smirk widened into a full-blown grin, and she realized that he hadn't been smirking at all. No; he was holding back laughter, his amusement dancing through the air around him like an electrical current. His big body practically vibrated with it. She considered telling him to just get on with it—to laugh at her, since she was sure she made a hilarious picture right now. But before she could work up the words, he spoke again.

"Are you stuck, Ms. Brown?"

She didn't miss the emphasis he put on her name, as sarcastic as the single eyebrow he raised. Goodness gracious, he'd better stop that. Looking at him was distracting enough; if he started to *emote,* her brain might short-circuit. Human beings so very vital should not be allowed to roam the streets unsupervised. Someone—Chloe—could die of fascinated envy and sheer self-consciousness.

"No," she said, with great dignity. "I am not stuck." It wasn't necessarily a lie, since she hadn't tried to get down yet.

"Are you sure?" he asked. "Because I wouldn't mind giving you a hand."

She snorted. How on earth would he *give her a hand* down a tree? "Are you on drugs, Mr. Morgan?"

His smile turned into a scowl. The expression didn't suit his catlike eyes or his upturned mouth, which just made it all the more effective. "No," he said shortly. Then he tutted loudly and shook his head, as if he despaired of her. Actually, he *did* despair of her; he'd made that rather clear.

For some reason, instead of ignoring him to prove how very

little she cared, she found herself blurting, "I didn't mean that in a bad way." Which was true, actually. She'd been joking, only jokes had never been Chloe's forte. Something about the delivery. "It's Sunday, after all. No work, few obligations. A perfectly acceptable day for recreational drug use."

He blinked up at her, his scowl replaced by bafflement. "Do you take drugs on Sundays, then?" he asked finally.

"I take drugs every day," she said. Then she remembered that he was the superintendent of her building and added, "Legal drugs. Very legal drugs. Doctor's orders."

His eyebrows flew up. They were the same amber-copper shade as his hair, so they stood out starkly against his pale skin. "Is that right?"

Time to change the subject. Otherwise, he'd start asking questions, and she'd answer out of politeness, and then they'd be sitting there discussing her medical history as if it were a topic as mundane as the weather.

"Do you know," she said, sinking her icy fingers into her troublesome cat friend's fur, "I think I might be stuck after all."

He folded his arms. Considering his height, the breadth of his shoulders, and the beaten-up black leather jacket he wore, the overall effect was slightly intimidating. "Thought you said you weren't?"

"Don't be a pain," she huffed, then immediately regretted it. The problem was, *she* was in pain, which tended to shorten her fuse. Her joints were stiff and aching, her lower back was screaming, and during physical catastrophes, her politeness was always the first function to go.

But Red, for once, didn't snap back. Instead he squinted up at her and asked slowly, "You okay?"

She stiffened. "Yes."

"Are you hurt?"

Hurt? No. Hurting? Always. "Are you going to help me or not?" she demanded.

He rolled his eyes. "You do know how to charm a fella." But he unfolded his arms and pushed off his jacket, clearly preparing for action. The leather landed at his feet like a dead thing, which she supposed it technically was. Unless it was fake.

"Is that real?" she asked, nodding toward it.

He arched an eyebrow again—the show-off—and approached the tree in his T-shirt and jeans. "That's what you're worried about right now?"

"I'm the sort of person who climbs trees to rescue cats. Clearly, I care deeply about animal welfare."

"You a vegetarian?"

Well. He had her there. "Not yet."

"Not yet?"

"I'm working on it." Ethical consumption had been easier at home, where they had a cook.

He grinned up at her, grabbed a branch, and started climbing. "Right. You only eat veal on Sundays, that sort of thing?"

"Certainly," she quipped. "Which is no worse than doing drugs on Sundays."

"Chloe. I don't do drugs on Sundays."

There; he'd used her name. Now was the perfect time to follow suit and use his. The one everyone else called him, not *Redford* or *Mr. Morgan*. But she felt so awkward about it that she couldn't figure out what to say, and in the end, after an uncomfortable pause, she . . .

Well. She simply blurted out, "Red."

And that was it.

He hauled himself up another branch—he was much quicker and more graceful than she'd been, the awful man—and cocked his head. "Yeah?"

Oh dear. "Um . . . do you know this cat?"

His climb continued. She tried not to stare at his hands and his forearms and the way his biceps bunched beneath his shirt as he lifted himself up. "Why," he asked, "would I know that cat?"

"I'm not sure. You are in a position of authority in the local community."

He eyed her suspiciously. "I change lightbulbs for old ladies and send out rent reminders."

"Sounds like authority to me."

The cat, which had been purring quietly, chose that moment to miaow again. Chloe scratched it between the ears. She appreciated the vocal support.

"Whatever you say," Red muttered, and then he was directly beneath her. Proximity to him unnerved her more and more every time they met. Which might have something to do with the mountains of guilt she carried after spying on him repeatedly.

At least she knew for sure, now, that he hadn't seen her last night. Because if he had, he probably would've left her to die in this tree.

"So, is it real?" she asked, mostly to divert her own train of thought.

"Is *what* real?" he shot back, sounding more than a little exasperated. His voice was gravelly, its cadence oddly musical, his words flowing together in an elision of consonants and shortening of vowels. He sounded as dynamic as he looked.

"The leather."

"No, Chloe. Don't worry. I'm not running around wearing a dead cow all the time." He reached up from the branch beneath her and said, "Can you hold my hand?"

Could she? Possibly. Should she? Debatable. His touch might stop her heart like an electric shock. Then again, she was hardly in a position to refuse. "Let me secure the cat," she mumbled.

"Fuck the cat. It's playing you like a violin."

Her gasp tasted of ice and pollution. "How *dare* you? This cat is an angel. Look at it. Look!"

He looked. His eyes were pale green, like spring pears. He studied the cat thoroughly before saying in very firm tones, "That thing could climb down any time it wanted. It's having you on."

"You're a heartless man."

"Me?" he sputtered, as shocked as if she'd accused him of being Queen Victoria. "*I'm* heartless?"

She drew back, affronted. "Are you trying to suggest that I'm the heartless one?"

"Well, you did—"

"Please don't bring up the post room incident."

"Actually, I was going to bring up the time you made Frank Leonard from 4J cry."

Chloe huffed out a breath. "I did *not* make him cry. He was already teary when the conversation began. It was all a mis-understanding, really."

Red grunted skeptically.

"Honestly, I see no need to rehash the past when I am in a tree, selflessly saving a cat."

"If you want to make this a competition," he countered, "*I'm in a tree saving a cat and a woman.*"

"You are absolutely not saving me, thank you very much."

"Oh? Shall I get down, then?"

"Fine. Throw a tantrum, if you must."

"Throw a—?" Red's incredulity was quickly cut off by a growl. "I'm not doing this with you."

She blinked down at him. "Doing what?"

"Arguing. I don't argue with people."

"That sounds dull," she murmured.

"You—just—hurry up before I lose my shit, would you?"

"You've not already lost it?"

"Swear to God, Chloe, you've got three seconds." He waved the proffered hand around for emphasis. There was a smudge of magenta ink beneath his thumbnail.

Chloe sighed, then picked up the cat to see if it would per-mit such familiarity. It did. Reassured, she unzipped her jacket a bit, stuffed the cat inside, zipped it up again. A furry kitty head rested against the hollow of her throat, a warm body curling up against her chest. The sensation was so wonderful, for a moment she almost forgot the pain clawing at her senses.

She rather liked this cat.

After fiddling for as long as possible, she put on her big-girl knickers and reached for the hand awaiting her. It was the third time she had ever touched Redford Morgan. She knew, because the first time—their first handshake—had sent a thousand tingling darts shooting up her right arm, darts that had dissolved into a strange, pleasurable sensation that was not unlike a muscle relaxant, and she had not approved. The second time, when they'd bumped into each other a few days ago, had only reinforced her decision to avoid all physical contact with the man.

Yet here she was, feeling his callused palm in hers, this time not for a handshake but a—she reluctantly admitted to herself—*rescue*. The usual darts of sensation returned. Red didn't appear to be sending them on purpose, so she decided, for once, not to hold it against him. Sometimes, when she saw him roaming the halls or the courtyard with a heartrending smile for everyone but her, she wished she had nothing at all to hold against him.

Usually when she'd taken her strongest painkillers and was therefore high as a kite.

"Can I keep it?" she asked, to distract herself, more than anything else.

"Keep what?" he frowned as he helped her climb down. His grip on her was steely; his other hand cupped her elbow. He supported almost all of her weight and pulled her onto a lower branch.

"The cat," she said, and concentrated on not falling tragically to her death.

"What are you asking me for? Put your feet here, look."

She put her feet where she was told. They were now a meter closer to the ground. Red climbed down a little bit, then reached up to help her again.

"I'm asking you," she said, as he maneuvered her like a particularly unwieldy doll, "because you are the superintendent, and pets are not allowed."

"Oh, yeah. You can't keep it then, can you? On your left, now," he added. "*Left*, I said. Chloe, d'you know your left and right?"

"Be quiet," she muttered, and finally put her feet in the right place. "Can't you bend the rules due to extenuating circumstances?"

"Extenuating circumstances such as . . . the fact that you're an extra special princess?"

"Precisely. I knew you'd understand."

"How d'you know the cat doesn't belong to someone?"

"No collar."

"Still, it—good God, woman, what are you doing? This branch. *This* one."

"Don't get snippy," she muttered.

"Are you trying to break your neck?"

"So dramatic. I'd break an arm at most. Of course, it has occurred to me that if I landed poorly, I could break my neck at any height. Especially since, as I'm holding a cat, I'd probably twist to avoid squashing the poor thing to death." She paused, considered. "But that's a worst-case scenario. I'm sure we don't need to worry about it."

Red halted his steady descent to stare at her. Then, from out of nowhere, he burst into laughter. It was a short, bright sound accompanied by a stunning smile, and she enjoyed it an unhealthy amount. She decided to ignore him and focus on studying the branches below. When she craned her neck a touch too vigorously, her body responded with a stab of pain through her shoulder blade. He, being a certified nuisance, noticed her slight wince and abruptly stopped laughing. Those sharp eyes excavated her expression. She'd seen him look at one of his paintings just like this, shortly before picking it up and throwing it against a wall.

He said, "Something's wrong with you."

She flinched. Her chest cracked wide open. "What is that supposed to mean?"

"You sure you didn't hurt yourself? Seems like you're in pain."

Oh. Of course. She shook her head, avoiding his gaze, her tension easing away. "It's nothing."

After a slight pause, he continued their descent. "You know," he said conversationally, "I think we're about the same age. I, too, enjoyed the era of *Xena: Warrior Princess* and Captain Janeway."

"How nice for you."

"And just because I'm rescuing you—"

"Incorrect."

"—like a proper knight in shining armor, don't mean I think you're all . . . you know. Damsel-in-distress-like."

Chloe huffed out a breath, a cloud of air pluming from her nostrils. Definitely more dragon that damsel. "Point?"

"Point is, if you've hurt yourself, I'm not gonna be a prick about it."

"Oh?" she asked through gritted teeth.

"Yeah. Like I won't *insist* you come back to mine so I can have a look at you."

"Good."

"But I will *suggest* that you let me see you home and get you settled. And make you a cuppa. To warm you up." Before she could quite get her head around that, he said, "Here we are, then," and jumped down. When his booted feet hit the ground, she realized they'd done it. They'd finished. Well, almost. She was crouched awkwardly on the last branch.

She wondered how badly the landing would hurt her already-screaming bones.

Red smiled up at her. It was the kind of sweet and effortlessly handsome smile that heartthrobs deployed in rom-coms, and she didn't trust it an inch. "Want me to catch you?"

"I'd rather die."

He shrugged, put his hands in his pockets, and started humming "Devil Woman."

She clutched the cat against her chest and jumped. Coincidentally, landing felt a little bit like dying. Her body had become a giant bruise. She swallowed a thousand curses, breathed through the urge to vomit, and felt like the silliest woman on earth. Why in God's name had she done this to herself? The cat licked the hollow of her throat, its sandpaper tongue warming her shriveled heart. *Ah, yes.* She'd done this because she was a pathetic ninny.

Red didn't bother to hide his concern. "You okay?"

For once, the apartment building's sweetheart was turning his nice-guy brand of nosiness her way. It might've been satisfying if she'd actually wanted his attention.

With great effort, she straightened up and attempted to smile. It felt more like a grimace. He winced at the sight as if horrified. She stopped. "I'm fine. Good-bye."

With that 100 percent believable lie expertly deployed, she made her escape. It was slow and steady, with little dignity, great pain, and greater determination. Being rescued from trees was all well and good, but she didn't need a rescue from herself.

CHAPTER FOUR

Red let Chloe limp off to her flat with a cat stuffed down her jacket. Then he found the motorbike he'd dumped shortly after spotting her, parked it, and settled in for a thrilling evening of minding his own damn business. He lasted about five minutes before grabbing his ring of master keys, turning up at her door, and knocking.

If she didn't answer, he'd assume she'd fainted or some shit and let himself in.

He was only checking on her because she was a tenant. Making sure she hadn't hurt herself was his job. The fact that she'd climbed up a tree to save a cat, and bantered with him in a weird, stuck-up, posh-girl kind of way, meant absolutely nothing. She was an unrepentant snob who'd possibly spied on him last night. He didn't give a fuck about her sarcastic sense of humor, or the cute little cardigans she wore, or her fantastic bloody face. But on a regular human-concerned-about-another-human level, he really wished she'd answer the door.

He knocked one more time, raked a hand through his hair,

and started worrying. When she'd left, her mouth had been tight, her skin gray beneath a sheen of sweat. Her words had grown rushed, strained, even sharper than usual. She'd moved stiffly, her body hunched with something more than cold. It was obvious she had some tree-related injury and didn't want to admit it, but Red was not above bullying it out of her. He had plenty of practice bullying his mother, after all.

He was reaching for his key when the door finally opened a crack. A large, dark eye peered suspiciously out at him.

Red arched an eyebrow. "Where are your glasses?"

"You're a very nosy man," she said. "What do you want?"

"Word on the street is, you've got a cat in there."

She looked him right in the eye and said, "Mr. Morgan. Would I ever?"

His lips twitched into a smile he didn't want to give. "I think I'll check, if you don't mind."

"I mind awfully."

"Still, though."

With a sigh gustier than a hurricane, she let him in.

Chloe was one of those women who always looked tidy. Even up a tree, she'd been in color-coordinated walking gear that could only be called *appropriate*. So the state of her home made him stop in his tracks.

She didn't appear to notice. She was too busy shuffling down the hall, dodging empty bottles of water lined up like bowling skittles and what seemed to be countless Amazon Prime delivery boxes. He picked his way through the chaos and followed her into an equally disordered living room, where fancy furniture was covered with pillows, books, empty mugs, and video-game cases that said PS4 on the front.

Oh, and then there was the cat.

It lay stretched across the glass coffee table, surrounded by a rainbow of prescription medication. Chloe picked up the boxes of pills, ignored the cat, and asked, "Happy?"

He stared. "The cat's right there."

"I have no idea what you're talking about." She hesitated, then took a nervous little breath. He wondered if she was about to confess to murder. Instead, she said, "I don't suppose you'd make some tea? Lavender for me, please."

He stared. Had she just—? Did she really think he would—? Well, holy fuck. The balls on this woman. "Used to servants, are you?"

"Oh, yes," she said.

It took him three solid seconds and one aborted scowl to realize that she was joking. Chloe Brown had just made yet another joke in that deadpan, oddly self-deprecating way of hers, which she really had to stop doing because he was starting to enjoy it.

She turned to leave the room while he questioned his grip on reality. "If you hear any ominous bangs," she called, "knock. If I don't respond, you can rush in to my rescue."

". . . Knock?" he echoed blankly.

"On the bathroom door," she told him, as if he was being particularly thick. "I've decided to use your presence as supervision."

"Super—?" Too late. She'd disappeared, mountain of medication in hand. "All right then," Red said to the empty living room.

The cat miaowed.

"Shut it, you. If she's hurt herself, you're to blame."

The cat was blatantly unrepentant.

Red went to make the tea.

The kitchen was comparatively tidy and reasonably clean. It had a few additions to the standard outfit, too: most notably a dishwasher, sleek and quietly efficient, which he had *not* authorized. She also had a plush little seat, the kind found at fancy bars, placed randomly by the oven. Odd. She had countless different flavors of tea, plus some PG Tips—thank Christ—all in the usual place. No milk in the fridge, but there was an army of juice cartons in there, plus a ton of stacked-up Tupperware boxes. Those boxes were filled with salad, chicken, tuna, sliced cheese, and more. Like a little pre-chopped buffet.

Someone was looking after her. Or she did all this herself because she was proper anal. Red looked out at her tornado of a living room and decided that the first option seemed more likely. Now, why would someone look after Chloe Brown? Maybe she was a spoiled brat. Maybe she needed the help sometimes. Maybe he should mind his own business and make the fucking tea.

He made it, helped himself to the biscuit tin as payment, enjoyed what appeared to be a homemade gingersnap, and grabbed a couple more. In the living room, he spotted empty packets of fancy chocolate among all the rubble. If he was going to bring Chloe Brown food, which he would never do, he'd bring something sweet. She seemed like a sweet sort of woman.

And he seemed like he'd lost his mind.

He made space for the tea on the table, between rubbish and

cats, and perched on the sofa beside a PlayStation controller and a spray of shiny business cards. The cat didn't seem particularly interested in the tea, but Red kept half an eye out even as he studied the cards.

Sublime Design Online
Web design, SEO, social media branding, and more

Chloe's details were on the back.

Huh. Fancy that. He needed a website; apparently, she made them. Not that he'd ever hire her. Ideally, he'd prefer a web designer he didn't want to strangle.

"Nosy, nosy, nosy," Chloe said.

He looked up to find her leaning against the doorway, not in a casually charming sort of way, but in a can't-stand-up-straight sort of way. He leaped to his feet. "Are you all right?"

"Absolutely. Are you eating my biscuits?"

He shoved the last one in his mouth and mumbled, "Nah."

"I saw you."

"I see the cat."

"Point taken." Her walk toward him was slow and painful to watch. She moved like someone who'd taken a beating. If he hadn't helped her safely down that tree himself, he'd assume she'd fallen. She was wearing her glasses now, at least, along with an enormous pink dressing gown and a pair of equally enormous bunny-ear slippers. The slippers surprised him until he remembered that Chloe used cuteness to disguise her inner evil. Sort of like Professor Umbridge.

Except he couldn't imagine Professor Umbridge saving a cat from a tree. Never mind. He'd think about that later.

Her eyes seemed a little too bright and unfocused. Her hair was down, floating around her face in fluffy waves that reminded him of thunder clouds. She patted at it self-consciously with hands that . . . shook? For fuck's sake. He barely resisted the urge to pick her up and carry her off to bed. Didn't want her to take it the wrong way. He also didn't want to care about her problems, but he knew himself well enough to realize that he'd care for a great white shark if given half the chance. He helped. Always. He just couldn't help himself.

"You shouldn't barge into people's homes," she said, "if you can't cope with a minor state of undress."

He sat down, realizing that he'd been staring. She seemed embarrassed by the scrutiny. "Sorry. I'm fine. I'm an intrepid home barger. Don't worry about me."

"I wasn't." She collapsed onto the mammoth sofa like a sack of potatoes, surrounding him with a cloud of soft, floral scent. "Give me the tea, would you?"

He gave her the tea. She cradled it like a baby and sipped with obvious relief. He watched her as closely as he could, which was pretty fucking close. And Red noticed things. Like the faint *V* between her eyebrows, the grimace she couldn't quite fight. The moisture that gleamed on her throat and collarbone, maybe left over from the shower, as if she hadn't dried off fully. The bare curve of her calves, visible beneath the hem of her dressing gown. That last part wasn't relevant to his suspicions, so he didn't know why his mind got stuck on it. Whatever.

Finally, he asked, "Are you going to admit that you're hurt?"

"I am not hurt," she said, "I am in pain." Her voice was bright in a dangerous sort of way, like a knife flashing in the sunlight. Like she was ten seconds and one irritating question away from skewering him.

He used his most patient, judgment-free tone. "Difference being . . . ?"

"I'm always in pain, Mr. Morgan. Especially when I do ridiculous things like climb trees for ungrateful cats."

"Red," he corrected absently, while puzzle pieces slotted together in his mind. "Chronic pain?"

She looked up at him, clearly surprised.

"What? I know things."

Her eye roll could only be described as epic. "How wonderful for you."

That, apparently, was the end of that. She didn't seem inclined to explain further, and if she wasn't hiding some urgent injury, the whole thing was none of his business. He told himself that very firmly: *None of my business. None of my business. None of my fucking business.* She'd have people to call when she needed them, the way his mum called him when she fucked up her insulin. There was no reason for him to hang around any longer.

But he should finish his tea, shouldn't he? It wouldn't be polite to leave it.

He sat and stared out of the window, sipping his almost-cold brew. Beside him, Chloe did the same. He could see his own window through hers, across the narrow courtyard. Could see his abandoned easel and even a few naked canvases piled around the room. Prime spying position, this was.

He gulped down the last of his tea and looked over to find that her eyes were closed, her face slack.

"You want me to bugger off so you can sleep?"

"I'm not tired," she said instantly. "I'm just resting my eyes."

Since that was clearly bullshit, he should leave. Yet he found himself hanging around and blurting out pointless crap like "So you're a web designer."

"Yes," she murmured.

She was so quiet, her usual snap-crackle-flame extinguished, that he found himself wanting to bring it back any way he could. Even if that meant pissing her off. "Wouldn't have thought you'd bother with a job. What with your family being loaded and all."

It worked, kind of. She cracked open one eye like a sunbathing lizard and managed to look haughty while doing it. "You don't know my family is wealthy."

He snorted. "You gonna tell me they're not?"

She closed the eye.

"So why do you work?" he asked, not because he was genuinely curious, but because he wanted to keep her lively. That was all.

She sighed. "Perhaps the monthly amount I receive from the trust is not enough to keep me in sea-salt chocolate and tea. Or maybe I am addicted to ordering antique Beanie Babies for thousands from eBay. It is possible that all my clothes have tiny diamonds sewn into the seams."

He couldn't help himself. He laughed. "You're so fucking . . ."

So fucking unexpected. Like maybe she wasn't the vicious snob he'd once assumed. Like maybe she was just an awkward, sarcastic grump, and he should stop losing his temper around her.

Christ, he didn't even *have* a temper unless he was around her. And he'd learned the hard way that letting a woman fuck with his contentment was a stepping stone on the way to bad shit.

Maybe that was why he found himself saying, "Just so happens that I need a website."

"Really?" Her tone was dry as sandpaper, but somehow, he could tell that she was interested.

Or maybe that was just wishful thinking.

"You're probably one of the posher designers, right? Bet you charge out the arsehole."

"Indeed I do." She opened her eyes, and something zipped up his spine when their gazes met. It was hot and cold all at once, unexpected and unexplainable. He was still trying to figure it out when she added, "Since you're being so decent about the cat, I might give you a discount."

Red arched an eyebrow. "What cat?"

The tilt of her lips was so tiny, it could barely be called a smile. If he *did* decide to call it a smile, well—it would be the first time she'd ever smiled at him. Not that he'd been keeping track.

"This is only until we find the owners, mind," he added quickly.

Her not-smile widened like a waxing moon. "It has no collar."

"Don't look like a stray to me, though. It'll be chipped."

"I'll find out," she said.

"Good. And keep it inside, yeah?"

"I'll see if one of my sisters has time for an emergency kitty litter run."

Red sighed, resigned to the pitfalls of his own nature. "I'll do it."

She gave him one of her usual looks, all irritated and snooty. He was trying not to bristle when she followed up with actual words, words he really hadn't expected. "You're so *lovely*," she scowled. "I don't think I can stand it."

He blinked, an unsettling warmth creeping up the back of his neck. Which meant—bugger this skin of his—that he must be flushing like a teenager. He looked away and shoved his fingers through his hair. His voice was gruff when he said, "It's nothing."

There was a pause before she laughed, the sound low and disbelieving. "Oh, my goodness. You *blush*."

"Nope." He knew full well his face was bright red, but he lied anyway.

"You *do*. This is hilarious. I should compliment you more often."

"Please," he said wryly, "don't." Clearly, he couldn't take it.

"Fine. I promise to be consistently awful." She smiled, *really* smiled. It was bright and lopsided and absolutely stunning. It only lasted for a second, but he saw the impression of it behind his eyelids the way he might see a firework that had gone out. Then she frowned and raised her fingers to her lips, as if she was confused by her own moment of happiness. Which, aside from anything else, was pretty fucking depressing. She looked at him, her eyes narrow and considering, like he was some kind of lab rat. "Alive," she murmured under her breath. "Hm."

His eyebrows rose. "Pardon?"

She cocked her head. "I think . . . I do believe I have a proposition for you."

There was nothing seductive in her tone, but the words sent a twisted kick of *something* through his chest. He'd watched too many rubbish spy films where propositions always ended in blow jobs. "What's up?"

"It's rather a long story." She bit her lip. "Actually, never mind the story; you don't need to hear it. The short version is that I need to ride a motorbike."

He'd have been less surprised if she'd gone with the blow job thing. Chloe Brown. Motorbike. Didn't really compute. He wracked his brain for a passable response and finally came up with "Okay?"

She nodded. "And you, obviously, *have* a motorbike."

". . . Yeah, I do."

"Would you like a free consultation? For your website?"

". . . I might."

"Then it's settled." She closed her eyes again. "I'll give you one, and you'll take me for a ride. Do you mind if we handle the details another time? As it turns out, I *am* rather tired."

He opened his mouth to say something like "Now wait a fucking minute," but all that came out was "Uh."

"I'll be in touch."

That's what she said. *I'll be in touch.* Like she'd just interviewed him for the position of motorbike chauffeur and would let him know how he'd done in due time. Christ, she was so far up her own arse, it was a miracle she could see the sun.

"Good-bye," she added.

He was stuck between telling her to piss off, remembering that she was a tenant, and wanting to die of laughter.

Then she cracked open one eyelid and said suspiciously, "You're not one of *those* men, are you? Because you'd be surprised by how loud I can scream. Years of vocal training."

Red stood. "Nope. No. Don't worry. Going."

"Thank you," she murmured.

He went.

Ten minutes later, he was in his own living-room-slash-studio, watching Chloe "rest her eyes" through the window. She looked pretty fucking asleep to him, but that was none of his business. He just wanted to check that the cat hadn't curled up on her face and suffocated her or something. Cats couldn't be trusted, as Vikram was telling him through the phone.

"Nasty little buggers. They piss behind sofas, you know."

Red ran a hand through his hair and turned away from the window. "If you say so. Look, it's just until we find the owners. Woman from 1D grabbed the thing out of a tree, so she's not about to chuck it over to the RSPCA."

"Hm, 1D," Vik mused. Red shouldn't have mentioned specifics. Vik was too clever for his own good and had a fantastic memory. "Ain't that the one you're always moaning about?"

Red glared at thin air. "*Always?*"

"Always."

"Nope."

"Alisha!" Vik bellowed. "Red's on about the rich bird from 1D again."

In the distance, he heard Vik's wife holler back, "Oh, he isn't. Tell him to bloody shut up about her."

"See?"

"Fuck off."

Vik sighed dramatically. "There's no shame in having a type, mate. The posh ones never did it for me, but—"

"Vik."

"—your tastes leave a lot to be desired."

"*Vik.*"

"One month, and the cat's got to go," Vikram said, smoothly changing the subject. *Thank Christ.* "And don't let it out of the flat. If anyone sees it, there'll be hell on earth."

"That's what I told her. I'm dropping some litter off in a bit."

"Oh yeah? She can't get it herself?"

Well, no, she probably couldn't. "I'm the superintendent."

"Right," Vik snorted. "That's exactly why."

"Yep."

"Not like you're soft on her."

Not bloody likely. "You know me. I'm soft on everyone."

"True enough, mate. True enough."

Red put the phone down. He spent the rest of the day avoiding his window.

CHAPTER FIVE

Chloe's youngest sister played five different instruments, but her greatest asset was her voice. Eve Brown had, as Gigi would say with great significance, *lungs*. So when she burst into Chloe's flat belting out "Defying Gravity" like Idina Menzel on Broadway, the cat reacted as if an earthquake had hit.

Chloe watched her placid companion fly into a state of major feline alarm. She'd learned since rescuing it a couple of days ago that this particular cat was not like most others; it lacked all grace and spatial awareness, as evidenced by its current path of evacuation. Streaking off in the direction of the bedroom, it managed to hit the sofa, the base of a standing lamp, and the door frame before making good its escape. Chloe had decided that this nervous clumsiness marked the two of them as a fated pair. She had also, in moments of exhaustion or panic, been known to bump into a door several times on her way through.

Eve bounded into the now cat-less living room and trilled, "We come bearing snacks!" Then, seeing Chloe's wince, she removed one of her ever-present AirPods and stage-whispered, "Oh, sorry. Do you have a headache?"

"No."

"She's lying," Dani said, appearing in the doorway with far too many shopping bags. She wore a fluffy gray hat to protect her shaved head from the cold. "I always know when you're lying, Chlo. I've no idea why you bother. Tea?"

Chloe rolled her eyes and snuggled deep into the nest she'd made on the sofa. "Is it tea? Or is it one of your bush concoctions?"

Dani waggled her eyebrows menacingly and raised the shopping bags. "Don't worry, darling. Evie baked devil's food cake to make the medicine go down."

Ten minutes later Chloe was indeed armed with a steaming mug of mysterious, spicy liquid and a fat slice of gooey chocolate cake. She shoved the latter into her mouth with shameless enthusiasm and let her eyes roll back, headache be damned. "This is divine."

"I made it just for you," Eve said, and patted Chloe's knee like a concerned mother. It had been three days since the Grand Climb, and Chloe had been on the sofa throughout because her body was throwing a tantrum. Her sisters, being painfully nosy, had finally caught wind, and had therefore descended upon her to treat her like a baby. It was mildly irritating and simultaneously endearing, because it involved both pats and heavenly chocolate cake.

"Thank you. You're a very good baker."

"I'll put that in the window of my cake shop one day," Eve said brightly. "*I am a good baker. My sister says so.*"

Chloe raised her brows. "Cake shop?"

"That's the latest plan," Dani called from the hallway. "But don't ask her about it, or she'll start whining about the tyranny of skeptical parents who refuse their daughters business loans, and you know I can't stand her spoiled-brat routine." Ignoring their youngest sister's outraged gasp, Dani marched back into the room with a hissing cat in her grip. "Now," she said, holding up the squirming bundle of fur. "Is this the creature you rescued?"

"No," Chloe murmured. "That's one of the countless other cats I acquired two days ago."

"Shut up." Dani squinted into a pair of narrowed, feline eyes, her expression stern, her jaw set. She had a habit of grinding her teeth when she was concentrating especially hard. Finally, she ended the interspecies staring contest and announced, "I judge this cat to be . . . a boy."

"Excellent," Chloe said, quite satisfied. "We'll name him Smudge."

"Oh, Chloe," Evie tutted. "You ought to name him Cat, like Holly Golightly."

The nerve of little sisters. Bossy boots, the lot of them. With a withering glare, Chloe said, "Don't tell me how to raise my children. His name is Smudge. The end."

"Wonderful." Dani set Smudge down and he ran off in a blur of smoke. After a minor collision with a table leg, he was gone. Dani snorted and slipped into their old Nana's patois. "Him 'fraid like puss."

"Of everything," Chloe admitted. "I think that's why he was stuck in the tree, actually: he could've gotten down, but he was too scared."

The air in the room changed, excited grins blooming like

flowers, all eyes turning to Chloe. "Ohhh, yes," Eve sang, lean-ing back against the cushions. "The *tree*. That you *climbed*. Like a *badass*! Care to share?"

Ah. Chloe smiled coyly. "It was rather impressive," she murmured, feigning modesty.

"Do tell," Dani drawled from her position sprawled out on the floor. Honestly, the woman was allergic to chairs. She was also good at ferreting out lies. But would she notice a minor (read: huge and ginger) omission? Hopefully not, because Chloe had no intention of bringing up Red's role in the palaver.

"I saw the cat, I got the cat. It was all very athletic. I climbed that tree like . . . like Lara Croft!"

"With sweaty cleavage and frequent, strangely sexual grunts?" Dani mused.

"With effortless expertise," Chloe corrected. Inaccurately.

"I'm sure you were quite Byronic," Eve said.

There was a short pause before Chloe deciphered that one. "Darling, do you mean *heroic*?"

"No."

Dani rolled her eyes. "Regardless, I'm glad you did it. Climbed the tree, I mean. Sorry that it triggered a spell, but also glad."

"Are you really, Dani?" Chloe narrowed her eyes, all suspicion. "Because it was part of my plan to be fabulously reckless and extremely exciting, and a little birdie tells me that you have a personal investment in my failure."

"Oh, don't be like that, darling. It's only fifty pounds; of course I'd rather lose. And anyway, I don't remember 'cat rescuing' or 'tree climbing' being on the list. Am I wrong?"

"No," Chloe admitted. "This was an extracurricular activity."

"Well, then. My fifty pounds is safe. But what will you do about the cat, long-term? Pets aren't allowed here, are they?"

"I've made a temporary arrangement with the superintendent," Chloe said, then mentally kicked herself.

Her sisters, predictably, collapsed in a chorus of lustful shrieks and sighs. "*Red,*" Eve said with such feeling you'd think she and the superintendent were Romeo and Juliet made flesh.

"*Redford Morgan,*" Dani purred, vixenish in a way Chloe had never mastered. Danika Brown was a left-wing academic and amateur spiritualist who shaved her head because "hair is just *so* much effort," but beneath it all, she took after Gigi. If Dani had been the one rescued from a tree by a handsome man, or woman, for that matter . . . well, she'd have secured said rescuer's affections by the time they hit the ground.

"How *did* you broker this deal?" Eve asked innocently, fluttering her lashes.

"She offered her body of course," Dani grinned.

"Oh, be quiet, the both of you. I'm not so desperate as that."

"Because sleeping with that man would be such torture," Eve snorted. "He is sex on a stick, Chlo. And he's so *sweet.*"

"Sweet?! Clearly, you barely know him."

"Which is why I'm not yet pregnant with his babies. What's your excuse?"

"Her excuse," Dani said, "is that he's so hot, he short-circuits her little robot brain."

"My robot brain is huge, thank you very much," Chloe sniffed. "And he does not *short-circuit* anything."

Dani gave a slow smile, an action that had been known to cause proposals, jealous fist fights, and in one notable case, a minor car accident. "Wonderful," she purred. "In that case, I expect you to sleep with him as soon as possible. Isn't sex on your list?"

Chloe narrowly avoided choking to death on her own astonishment.

"It *is*," Eve piped up. "Oh, go on, Chlo. Shag him. Tell us all about it."

Good gracious, sisters were a nightmare. "Men," Chloe said firmly, "are not for me." *Especially not* that *man. I wouldn't know what to do with him.* But her mind proposed several heroic suggestions, and her mouth went dry.

Dani cocked her head. "Finally decided to try women? Wonderful."

"I am trying no one, thank you very much." Clearly, her subconscious needed the reminder as much as her sisters did.

"Why not?" Eve demanded, her romantic nature clearly offended.

"You know why not."

"Clearly, I don't."

Sigh. "It's too much work. I can't be bothered."

Two sets of dark, unimpressed eyes speared her.

She doubled down. "It's very awkward, dating while disabled. People can be quite awful. And you know I don't have much energy to spare for social nonsense."

"*Social nonsense*," Eve snorted. "I swear, Chloe, you are so full of it."

Eve clearly didn't realize that "social nonsense" was Chloe's succinct way of phrasing "the constant disappointment that is human nature." She'd learned the hard way that people were always looking for a reason to leave, that affection or adoration or promises of devotion turned to dust when things got tough. Losing Henry had shown her that. Waking up one day to realize that her friends, bored with lists and rain checks and careful coping mechanisms, had left her behind . . . that had been unnecessary emphasis on a painful lesson. Chloe's family was abnormal in their loyalty, and she loved them for it, but they didn't seem to understand that others couldn't be trusted. Better to be alone than to be abandoned.

She refused to let that happen again.

But if she explained those facts, her sisters would insist she'd simply had a bad experience, then start insulting everyone who'd ever left her. And then Chloe would be forced to remember all the things she'd lost, and to wonder, for the thousandth time, what it was about her that made her so easy to leave.

It was time to change the subject, and also her pajamas.

Pushing off her blankets and rising to her feet caused a moment of dizziness, but she'd been ready for that. She waited. The encroaching blackness faded. "There," she smiled, pleased with herself. "Right as rain."

Dani looked up in alarm. "Where are you going?"

"I'm just popping into the shower. Won't be long." That was an unrepentant lie. She would indeed be long, and everyone present knew it.

"Would you like some help?" Eve asked.

"I'm not that bad." Chloe rolled her eyes and left her sisters in the living room. As she peeled off her worn-in pajamas and settled into the bathroom's plastic shower seat, she thanked God for the disability aids all ground-floor flats came with. After grabbing her shampoo and conditioner, she switched on the water and tipped her head back under the spray.

It had been a frustrating few days. She'd fallen into an infuriating cycle when she'd climbed that tree. Physical overload led to pain and a complete dearth of spoons, also known as mind-numbing exhaustion; which led to extra meds and insomnia; which led to sleeping pills and too much brain fog; which led to, in a word, misery.

When she found herself trapped in that cycle, Chloe was supposed to do certain things. Things like socializing with all her nonexistent friends, despite her inability to brush her teeth and change out of her pajamas. Things like forcing her battered body into excruciating Pilates positions, because it was *sooo* good for the muscles. Things like meditation, presumably so that she could think more deeply about how much she resented her own nerve endings. These, obviously, were the suggestions of specialist consultants who were rather clever but had never lived inside a body in constant crisis.

What Chloe actually did to cope was take her medication religiously, write fanciful lists, play *The Sims,* and live through it. Sometimes it was hard, but she managed by whatever means necessary.

Right now, her aches and pains had faded to a low background hum and her mind felt clearer than it had in ages. She scrubbed the three days' fever sweat from her scalp, smiling as she fingered the cute little kinks growing out at her roots. It was almost time for another chemical relaxer; she didn't have the endurance to care for her natural texture, pretty as it was. After conditioning, she lathered herself with entirely too much scented soap, standing long enough to rinse all the necessary bits. She watched the water send white suds sliding over her skin, like clouds moving over the earth. When she was sick and tired of being sick and tired, she clung to moments like this: the first shower after a flare-up.

Bliss should be held on to with both hands.

Some time later, Chloe was clean and dry and neatly outfitted in a tea dress and matching jumper—though her jumpers were all designed to look like cardigans. She liked the little buttons, but her fingers couldn't always handle slipping them in and out of holes. Her glasses were freshly polished and her hair was in a sleek bun. She'd taken her anti-inflammatories, her weakest painkillers, and the pills that protected her stomach lining from the damage caused by her other pills.

Then she'd returned to the living room, largely ignored her bickering sisters, and written several lists: people to email, jobs to catch up on, mood and diet diaries to fill in. Last of all, she'd put a note in her journal, under the weekly to-do section. It was a single word.

Red.

She hadn't been sure what else to put. What did one write about a man with hair like a fall of fire and silver rings on his fingers, a man who smiled at everyone and didn't feel awkward about it, a man who was the exact opposite of boring Chloe Brown?

Apparently, just his name.

She drifted back to reality to find her sisters arguing about Lady Gaga, because of course they were.

"It was a stepping stone. Everyone stumbles during a period of growth."

"It was ruinous, Evie. I mean!" Dani threw up her hands. "After the majesty of *Born This Way*—"

"You only like *Born This Way* because it's all dark and evil and rah-rah-rah."

"Don't be ridiculous. I like it because it's unapologetically sexual and ironically German."

"You're ridiculous."

"Says the woman who prefers 'Paper Gangsta' to 'Judas.'"

"Oh, please," Eve scoffed, clearly disgusted. "That track is the biggest waste of vocal talent ever created."

Dani arched an eyebrow. "Darling. You act as though you've never heard a Miley Cyrus song."

Eve's scowl wavered, then disappeared. She giggled. Dani laughed.

Chloe rolled her eyes. "If you two are quite finished . . ."

Truthfully, they shouldn't be here at all. Dani had a never-ending list of Ph.D. things to accomplish, and Eve was always embroiled in some favor or other for one of her many friends. But they'd come anyway, because they were her parents' agents in the secret war to Monitor Poor Chloe's Health—and because they wanted to make sure that she didn't pass out in the shower and crack her head open. Chloe wanted to make sure of that, too, so their presence was always appreciated on days like these. But they had other places to be, lives to live, et cetera.

And Chloe had an item to check off her Get a Life list. All she had to do was get the ball rolling.

So she shooed her sisters out of the flat, kissing cheeks and arranging a film night, vowing to visit Gigi soon—Eve would pass on the message—and showering them in sarcastic remarks because she'd rather die than actually say *Thank you*. She hadn't always been like this, a tongue with the tip bitten off, her feelings squashed into a box. But help and concern, even from the people she loved—even when she needed it— had a way of grating. Of building up, or rather, grinding down. Truthfully, guiltily, sometimes simple gratitude tasted like barely sweetened resentment in her mouth. So she didn't express it at all.

When they were gone, she felt deflated and unusually alone, even though Smudge had reappeared from his hiding place. She stood in her empty living room, which was now tidier, thanks to Dani, and stared at the window across the courtyard.

She'd googled Redford, of course. She'd even used her proper computer, the dual-monitor desktop in her bedroom, despite the fact that her touchscreen laptop and a small mountain of pillows were far more comfortable. She'd simply needed as much visual detail as possible. It had been a purely professional exercise: she'd wanted to find out if he already had an online presence, and if she was right in assuming that the website he needed had something to do with his art. She didn't know what she'd been expecting, exactly—but what she'd found were images of his work, images beautiful enough to take her breath away, shared on multiple sites and social media accounts by fans who asked each other where Redford Morgan had gone.

He's busy charming tenants in a block of flats in South Nottinghamshire. And yes, to answer your countless questions, he is indeed still creating.

She'd also found tabloid photographs, ones that surprised her far more than his talent and popularity. They'd shown big, rough Redford Morgan exiting glittering events on the arm of some society blonde with huge teeth. The woman was pretty and well-dressed, with glossy hair and designer shoes. She looked at Red the way a wolf eyed a sheep.

That was when Chloe had stopped googling. Something about that look sent a shiver creeping down her spine. Something about *witnessing* that look felt like . . . snooping. Which she had vowed to stop doing. For that very reason, she'd decided to forget all about her research, to act as though she knew nothing of Red's life. She would be the picture of ignorance, and therefore innocence, at their website consultation.

She hoped.

CHAPTER SIX

When Red was six or seven, he'd had a babysitter named Mandy. Mandy was only about thirteen herself, but she'd watched him in the evenings for a tenner a week, which in those days was enough money to keep her rolling in snacks and the occasional sneaky cigarette. She was a proper bookworm, but she'd wanted to do a good job watching him and all. She'd compromised by shoving him into bed early and reading aloud from her book of the moment for an hour or two. He blamed Mandy, to this day, for the strange quality of his dreams.

Thanks to her copies of *Alice in Wonderland* and *Peter Pan*, Red's nights were always a bit too vivid. He had Technicolor dreams, through-the-looking-glass dreams, down-the-rabbit-hole dreams. Dreams where shooting stars streaked fuchsia across bruised, sunset skies, and people didn't move so much as swirl into existence toward him, and music lived under his skin. It wasn't exactly normal, but it was what he'd grown used to. Which was why last night's dream had disturbed him so much.

Last night's dream had been different.

Dark, for one thing, pitch black, as if the lights were off inside his mind. Hot, hot like a midsummer evening, the air sultry and rich. And he'd been with a woman. Touched her, kissed her, woken up with his own come painting his belly and her name on his lips. *Chloe.*

Suffice it to say, he wasn't too happy about the implications. His wet dreams were few and far between because he was a grown man, and when they did happen, they involved cheerful, faceless women who didn't mind getting come on their tits. Maybe Chloe wouldn't mind getting come on her tits, either—Dream Chloe certainly hadn't—but she definitely wasn't cheerful or faceless. She also wasn't orgasm safe.

He couldn't stop reliving that dream, though. That fantastic fucking dream.

After a morning of mucking up basic maintenance, and an afternoon of struggling to bleed 3B's radiator—which was impressive, since it should be categorically impossible to fail at bleeding a radiator—he'd given up and gone home. He was now sitting in his bedroom like a lemon, as if returning to the scene of the crime would render him able to focus again. Un-bloody-likely, but Christ, something had to give.

Red fell back against the pillows and sighed. He was beginning to think he had some kind of fetish for unsuitable women. First there'd been Pippa, and now this disturbing interest in Chloe. It wasn't *attraction,* exactly, couldn't be, because Red had only ever been attracted to women he actually liked. No, this was something else. Something that whispered to him even now, heating his skin with memories of last night, swallowing up his good intentions and making his cock swell against his thigh. He took a breath, then another. He closed his eyes and drummed his fingers against the sheets. He resisted sudden, twisted temptation for as long as he could.

Which turned out to be about five seconds. Then he cracked like a perverted egg.

He was still wearing his uniform overalls, so it took one hand to pop open the buttons, reach past the waistband of his shorts, and palm his cock. When his mind helpfully produced the three-day-old memory of Chloe's bare calves and gleaming collarbone, he was caught between self-disgust and relief. On the one hand, it was incredibly weird that those glimpses were enough to get him going. On the other, it was also pretty convenient, since he would never actually see her naked body.

He could imagine it, though. And he did. Inside his mind, Chloe Brown was in his bed because she belonged there. He had no idea *why* she belonged, and Dream Chloe was in no state to explain it to him, but she definitely did. He could feel her soft skin against his, her breath in his ear, her nails digging into his biceps. A phantom scent haunted him, salty like the ocean air on a seaside holiday—or like the sweat between the bodies of two people chasing sensation.

He squeezed the base of his shaft and felt an electric pulse of pleasure. His other hand moved to cup his heavy sac, full and firm and tight against his palm. He didn't know whether to be relieved or worried by the realization that this wouldn't take long. A minute, at most. He stroked himself hard, twisting his fist as he reached the swollen head, smoothing slick pre-come over sensitive skin with his thumb.

Sinking into her was tempting, but he moved down her naked body instead. Eyes shut against the truth of his own weakness, he breathed her in, bathed in her heat. Lowered his head. Swept his tongue over her, parting plump labia to tease her clit and taste the wet, scorching center of her cunt. In the real world, he shuddered, as if his body was overwhelmed. His next breath sounded more like a gasp. He stroked himself faster and thought about how she'd react, how her thighs would tighten around him and her hips would arch up toward him and that dangerous voice of hers would crack on his name—

Someone knocked at his front door.

Red shot out of bed and stared down at himself. His overalls gaped open in a helpful little window of perversion, display-ing his jutting cock—also known as the undeniable evidence of what he'd almost done. But, he told himself feverishly, last night didn't count since it had been a dream, and this didn't count because he hadn't actually come. *It didn't count.* Everything was fine. He cleared his throat, shoved his traitorous dick out of sight, and headed for the bathroom. On his way, he called in the direction of the door, "Just a sec."

The last voice he'd wanted to hear replied, "Please, don't hurry on my account." A crisp, deadpan tone that he now knew signified a joke.

Red froze, asked God what he'd ever done to deserve this, then remembered his activities of approximately sixty seconds ago and realized the answer. Hoping he was wrong, knowing he wasn't, he choked out, "Chloe?"

"Very astute, Mr. Morgan."

Shit.

"Just . . . hold on," he ordered, jerking back to life. He rushed to the bathroom, his heart pounding. Hands were washed, uncomfortably warm cheeks were cooled with tap water and his overalls were buttoned up. Completely. To the very top. He had the strangest idea that his virtue wasn't safe around her, which was the single weirdest thought he'd ever had. He pulled himself together—eventually—and went back to answer the door. And when he saw her, he understood why he hadn't been able to get her off his mind.

His dreams couldn't truly re-create her. Something about her was too striking to remember accurately, as if his brain didn't have the right tools. She watched him with those endless eyes, folding her arms under her breasts—but he wouldn't look at those—and arching her eyebrows. One, as always, winged higher than the other. Just like one corner of her lush mouth tilted a little higher, making her look as if she was smirking.

Actually, she *was* smirking. She cocked her head and asked, "What on earth has happened to you?"

Red looked down sharply, searching for whatever had given him away. The baggy cut of his clothes hid the fact that his cock was, for some reason, still hard. He stared at his own hands and found them unusually paint-free and, more important, come-free. Because he hadn't actually come. Which was key information. He met her gaze and said, as calmly as he could manage, "What do you mean?"

She studied him suspiciously. "You're all flushed. Your hair is a mess. And . . ." She leaned forward, squinting at his chest. "I think you've done your buttons incorrectly."

Oh, for fuck's sake. She knew. Somehow—perhaps because she was a witch who haunted his dreams—she *knew*. And now she'd hold it over his head, use it as a weapon, because that's what people like her did. He knew it. He'd learned it well. He—

"Redford Morgan," she said severely, "have you been sleeping on the job?"

He was so relieved, he almost passed the fuck out. He clutched the door frame and released a heavy breath, his hair hanging around his face as his head fell forward. Then he remembered that he was trying to seem normal, unsuspicious, and not at all like a man who wanked over women—*tenants*—he barely knew. He straightened and cleared his throat in what could only be described as the guiltiest move of all time. Chloe was eyeing him with obvious confusion.

"I was," he lied. "I was taking a nap."

"Hmm. I expect you're one of those people who doesn't respect the power of ten hours a night."

"I thought it was eight?"

"Rubbish. It's definitely ten."

The glint in her eye said she was prepared to argue. He decided not to push it and searched for another subject. His gaze landed on the sturdy black case hanging from her shoulder. "Got something for me?"

"In a way. It's my laptop. I thought I'd call round and see if you were free for the consultation." She stepped forward. There was so much authority in that single step that he automatically stepped back. All of a sudden, she was in his flat. How the fuck had that happened? And how the hell was he going to get her out again?

He opened his mouth to say, *Please go away,* then remembered that he wasn't a rude prick and closed it. Fact was, he couldn't stand men who treated women differently because they were desirable. And really, the dream wasn't that big a deal. He just needed a good shag, and she was undeniably gorgeous, and his subconscious had slammed both facts together. That was all.

Red shut the door and said, "Yeah. Now's good."

"Wonderful." Her smile was small and impossibly sunny. Her skirt swirled around her legs as she turned to face him. It was a floofy sort of vintage skirt, white with bright red poppies creeping up from the bottom. He liked it. But then, he liked all the prissy shit she wore. Despite himself, he let his gaze drift to her legs. He could see her calves again today, and her ankles, circled by the leather straps of her shiny shoes. He drank in every detail like some sexually deprived Victorian bloke.

"Are you all right?" she asked.

"Fine."

From behind the turquoise frames of her glasses, her gaze narrowed. "You really don't seem like yourself."

"You don't know me."

There was a pause before she admitted, "True." Her shoulders were still thrown back and her nose was still firmly in the air, but for a moment she seemed . . . vulnerable. Like he'd upset her.

His first instinct was to apologize. Then he remembered that he'd told the truth, that he didn't like her, and that she'd definitely spied on him. He shouldn't care about her feelings. He was determined not to care about her feelings.

She followed him to the living room until, halfway down the hall, he remembered that he didn't actually *have* a living room, since he'd turned it into a studio. He recalled the little chair in her kitchen, and how plush and cushioned it had been, with a proper back to it. He stopped. Scowled at nothing in particular, or maybe at himself, and said, "I don't suppose you'd be too comfortable on a shitty wooden stool, would you?"

She gave the fastest, tiniest wince, but he saw it, somehow. *Note to self: stop looking at Chloe so hard.*

"Not comfortable, no," she said awkwardly. Judging by the way she avoided his gaze, she didn't quite know how to say, *I absolutely cannot sit on a shitty wooden stool.* He'd chalk that up to shyness, but he knew she wasn't shy. So why wasn't she making unselfconscious demands, like she had three days ago?

Maybe she's uncomfortable because you're being a broody twat.

Oh, yeah. Maybe. A slight glower had sneaked onto his face while he wasn't looking. The air in the hall vibrated with tension that was all his. Guilt dragged at him. He, in turn, dragged a hand through his hair. "Listen . . . Sorry if I'm being a bit of a prick. I'm, er . . . still tired."

She gave a tight smile and a shrug. "It's all right if you've changed your mind, you know."

He said, very intelligently, "What?"

"About our deal. A consultation for a ride?"

Not that kind of ride, he told his cock firmly.

"I'm aware that I browbeat you into it," she went on. "I have a tendency to do that."

He'd never have guessed.

"But if you're having second thoughts, please feel free to say so. Don't worry about my feelings. I have very few."

He could tell by the tone of her voice that she was taking the piss with that last part. When Chloe joked, she sounded slightly more serious than when she was *actually* serious. Still, he couldn't stop himself from protesting. "I'm sure you have more than a few."

She shrugged again.

"I haven't changed my mind," he told her.

She smiled a little bit, and his heart stammered. She looked so quietly, secretly pleased, so impossibly sweet, and he just—he couldn't—oh, for fuck's sake.

"All right then," she said, tentative warmth in her voice.

Oh, for fuck's *sake.* Even if she was rude and she made him feel like a monster of a man, he could not be a dick to Chloe Brown, not anymore. He accepted that fact and reassured himself that this wouldn't be like the last time. He wouldn't trip and stumble into the life-ruining black hole of making excuses for a seemingly perfect woman. He couldn't. For one thing, he didn't think Chloe was perfect at all. For another, they weren't in a relationship and never would be. So there. He was safe.

They stood for a moment, staring at each other like a pair of tits. He cleared his throat and said, "Change of plans. Do you mind sitting in my room?"

Her lips didn't smile but her eyes sparkled like diamonds. "I don't know. You're not going to ravish me, are you?"

He almost choked on his own tongue.

"Good Lord," she laughed, while he caught his breath and his wits. "Don't look so horrified!"

"I'm not—I mean—*horrified* is a strong word."

She shook her head. "Really. I was only joking, Redford."

"Red," he corrected, because he had nothing else to say.

"I was only joking, Red."

He cleared his throat. "Just to, ah, just to be clear, you're not . . . horrifying."

"Of course I'm not," she said. "I'm extremely attractive. Now, shall we go and sit down?"

He bit back a smile and took her to his bedroom. Then he wondered what the fuck he'd been thinking. Did blue balls lower intelligence? Maybe. It was the only reasonable explanation for him setting Chloe loose in his room, also known as the scene of his almost orgasm. He couldn't look at her. He also couldn't look at the bed, but he knew the blankets were rumpled where he'd lain, and . . .

Well. He'd rather not think about it, to be honest.

"This isn't very artistic," she said wryly, her eyes everywhere. She stared for a long time at the art history books stacked on his dresser. He found himself wanting to check that he'd closed his underwear drawer.

"What were you expecting? Finger paintings on the walls?"

"Is that your area of expertise? Finger painting?" She looked down at his hands. His palms tingled with the false memory of touching her.

He curled his hands into fists and shook his head. "Figurative. Acrylic. I—never mind. I'll have to show you, won't I? For the website?"

"Yes," she said faintly. "For the website."

Red grabbed the armchair he kept in the corner of the room and shoved it closer to the bed. Chloe sank gracefully into its tattered, tartan depths. She crossed her legs, which probably made her skirt ride up a little bit, but Red wouldn't know, because he absolutely was not looking. He had firmly instructed his eyes to focus only on her ears (which, while cute, weren't especially arousing) or her nose (ditto) or the wall behind her. So far, things were going okay-ish.

Once she was settled, he went and grabbed a piece to show her, something he'd finished just last week. After all, there was no use in showing her what he *used* to do, how it had all been lucid and bright and hopeful. He wasn't the same anymore, and that was that.

But when Red returned with the canvas, he found himself hesitating before his bedroom door. Something uncomfortable tightened in his stomach, making the back of his neck prickle. Nerves. He was absolutely shitting it, which was how he'd felt the last few hundred times he'd tried to show someone his art. Ever since it had changed, that is. Ever since he'd fucked almost everything up, and the bits of his life that he hadn't messed with had been fucked on his behalf. But this, he decided, was the perfect way to get over his weird performance anxiety, because he didn't actually care about Chloe's opinion.

The thought clanged in his head like a lie, but he stepped into the room before he could figure out what that meant.

"Here," he said gruffly, handing her the canvas and perching on the edge of his mattress. She was silent as she accepted the piece, studying it for long moments while he looked anywhere but her.

Then the quiet stretched so far that his attempt to remain cool wore thin, wavered, snapped. He gave in and looked, needing to see her reaction, even though he absolutely did not care.

The awed expression on her face gave Red the shock of his fucking life. Really. It was a near-violent jolt of power to his system, one that left his blood pumping harder and his vision clearer, sharper. A slow smile of surprise tugged at his lips. Surprise, and dizzying, hard-exhale relief.

Chloe was . . . delighted. That was the only word for it. She stared at the eerie, blood-toned landscape with its impossible hues and fantastical proportions as if she knew exactly how he'd felt when he painted it. As if every emotion he'd poured onto the canvas had remained like a little slice of leftover soul, and now that slice was slapping her in the face. Energy. Exuberance. Mystery. Strength. Giddy satisfaction with your own bad behavior. That was what Red had shoved into his paint on the night he'd created this piece, *Neverland,* and that was what he saw reflected in her eyes.

Finally, she cleared her throat, seemed to school her expression, and said, "You're very talented. Not that I know what I'm talking about."

Her words were measured and polite, but it was too late. He'd seen. He'd seen, and it had touched something deep and wild in him that was probably best left undisturbed. Something that made him feel more firmly settled in his own skin. He wanted to touch her, just to see if things felt different now. Now that he knew she saw something the same way he did.

But if he went around grabbing her for reasons he could barely explain, she'd probably whack him over the head, and she'd be well within her rights. So he curled his suddenly curious hands into harmless fists and told himself that the air didn't taste like reassurance or renaissance or redemption. He'd always been dramatic when it came to things like this. He was a puppy and someone loving his art was a killer scratch behind the ears. That was really it.

She handed him the canvas and he tossed it onto the bed and returned to his earlier tactic of looking anywhere but her face. It didn't help. He'd almost managed to forget that he wanted her, but the raw emotion he'd just seen had brought the need right back. He knew he was supposed to say something, but his scattered brain couldn't quite remember what.

Oh. Yeah. She'd complimented his work. So this was the part where he said . . .

"Thanks." He tried not to wince at his own voice. Too low, too rough, too obviously affected.

She pursed her lips and looked down at her knees, her dark lashes fluttering behind her glasses. She wasn't cursed with translucent skin like his, but he could've sworn she was blushing. Probably because he'd been so obviously grateful for the slightest compliment.

Feeling the need to explain, he said, "I haven't shown anyone my new stuff in a while."

"I know," she said, then looked up with wide eyes and clapped a hand over her mouth.

He arched an eyebrow, smiled at the *Oh, shit* expression on her face. "You know, huh?"

"For goodness' sake," she murmured.

"What's that?"

"Forget I said anything."

"No, thanks." He leaned forward. "Explain that, please."

She looked tortured as fuck. It was great. "I—well—I had some time free over the past few days, and so, in the name of preliminary research and everything, I, erm, googled you."

Ah. Why was he not surprised? "You know," he drawled, "for a woman who called me nosy about a thousand times the other day, you have a bad habit of peeping through windows."

She froze. Stuttered, "What—what do you mean?"

He smiled easily and felt evil. "Turn of phrase."

"Oh." The tension flooded out of her so fast, she deflated through sheer relief. If he'd had any doubt that her spying had been intentional, rather than a passing glimpse at her weird, shirtless neighbor . . . well, that doubt was officially dead. Chloe had watched him, and she felt guilty about it. He wondered when she'd confess.

Because she would confess. She had no filter, as most of the building had already learned.

She shifted uncomfortably and said, her voice brisk, "As an artist, you should really be on Instagram."

"Don't change the subject. Are you nosy with everyone, or just me?"

"I could link the feed to your website," she said desperately. "People do that. It's very pretty."

Instagram? Throwing his work up, not just for people to see, but on an app literally designed to display your fucking approval rating? The whole concept of internet likes had always unsettled Red, even when he'd been more confident in his abilities. "I'll think about it." *Lie.* "We're still talking about you."

"We are not." She looked horrified, so he had to keep going.

"You like to research everything," he guessed. "No; you like to know everything. You're one of those 'knowledge is power' people."

"Knowledge *is* power," she shot back.

"I bet you were a massive teacher's pet at school." He was grinning. Hard.

"I bet you were an aimless slacker," she said archly.

"I bet you always file your taxes on time."

She was clearly scandalized. "Who doesn't file their taxes on time?"

He burst out laughing. "Oh, Chloe. You're cute as fuck, you know that?" He had no idea how any of those words had slipped out, but he couldn't exactly snatch them back. And he didn't quite regret setting them free.

"Cute?" She wrinkled her nose. "No. No, I'm not."

She shouldn't be. "You are."

Primly, she threw his own words back at him. "You don't know me, Red."

Which was when he realized that he *had* upset her earlier, when he'd said exactly the same thing. That bothered him. A lot. He said, "I'd like to know you," then realized it came off like the world's worst chat-up line. Quickly, he added, "If I'm gonna let you on my bike, I need to know you're good people."

"Well, that's easy enough to discern. I saved a cat the other day, remember?"

He shrugged and leaned back, resting his weight on his hands. Slowly, reluctantly, he realized that he was comfortable around her—which made about as much sense as a toothless shark. "I remember. But I don't know if I care. I'm not a fan of cats."

"And why not?"

"They're judgmental."

"I had no idea that it was such a reprehensible trait. I expect to see you on the news soon, protesting the judiciary."

He snorted and tried again. "Cats are snooty."

"Or perhaps," she said wryly, "you're simply projecting your expectations."

"Perhaps," he replied, mocking her crisp words, "I prefer pets who aren't afraid to get dirty and don't lounge around looking down on people like the queen of bloody Sheba."

"Actually, Smudge would be the *king* of Sheba."

Red smiled despite himself. "Named him, have you?"

"Clearly."

"Took him to the vet's yet?"

"I've been indisposed."

He was going to have to buy a bloody dictionary to keep up with her vocab, but he could read between the lines. "All right. So, Smudge. Has he been . . . ?" Red trailed off politely.

Her eyebrows rose in question, one winging higher than the other. He felt that delicate, uneven arch in his gut. She really was beautiful.

And he really was easily distracted, staring at her like this. He cleared his throat, gave her a significant look, and said, "Smudge. Have they . . . You know."

Judging by her frown of confusion, she did not.

Give him fucking strength. No way was he saying this plain to a woman like her. She'd get it eventually.

Only, she didn't. He raised his eyebrows. He cocked his head, clicked his tongue, and looked down. Nothing worked. Chloe remained blank as a computer with no power. In the end, he gave up on subtlety and blurted, "Someone got rid of his knackers yet?"

She blinked, looking completely unoffended by his choice of words—while he, for some reason, could feel heat creeping up his neck. Irritating, irritating, irritating. Cool as anything, she told him, "I have no idea." Like it was ludicrous to think she would.

"No idea?" he echoed.

"I haven't looked." She wasn't looking at him, either. Her eyes wandered around the room with the sort of interest aliens and androids showed in sci-fi films when they came to earth for the first time. Meanwhile, he couldn't take his eyes off her. Great.

Probably sounding more annoyed than he should during a

conversation about a stray cat's bits and bobs, he demanded, "How'd you know he's a boy, then?"

She arranged her skirt over her legs, an action he saw in his peripheral vision but absolutely refused to focus on. He was focusing on her ear, and that was that. But the smooth, inviting sound the fabric made, like she was running her palms over it, pressing it tight . . . Maybe she secretly knew he was developing a minor obsession with her thighs, and this was her subtle and ingenious torture. Yeah. That sounded likely.

He was so busy thinking ridiculous thoughts, he almost missed her baffling explanation. Calmly, she told him, "We know Smudge is a boy because Dani decided he was."

He sighed, running a hand through his hair. He was almost afraid to ask. "And how did she do that?"

"Do you know," Chloe said, apparently confused, "I'm not sure I understand your obsession with genitals, Red."

His eyes, which had been doing so well, slid from the safe zone of her left ear to the decidedly *un*-safe zone of her skirt-covered lap. *You and me both, love.*

"Why do you ask, anyway?"

He jerked his eyes back north. "If he'd had the chop, that'd suggest owners."

"You don't need to worry, you know. I *am* going to take him to the vet. I'd hate to steal someone else's pet."

"Yeah, well, maybe I'll come with you. Just to make sure."

She gave him a look. He saw humor dancing in her eyes, a bright sparkle that matched the strange fizzing in his own chest. "You're a very rude man," she said.

"*I'm* rude?" He snorted out a laugh. "God almighty, that's rich, coming from you."

"And what is that supposed to mean?"

"Sorry, I thought I was being obvious. It means you're rude as fuck."

Apparently, she was actually shocked by that information. She gaped at him as if he'd started speaking in tongues, and then she made an odd little wheezing sound. Finally, she said, "Well, I *never.*"

"What? No one's ever told you that before?"

"Of course they have! But I've been on my best behavior with you."

He couldn't stop grinning. "Seriously? You're serious. *Seriously.*"

"Well, this week, at least."

He'd have loved to respond to the outrage in her voice, but he was laughing too hard.

"Stop that," she commanded, but she was smiling wider than he'd ever seen before. Her cheeks plumped up and her eyes danced and goddamn, she was even prettier than usual. "Stop! It's not that funny."

But, for some reason, it was. It was fucking hysterical. His breath came in gasps and his belly felt tight and his laughter bounced around the room. Then she reached out and pushed him. *Shoved* him, really, her palm flat against his chest, sending an odd warmth through his body. He fell back against the bed, still laughing helplessly—but he grabbed her wrist as he went. And pulled.

And she came tumbling onto the bed with him.

Yeah. He stopped laughing then, that was for sure.

She landed almost on top of him. Her wrist felt oddly delicate, like the bones were made of china. Her palm still rested against his chest; her other hand was on the bed, holding most of her weight. Still, she was close enough that he could feel the swell of her tits against his ribs, the curve of her belly against his hip, the weight of her thighs over his. Red swallowed hard, gritted his teeth, and willed his cock not to embarrass him, even though it already was. In a last-ditch attempt to maintain control, he closed his eyes.

Which was a mistake.

"I—sorry," she murmured. He felt her breath against his throat as she spoke and remembered a night they hadn't shared. *Fuck.*

"My fault," he replied. His voice was rough; his eyes still closed; his hand still curled around her wrist. He could feel her pulse racing. He could feel his own good sense flying out the window. The little demon that sat on his shoulder and whispered bright ideas like *Drop out of college,* and *Let your mate tattoo you in his kitchen,* and *Follow your heart,* said slyly that now was not the time for website consultations. Now, according to that demon, was the time to roll her over, push up her skirt, and make her beg.

Thankfully, he was old and wise enough to ignore that suggestion. He let go of her wrist, and she clambered off him. He sat up. They stared at each other. She straightened her glasses and tugged at the sleeve of her cardigan and gave a nervous little laugh.

The idea of mouthy, snotty Chloe Brown being *nervous* made him itch. Wasn't right and it wasn't natural. He needed to fix it. "How about we postpone the consultation?"

The subtlety of her expressions—the way she beat them down before they could fully form and shoved them into a box—wasn't enough to fool him anymore. He saw the slight slump of her shoulders and the way she blinked too hard, and knew she was disappointed.

"Can't seem to concentrate today," he went on.

"All right," she said briskly, bending to pick up her laptop. She hadn't even got it out of the bag. "I quite understand. I'll just—"

He ignored her. "Usually, when I get like this, I go for a ride."

She looked at him, her eyes even wider than usual behind her glasses.

"Fancy it?"

There was that smile of hers. Like the rising sun.

CHAPTER SEVEN

The neat little car park was at the rear of the building. Its flat tarmac and faded white lines were brightened up by intermittently placed leafy things, as if the designers had some sort of greenery quota and had shoved in a few plants to meet requirements at the last minute. Red's monster of a bike stood next to one of those plants, the shiny, electric-blue chrome a harsh contrast to the pale branches of the spindly birch sapling.

Chloe imagined that if the things in this car park were characters in an American high school movie, the motorbike would be a big old bully, and the poor little tree would be one of its victims. In its final year of compulsory education, that bike would be voted "Most Likely to End Up in Jail." She didn't think she should ride a school bully that was likely to end up in jail. She'd put this on her list because it seemed the epitome of reckless insouciance, but now that it might actually *happen,* she was feeling neither reckless nor insouciant.

But she took a deep breath and told herself sternly to buck up and get on with it. She would stick to her list, fear be damned, because people didn't change their lives by meekly giving up at the first heart-pounding hurdle. She was ready for this. Actually, she wasn't, but she'd do it anyway. She'd already agreed. She'd even made Red wait while she went home to put her laptop away. She couldn't back down now, just because one little crash might result in her brain being decimated.

Although, she did rather need her brain. For things. And stuff.

"Chloe." Red's voice was loud in the deserted car park, so deep it almost made her jump out of her clothes. Wait, no: *skin*. She meant skin.

"Yes?" she squeaked, dragging her gaze from the enormous bike to the enormous man standing beside it.

His eyebrows were raised, his lips slightly tilted. That was his resting expression, the opposite of her chronic bitch face: happy, curious, open, friendly. Why did she even like him?

Wait a moment—did she like him?

"You okay?" he asked.

"Fine," she said brightly. "Just thinking about the potential likelihood of brain decimation."

His smile widened at that, slow and steady and achingly handsome. Ridiculous man. Brain decimation was a serious business.

"You got any hard numbers on that?" he asked. "Odds, percentages?"

She scowled. "No, but if you'd give me a minute I could probably calculate some." That would wipe the amusement off his face, guaranteed. She pulled her phone out of her pocket, because *of course* her vintage-replica swing skirt had pockets.

There was a reason sartorial upheaval hadn't been mentioned on her Get a Life list; Chloe was already the coolest dresser on the planet. "Where do you think I'll find the most reliable crash statistics? Gov.uk?"

"Maybe," he mused. "Or maybe, I don't know . . . ScaredyCats .com?"

She looked up with a scowl, outraged. "What on earth is that supposed to—?"

He held out a big, clunky-looking helmet and interrupted her quite happily. "Give me your glasses."

"I'll do no such thing," she snapped, yanking the helmet out of his hands. She eyed it suspiciously, then studied the motorbike compartment he'd pulled it out of. The compartment that also doubled as a seat. *Hmm.* That didn't suggest the sort of structural integrity she typically desired in a vehicle.

"Glasses might not fit under the helmet," he said mildly. "It's full-face. You know, to reduce the chances of brain decimation."

She snorted, was silent for a moment as she studied the helmet. Then, in a fit of irritation, she muttered, "Don't act as though it hasn't crossed your mind."

Something hot and wild sparked in his gaze, a sort of sharp-edged teasing that reminded her of a wolf on the hunt. He leaned toward her over the bike and asked, "As though *what* hasn't crossed my mind?"

She shivered slightly, despite the thermal vest under her clothes and the jacket she'd picked up from her flat. And she remembered what had happened in his bedroom, when she'd fallen on top of him like a ninny, and sparks of sheer sensation had taken over her entire body. After a shamefully long silence, she blurted, "Brain decimation. The risk of brain decimation has definitely crossed your mind."

He gave her a crooked smile that seemed, for a moment, oddly triumphant. Then he straightened, shrugged, running a hand through all that glorious, sunset hair. "I don't let myself worry about that. If I die, I die. Could happen on this bike if I'm not careful or my luck blows. Could happen tomorrow morning if I trip and fall in the shower." He grabbed his own helmet. "You still in? It's okay if you're not."

She swallowed down her instinctive response, the worries she never voiced. Things like *I could get hit by a drunk driver in broad daylight while walking down the street. I could fall in the shower, not by chance, but because that's what I do. I fall sometimes. I could fall right now, and hit my head, and die.*

Except, if she fell right now, she had the oddest feeling Red wouldn't let her hit the ground.

She took off her glasses, turning his face into a pretty haze of pale cream and red-gold. "I'm in."

"Good." She could hear the grin in his voice. While she shoved on the helmet, he put her glasses . . . somewhere. The fact that she didn't know exactly where, and didn't really care, was testament to her new footloose and fancy-free attitude. She'd been right about her plan, about her list: the process of completing each task involved multiple adjustments in attitude and countless bite-sized moments of bravery, and those would all add up. By the time she finished, she'd have more than check marks and a few stories to tell.

She'd have a life.

The world beneath the helmet was strange and insulated, and her lack of sight didn't help, but Red talked to her. Like he knew she'd need some kind of guiding light, some reassurance. He said, "I'm touching you now," and then he did. His hands began fiddling with her helmet, adjusting it until it felt more comfortable. Then he zipped up her jacket. The action was brisk, over in a second, but it felt weirdly intimate in a way that made her stomach dip.

Which was silly. So, so silly. Who cared if he'd zipped up her coat? That was something parents did for their children. Clearly, he thought of her as a child. Which annoyed her on multiple levels, a few of which she didn't feel comfortable examining right now.

He, of course, was completely unaffected throughout her mental debate. "All you need to do," he said, with his typical mix of easygoing authority, "is keep your feet on the rests and hold on to me. I'll get on first and hit the throttle. It's loud. Don't freak out."

Apparently, despite witnessing her Lara Croft–like tree climbing the other day, he still thought she was the sort of woman who needed to be warned about loud noises. Depressingly, he was right.

He straddled the bike, and she wondered absently if he might be persuaded to straddle her. Purely so that she could cross item number five, meaningless sex, off of her list. She dismissed that rogue thought instantly, however; Redford wasn't a suitable candidate. Aside from the fact that his hotness was vaguely terrifying, she couldn't sleep with men who were clients, or men who lived just across the courtyard, or men who already knew certain things about her health and would therefore nervously reject all advances as if her vaginal canal were made of glass.

The bike roared to life like an angry lioness. She managed not to jump and was very proud of herself.

"Get on," Red told her.

She held her skirt down awkwardly as she swung one leg over the chrome beast. And then, there she was, sitting casually on a motorbike. It thrummed, huge and hot and weighty, between her thighs. And right in front of her was Redford, his back looking extraordinarily broad in black leather. She wasn't sure if she was intimidated or aroused. She checked in with her nether regions and discovered that she was both. Righto, then.

As if he'd heard her thoughts, Red's long, strong fingers wrapped around her calf and she almost fainted. He squeezed and something inside her clenched. Okay, not "something": her pussy. Good Lord. Then she realized abruptly that he was trying to tell her something. Right, yes, she was paying attention. She was a Very Good Chloe and she was taking this Extremely Seriously.

Gosh, his hands were big.

"Right there," he shouted, and squeezed her calf, and let go. *Boo.* But at least she understood what he meant: *Keep your feet where they are, right on those convenient little rest things I mentioned.* As if she'd forget. She'd be following his disgracefully minimal instructions to the letter, thank you very much.

Then he reached back, caught one of her hands, and pulled.

Next message, presumably: *Hold on to me.* He didn't need to remind her of that, either; she'd watched enough teen romance films to know how one behaved on the back of a hot guy's motorbike. She committed fully, shuffling closer to wrap her arms around his waist, lacing her fingers over his taut abs. She'd seen those abs naked. He wouldn't be giving her a ride if he knew *that,* now would he?

Guilt whirled in her stomach, making her feel slightly nauseous and extremely evil. It was wrong of her, to let him treat her so nicely when she knew he had reason to despise her—actual reason, rather than misunderstandings and awkwardness. She should confess. She had to. It was the right thing to do.

"Ready?" he shouted.

Not in the slightest. "Ready."

The engine growled. The world began to move. She reflected that her god-awful guilt had been a blessing in disguise because it had distracted her from reasonable concerns about her impending doom. Her stomach lurched even though she knew they were only going five miles per hour, because that was the car park's speed limit and Red was a very good and rule-abiding superintendent. Under her breath, beneath a helmet that was suddenly far too small, dark, and hot, she murmured, "It's only five miles per hour. It's only five miles per hour. It's only—"

They turned out of the car park and the bike shot forward like a bullet.

"*Good Lord,*" she shrieked at the top of her voice. She hadn't thought she could get any closer to Red, but she was now in danger of crawling into his skin. Her grip on his waist had become more of an "iron bar" situation. He probably felt like he'd been strapped into an electric chair on death row. *She* felt like she'd been strapped into an electric chair on death row, because anything that made her unprotected human body move as quickly as this was clearly a death sentence, and she couldn't exactly escape by throwing herself off, now could she?

Out of nowhere, she felt Red's glove-covered hand on hers. He squeezed, once, and she remembered that he was driving, actively controlling the beast beneath her. They weren't just flying through the world willy-nilly on a murder machine. An odd sort of calm moved through her and she remembered what he'd said earlier. *If I die, I die.*

If she died, she'd be doing so on the back of an intensely sexy superintendent's motorbike. Not a bad way to go, all things considered.

The blurry world grew even blurrier as their speed increased. She felt like data lost in the stream. Cars and buildings whipped by, as if the two of them were moving through time and dimensions rather than just space. It reminded her of the way she'd been years and years ago, running through crisp air as if she were flying, the thought of pain and life-changing fatigue never even crossing her mind.

The thrumming heat of the engine beneath her began to feel like a comfort, and then, all at once, like a tease. So did the body in front of her, though he wasn't doing a damned thing to make her feel that way. It was past time to accept that Redford Morgan made her as hot and bothered as Enrique Iglesias in the "Hero" music video, with considerably less effort. That was why she felt so odd and unsettled around him: because he shoved her into motion the way he had this motorbike, as if he had the key to her motor. Being around him without melting was another bite-sized step of bravery, just like every item on her Get a Life list.

Maybe he could help her come alive. Maybe he could help her with the rest of her list.

She bit her lip and her teeth felt too sharp for her mouth, as if she'd turned into a predator. She couldn't see a damned thing without her glasses but suddenly it didn't matter; she had wild eyes, that was all, wild just like the rest of her. Her skin was electrically charged, so she could do whatever she wanted— including make another deal with the boldest man she knew. There was safety in transactional relationships, after all. If he refused to help her, or if he tried and got tired and gave her up as a lost cause, it wouldn't rip her heart out like every other exhausted abandonment had.

It would just be the end of a deal.

But then she remembered that, when this ride ended, she'd have to confess what she'd done. That she'd invaded his privacy, that she'd practically stalked him. She highly doubted any deals would be forthcoming after that.

Would they?

Pippa had ridden with him once.

She hadn't liked it, which was fine. Red knew perfectly well that certain thrills weren't for everyone. The fact that his girlfriend had no tattoos hadn't bothered him—why would it?—so the fact that she'd hated the bike hadn't bothered him, either. He still remembered the way she'd stumbled off it that first time, yanking off her helmet so her glossy hair spilled out like a waterfall. He always remembered images like that.

She'd spat, "Never again, Red!" and when he'd laughed, she'd lost her temper and called him an imbecile with dog-shit sensibilities. For some reason, at the time, he'd thought that was a fight with his feisty girlfriend rather than an insult that would gnaw away at something vital in him. Maybe that was his problem in a nutshell: he'd seen cruelty like that as a challenge. And he'd felt rewarded when she wanted him, grateful when she stood at his side with all her poise and polish and easily recognized *personhood* in galleries where he felt barely human.

So, when she'd posed for Instagram photos on his bike, the one she hated so much, he hadn't let himself think it was odd. He'd watched her post the pictures with captions implying she was some badass biker chick, and then he'd locked his bike up and gotten in her chauffeur-driven car, just the way she liked it. Everything was for show. He'd been an accessory in more ways than one.

He had no idea why he'd taken Chloe out today. Why he'd agreed to her deal when he knew damn well he could pay for the consultation with actual cash. This was supposed to be his personal pleasure, now, never to be used again. Maybe he was falling back into bad habits, seeing cruelty as a challenge. But everything in him rejected the idea that Chloe could ever really be cruel. And besides, he didn't see her as a challenge; he saw her as an enjoyable pain in the arse. She made him irritable, yeah, but worse, she made him . . . curious. Oddly energized in a way he'd been craving, a way that felt so simply *good*.

And the way she felt sitting behind him right now? That made him satisfied.

Her thighs squeezed him as she screamed, which he liked more than he should. The screaming because it was so wild, so unexpected, and so full of glittering excitement. The squeezing because she was so soft and so hot, plastered against him like they were the only two people on earth. As if his physical fascination with her needed any more fuel. He'd only meant to run around the block real quick, but he was worried that if he stopped now, he might do something awful, like kiss the fuck out of Chloe Brown. And Christ, wouldn't that be the end of the world?

It would, he told himself. It really fucking would.

He spent the next ten minutes concentrating harder on the road than he had since his very first ride, forcing himself to calm down. By the time they pulled into the same car park where this fiasco had begun, his body was mostly under control. There was just the secret, burning core of him, smoldering for her. Good thing she'd never see it. He could almost pretend it wasn't there.

He cut the engine, toed the stand, dragged his helmet off, and sucked down some much-needed air. Behind him, he felt her fidgeting like a little kid. He held out his hand in silence, and she gave him her helmet and slipped off the bike. He stood. Wondered if, despite that one exhilarated scream, she'd actually hated it. Wondered why she'd wanted to go out in the first place. Opened his mouth to ask.

And was hit by an asteroid that felt suspiciously Chloe-shaped, slamming into his side and throwing its arms around him.

"That was amazing," the Chloe-shaped asteroid murmured. Didn't sound like Chloe; there wasn't an ounce of sarcasm in those three words. No hesitance or snooty distance, either. Just all this intense *feeling,* like she was full of the same white-lightning thrill he'd always chased and savored, like touching her should give him an electric shock. And it kind of did—not because of the palpable excitement coming off her, but because of the way her breasts pressed against his arm. Asteroids weren't supposed to have fantastic tits.

He patted her awkwardly on the shoulder and tried to seem disinterested. After dinner at Mrs. Conrad's, Vik had made it clear that friendship with tenants was fine—but the last thing Red needed was for someone to wander out here and see him grabbing the prettiest woman in the building. Knowing his luck, they'd investigate further, find out about Smudge, and decide that Chloe was trading sexual favors for pet privileges. Tenant wars could be ruthless and she might end up with a scarlet letter painted on her front door, which would take him fucking forever to scrub off.

"Thank you," she said.

"Uh," he replied, smooth as fuck. ". . . No problem." To add to his air of charm and intelligence, he patted her shoulder again. Brilliant. Bloody brilliant.

She pulled away abruptly, as if she'd just realized who she was hugging. Somehow, she managed to put a good three feet between them in about a second. The woman moved like a shot when she was embarrassed—and she *was* embarrassed, with her eyes focused on the tarmac and her lips pressed tight, awkwardness rolling off her in waves. He could tell now, as if he knew her, all of a sudden.

As if he'd put on those 3-D glasses at the cinema and was finally seeing every side of her.

She was fiddling self-consciously with her hair, smoothing down frizzy little flyaways that popped right back up again. Cute as fuck, this button of a woman. He tore his gaze away and opened the bike's pannier, retrieving the case that usually held his shades, but currently held Chloe's glasses. Her eyes were all soft and unfocused without them. For a moment he wondered if she took them off when she had sex, or if she wouldn't want to give up even that ounce of control.

Then he told himself to stop being such a fucking weirdo and held out the specs. "Here you go."

"Thanks." She took them, quick and wary, like a squirrel snatching nuts from his hand. "What are you smirking at?"

He couldn't help himself. He said, just to piss her off, "You hugged me."

She narrowed her eyes behind those familiar blue frames, set her jaw, crossed her arms. "*And?*" She could have silenced a thousand men with that one scary syllable. He wondered how many people had been shocked to realize that, despite the posh accent and the prissy outfits, she was a tough motherfucker all the way to her bones.

"I didn't have you down as a hugger," he drawled, locking up and strolling back toward the flats.

"I should hope you don't have me down as anything," she said primly, falling into step beside him. "I am, as I've just proved, an eminently unpredictable woman."

He barely managed to choke back his laughter, turning it into a mangled sort of cough.

She shot him a glare and said, "I *am*."

Red had to lean against the nearest wall for support. He doubled over in the narrow walkway leading to the back entrance, laughing so hard he might break something.

She stood in front of him with her hands on her hips and a mutinous expression that clearly hid a smile. That mouth of hers said one thing—abject irritation—but her eyes shone and crinkled at the edges in a way that felt like champagne bubbles looked. A way that let him keep laughing.

When he finally managed to calm down, she asked archly, "What, exactly, is so amusing?"

He let his head rest against the wall for a second, let his eyes slide shut while he savored the ache in his abs. He hadn't laughed this much in a fucking century and it felt better than a three-hour massage. "For one thing," he said dryly, "if you were such a wild card, you probably wouldn't have to tell me."

She sniffed. "Maybe I simply don't trust your skills of observation."

"Fair enough. Observation's more your thing, ain't it?"

She stared at him, biting her lip. Her laughing annoyance faded away, along with most of the warmth in her brown skin. "Red, I—" She stopped, swallowed, squared her shoulders. "I have something to tell you."

Ah, shit. He couldn't resist prodding her guilty conscience, and now she was going to confess. She'd open her mouth and spill the secret of her spying into the open, and then he'd have to ask her why she'd done it, and she'd make it clear she saw him as a creature in a zoo, and he'd have to go back to disliking her.

Suddenly, he didn't want to dislike her. It had been difficult. This new, laughing, teasing thing was easy.

"You going to tell me why you wanted to ride a motorbike?" he asked lightly. "Because I've got to be honest, I'm dying to know." He was giving her an out. She'd take it, right?

Wrong. She rolled her lips inward, shook her head, and he thought, *Come on, Button, don't be so bloody decent.*

Behind his back, he pressed his palm to the wall until the brick bit into his skin. He didn't want to hear her admit how little she thought of him when she'd just made him feel so . . . free. So he did the only thing he could think to do; he kept needling her. "Is it because you have a biker fetish?"

Just as he'd hoped, her mouth popped open in a shocked little *O* and her dark eyes flooded with outraged humor instead of cold anxiety. "I—*what*? No. No, I do not have a biker fetish." She wrinkled her nose at the words, as if the idea horrified her.

For some reason, he felt compelled to point out, "I'm not technically a biker, myself."

She blinked.

"Not that it matters." For fuck's sake, what was he doing? Shaking his head, Red got back to the point. "Tell me, then. Why?"

He could see the indecision in her face, where last week he'd have seen nothing but cold blankness. She was trying to decide if she should tell him—or rather, *what* she should tell him. In the end, to his relief, she didn't broach the topic that would change everything between them.

Instead, she said, "I have a list."

His eyebrows rose. "A list?"

"Yes. A list of fun or exciting things that I intend to do, for . . . for reasons. And riding a motorbike was on the list."

He grinned. So, Chloe had some kind of bad-girl bucket list? Hilarious. "Reasons, huh? What reasons?"

"It doesn't matter," she said quickly, which only fed his curiosity. "What matters is that I have a proposition for you."

Goddammit, his dick just wouldn't stop reacting to that phrase. "Yeah?"

"Yes," she confirmed crisply. "But we probably shouldn't discuss it here. We'll need to make some sort of appointment. Set the time aside. It's quite in-depth."

His lips twitched. Did she know she was adorable? Was she *trying* to be adorable? Maybe this was something they taught at private schools. Maybe she was reeling him in right this minute, and he'd wake up in a year's time with his life in pieces, her perfume all over him, and a distinct feeling that he'd lost his fucking mind. But no, he reminded himself; these days, no one could reel him in unless he let them.

"Just tell me," he said. "Give me a hint."

She rolled her eyes. "Where is your patience?"

"Same place I left my shame."

"I pity your mother. You must have been an infuriating child."

"I'm her *favorite* child," he corrected.

"You can't have any siblings, then."

"Wow. That hurts, Chloe. Gets me right here." He clapped a hand over his chest because he was gravely wounded.

She snorted, zero sympathy. "Since you apparently *have* to know, I was thinking that perhaps . . . well, perhaps you could help me complete some other items on my list, the way you helped me today. And in return, I could build your whole website for free."

His scowl was automatic. "I may not be loaded, but I can pay for the bloody website. I have savings. And anyway, it's a business expense." Been a while since he'd had any of those, but since he was about to be back *in* business . . .

"No. If you help me, I have to do something for you in return, so it's fair. Even. A deal, like this. And the website's all I can offer. It would be an exchange."

He frowned at her insistent tone. "Just exactly how much 'help' do you need? What's on this list?"

"Well, as I said, we should probably discuss it elsewhere." Her gaze darted around like government spies might be lurking in piles of dead leaves. Like her list was some big, dangerous secret.

"The more you hesitate," he told her, "the more I imagine terrible and/or kinky explanations."

"*Kinky?*" she echoed, then slapped a hand over her mouth like she'd just blurted out, *Fuck the pope.* "I—no. It's not. It's just a list of things I want to do. Fun, exciting things."

"Like bondage?"

"Like *camping*," she snapped.

He'd been hoping she'd get all flustered and give it up, but he really hadn't expected her juicy secrets to include . . . camping. "Seriously? You want me to help you *camp*?"

She nodded stiffly. "You're probably much better with the outdoors than I am. You certainly couldn't be worse. I also need to go out drinking. You know, partying. Which I'm sure will be much safer with someone who, erm . . . looks like you."

Well, he couldn't argue with that. "What else?"

"As if that isn't enough?" She shook her head ruefully. "There's more on the list, but nothing you can help with."

"What. Else?" Not that he was desperate to know, or anything. He was just curious. This list was . . . unexpected, like jigsaw pieces that didn't quite fit together yet, but hinted at a surprising picture. He wanted to see the picture. That was all.

"Oh, well, I want to travel the world with nothing but hand luggage." The words eased out of her like a creak from a carefully opened door, as if she were tiptoeing around the idea. Like it was silly. Like he would laugh.

The truth just up and fell out of his mouth. "As goals go, that's fucking amazing."

Her face lit up, then closed down as she wrestled it under control. She was the queen of deadpan, after all. "Do you think?" she asked in a tone that said, *I don't give a shit, but go on.*

"I do," he said, and she gave in and smiled. She might as well have stabbed him in his dignity, the way his body responded to a measly curve of those full lips. He'd always thought she was beautiful, but she seemed to get prettier every time they spoke, which was bloody inconvenient. He cleared his throat and said, "So . . . you want my help with your adventure list."

Although, going out for a drink didn't seem like an adventure. More like a Friday night.

"My Get a Life list," she corrected.

He frowned. "What—?"

"And in return," she cut in, "I'll build your site. It's a fair trade. Trust me."

Trust her? He didn't. These days, he barely trusted himself. And the way she talked about this list . . . it wasn't sitting quite right with him. He should say no. He opened his mouth to do just that, but a question came out instead. "How did something as ordinary as camping end up on the same list as traveling the world?"

She shrugged, wandering over to the wall opposite his. And then she was leaning, just like him, like they were mirror images. "Life experience tends to start small and build up, doesn't it? You might camp as a child and end up traveling in your twenties. But mine didn't build up, exactly, for all sorts of reasons. I have these different levels to catch up with. I chose the ones that seemed important, and I suppose I . . ." She shrugged, let out a self-conscious little laugh. "Well, I suppose I shoved them all together. Is that silly?"

Say yes. "No. Do you need to sit down? Shall we go inside?"

"I would love to sit down," she said, "because I happen to be happiest when curled up on something soft. But I don't strictly *need* to sit down, not yet, so I will push myself a little."

Push herself. Sounded like she pushed herself a lot, in a lot of different ways. He should find out why. Better yet, he should avoid getting tangled up in her mysterious list, because he knew himself, and he knew it would lead to getting tangled up in *her*.

Red was trying to avoid tangles right now. He had enough in his own head, and they'd happened because he'd been here before. Because he'd felt this same urge to get swept up by a pretty, posh girl's charming quirks, and it really hadn't ended well. He'd rather ride naked through Trinity Square than get himself wrapped up in yet another mess. He'd rather eat a damned rock. He'd rather—

"So," she asked softly, "will you help me?"

And he, Mister Shit for Brains, said, "Yeah."

CHAPTER EIGHT

He still didn't know why he'd agreed. Why he'd jumped headfirst into the murky waters of someone else's weirdness when his focus should be on his own issues. He was so completely pissed with himself that irritation kept him up all night, distracted him the next morning, and ate at the edges of his concentration while he made his way to Vik's house.

Luckily, when he arrived, Vik was too busy eating some foodie salad to notice anything was up. The guy was usually sharp as a tack, his big, dark eyes like CCTV cameras, but stick some grub in front of him and he lost track of every fuck he'd ever had to give.

After letting Red into his fancy three-story town house, Vik jerked his thick head of curls toward the stairs and said around a mouthful of bright leaves and white cheese, "You still want to paint that view?"

"No," Red said dryly, hefting the art supplies slung over his shoulder. "I'm just here to flirt with Alisha."

"Yeah, well, she's out. I knew you were coming."

Red snorted, kicked off his shoes, and made his own way up the stairs. Vik followed like a lanky shadow, face still buried in his bowl. Every now and then, as they climbed to the attic floor, he'd give a disturbingly orgasmic groan and mumble, "You really have to try this."

"What is it?"

"Spinach, pomegranate seeds, feta cheese, balsamic—"

"I'll have the recipe for Mum." When they reached the attic, Red peered into the mysterious bowl, surprisingly drawn to the colors, the textures. Deep, gleaming pink that reminded him of biting kisses. Soft, creamy white, like gasping murmurs of pleasure. The contrast made him think of other juxtapositions, like shiny shoes and velvet skin.

Christ, he was in a strange mood today.

He turned away from the surprisingly inspiring salad to survey the bare and slightly dusty attic space. Alisha hated what she called "tat," so the Anand house was the tidiest, most streamlined space he'd ever seen, with no drawers full of crap or biscuit tins filled with thread, or spare rooms stuffed to the brim with old record players and books that would never be read. They had no use for the attic at the top of the house, and so it remained empty, the walls a neat, plain white and the floorboards pale blond. All of which made the play of light through the roof windows absolutely stunning at a certain time of day.

This time of day.

Red loved light. He craved it. Once upon a time, everything he'd created had been all space and glow and refracted rainbows through crystal. But these days, all he seemed to produce were vivid fever dreams that he occasionally liked, until he remembered what he'd been before.

Did that mean he was ruined, or just changed? He hadn't decided yet, but he'd known for a while that this space would be the perfect place to find out. That, if he couldn't catch his old self here, it was really gone. He needed to know so he could move forward, but he'd been almost afraid to find out.

Then he'd shown Chloe that painting. He supposed having someone else's eyes on his work had made it more real. He supposed the fact that she liked it, too, had made him brave, which said a lot about his strength of character—or lack, more like—but fuck it, he needed all the encouragement he could get. He focused on his breathing as he set up by the windows, and by the time he was ready to paint he was almost in a meditative state.

Which Vik, of course, immediately shattered. "So," he said, as Red stared at the mess of blue and white on his palette. "You're painting again. That's new."

"Not," Red grunted, half of his mind elsewhere. He could talk while he worked, but it usually wasn't polite.

Luckily, Vik had years of experience in interpreting. "It's not new? You've been holding out on me."

Red squinted up at a sky of solid, slow-moving, cotton-wool cloud. Today, autumn was cruelly bright instead of dully gray. This was perfect. But how perfect would it be if he inverted the shades, to catch the way all that white sent the softest, slightest pain shooting through sensitive eyes? After a moment's thought, he grabbed a different tube of paint.

"Ah well," Vik went on between mouthfuls of salad. "If you've been hiding it, this is progress, right? You're not hiding anymore."

It took a moment for Red to really hear those words as he built up color on his little canvas. His new work habit—standing in front of his courtyard-facing window half naked—hadn't felt like hiding at the time. But now he found himself noticing that, for months, he'd only ever painted at night. Even though he'd chosen that room as a studio, set up by that window, for the light itself.

Hiding. According to the pang in his chest, he had been. He shrugged as he daubed cerulean over violet. "Getting my shit together."

He could hear the smile in Vik's voice. "Yeah? You feeling good?"

Red snorted. "Who are you, Dr. Phil?"

"Ah, don't start that manly crap. We talk about our feelings in this house, boy."

"Can I talk about my feelings for your wife?"

"This bowl would be a great hat on you."

Red rolled his eyes and studied the skyline. On the outskirts of the city, there were plenty of bleak council flats, like grim obelisks kissing the clouds. Like a monument to the massive gap between rich and poor in this country, they symbolized a truth the wealthy preferred to avoid. Usually, he'd paint them out of the picture, replacing them with coppery autumn trees or a gold sunset—with bright, brilliant beauty. But for some reason, today, he couldn't make himself do it. His changed mind kept demanding, *Why should I?*

Why should he create a more palatable version of reality? Why should he paint for anyone but himself?

He'd grown up in flats like those, his home one monstrous headstone among a row of eight. Looking at them now, he *felt* something. It wasn't clean or simple, but it was powerful, and it was worth sharing. He mixed a deep pink, like love's blood, and tried his best to do that feeling justice.

As Red worked, Vik's chatter slowed, then stopped. Silence rose up to cradle Red like soft blankets, and before he knew it, he wasn't thinking anymore. He used to take it for granted, that lack of thought, the ability to turn off the constant churn of his mind. But when he put the final touches on his work, and came back to himself, it was a shock to realize he'd "gone" somewhere else. That he'd escaped constant self-awareness for a while. He hadn't known he had it in him anymore.

But apparently, Vik had. He clapped Red on the back as he came over, his eyes stuck on the charred carcasses, swallowed up by wild, thorny nature, that Red had turned the flats into. Vik had grown up in flats like those, too. Red held his breath.

The rubber-band tension stretched, then snapped back. The sting was the kind that made you feel alive. Vik squeezed his shoulder and muttered, "Proud of you, mate."

For a second, Red was proud of himself—of his work—too. Then came hesitation. He hadn't produced anything like his old stuff. He'd forgotten to even try. In front of him was a vivid, half dream, half nightmare of a landscape, the kind that made him feel flushed and frantic and reckless. So he had his answer. He'd lost himself. He took a moment to breathe through that realization, to sit with the finality of it. Oddly, it didn't choke him. In fact, knowing it once and for all felt a little like lifting a weight.

He swallowed and wiped his paint-spattered hands on his jeans before turning to drag Vik into a hug. They stood like that for long moments, until Red managed to form a half-decent sentence. "You're always behind me."

"Well, not always. That'd be a bit fucking weird."

They both laughed, Red's sounding rusty—but not as rusty as it had been. He'd laughed with Chloe yesterday, first a bit, then a lot, and it had loosened something in him.

Maybe that was why he'd agreed to help her. Yeah, that must be it.

Now, if he didn't know any better, he'd think she could hear his thoughts—that she'd been waiting for him to figure out his shit and truly accept the deal between them. Because when he pulled out his phone to take a picture of what he'd done, to commemorate it in some wild, nervous moment of *just-in-case*, there was an email from her in his inbox. He probably should've left it, should've looked at it later, but something curious zipped up his spine and he found himself opening the curtest email he'd ever received.

Red,

Our in-person consultation efforts failed miserably due to a lack of focus on both sides. From now on, email seems the most efficient choice. Questions:

1. Do you own a domain name, and if so, where is it registered?
2. Do you have any ideas or examples of websites you find pleasing/effective?
3. What is/are the main purpose(s) of this site? Exposure, direct sales, portfolio, etc.?
4. Do you participate in social media, and if so, which platforms?
5. Do you have an ideal time line in mind?

Rgds.,
Chloe

Rgds., she said, like she was too bloody busy to type out the full word. And anyway, wasn't that email-speak for *fuck off*? But she was the one in his inbox, talking about things like "a lack of focus on both sides."

That phrase in particular gnawed at him, the way his granddad's soft old mongrel used to gnaw at people's knuckles. Both sides, huh? He wondered if her lack of focus had anything in common with his. If she felt this insistent, dizzying tug toward someone she should barely like, the way he did. The idea made something inside him coil up tight, like a spring. Made him remember the wide-eyed look she'd given him when they'd tumbled onto the bed together yesterday.

He must be petty as hell, because he hoped prim and proper Chloe was an absolute mess over him, that she'd stayed up last night thinking about him with every ounce of the frustration he'd felt over her. No—double the frustration, just because.

Imagining her tangling the sheets as she rolled around, irritated, unable to get his name out of her head, made him feel . . .

"What are you grinning at?" Vik demanded, craning his neck to see the phone.

Red locked the screen. "Email."

"Since when do you get so jolly over emails? Hate to be the one to tell you this, but those foreign princes are usually—"

"Ah, fuck off."

"Who was it from?" Vik asked, nudging Red's shoulder. "Because I'll use my considerable stalking talents to find out anyway, so you might as well just tell me."

Red sighed, wishing that was a joke. "It's from a web designer. I'm getting a site done."

"No fucking way. Look at you, off like a shot all of a sudden. You're on it."

Red put the phone in his pocket, already mentally typing his reply. "Yeah. I suppose I am."

Dear Chloe,
   I don't think we failed *miserably*. You didn't seem miserable on the back of my bike, unless I misunderstood the screaming.

And, about yesterday—I already knew I couldn't focus, but I had no idea you couldn't, either. What distracted you? I'm curious.

So, these questions.

1. I don't have any of the shit you need for a website.
2. Copying sites I like is a smart idea, so I went and found some for you. Is this what doing homework feels like? I usually skipped mine.
3. The site is for exposure, but I like the idea of direct sales. Would that mean building a shop?
4. No social media. Hate that shit.
5. As for time line . . . I'm not picky. This is a favor, after all. Fit me in around your actual work.

Speaking of favors—where are we at with this list of yours?

Regards (see how easy that was?),

Red

Red,

No, I wasn't miserable on the back of your racing death machine. As for my lack of focus: concentration is something I occasionally struggle with. Not that I allow it to impact my work.

Re: direct sales, yes, we would build a shop into the site,

and you—through that avenue, at least—would control your own sales, etc. Examples attached.

An Instagram feed on the site would add a dynamic, social element. As an artist, it seems wise to have an account. Consider it.

I don't think we should discuss my list until we've at least hammered out these details. You helped me tick off an item yesterday. I should start my end of the deal before we go forward. I don't want you to feel you're being taken advantage of.

REGARDS,

Chloe

DEAR Chloe,

If you weren't miserable on the racing death machine, what were you? Describe it to me, just so I can make sure I haven't traumatized you.

I'd definitely like a shop. The direct sales thing sounds right up my alley, and if I don't sell some of these pieces soon I'll end up drowning in canvas.

I'm not joining Instagram, though.

And I don't feel taken advantage of. You're really into balance, huh? Why is that?

(Since you did so well with regards, let's push it a bit.)

Best wishes,

Red

To one Mr. Redford Morgan,

You haven't traumatized me. The ride . . . surprised me. But I liked it. Please don't worry. I really did. And even if I hadn't, I liked making progress on the list.

The shop is a go, then. As for Instagram, you really should get over your Too Cool for School reluctance and just sign up. This behavior is modern hipsterism.

I don't think anyone needs a specific reason to avoid incurring excessive debt. We've made a deal and I am taking it seriously. The end.

Best,

Chloe

Dear Ms. Chloe Button Brown,

Glad to hear you're not traumatized. Confession: I already knew you liked it, because afterward, you stared at me like I'd just rocked your world. Which is a great look on you, by the way. Feel free to shower me in hero worship more often.

But—let me get one thing straight—are you saying that finishing the list and enjoying the list are two separate issues, or something? Isn't the list made up of things you *want*? Things you fantasize about, maybe?

I'm really hoping you didn't just call me a hipster, by the way. I've read that sentence like ten times, hoping you wouldn't dare. I am not a fucking hipster. I don't even have a mustache. I just think Instagram is where self-esteem goes to die.

"Debt" is an interesting word to use, when you're talking about two people helping each other out. Are you scared I'll help a little too much, and you won't be able to help me back, and next thing you know, I'll be banging your door down like a bailiff and I'll take your laptop as retribution? Because that's definitely not going to happen.

Yours *sincerely*,

Red

Dear Red,

(You write emails as if they're letters, and it's ridiculous, and now you've got me doing it. Disgraceful.)

"Button"? I do have a middle name, but that definitely isn't it. As for my supposed hero worship of you, I am sorry to say that you have made a mistake. The truth is, I am occasionally mesmerized by how outrageously ginger you are. I do hope that doesn't hurt your feelings.

The list has nothing to do with "fantasies." I told you before, it's about building life experience. I suppose I should tell you that I was almost hit by a car. When my life flashed before my eyes, it was rather uneventful, so I'm taking the necessary steps to rectify that. It's really quite simple.

I think your definition of a hipster is roughly a decade behind the times, which frankly makes you even more of a hipster. Read my words now, very carefully: You. Need. An. Instagram. Account.

I'm so glad we had that talk.

I'm also very happy to hear that you don't ever plan on trying to take my laptop, because, while I do spend a lot of time indoors, the length of a murder sentence might be a touch too long, and prison beds would absolutely ruin my back.

Yours, supposedly,

Chloe

Dear Chloe,

(Emails are internet letters, so my way is the right way. You're welcome.)

"Button" because you always seem to be wearing them, and I don't know where you find all those old-fashioned clothes. What's your actual middle name? I bet it's something ridiculous, like Fenella.

You should be really proud of yourself, by the way. It takes a lot of guts to admit to a man that you're mesmerized by his amazing hair, and I appreciate the compliment. I promise not to bring it up too often. Once a day, tops.

That's rough about the whole "near death" thing. Really, it is. But—and I'm not trying to tell you what to do here—but don't you think, if your life ever flashes before your eyes again, you should remember all the shit you enjoyed?

Rather than the stuff other people care about? I don't know. Just a thought.

As for the Instagram account . . . you really are so damn bossy. I thought maybe the bossiness was a case of speaking before you think, but you're typing these emails out. You're reading them back to yourself. And you're still so fucking bossy. Incredible. I mean, don't get me wrong—I'm not even complaining anymore. I respect it.

Still not getting an Instagram account, though.

Yours SINCERELY,

Red

Dear Red,

Buttons add a certain dignity to an outfit, in my opinion. And I'll have you know that my clothes are actually retro, and they are very stylish.

My middle name is Sophia. I suppose it has a similar ring to Fenella, but it's not quite as ridiculous. Sorry to disappoint.

Perhaps I should've been clearer on the hair—*mesmerized* is such an ambiguous word. What I meant to say was, is it true that gingers have no souls?

The list is really not up for debate, since it has already been immortalized, and since I am committed, and also because I'm right and you're wrong. I trust you understand.

I'm starting to think that your aversion to Instagram hides

some deeper-seated issue. You mentioned it being where self-esteem goes to die. I hope you know I'm not suggesting that you use it for selfies and the like, though really, there is no need to be shy. You generally look passable.

Yours sincerely (this is beyond silly),

Chloe

Dear Chloe,

Just so you know, I like your clothes. Not that I go around telling women about their clothes, like anyone cares, but I realized it sounded like I might *not* like them, and that isn't accurate. I know you're into accuracy. So. There we go.

Although I hate to break it to you about those buttons, Button—they're more cute than dignified. Sorry.

Sophia isn't even slightly ridiculous, but I forgive you. And, on the subject of my soul, the rumors are true. Don't have one. So watch your step.

If you want to talk about my Instagram "issues," I want to talk about how hung up you are on this list, and why. Does that sound like a fun conversation? Because I'm ready when you are.

Good to know I look passable, though. For a soulless ginger, and everything.

Yours sincerely (not silly),

Red

Dear Red,

Well, thank you. You are, of course, correct; I always look excellent. But if you actually intend to start calling me Button, I may sew one into your tongue.

While it would be very thrilling to think I rode on the back of a soulless demon's motorbike, I feel compelled to point out that your behavior suggests you do in fact have a soul. For example, the way you let that very boring man from the third floor barge up to you whenever he likes to whine about the lightbulb that keeps going out. Clearly, he's doing something questionable with that lightbulb. And yet, you keep replacing it.

I have seen sense and decided to abandon the Instagram topic. For now.

And, since I feel like you might have misunderstood, I wasn't being serious before. You really do look fine. Nice, even. And you have lovely hair.

Yours sincerely,

Chloe

Dear Button,

I would love to see you try and sew something into my tongue. Really. I need to witness this in action. I'm sure you have a detailed plan. Are there drugs involved, a good whack over the head, or are you just planning to hold me down somehow?

I can't really comment on a tenant's behavior, but I can

confirm that, considering the number of times I've been up to SOMEONE'S flat to change *the same fucking lightbulb,* I really must have a soul. An extra shiny, golden one.

And don't worry; I knew you were joking. I was joking, too. But I might fish for compliments more often because you really snapped up that bait.

By the way—you've now spent the whole day emailing me, a client. That's a lot of hours, really. So maybe we should talk about your list tomorrow, just to make sure everything's even.

Yours,

Red

Dear Red,

You'll soon get to see my violent plan in action, since you flagrantly ignored my button threat, and extorted compliments from me, too. Come over tomorrow when you finish work, and I will attack. Or show you the list. We'll have to wait and see.

Yours,

Chloe

CHAPTER NINE

For some reason, emailing Red all day made Chloe alarmingly upbeat. Of course, the universe put a stop to that cheer the moment she went to bed by cursing her with a numb right foot that kept her awake all night.

Some people (like singularly unhelpful and clearly under-qualified physical therapists, unsympathetic GPs, and that supremely irritating second cousin who ate all the stuffing at Christmas) assumed that a lack of feeling in certain body parts shouldn't affect sleep at all. Her insomnia in such situations, they said, was something she could easily overcome. Chloe liked to remind those people that the human brain tended to keep track of all body parts, and was prone to panic when one of those parts went offline. Actually, what Chloe *liked* to do was imagine hitting those people with a brick. But she restrained herself to scathing explanations and used her brick-hitting fantasies to occupy her when sleep refused to come.

After hours of numb-footed hell, she dragged herself up to feed Smudge, who had spent the night beside her offering moral support. If she was going to get any work done today, she needed to feed herself, too. She should brew green tea for the antioxidants and make a healthy breakfast rich in whole grains for slow-release energy. However, since that sounded extremely difficult and her body ached as if she'd been stomped on by a god, she improvised by eating handfuls of Coco Pops straight from the box and gulping apple juice from the carton.

Thus fortified, and wrapped up in her favorite plush, gray onesie, she settled on the sofa and opened her laptop. Sitting at her desk wasn't happening today, no matter how much fine detail her monitors allowed. In the end, though, Chloe's choice of computer didn't matter—because, after 0.5 seconds of staring at a pixelated screen, she developed a sudden headache. Or perhaps someone had shot her. It felt roughly the same.

She closed her eyes and took a deep breath. "I will not be defeated."

Smudge miaowed supportively.

She opened her eyes and got to work.

Hours later, a knock came at the door. Chloe sat bolt upright and realized three things in quick succession:

1. She had fallen asleep. Oops.
2. The flat had warmed up considerably since this morning, because she was now far too hot in her onesie.
3. It was after five o'clock and Redford Morgan was here.

"*Fudge*," she muttered darkly, swiping the drool off her cheek. Judging by the fine lines and indents under her fingers, she had a mess of pillow creases on her face, too. Wonderful.

She glowered at Smudge, who was stretched out across her PlayStation with outrageous disregard for the house rules. "Why didn't you wake me?"

He waved his tale with open belligerence.

"Oh, you are *useless*. I bet you wouldn't nudge me awake during a fire. Get off there, would you?"

He casually kicked out his back paw, knocking her copy of *Overwatch* off the TV cabinet.

"I swear," she huffed, rising to her feet and adjusting the Velcro straps of her wrist supports. "I've no idea what to do about your attitude. This is your last warning."

She tried to sound stern, but as she hurried to answer the door, she heard mocking kitty laughter echoing behind her.

Still, she couldn't worry about feline insubordination right now. She was too busy worrying about other things, like how utterly unprepared she was for Redford's arrival. This wasn't the way things were supposed to go. She'd had a *plan*—one that involved her looking calm and put together, not half asleep in a onesie designed to make her resemble a giant lemur. She hovered awkwardly by her own front door, smoothing flustered hands over her hair, wondering if her and Red's increasingly familiar emails yesterday meant they were now proper friends, or if she'd simply read too much into things.

Well, she was about to find out.

Her heart pounding thickly at the back of her throat, Chloe

opened the door. And there he was, her exact opposite: cool, calm, hands in his pockets, a slow, easy smile spreading over his face. Her stomach swooped along the roller coaster curve of his mouth, the defined cupid's bow a pulse-racing drop. She ordered her lungs to continue breathing normally, but it was too late; they'd already decided to gulp down air like it was going out of style.

"Hey," Red said.

"Hmm," she replied, because coherent speech was for other people. She looked away from his disturbing smile and found herself confronted, instead, by his eyes: warm, pale green, like sun-baked grass, with fine lines at the corners that might as well be a smile in themselves. Her cheeks flushed hot. She abandoned his face entirely, in favor of his body. He was wearing a gray T-shirt that clung slightly to his broad chest, and black jeans that hinted at his heavy thighs. She could just *lick* him. South of the belt.

"Chloe," he said.

She looked up sharply.

He arched an eyebrow, cocking his head at her until his hair slid over his shoulders like silk. Had she told him, yesterday, during those funny, giddy, friendly emails, that he had lovely hair? *Divine* would've been more accurate.

"You okay?" he asked.

Was . . . she . . . okay . . . ? No. He was disgracefully, disgustingly handsome, and her head still ached, she was still exhausted, and her numb foot was tingling painfully back to life. But that was really no excuse for gaping at him with her tongue hanging out, so she pulled herself firmly together.

"I'm fine. Just tired. Sorry." She stepped back to let him in, running her thumbs over the line where her wrist supports ended and her skin began. *Whatever's gotten into you, Chloe Sophia Brown, exorcise it before you make a fool of yourself.*

He gave her a sympathetic, head-to-toe glance that reminded her—as though she could forget—of how terribly pathetic she must look. "Were you asleep?"

"Ah, yes," she admitted, trying for an airy laugh. It came out a bit too strained, but she forged on. "Now we've both caught each other napping, haven't we?"

She'd thought that joke would make things less awkward, but he flushed abruptly, brilliantly red. Scarlet heat colonized his whole face from the throat up.

"Yeah," he said after a strange little pause. "Napping." He cleared his throat and nodded down the hall. "So, shall we . . . ?"

Right, yes. He was here about the list, and she'd decided last night while lying awake—in between chatting with Smudge and imagining violence against everyone who'd ever wronged her—that she would treat said list as a professional endeavor. Of course, her lack of preparation today put them off to a bumpy start, but as she led Red to the living room, she felt confident she could put things back on track.

"Nice tail," he said from behind her.

She'd forgotten the onesie had a tail. Dear God, how could she forget it had a tail?

"Thank you," she said stiffly, because she was committed to regaining control over this situation. She even arranged her tail carefully before sitting down on the sofa, just to prove how utterly unconcerned she was by it.

The corner of Red's lips curled into a faint half smile as he watched. He hovered over her like an alien spaceship, seeming even huger than usual from this angle, his hair swinging forward to frame his sharp cheekbones. He didn't say another word about her tail, despite his little smile. Instead, he simply asked, "Can I sit down?"

Oh—there wasn't any more space on the sofa. She shoved away a few stray notebooks, two of her twelve pencil cases, an unopened bank statement, and a bar of sea-salt chocolate.

He snorted and sat. His weight made her sofa sink in the middle, like a marshmallow being poked. Her fleecy bottom started to slide toward the dip, closer to him. She grabbed the sofa arm and held on for dear life. Then she realized how silly that must look and let go.

"So," she said brightly. "The list! Let's discuss."

He leaned back, propping his right ankle on his left knee in that way people did when they didn't mind taking up space. Chloe had never really gotten the hang of it.

"Is that why I'm here?" he asked lightly. "For the list? I thought you were going to hold me down and sew a button onto my tongue."

Good Lord, had she really said that yesterday? What on earth had come over her? She typically saved that sort of lunacy for her sisters. "Upon reflection, I decided that holding you down would be beyond my physical capabilities."

"I don't know about that," he said. "You're shorter than me, but you're pretty tough."

For some reason, the fact that he thought she was tough made a pleased little smile curve her lips. She wiped the smile away instantly, however, because it was ridiculous. She *was* tough. Basic facts being acknowledged should not make her chest all tingly and light.

She found the right notebook, a deep, glittering blue with black-edged pages, and turned to face him. "Since you haven't actually called me that cursed name today, I think we can hold off on your punishment."

His eyes caught hers, and he grinned in a flash of soft lips and white teeth. "I appreciate that, Button."

She slapped the notebook against his chest, biting her lip so hard she was surprised she didn't taste blood. "Shut up. Focus. We have a list to discuss."

To her surprise, he actually obeyed, the humor in his gaze replaced by something calmer, more curious. He took the notebook, and for one breathless second his thumb brushed the side of her hand, just above the straps of her wrist support. Then he was opening the book, intent on the words she'd written inside, while she was left staring at her own hand like a ninny, wondering why it seemed to fizz.

"This it?" he asked, studying the first page—the only one she'd used. "Seems kind of short."

"That isn't the original version," she told him, fiddling with the zip of her onesie. God, she was hot. "I wrote a new one that only includes the things you'll be helping me with."

Because she'd rather die than hand him the actual list, complete with item number five (meaningless sex) and the ticked-off item number seven (do something bad, e.g. *spying on him*). This safe, censored version only featured three things: riding a motorbike—which she'd included just to cross off, for the encouragement factor; a drunken night out; and camping.

"See?" she said, nodding over his shoulder. "Just like we discussed."

"What about your traveling?" he asked, still studying the list. He had the most adorable frown of concentration, three vertical lines between his eyebrows. A tall middle one, and then two shorter ones on either side, like a hug.

Chloe blinked. She was losing her mind.

Clearing her throat, she said, "You can't help me with traveling, so I didn't include it."

"I don't know," he shrugged. "I thought we should talk about that. I want to make sure you realize that traveling the world with hand luggage is basically backpacking."

She shrugged, unzipping her onesie ever so slightly. A tiny bead of sweat had started to drip down her spine. "Well, I was envisioning a rucksack containing a large supply of clean knickers, painkillers, chocolate, and a toothbrush. If that's what backpacking is—"

"Close enough," he cut in dryly.

"Then a backpacker I shall be." She had this wild idea that it would feel more like an adventure if she was missing most of the things she needed to survive. She'd be an intrepid lady version of Indiana Jones.

He looked up, and she swallowed. It turned out his concentration frown was even more arresting when it was aimed at her. "It just doesn't seem like your thing. That's all."

"It isn't. That's the point." She *did* want to travel, but the "only-hand-luggage" part was supposed to be a challenge. "Once I've completed the rest of the list," she told him, "I'll be so used to daring exploits that backpacking will seem completely manageable."

He laughed, then realized she was serious. "Ah. Okay. But aren't you worried about your—?"

"If you ask about my health I will strangle you."

He choked down another laugh and nodded gravely. "Fair enough. You know what you're doing."

Debatable, but she was working on it.

"All right," he said, with that abrupt firmness that usually indicated someone was ready to take action. "You got a pen?"

Her mind blanked with confusion for a second—she really wasn't firing on all cylinders today—before she nodded and found one among the debris. Smudge had moved, at some point, from the PlayStation to the equally forbidden coffee table. She shot him a warning glare, which he haughtily ignored, before handing Red the pen. It was gold, with a clear little ball at the top filled with glitter and pink stars.

Red held the pen up to the light for a moment, staring at it with the oddest expression on his face—a sort of quiet, bone-deep pleasure, his smile slight and fond. He asked, "Where'd you get this?"

Of all possible interests they might share, she hadn't expected pretty pens to be one of them. But she supposed an artist would like beautiful things. "A shop on Etsy. I can email you the page."

"Yeah," he said, shaking the pen, watching the glitter dance. "Thanks. Can I write in this?" He tapped the notebook.

"You can." Although she really hadn't expected him to.

"All right. Let's see . . ." He flipped over to a clean page and wrote something down, those sharp eyes narrowed, his big, work-roughened, paint-spattered hand dwarfing the golden pen. "You free tomorrow night?"

"No. I promised my sister I'd watch *My Fair Lady* with her to make up for my lack of commitment to karaoke."

Red looked up, his expression a cross between confusion and wry amusement. "Uh . . . what?"

"Nothing," she muttered, waving a hand. Apparently, she overshared now. Wonderful. Very cool, extremely professional, everything was going swimmingly. Kill her now.

"Okay," he said slowly, a knowing light in his eyes. "Babysitting Eve. Got it. Saturday?"

She didn't ask how he'd known the sister in question was Eve. "I'm free on Saturday."

"Great. I'll take you out for drinks then."

For some reason, it wasn't until he said those words that she realized where he was going with his questions. Or rather, where he'd already gone. Her mouth dried up as if she were hungover in advance, and her onesie grew even warmer, like a furry torture chamber. "Saturday night," she laughed nervously. "So . . . so soon."

He looked up again, his three-line-frown back. "Is that okay?"

"Oh, yes. Why wouldn't it be?" she squeaked. Saturday night, drinking and dancing, just as she'd planned. Lovely. Delightful. The stuff of dreams.

"Because," Red said slowly, "if you don't want to do it—"

She sniffed. "Don't be ridiculous."

He ignored her. "—you could just . . . not do it."

"Preposterous."

"Since this is *your* list and all," he finished gently.

She glowered. "The list is not up for debate. I look forward to Saturday, when we will go to various shady establishments and drink far too much alcohol together."

"Yeah," he said dryly, scribbling something on the page. "I bet. Anywhere in particular you want to go?"

She wracked her brain, trying to remember the places she and her friends used to visit—back when she'd had friends. But she'd been at university then, in another city. She had no idea what was good here, where was fun. She sat up straight, cleared her throat, and said calmly, "I shall leave all major decisions to you. Just—make it, you know. Edgy."

He arched an eyebrow, scribbling a few more lines. "Edgy. Aye aye, Captain Button."

"Oh, shut up."

"Next," he said, "camping. Want me to handle that, too?"

Since he was turning out to be surprisingly organized, it wasn't difficult to say "Yes." He was supposed to be helping her, after all. And, since he was ordinary in all the ways Chloe and her family were not, he presumably had a touch more experience in outdoor pursuits than she did.

"All right," he said, then seemed to stop and think for a second, all his swirling vitality pausing along with his hands. She recognized this considering stillness from the nights she'd spied on him.

But she wouldn't think about spying on him. She was overheated enough without guilt adding to the issue, and one of the many curses of fibromyalgia was an inability to maintain homeostasis. If she got *too* hot, she'd simply pass out. She decided to open a window while Red was too distracted to ask why. He was staring at nothing beside her, running his knuckles back and forth over his lower lip.

She'd never seen him do that before. How fortunate that, the first time she witnessed it, there was a mountain of fleecy fabric in place to hide the way her nipples reacted.

She opened the window—ah, sweet air—and returned to the sofa just as he started writing again. His voice absent, he asked, "How long did you want to camp for?"

As little time as possible. "Oh, just a night should do," she said awkwardly. "I know you're very busy."

"I could do Saturday to Sunday, next week?"

She didn't need to check her schedule to know she was depressingly unengaged on those evenings, and most evenings, forever after.

No. Not forever. You're getting a life, remember?

"That should work for me," she said brightly.

"Cool. I have a place in mind, but I'll look into it and let you know." He finally put the pen down. His writing, she noticed, was surprisingly neat. There was wildness there, but it was carefully restrained. Every now and then it trickled from the swooping curl of a *g* or *y*, burst from the seams of an *I*. Before she could stare any longer, he snapped the notebook shut and put it on the coffee table, along with the pen. "There's something I need to ask you."

The slow, deliberate way he said those words, as if he were plotting his way through a booby-trapped room, put her on her guard. "Yes?" she asked crisply.

He turned his whole body toward her, his right knee disturbingly close to her thigh. She could feel the heat and the life and something else, something that tightened her belly, radiating off him and sinking dangerously deep into her. She stiffened and stared straight ahead.

"Come on, Chlo," he said softly. "Don't do that. We're . . . friends, aren't we?"

She didn't know what surprised her more—that casual shortening of her name, the kind of easy intimacy she'd had from no one but her sisters in years . . . or the fact that he thought they were friends. "A week ago you barely even liked me."

Most people would probably deny that, but he just shrugged, smiling slightly. "You didn't like me, either. But now that I know you better, I think you're funny and secretly sweet, and I *do* like you. I'm hoping you like me, too."

A weightless, tingling warmth suffused her as she battled a big, silly smile. Yesterday, she'd almost convinced herself that the dizzying tone of his emails was just his natural charm, the one she'd seen him flashing around like fifty-pound notes plenty of times. Apparently not. Apparently, he'd meant the little jokes and the kindnesses.

What a relief, since she had, too.

But her pleasure at his words, at the way he described her, was too enthusiastic, so she reined herself in. Changed the subject. Reminded herself he wanted to ask difficult questions. "Fine. We're friends. Now what is it?"

His smile didn't waver, as gentle as his words. "I know you're sick," he said. "I'm not trying to get full details, or anything. But if you've never done this stuff because of your health, I need to know what the risks are. What to do if you need help. All that shit."

Sigh. "I have fibromyalgia. Chronic pain, chronic fatigue, migraines, random periods of muscle weakness. Physical exertion can result in flare-ups, but I know my limits."

He arched an eyebrow. "Except for the times when you climb trees to save cats."

"I knew my limits then, too," she sniffed, relaxing a little, leaning closer to him. God, why was she leaning closer to him? "I simply decided I wanted to rescue Smudge more than I wanted to be sensible. But I wouldn't do that with you," she added quickly. "And I won't need to. I'm not physically incapable of completing those tasks, though I might require accommodations that others wouldn't. I don't need your help because of my disability. The list is about . . . something else."

Red nodded slowly, his gaze focused on her like a laser. There was an unexpected warmth in that gaze, one that tricked her into speaking further when she should have shut her mouth.

"I didn't used to be, you know . . ." She waved a hand. "A socially inept control freak."

His lips curved. "That's not exactly what I'd call you."

"I'm sure you'd choose something more blunt."

"No," he said, but that was all he said. And now she wanted to know what he'd been thinking. Too late; he swept the conversation along. "So what changed? What made you start thinking of your life in two halves—before and after?"

Her heart stuttered for one dangerous moment. "I . . . how did you—?"

"I have some experience with that feeling myself," he said, raking a hand through the silken sunset of his hair. He sounded vaguely sad. "I guess I recognize it in you."

"Yes," she murmured, because that made sense. "I see it in your paintings."

His eyes widened for a moment and color appeared on his high cheekbones. "Oh."

Now she was blushing, too. She hadn't meant to embarrass him. She certainly hadn't meant to admit so much knowledge of his art. She got too comfortable around him and things slipped out when they shouldn't. "I only meant—I was researching, for the website, and I found some of your older work, and there's a distinct—"

With a kindness she didn't really deserve, he cut her off. "I know what you mean. It's fine." He studied her for a moment as if her skin were translucent, and he could peer inside her head if only the light hit her just right. She felt uncomfortably like the light was hitting her just right. "You know, for someone who happily admits to being rude, you seem to care a lot about hurting my feelings."

Her derisive snort was automatic, a familiar shield. "Don't flatter yourself. I care about everyone's feelings."

"Yeah? What about your own?"

She sucked in a breath to say something cutting or witty or otherwise distracting, only it got caught in a tangle at the back of her throat.

"Tell me what happened," he said, his proximity turning her pulse into a tempest. "Tell me about your before."

CHAPTER TEN

Red didn't know why he was pushing, why he felt so ravenous for any scrap of the woman sitting before him. But when she curled her knees under her and faced him completely, when those spilled-ink eyes met his and her velvet voice wrapped around him, it felt right. It felt like exactly what he'd wanted.

Even though her quiet words ripped into his chest.

"I used to have friends. I used to have a fiancé, even." She said that with a wry smile and an arch of those winged eyebrows, like she thought that might surprise him. It did, and it didn't. She wasn't a social person, exactly, but she was damned hypnotic. Of course she'd had friends. And yet, apparently, she'd also lost them.

"I suppose the end of all that started when I got pneumonia," she said, hooking her arm around a nearby cushion, pressing it to her chest. "Apparently, I nearly died. All I remember is how it felt." He wondered if she noticed she was squeezing that cushion, the sort of vulnerable move she usually avoided like the plague. Probably not. In the space of a few seconds, she'd somehow become so distant.

"My bones were like eggshells. There was this cold, wet toad squatting on my chest, too heavy and chilling for me to breathe right." She said it so steadily, but he saw a hint of remembered panic in her eyes. "I remember being so angry with myself, because it was so silly, the way I got sick. I used to play netball, and I'd been nervous about a particular game. I stayed out in the rain with some of my friends, running drills. We won the match, but I was in the hospital a few days later. Obviously, I survived," she quipped, as if he needed a reminder of her continued existence.

He didn't laugh. "But . . . ?"

"But," she went on grimly, "my body was different. The weight on my chest, and the cold—they faded, as I got better. But my bones still felt fragile. It never went away. Over the months, I noticed more and more problems. I was exhausted all the time. I got these awful headaches for no reason. And there was the pain—always, so much pain. I'd go for a walk and feel like I'd worked every muscle to the point of tearing. If I spent too long on my laptop, my hands would hurt so badly I cried. I started feeling afraid of my own body, like it was a torture chamber I'd been trapped inside.

"But when I asked for help, no one would listen. I'm lucky my family believed me, because for years, they were the only ones. I remember one doctor asked to speak with my father, even though I was an adult. He told my dad I was physically fine, but they should look into my mental health." She laughed, but the sound was too loud, too edgy, grating against his skin.

Red curled his hands into useless fists in his lap, fighting the urge to touch her. To stroke her hair or pull her into a hug, the way he might if she were someone—anyone—else. Usually, he offered comfort to help other people. But she looked so determinedly brittle right now, eyes sharp, jaw hard, chin up, he knew comfort wasn't what she wanted. He'd only be doing it for himself, because he could see how trapped she'd felt, and it made him feel hollow inside.

"I mean, don't get me wrong," she said dryly, "my mental health *was* a mess at that point. And having actual medical professionals dismiss me really didn't help, so . . ." She squeezed her eyes shut for a moment.

"Of course it didn't," he said, his voice rough, almost rusty, with the anger he didn't want to show. "Whether something bad is coming from your body or your brain, it makes no difference. Still feels like shit, right? Still hurts. Still needs fixing. They shouldn't have dismissed you, even if it was in your head. When it comes down to it, everything we feel is in our heads."

She opened her eyes. Wet her lips. Nodded slowly, and looked a little bit less tortured. When she spoke again, her voice was smooth and arch and familiar. "I do hate to admit when you're right, but you happen to have stumbled upon a sensible opinion, there."

Somehow, for her, he dredged up a smile. "Must be a blue moon. Keep going."

She swallowed so hard, he heard it. "Right. Yes. Well. I was diagnosed, in the end. My consultant believes major physical trauma can trigger conditions like mine. She thinks it was the pneumonia. But that doesn't really matter. What matters is that, for years, I had no idea what was really happening to my body.

No painkillers, no physical therapy, no medical support what-soever. So I did what I had to do. I developed my own coping mechanisms. The problem is, they weren't particularly healthy."

He wondered what it was like, to cope constantly. Tiring, probably. Stressful, definitely. Doing it alone didn't sound healthy at all.

"I avoided anything that might make me feel worse," she said. "I was afraid." No inflection. No emotion. As if she was read-ing someone else's story from a sheet of paper. "I quit netball. I quit my postgrad degree. I stopped going out with my friends. I didn't stay up late because sleep was too precious. I refused to make plans because I never knew when my body might force me to change them. My friends disappeared one by one. I suppose my problems made them feel guilty."

"And your fiancé?" Red asked softly.

"Oh, Henry," she laughed. "He lost patience almost immedi-ately. He didn't believe me."

"*What?*" Red had been trying to stay calm throughout this story, to avoid showing his own reactions in case they affected what she chose to share. But he couldn't have hidden his dis-gust in that moment, not even if he'd pulled out his own fucking tongue.

She shrugged, but a smile teased the edges of her mouth, as if she found his obvious horror amusing. "There was no blood test or scan or injury to prove that I was really in pain. He was very logical, you see. He needed evidence and I had none."

"Your word isn't evidence? Your feelings aren't evidence?" Red demanded, his tone harsher than he'd intended. But he couldn't help it. He'd seen the change in Chloe when her pain got too serious to handle. Fuck, he saw her *now,* when she was trying to seem fine but was clearly exhausted. Black circles under her beautiful eyes, weariness clinging to her like a shadow. How the fuck could someone who planned to marry her just ignore all that?

"Henry thought I was malingering," she told him. "That I was being pathetic, I was too demanding, I needed too much support." Her lip curled, displaying a flash of anger that had been absent so far, one he was actually relieved to see now. "He disappeared on me without much remorse, but I consider that a lucky escape."

So did Red. "He doesn't sound like marriage material."

Her eyes slid to his, sparkling with humor. "No."

"He sounds like the type of guy who finds out his wife has cancer and starts screwing his secretary to relieve the stress."

"Yes," she said, smiling now.

"Fuck him."

"I pity whoever is," she smirked. Then she waved a hand and the moment of camaraderie passed. "I've learned how to manage my symptoms, now, of course. I have medication, physiotherapy, cognitive therapy. I'm fine, really. But I feel like a part of me hasn't caught up with that. Like I'm still afraid of myself. That's what the list is for. To help me get my bravery back."

She began that speech sounding like her usual self, but toward the end she started to mumble, her voice growing smaller, her eyes skating away from his. Like she was embarrassed to say the most badass thing he'd ever heard.

He couldn't let that stand. "Hey."

She pursed her lips and glared at him without much heat. "What?"

"If this list is supposed to make you braver, you're gonna be fucking Wonder Woman by the time we're done."

She snorted, rolling her eyes, but he could tell she was pleased. It oozed out of her like jam from a layer cake, and he was lapping the sweetness up, desperate for more.

"Also," he added, "just to make it really clear: your fiancé was a fucking donkey cock for leaving you."

He liked the way she laughed at that, not her usual, low chuckle, but a gasping, breathless giggle that she clearly hadn't meant to show him. She pressed her hands to her plumped-up cheeks as if she could push the laughter back inside, but it didn't work. She just kept going, and his grin grew wider and wider.

"Your friends were fucking useless and all," he told her. "Load of twats, the lot of them."

She pressed a hand to her chest, over the ridiculous, furry all-in-one thing she was wearing. "True," she managed between giggles. "Very true. Although, I don't know why I told you about that. It's not the point. It's incidental."

Did she really believe that, when he could see her pain a mile off? When her eyes shuttered with sadness as she talked about the people who hadn't stuck by her? His voice softened. "You should make new friends now. You shouldn't be lonely."

That wiped the smile off her face, though not from her eyes. She scowled at him, trying to look outraged. For some twisted reason, he liked it. "I don't need new friends," she said, "and I am not lonely."

"You are," he insisted, partly because it was true, mostly

because he enjoyed pissing her off almost as much as he enjoyed making her laugh.

Stubborn as fuck, she shot back, "I am not."

"You are."

"Redford Morgan, I will throw you out of my flat."

He grinned. "But I have a key."

"Which you would never use without due cause," she countered, "because you are a very good superintendent."

There was that flash of dizzying sweetness, the one she kept teasing him with. The one that made his grin turn wicked and his voice dip low, even as his logical brain screamed that flirting was a shitty idea. "Oh yeah? How good?"

She blinked rapidly, and he could've sworn she was blushing. "Well, I . . . I don't know," she muttered awkwardly. "I don't actually have much experience with superintendents."

"So I'm your first. Good to know."

She was definitely blushing now. "*Red*."

"I'm just teasing you, Button." He was, wasn't he? Teasing her, and enjoying it way too much. "Don't faint on me now."

"Right," she said dryly. "Excuse me while I swoon."

She looked hot enough to, in that outfit. The fluffy, gray pajamas swallowed her whole, and even though she'd opened a window earlier, he could see a bead of sweat creeping down the line of her throat. His eyes followed that tiny drop's path like he was a wolf and it was lunch. Now he'd noticed it, he couldn't look away. Couldn't drag his thoughts away. Couldn't remember what, exactly, they'd been talking about—only that he'd made her blush and he'd enjoyed it.

The drop had reached the hollow between her collarbones now, exposed by her slightly lowered zipper. He wanted to lick it away.

Wait—no he didn't. No. He. Didn't.

Oh, for fuck's sake. Yes he did.

"Red?" she said, her voice a little bit shaky. But not the way it had been earlier. This time, it shook the way his muscles did when he was pushing it at the gym. Like she was aching with adrenaline.

"You should really take that off," he said, his throat dry, his mouth moving like it belonged to someone else.

Her tongue darted out to wet her lips. She patted nervously at her hair. "Take what off?"

"Your clothes," he said, because he was concerned for her health, obviously. "Whatever that thing is you're wearing. You should take it off."

Chloe replied, rather intelligently, "Eep."

"You're sweating," Red went on, his gaze oddly fixated at the base of her throat. Probably staring in mild disgust at the afore-mentioned sweat.

For approximately the thousandth time that day, she cursed her numb-footed, sleepless night and all that it had led to. There he sat, devastatingly handsome, and she was sweating in a lemur outfit like a child who didn't know how to dress herself.

She tangled her fingers in the fabric, scrabbled for the last scraps of her dignity, and said firmly, "I'm fine."

"You don't seem fine." His gaze moved from her throat to her face, studying her with a stomach-clenching intensity that made her blood shudder its way through her veins.

The way he watched her made Chloe feel so . . . present. Noticed. Touched, and not in the emotional way. Her skin tingled in anticipation of a contact that would never be made. She was suddenly, disturbingly conscious of the fact that she wore very little under this onesie. *Very little,* as in, he could rip down the zip and she'd be standing there in nothing but her knickers.

This odd attraction she felt toward him was getting out of hand. She kept hearing a feral edge to his voice that couldn't possibly be there, felt a heat in his gaze that must be 100 percent her imagination. She tried to control her breathing and look innocent, as opposed to looking like the depraved mess she was. It didn't work.

"Chloe?" Red nudged, his little frown returning. She wanted to smooth it out with her fingers.

"What?" she asked faintly.

Gigi appeared helpfully on her shoulder and said, *"Don't mumble, darling. Nice big voice. Repeat after me: 'I want to ride you like a stallion.'"*

Dani appeared on Chloe's other shoulder and drawled, *"Don't forget to say, 'Please.'"*

A tiny, phantom Eve joined the fray and said, *"Don't listen to those two. Actions speak louder than words. Jump him."*

"You're too hot," Red said.

"I'm not."

He pressed the back of his hand to her cheek. The contact

sent a jagged shock of arousal through her. She didn't mean to react, but her next inhale came rather sharply—so sharply she made a soft, hungry sound. And he noticed. Oops. After a pause, he caught her chin and turned her to face him, which was unfair, because staring straight ahead had been her only coping strategy. His gaze unraveled her expertly in approximately 2.3 seconds. She saw the precise moment that he realized she was a breathless, horny little demon with a ridiculous crush on him. His eyes widened slightly, as if she'd shocked him witless.

Then those spring-green irises heated, were slowly swallowed up by dark pupils. He sighed, almost shakily. He leaned closer and bent his head until his brow rested against her temple, skin on skin, technically chaste. And yet, it felt so reckless, so charged, so shockingly intimate. His hair was a curtain cutting the both of them off from reality, silk swinging softly against her cheek. The scent of him, warm and earthy and comforting, imprinted itself in her mind, forever associated with this moment. This trembling, achingly close moment when they breathed, deep and desperate, in sync.

Once upon a time, Chloe remembered, she had absolutely loved sex.

"So, it's like that," he murmured, the words almost tender, sinking into her skin.

"No." Her voice was a ragged whisper, broken by sharp inhalations. She was drinking down his presence before he could take it away.

He laughed softly, each puff of air a kiss to her sensitive throat. "You are such a shitty liar."

"True." She closed her eyes. The way he drew her in, from his smile to his confidence to his honest charm . . . this attraction was forceful and unexpected, a riptide lying in wait beneath the smooth surface of her own mind. Now she'd sunk a bit too deep and been snatched under.

She wasn't sure which way was up anymore.

He found the fingers she'd tangled up in fleecy fabric and eased them gently apart, which was a relief, because she'd been in danger of clenching her fists hard enough to hurt herself. It took her a second to realize that he was holding her hand. She could feel his cool, dry palm against her clammy one, right up to the point where her wrist supports covered her skin. *He was holding her hand.* He was lacing their fingers together carefully, as if to connect them. Why?

She didn't know how to ask, and since she liked it, asking seemed silly anyway. He might come to his senses and let go. *She* might come to her senses and pull away. Far better to keep quiet.

He kissed her jaw. Softly, so softly, but she still whimpered.

He'd been so slow and languid, but at the sound of that whimper, everything about him tensed. He murmured roughly, "I like that," and brushed his lips over her skin again, as if to tease out more sound. Her nipples tightened, but she swallowed her breathy sigh. So he tried harder, though it felt lighter. His tongue flicked her earlobe, traced the shell of her ear. She moaned. He made a low, raw noise of satisfaction and held her hand tighter, as if he were sinking, too, and he needed something to cling to.

She was dissolving like sugar in hot tea. Her breaths were shallow, her temperature was rocketing in a way that had nothing to do with her outfit, and her desire was a drumbeat pulse pounding between her legs. Her pussy was so swollen it felt like a fist clenched between her thighs. She was coming apart at the seams. Thank her lucky stars that all he'd done so far was tease, because if he really bit into her the way she wanted him to, she might faint dead away.

If he really bit into her the way she wanted him to, she might bite back.

And then what? Would he strip her naked, shag her senseless, and see her on Saturday night to continue the list? She didn't know. She didn't know. What did it mean, when a man you made deals with and sent slightly flirtatious emails to licked your ear and held your hand? What did it *mean*? It certainly wasn't professional, or transactional, or simple. Not in her case, anyway. She was quite sure of that.

He slid a hand over the back of her neck, warm and solid and deliciously firm. Sensation spiked between her legs. "Chloe," he said, his voice like gravel. "I want to kiss you. Can I kiss you?"

He turned her on so badly she felt dizzy. She couldn't look at him, because she knew what she'd see: living, breathing sex, a man who could so easily make a mess of her. She was melting for him and they barely knew each other. She wanted to sob out her pleasure and he'd barely done anything to cause it. She. Was. Losing. Control.

She made herself whisper, "Stop."

He obeyed her the same way he did everything: calm, easy, as though it had been his idea. His mouth left her skin before she'd even finished speaking the word. The warmth of his proximity faded and she knew he'd pulled back. He squeezed her hand once before he let go.

His expression was unreadable—but his cheeks were flushed. Her mind fixated on that because it seemed so impossibly vulnerable. Impossible full stop. Why would he be flushed? He was cool and confident and probably made women wet with a bit of hyper-sexy hand-holding a few times a week, just to keep himself sharp. Except, according to the kiss of crimson painting his high cheekbones, maybe he didn't.

The sight of that flush—of the slightly glassy look in his eyes, of his soft, parted lips—filled her with reckless regret. She wanted to grab him by the hair and drag him back. She wanted to twine their fingers together again and ground herself in him. It was on her list, after all—meaningless sex. But some wise and protective instinct, hidden deep in the prehistoric part of her brain, warned her that nothing would be meaningless with someone like Red. And if it wasn't meaningless, she didn't want it. When it came to feelings, to relationships, to *more*, Chloe was off men.

He shut his eyes for one long moment, and when they opened again he looked a little more like himself and a little less like a creature sent from Planet Lust to sex her to death. Which was good. Very, very good.

"Are you okay?" he asked softly, clearly concerned. "Did I . . . ?"

Gosh, he was sweet. She needed to get him out of here before she cracked completely.

"I'm fine," she said brightly. Possibly a touch *too* brightly, but it was too late now; she was committed. "I'll see you on Saturday, to continue with the list." She sounded like a chipmunk on helium.

He hesitated, then said quietly, "Do you still want to do that? With me, I mean? It's okay if you don't."

Oh, I want to do a lot with you.

She was going to have to start tapping herself on the nose with a rolled-up newspaper. Her mind was out of control and needed training.

"Yes, I still want to do that. With you. I promise, everything's fine." She stood up and made vague, shooing motions in his direction. "Off you go, then."

He stood, too, smiling now. "I wrote the details in your little book. I know you like plans."

"Wonderful. Fabulous. Much appreciated." She shoved him bodily out of the room.

His smile widened. "I take it you don't want to talk about—?"

"Good-bye, Redford!" She herded him toward the hall.

"—about me kissing your—"

"Ah, ah!" She strode past him to unlock the front door, holding it open. "No more talk. I am a poor, disabled woman who is not to be harassed with unnecessary conversation."

He burst out laughing.

She pushed him out of the door.

CHAPTER ELEVEN

Saturday evening had never been so fraught.

Two days—and a few too many flushed, forbidden daydreams—after that Very Professional Meeting with Red, Chloe sat with her laptop perched on her knees and her sparkly blue notebook in one hand. He had indeed written out the details for her, right down to the bars and nightclubs they would visit. And, as she passed the time until his arrival by researching those establishments online, she couldn't help but notice that they were all very close together.

Close enough that walking from building to building probably wouldn't tire her out.

She closed her browser window with a tut, still not sure if she was pleased by that discovery or if she found Red's behavior presumptuous. She had a feeling it was the former, but she so wanted to believe the latter. It would make it considerably easier to resist feeling mushy things toward him. And, since escaping his intoxicating presence and remembering that men possessed less loyalty than the average flea and caused more emotional trouble than they were worth, Chloe had decided she must indeed resist.

It wasn't that she assumed he'd leap at the chance to become the next fiancé to abandon her. But, whatever their relationship, he would leave her life eventually—everyone did, in the end—and it would be easier to watch him go if they kept the kissing to a minimum. It would probably be easier if they kept the funny, flirty emails to a minimum, too, but he'd kept sending those, and . . . well. Ignoring him would be rude. Plus, he took her mind off of certain things. Somewhat.

On the coffee table, Smudge was delicately licking his own arsehole in flagrant convention of the established house rules—a sight that, bizarrely, plucked at something sad beneath Chloe's breastbone. Beside him sat Chloe's phone, and from the speakers a familiar voice was emanating. It had not stopped emanating, in fact, for the last ten bloody minutes.

"You're very grumpy today, darling," Gigi said. "Are you feeling delicate?"

"No," Chloe said, the word both flat and honest. She was physically passable; her misery was 100 percent emotional today. Being unhappy made her irritable. Even more irritable than severe back pain.

"Well, whatever is the matter, then?" Gigi asked.

Redford-based confusion and Saturday-night anxiety aside, Smudge was the matter. Chloe had finally taken him to the vet's yesterday, and what had she discovered? Why, that he had an owner, of course. An owner who'd put a chip in him like he was some sort of computer. The vet assured her that chips were both humane and safety conscious, but since Smudge's chip meant that she absolutely could not keep him, she found herself violently opposed to the concept.

"Darling," Gigi murmured, "are you growling?"

Chloe gave herself a little shake. "Absolutely not. Why would I ever do such a thing?"

Gigi sighed fondly. "Such strange granddaughters I have. I'm so proud. Your father is depressingly ordinary."

Chloe's dad was a financial analyst with zero inclination toward the outrageous, which disappointed Gigi no end. He never took off his herringbone coat, and speed-walked everywhere, and said things like "Bear with me a moment, please." He'd spent Chloe's entire school career slipping encouraging notes into her book bag because he knew how much she hated English class. If Martin Brown was ordinary, she wished everyone else would be. But she didn't bother saying any of that, because Gigi would roll her eyes and call his tie choices *utterly uninspired*.

"I'm not strange."

"You are, darling. Not as strange as Danika, I'll grant you, but still. Now, what have you been up to today, my sweet little onion?"

Onion was not the weirdest thing Chloe had ever been called by her grandmother. "I took my stray cat to the vet and discovered that he belongs to a control freak with no respect for the sanctity of the feline body. Her name is Annie."

"*Annie?* Outrageous. I despise her already."

"She is on holiday, if you believe it," Chloe said acidly. "Her cat is missing, and she has gone abroad!"

"*Thoroughly* shocking," murmured Gigi, who had once gone on a cruise of the Mediterranean while her third husband remained at home with a shattered femur. Of course, as she had informed all who questioned her decision: "I *did not tell the fool to shatter his femur during a perfectly lovely July.*"

"When she returns," Chloe bit out, "she will phone me, and I will be expected to hop to it and give back her cat. Well, I don't know if she's fit to own a cat. I found Smudge in mortal peril!"

A reasonable person might have pointed out that no cat had ever died of falling from a tree, and also that cats were uncontrollable creatures, but luckily, Gigi wasn't reasonable. She said in soothing tones, "The woman is an unfit mother. I'm sure of it."

"So am I! Do you know—" Chloe was cut off by a knock at the door. Her middle melted like chocolate fudge cake. She hadn't realized the time. It was Red. The skin over her collarbone tingled, as if he'd marked her with his heated gaze.

"Are you there, darling?" Gigi nudged.

Chloe cleared her throat and locked her inappropriate thoughts away. *Back in the vault you go.* "I have to go. Someone's at the door."

"*Someone,* hm?" Gigi said gleefully. "Why, darling. Whoever could it be? You sound flustered."

"I'm not flustered. And I don't know who it is."

"You sound," Gigi murmured, "as though you are telling fibs."

How could she tell? She could always tell. It must be a grandmotherly superpower. "We'll talk about this later," Chloe squeaked. "Got to dash love you bye!" She ended the call, huffed out a breath, then patted her robe self-consciously. Between wor-

rying about tonight and worrying about Smudge, she'd somehow
managed to lose all sense of time—and now Red was here, and
she was barely dressed, and oh, God, this was all going horribly.
She grabbed Smudge for good luck and rushed to get the door.

Still, she felt oddly buoyant—almost giddy—as she went.

Redford was big and broad on her welcome mat, his smile
almost tentative, his hair spilling over his shoulders like liquid
fire. He was wearing jeans and a flannel shirt, the sleeves rolled
up to expose forearms ridged with fine veins and thick tendons,
and sprinkled with barely visible, golden hair. Not that she was
staring, or anything.

"Evening," he said, his voice low and rich. And calm. Always
calm. Clearly, he was not at all bothered by the fact that the last
time they'd seen each other, he'd slid his *tongue* over her *ear*.

Well, if he wasn't bothered, then neither was she. "I'm very
sorry," she said, holding Smudge against her chest. "I'm afraid
I'm going to make us late."

Chloe's email that afternoon had been short and to the point,
but Red must have learned her language these past few days,
because he'd known straightaway she was upset.

Took Smudge to the vet. He's chipped. Has owner.

Oh, yeah. She was upset. But she obviously didn't want to talk
about it, so he hadn't planned on bringing it up.

Then she answered the door with that apologetic frown, her lip caught between her teeth and Smudge held against her chest, and he couldn't have kept his mouth shut for all the money on earth. "Are you okay?" he asked, completely ignoring what she'd just said, because apparently he was that kind of guy now.

She raised her eyebrows, that divine, Rococo face as striking as ever. "I'm in a mood, but then, I usually am. Why?"

"I got your message about Smudge, and—"

"I don't want to talk about Smudge," she said, her voice sharp.

Not so long ago, that sharpness would've jabbed him like a thorn. Now it popped his heart like a balloon, because he knew it meant that she was hurting, and hiding, and dealing with her feelings all alone.

Women who saved cats and wrote ridiculous lists and took deals painfully seriously shouldn't deal with their feelings alone. No one should.

But before he could tell her that, something about her seemed to soften, and she said quickly, "We're going to have fun this evening. It will be a list-ticking success. That's what I want to think about. Not Smudge."

He ran a hand through his hair and nodded, holding her gaze. Her eyes were big and dark and a little too bright behind her glasses. He wanted to touch her, but all things considered, that was probably a bad idea. So he kept his clumsy hands to himself, and swore silently that he'd make her smile tonight. One way or another. "All right," he said.

The tension between them dissolved, or maybe it had just faded for a while. "Come on, then," she said brightly, stepping back to let him in. Which was when he noticed her outfit—or her lack of one. She was wearing some silky robe thing, and the skirt ended just above the knee. He'd been drooling over her fucking ankles for weeks. Now he stared at the inch of thigh just above her knees and decided he should've jacked off before he came over. Twice. Three times, even. His balls ached just looking at her. Was this normal? This couldn't be normal.

She shoved the cat at him, turned in a dangerous whirl of short, silky skirt, and started off down the hall.

Red stared at the cat. The cat stared at him. If he were the kind of man who really understood animals, he might say this particular cat was sending him a telepathic message that went something like, *Get your dirty pervert eyes off my mum.*

"Sorry, mate," he muttered, and shut the door, and made his way to the living room.

She was bending over by the TV, switching off all the plug sockets. The hem of her robe lifted for a split second and he caught a flash of bare, brown skin before he looked away. All his nerve endings sparked to life, even as he begged them to calm the hell down. Everything in him turned hot and liquid, except his dick, which was, of course, rock fucking hard. He sat down and held Smudge over his lap.

And, because God was having a great time taking the piss out of Red today, Chloe turned around and zeroed in on the sight with a smile. "I thought you didn't like cats?"

"Yeah, well." He cleared his throat. "Maybe I judged before I really got to know them. They're not as snooty as they seem. My bad."

He watched as surprise flickered across her face. "Oh." She shot him a quick, shy smile and his heart burst like a firework. "Okay then. Um . . . I'm just going to get dressed. I'll be five minutes."

"Don't rush. It doesn't matter if we're later than we planned."

She gave him the same indulgent nod mothers gave their nonsense-babbling toddlers and hurried out of the room, probably intending to ignore him.

While she was gone, Red decided to occupy himself by listing the many, many reasons why he shouldn't lust after Chloe anymore, even if he desperately wanted to, really enjoyed it, and wasn't totally sure he could stop.

1. He'd come on to her and she had very firmly shut him down. No matter how much he thought about the taste of her skin, or the sound of her moans, it wasn't happening. So he should stop torturing himself now.

2. If he didn't stop, she might notice, and then she'd be uncomfortable. He was her superintendent, for Christ's sake—which he probably should've thought about before he'd put his hands on her. He couldn't make her uncomfortable. It just wasn't right.

2.5. Vik would slaughter him. And then Alisha would beat his corpse with a hairbrush.

3. Thoughts of her were starting to distract him at work.

4. He hadn't masturbated this much since he was a kid, and he was worried his balls might permanently shrivel up like walnuts.

He was just working on number five when Chloe reappeared, ruining everything. He'd thought the robe was bad, but now . . . now, she wore a dress the color of gold-edged moonlight, the fabric stretching tight over roller-coaster curves that deserved their own hazard warning. That outfit cupped every inch of her the way his hands wanted to. Her cleavage was so deep she might as well just throw in the towel and go topless. He consoled himself with the fact that the dress was longer than the robe, until she moved and a thigh-high slit made itself known. Fuck.

Her face wasn't any easier to look at. Her eyes yanked him in like twin black holes and her lush lips shone with some kind of makeup. Her hair was different, pulled back in a thick, fancy braid he didn't know the name of, one he'd like to wrap around his fist while he kissed her pretty mouth.

He was fucked. He was absolutely fucked.

She came to stand in front of him, clutching a little gold bag. "Is this appropriate?"

Appropriate? He cleared his throat. *Don't fuck up. Don't fuck up. Don't fuck up.* "Well. It doesn't have buttons, but it'll do."

She laughed and hit him on the shoulder with her bag. He wondered absently if he'd survive the night.

CHAPTER TWELVE

Walking toward the entrance of a nightclub was like leaping back in time. Except, in her teens and early twenties, Chloe had never felt the cold, whereas right now she was shivering her barely supported tits off.

The night was made of layered shadows and flashing, neon lights, rain an icy threat in the air that kissed her overheated skin, freezing her nervousness dead. She was too busy regretting her skimpy outfit to question if she should be here at all. That, she supposed, was a solid silver lining.

Red was in front of her, his big body a wind barrier she shamelessly huddled behind. He was holding her hand, tugging her along like a boat, and she knew he did it so they wouldn't get separated in the busy dark—only, she couldn't help but remember the last time he'd held her hand. Her heart pounded now just as fast as it had then. He'd been so tender, to touch her like that as he pulled her apart with his kiss. She still couldn't decide what it meant. Her logical brain said, *It means he* likes *you, obviously!*

And maybe—probably—he did. But it couldn't be that simple, or that lovely. Things never were, for Chloe.

Their first stop of the night had the cheapest drinks, which, Red had explained in the taxi, was strategic. She'd tried to point out that expensive drinks wouldn't bother her, but he'd muttered something about posh money wasters and told her to get into the spirit of the thing. So here they were, heading toward a slightly shady-looking club with a small field of cigarette butts littering the pavement in front of it. There was a sign the color of her glasses above the door that read BLUEBELL. Bluebell's pounding music took every other nightclub's pounding music by the throat and squeezed. The closer they got, the more she wondered if she ought to have brought some earplugs.

Red nodded at the massive, black-coated bouncers, dragged her through the doors, and then they were inside. Everything was dark, flashing, and sweaty. She didn't like it.

No—that wasn't right. She simply wasn't used to it, or drunk enough to enjoy it yet. Of course, a little voice in her head muttered that the hangover she would incur from drinking enough alcohol to make this place palatable would also leave her bed bound for a week. She squashed that voice. It was a party pooper and it belonged to the old, boring Chloe, not the Chloe who rescued cats.

Wait. She wasn't supposed to be thinking about Smudge.

Red somehow carved out a space for them at the bar. She found herself caged between his chest and the sticky surface, his hands braced on either side of her body. He bent his head to her ear, and the feel of his breath against the side of her throat made everything between her legs tingle. She pressed her thighs together while he shouted over the music, "What do you want?"

Good thing she'd already decided on this, or her poor, scrambled brain wouldn't have been able to produce an answer. "Cherry Sourz." It used to be her favorite.

Apparently, Red didn't approve, because he snorted, the puff of air hot against her skin. Still, he caught the bartender's attention, and before she knew it, three vivid pink shots were lined up in front of her, along with a glass of something dark. She was supposed to be paying for everything tonight—that had been her intention, anyway—but Red had handed over a note before she got the chance. She tilted her head back to glare up at him. He winked at her and picked up his glass. Coke and something, she thought, or maybe just Coke.

Then he brought it to his lips, and she caught the sharp scent as his throat bobbed with each long swallow. Coke and something, definitely. As definite as the slick arousal growing between her legs.

It really had been too long, if the heat of his body and the sight of him swallowing were enough to make her jittery like this. She faced front and grabbed a shot. It went down easy, but she found herself making a face. It was sweeter than she remembered. And, speaking of memories—this had been a lot more fun when she'd shared a row of shots with her girlfriends, drinking one after the other, shrieking foolishly afterward like they'd done something shockingly wild. But Beth wasn't here, Sarah wasn't here, Catie wasn't here, none of them were here, and this wasn't ten years ago. She bit her lip and downed the next shot.

Then she felt Red's hot breath against her skin again, smelled sharp alcohol as he spoke. "You okay, Button?"

She held up the last shot of cherry Sourz and shouted, "Will you drink this?"

"You don't want it?" He narrowed his eyes.

Awkwardly, she told him, "I want you to have it."

He nodded as if that made a lick of sense, took the shot, and downed it. She took his glass in turn and had a taste, pretending it didn't thrill her that they were now sharing a glass. He'd ordered rum and Coke. She licked his drink off her lips and tried not to enjoy it too much.

"Hey." He took the glass back, his free hand running down her arm in an action he probably meant to be soothing. It set her on fire. "Slow down," he said. "Give yourself a second."

She bristled, all—okay, *most*—of her arousal forgotten. She was seconds away from a scathing comment on men who thought they could tell women what to drink when he leaned down and spoke again.

"Getting properly wankered," he said in an academic sort of tone, "is a fine art. It is if you want to avoid the messier side effects, anyway." While she absorbed that, he caught the bartender again. She didn't know how he managed it. Must be one of the benefits of giant gingerism: he was impossible to miss.

The bartender produced two bottles of water—*boo*—and four more shots. Red shoved a water at her and paid again. Then he finished his rum and Coke in two impressive gulps, and drank his own water, which made her feel less indignant.

"All right," he said finally, splitting the shots in half. "You and me. Let's have it."

Surprise filled her, chased by pure pleasure. She swallowed her share easily this time, barely shuddering at the taste, and when he did the same, something inside her felt lighter. Warmer. Chloe giggled at nothing and let her head tip back onto his shoulder. For one dangerous second, his arm wrapped around her waist and squeezed. His hair spilled over her skin as he bent his head closer.

Then he let her go, as if it had never happened at all. He caught her hand, stepped back, and they were moving again, their clasped palms their only connection now. Chloe wobbled behind him like she was on stilts. She hadn't realized just how integral Red's chest had been to her structural stability during the last ten minutes. Stumbling after four shots? How mortifying. But fun, too.

Until she realized where Red was leading her, anyway. To the dance floor. Because that was what she wanted. She'd told him so in the taxi: she wanted to go out, get drunk, and dance. Except, now that they were headed in that direction, deep into a churning mass of bodies, she didn't want to do that at all. It was flooding back suddenly, how much she'd always hated this part. With her friends, she remembered, she'd bobbed awkwardly at the edge of the group, feeling like a ninny.

That wasn't how she wanted to feel tonight.

She tugged at Red's hand and he looked back at her, raising his eyebrows in question. When she looked at the dance floor and shook her head, he changed course without a word, pulling her smoothly toward the sticky, shadowy booths in the corner. They slid into one beneath an alcove, and by some audio-architectural miracle, the volume lowered just enough for Chloe to hear herself think. Thank God. All this pounding and pulsing was making her vaguely homicidal.

"What's up?" Red asked, his knee nudging hers. She looked at their legs beneath the filthy table and a thought danced wildly through her mind: he could touch her. He could slide his hand up her skirt right now, and no one in this hellhole would be any the wiser.

Then she looked up, met his endless eyes, and could've sworn he was thinking exactly the same thing. Each flash of strobe lights in the room lit up another facet of the hunger on his face. But he didn't move. He sat and waited patiently to hear that she was okay.

And suddenly, she was bored with lying to him. Must be the alcohol. "I don't like it here," she shouted.

He gave her a look that seemed to say, *Color me shocked*. But there was no gloating in his response. "Want me to take you somewhere quieter?"

"Yes. No. I—" She hesitated, her mind whirring. This, tonight . . . It wasn't what she'd really wanted. Because she hadn't known what she'd really wanted when she'd put this on the list. She'd been hunting for an indescribable thrill, a feeling she remembered from nights out with her friends, but she'd misunderstood where the feeling came from. It wasn't about drinking and partying in some dingy club.

It had been about the people. The constant laughter they shared, too high on each other to care that they were being obnoxious. Group trips to the bathroom like a small army unit, where the mission objective was helping each other squat over filthy toilets without their dresses touching the seat.

Belonging.

Maybe her list wasn't quite as perfect, or as clinical, as she'd assumed. Because this was the first item she hadn't enjoyed crossing off, and she couldn't deny that she was disappointed.

But she could fix this, couldn't she? Plans changed, didn't they? Wasn't that why she'd written the list in the first place—to become the kind of woman who turned disappointments around, who thought flexibly and did what she wanted to do?

Yes, she decided. Yes. That was exactly why.

She turned back to Red, found him waiting with those three little lines of concentration between his eyebrows. "I want to go somewhere else," she shouted.

He nodded. "We can do that."

But she wasn't done. "I want to know what you do for fun."

His frown cleared, replaced by a startled, hesitant pleasure. "Yeah?"

"Yes. Show me."

They left the club, and Red put his jacket over Chloe's shivering shoulders. He wouldn't miss the warmth—when he was around her, he burned from the inside out. She must be tipsy as fuck, because she didn't push him off or say something smart; she just smiled all pretty and held his hand as they cut through the cold, wet night.

Since the moment she'd decided to abandon their plan, she'd been electric. Vibrating brilliance, her walk slow and loose hipped, all the barriers and little hesitations he was used to from her fading away. Like she'd turned fearless.

He liked it. He liked her so happy that her soft, full lips had a permanent curl, that her eyes sparkled and her cheeks plumped. Tiny drops of rain spattered the lenses of her glasses, beaded on the flyaways frizzing from her hair, slicked her skin until she gleamed under the streetlights like a jewel. He slung an arm over her shoulders and she let him. Joined together like that, they strode through familiar, sleepless streets.

Leaving this city for London had been Red's first mistake of many. He'd thought he needed to do things in a certain way, as rigid then as Chloe was now about her list. But being around her was really driving home how wrong he'd been: there was no single way to reach any goal. He should've been flexible, should've stayed in the city he loved and tried to succeed as himself, instead of going somewhere else to be someone else beside a woman who'd never really given a fuck about him.

He still wasn't sure how to take things back to the start, how to build the life he wanted on his own terms—but tonight, he looked up at the stars and knew, really fucking knew, that he'd figure it out. He *was* figuring it out.

The funny thing about Chloe was, when he wasn't busy panting after her . . . she made his head a hell of a lot clearer.

"I think you'll regret asking me to do this," he admitted, his voice rising over passing traffic and distant music and the shouts of drunken students waiting at a nearby bus stop.

"Why?" Her shoes made little squeaking noises against the wet pavement. "Are your hobbies so depraved?" Her voice was rich with a flirtation he didn't quite trust. If she could sound that unreservedly into him, she was a little bit drunk.

Lightly, he said, "I think you'd like it if my hobbies were depraved. But no, they're not. They're boring."

"I'm supposed to be the boring one. You're supposed to cure me."

Was that what she thought? His chest tightened, his frown automatic. Chloe Brown was the furthest thing from boring on this planet. He didn't say that, though, because she wouldn't hear it. "This definitely won't cure you."

"Oh." She pouted. He tensed every muscle in his body to stop himself from leaning down and biting that plump lower lip. Then she stopped walking, cocked her head, and murmured, "Let me guess. We're here?"

He looked up with a start, and shit, she was right. He hadn't even noticed. She split time into something endless and wonderful, like crystal splitting light into rainbows. Or maybe he was so fucking hungry for her he was slowly losing his grip on reality. One of those.

"Yep," he confirmed. "We're here."

In a tucked-away section of the city, the kind lined with boutiques where only the rich bothered to window-shop, there was an alleyway. It was the kind of alleyway that would look suspicious and possibly dangerous in any other part of town, but here it just seemed mysterious. It helped that they could see light twinkling at the other end, and hear raucous nightlife a few streets over. It also helped that the alleyway itself was lined with art, fairy lights wrapped around the easels.

The first piece was an abstract vinyl print that, when you squinted just right, looked like a huge, pale, flower petal. When you squinted just wrong, it looked like dead skin. The second was a stark, stylized oil painting of a panda on acid. The third canvas, the last dropped bread crumb, looked like Roy Lichtenstein had taken on Klimt. He didn't hate it, exactly.

"Random art in an alley," Chloe said. "Is this really what you do for fun?"

He tensed a little, wondering if she'd say something that stripped him painfully to bloodied flesh, like Pippa would have. But then he remembered that Chloe was nothing like Pippa, which was why he'd brought her here. Because watching her chase what she wanted made him realize it was time. Because this would be easier with her than it would be alone. Because she'd asked him to show her something honest, whether she realized it or not, and this was as honest as he knew how to be.

And because she was too careful, too sweet, too cautiously loving to ever smash anyone's heart to pieces for a laugh.

"Yep," he said finally. "This is what I do for fun."

They were a few paces from the open doorway that was his goal. A distressed sign hung over it that read JULIAN BISHOP ART GALLERY.

"Adorable," she murmured.

Sounded like she was talking about him, but she couldn't be. He looked at her. She was. He started to speak, but his voice came out a little too rough, so he stopped, cleared his throat, tried again. "You calling me cute, Chlo?"

"I am. You giant, blushing art nerd."

Well, if he hadn't been blushing before, he surely was now.

Stepping over the threshold after avoiding this world for so long was like getting something pierced. He'd had his nose done when he was twenty-one, which had been a mistake on a face like his, and now he remembered the sudden, sharp push and watering eyes. He felt half a second of panic before deciding he couldn't be arsed to make a big deal out of this, even inside his own head. He was here. It was done.

Because of Chloe. Strange, that.

The gallery's entryway was tiny, housing a flight of spiral stairs. "You all right with those?" he asked.

"If I said no, would you give me a piggyback?"

His lips twitched. "Yeah."

"Good to know," she murmured wryly. "But don't worry, I'll manage." She turned, studying the little space around them. It was sparse and pretentious, which was all part of the fun. The white paint on the walls flaked horribly and the floors would probably give your bare feet splinters, but the paintings left to stand in the street had price tags in the low thousands. The stuff upstairs would be even more expensive.

Artists were all a lost cause, he thought, himself included.

The only interesting thing in this cramped space was the pink-painted garden chair jammed into a corner. A sign was tied to its seat with clashing red silk: DON'T SIT ON ME, I'M FAMOUS.

Chloe arched a brow. "Gosh. A chair that reminds me of my grandmother. I feel so at home."

Here was something he hadn't considered: how hilarious Chloe's sarcasm would be in a place like this.

"Always wondered what the chair's famous for," he said.

She flashed him a look. "You don't *know*?" Her face took on the faintly bored, slightly amused expression he'd seen on countless classy women in galleries fancier than this one. He'd never been in on the joke, even when his girlfriend was leading the jokes, but Chloe was about to bring him in. "Madame Chair comes from money, of course."

"Oh, of course. I remember now. She was on *Celebrity Big Brother.*"

Chloe arched an eyebrow, bit down on her growing smile. He could almost see the laughter trapped in her throat, but she refused to let it out. "Was she, indeed? And how did she do?"

"Not great," he sighed. "Long story short, Madame Chair got into an argument with a *Hollyoaks* actress about the ingredients of fast food. Ended up stuffing a frozen chicken nugget down the poor girl's throat live on national TV."

Chloe choked, coughed, wheezed. Red patted her helpfully on the back. Apparently that knocked the last of her control loose, because she dissolved into helpless laughter. He stood there and watched as she bent double, clutching his jacket and gasping for air, completely carefree and unrestrained. Watching her made his heart feel oddly warm and . . . glowy. Like he could stand here and soak up her happiness forever.

That sounded a little bit like heaven.

After long, joy-filled moments, she straightened, dabbing at her eyes beneath her glasses. Her voice slightly hoarse, she said, "Now, then. Shall we go up, or did you bring me just to see the chair?"

CHAPTER THIRTEEN

Despite the poky hallway downstairs, Chloe wasn't surprised to find that the gallery itself was a loft space with cavernous ceilings, bright, clean lights, and scarred, white walls that gave the space an ancient sort of quiet. There was an exhibit, and people with champagne glasses wandered around muttering seriously to each other. Red ignored every curious and censorious stare aimed his way, leading her inexorably toward his destination.

Because there had been a destination all along. She realized that when he stopped in front of a trio of paintings and nodded at the little plaque beside them. It said, JOANNA HEX-RILEY, COURTESY OF THE WRATHFORD ART INSTITUTE. He said with a happy exhalation, "Joanie."

"Do you know her?"

"Met her in London. We were friends. Heard this was here a little while back."

"London?" she asked, and his face closed off like she'd yanked out his plug. She wet her lips and tried again. "What happened with your friend?"

He shrugged, coming back to life. A touch of amusement played at the corners of his lips. "Nothing happened. I left. I didn't stay in touch."

"Why not?"

"Lots of reasons. Lately I've been wondering if they were good ones. No, that's not true." He smiled wryly. "I know they weren't. So I'm gonna work on that."

Then he went all silent and brooding, which was highly unusual behavior in a man who handed out smiles the way traffic wardens gave out tickets. Luckily Joanna Hex-Riley's paintings were fascinating enough to stop Chloe from doing something silly, like hugging him until he softened again.

She couldn't begin to guess at how the artist had done it, but the pale, naked woman who took over each canvas managed to look almost transparent in places, as if pieces of her were fading into nothing. It was an interesting effect. It gave her interesting . . . feelings. Not entirely pleasant ones, but she was still impressed by them.

It was a while before Red spoke again. "We can go somewhere else if you want."

"I'm fine here. Will you tell me something?"

"Maybe."

"When did you know you wanted to do this?"

He didn't bother asking what *this* was. "School trip. I was nine. Almost didn't go because we didn't have the money to spare. But at the last minute my granddad scrounged it up from God knows where, so I went."

She smiled. "He sounds like a useful sort of man."

"Yep." Red held out one of his hands, those thick, silver rings shining dully under the bright lights. "He always wore these."

"And now you always wear them."

"Yep."

"I'm sorry for your loss."

His face tightened slightly, painfully. "Years and years ago. He was old. I only miss him sometimes."

"My Nana died when I was twenty-six. My mother's mother. I know what you mean."

He put a hand on her shoulder and the tips of his fingers brushed her bare skin, close to her neck. A shiver seemed to roll through her and into him, like he'd hooked into her current and now they were connected. Their eyes met. His were dark and hot and secret as a jungle, his mouth slightly parted in surprise, or maybe something else. She wondered what he'd taste like. Right now? Alcohol, probably.

She'd like to get drunk off that mouth. She'd like a lot of things. It was strange, and a little worrying, to realize that while she was rapidly sobering up, her thoughts weren't getting easier to control. At least, not when it came to him.

"You were saying," she nudged him, "about the trip. Go on." *Also, please take your hand off me before my uterus explodes with lust. Actually, does the uterus even feel lust? Note to self: learn more about own genitals.*

"We went to the National Gallery. Before that trip I never realized art could be a job. In my world, jobs were awful. They chipped away at you and made you miserable, deep inside where no warmth could touch. You only did them because you'd starve and die if you stopped. But that trip . . ." He shook his head and she saw the echoes of wonder in his expression. "It changed everything for me."

He was quiet for a moment and she watched him with a new kind of hunger. A hunger that came from an unfamiliar place, that had nothing to do with his vitality or with his beauty, but with the ordinary things about him that were starting to feel like oxygen. This hunger was urging her to sneak inside his head and devour everything she came across. But that would be a little creepy, possibly violent, and probably illegal, so she settled for asking questions.

"What's something you want to do but haven't yet, something that would affect you just as deeply as that trip?" *Something like my list?*

"Why?" he asked teasingly. "You gonna make it happen? Because my birthday isn't till June."

"I have a strict socks-only birthday present policy."

His eyebrows shot up. "What the hell does that mean?"

"It means the only birthday presents I give to people are socks."

He snorted. "Sounds like you." Then, just as she began to think he'd avoid the question, he said, "One day I'm going to MoMA. New York."

The Museum of Modern Art? She wasn't surprised. Nor was she surprised that he'd phrased it so decisively. *I'm going.* It wasn't a dream: it was a reality he hadn't gotten around to yet.

Fired up, she said boldly, "I'm going to New York, too. Not for the museum; I just want to go. As part of my list."

"You'll love it." He was wonderfully, achingly earnest, excited for her, not a hint of doubt on his face. He thought she would do it. The confidence he wore like a cloak was covering her, just as surely as his jacket. "Everything's instant," he said, his voice a mixture of awe, fondness, and bafflement. "It's all sharp lines. It's fucking wild."

"You've already been?"

"Oh, yeah." His hair fell in front of his eyes as he nodded, and the urge to push it back was so strong, she had to curl her free hand into a fist.

Of course, if she was brave, she'd reach up and do it. He touched her all the time. But he was confident in his way, and she was learning to be confident in hers. She asked another question. "You were there, but you didn't go to MoMA?"

His easygoing smile turned flat. "I went with my ex. We didn't get around to it."

She wondered if that ex was the blonde from the pictures online, the one with the shark eyes. Before she could think of a polite way to ask—or a subtle way to pry his deepest, darkest secrets straight from his head—they were interrupted. Which was probably for the best, since she'd been mentally shopping for futuristic brain scanners like a villain in a superhero film.

A tall, thin man in a black turtleneck came to hover a few meters away from them, huffing loudly and throwing pointed looks like knives. Chloe had noticed more than a few people shooting them suspicious or disapproving glances, but this wasn't as easy to ignore. Red turned his head, very slowly, toward the man. She couldn't see the expression on his face, only the long fall of his hair. And, of course, she saw the other man's reaction to that look. The way he blanched and scurried off like he'd seen a wolf headed his way.

Red turned back to her, rolling his eyes. "Nothing changes."

"Doesn't it?"

"You know," he laughed, "I used to think you were a snob. But when it comes to this stuff, you're just oblivious, aren't you?"

"You thought *what*?" She tried to look horrified. "*Gasp,* et cetera. I can't believe you thought I was a snob."

"Neither can I. You're just a cute little hermit who hisses at sunlight."

She laughed, because it was funny, and felt warm, because it was fond. But once her amusement faded, she couldn't stop herself from pointing something out. Or rather, she didn't *want* to stop herself. "I'm not completely oblivious. I am black, you know."

His eyes widened theatrically. "Shit, are you? I had no idea."

She snorted.

"Of course I know, Chlo. And I realize you must . . ." He trailed off, as if he wasn't sure how to finish that sentence.

Which was fine, because Chloe knew exactly what *she* wanted to say. "The thing is, Red . . . some of us have so many marginalizations, we might drown if we let all the little hurts flood in. So there are those, like me, who filter. I think you've noticed that I filter a lot. It's not some inbuilt shield made of money. It's just something I'm forced to do." She shrugged. "And that's not to discount the differences between us that fall in my favor. It's just an explanation." The fact that she'd even bothered to tell him this said something dangerous. It said that he might matter a little bit. But, hopefully, he wouldn't realize that.

His hand came to rest on her shoulder again and stayed there until she looked him in the eyes. His expression was . . . unexpected. Contrite, gentle, slightly amused. She understood that last part when he said wryly, "I'm an arse, aren't I?"

"Not especially, but I feel as though I should take any opportunity to call you one."

He chuckled softly. "Fair. Chloe, you don't need to explain shit to me. I'd say it's more the other way around. Though I'm grateful that you did. Listen . . ." His voice changed, becoming slightly uncertain. "I've got, uh, baggage? When it comes to class. And, in my head, I keep putting it all on you. But I'm sorry about that. I'll stop."

Sorry. He'd barely done anything wrong. He'd given her a slightly negative feeling caused by a series of implications based on practically nothing. Which wasn't to say those feelings didn't *matter*; only that it was rare for others to take them seriously. Yet here he stood, watching her with actual remorse. Something in her softened like warm butter.

She lifted her chin and made her words as crisp as she could. "I suppose I forgive you, then."

He laughed. "Not your fault you're a princess, after all."

"And it's not your fault you're in constant, tongue-tied awe of my sophistication."

He spluttered, choked, and then they were both snickering together like unruly children. She almost forgot they were in the middle of a gallery, until a cultured baritone cut into their laughter.

"Red. Still charming the ladies, I see."

The huffy turtleneck wearer was back, accompanied by the man who'd spoken. He was in his forties or fifties, dark-skinned and classically handsome, wearing a suit so sharp, it should be kept away from infants and waterbeds. He had a shiny white smile and twinkling eyes, and his clear pleasure at seeing Red was giving Turtleneck heart palpitations.

"Julian," Turtleneck spluttered indignantly. "These are the *individuals* I told you about. I'm quite certain they aren't guests of the—"

"Go away, Tom."

Turtleneck Tom blinked. "*Well,*" he said ominously. He was quivering with indignation. Nobody cared. He stormed off.

"Redford Morgan," Julian grinned—Julian Bishop, the gallery owner, Chloe presumed. Interesting. "You've not changed a bit. I know you secretly enjoy making my guests nervous."

"Ah, fuck off," Red said cheerfully, and dragged Julian into a hug. There was a collective intake of breath around them as the guests waited for Red to stab Julian, or shoot him, or perhaps rip out the other man's throat with his teeth. When nothing much happened, aside from Julian laughing and hugging Red back, the crowd slowly began to lose interest.

The two men clapped each other on the back and threw insults. "I heard you were home. I mean, I *heard* you, stomping around in those boots like a giant."

"Sorry we can't all be pocket-sized. Wish I was little like you, but . . ."

Julian, who was all of two inches shorter, rolled his eyes. "How's your mother?"

"Same as always. Can't do fuck all with her." Red's voice, always warm, became a blanket by the fireplace in winter. He loved his mother. Chloe probably should've guessed, what with the tattoo on his knuckles, but now she heard him and she *knew.* "How's your dad?"

"The same as always. Incorrigible. Where have you been?"

"Avoiding you, aren't I?"

"So it seems." Julian turned serious as the two men stepped apart.

"Nah, come on," Red said. "I've been busy." His easy charm was dialed up to ten, his smile slow and confident as ever, his broad body relaxed because he was comfortable in his own skin. Except, for once, she didn't believe it. For once, he seemed to be performing. She was absolutely certain that he was utterly uncomfortable. She remembered how quietly edgy he'd been at his flat, when he'd put his art in her hands and tried to pretend the moment wasn't ripping him open.

She knew Red's disappearance from this world had started about eighteen months ago. Now the question clanged in her head like slow, heavy church bells. *What happened eighteen months ago to make him feel like this?*

"Hmm. Will you introduce me to your friend?" Julian asked, twinkling in her direction. Someone should cover those pretty eyes of his. They might cause an accident.

"This is Chloe," Red said. "Chlo, Julian."

She nodded. "Hello."

"Hello to you, too," Julian murmured, taking her hand. He didn't shake it. He kissed it. His lips were firm and the kiss was light. She didn't want to smack him for it, nor did she find herself battling the urge to climb him like a tree. And so she didn't pull away.

Red didn't seem to approve, narrowing his eyes at his friend. "Leave her alone," he said, and put an arm around her shoulders.

"Why?" Julian grinned.

"She's a lady, she doesn't like shady art dealers. Do you, Chloe?"

Chloe said, very seriously, "I try not to judge people."

"That's bullshit," Red said. "She's being polite. She thinks you're obnoxious and your eyes are too small. Tell him, Chloe."

"You have lovely eyes," she said to Julian, quite sincerely.

"I told you, she's a lady. She can't insult you to your face, but she's thinking it. Anyway, we're in a rush. I just popped in. We have to go."

Julian snorted. "So soon?"

"We've got a hot date at McDonald's. Don't want to miss it. She gets pissy without regular carbs."

Well, that was technically true.

"Wait a moment," Julian said, and produced his card, smooth as silk. "Since you apparently lost my number . . ."

Red looked slightly guilty as he stuffed the glossy rectangle into his jeans pocket. "Yeah, sorry about that, mate. I'll ring you."

"It doesn't have to be about work. I want to know how you've been."

Red paused, then said again, "I'll ring you." Because it hadn't been true the first time. He dragged Julian into a one-armed hug, then caught Chloe's hand and led her out of the room the same way he'd led her in: with too much determination to resist. They passed Turtleneck Tom on the way out and Red actually growled at the poor man. He growled! Chloe tried not to be thrilled, but it happened anyway.

They broke out into the crisp dark and he didn't let go of her hand.

"So," she said. "You know the owner."

Red shrugged his massive shoulders, speaking simply, a restrained energy she couldn't name winding through each word. "Used to spend a lot of time in there, looking around, wondering how it all worked. Had no one to tell me. Then his dad—that was Julian Bishop the Second. His dad's the first. His dad asked me one day if I had any questions. He helped me a lot."

"That's lovely," she murmured as they wandered up the cobbled alleyway. Ahead, she saw a glimpse of city lights glinting like jewels in the dark. The rain had become moisture hanging in the air, and the cool, wet scent of it cleared her head. But even without the buzz of alcohol, she felt brave. Funny, that. "Julian Junior seemed rather nice."

"He's a twat," Red muttered. "Kissing your fucking hand."

"Why shouldn't he kiss my hand?" she asked, because she was an attention-seeking little monster, hunting gleefully for evidence of jealousy.

He snorted, his breath a white cloud in the cold air. "First time I shook your hand," he said, "you acted like I'd electrocuted you."

Ah. He'd noticed. Well, subtlety had never been her strength. "I felt as if you had," she admitted.

He turned to look at her. He was shadowy, his hair catching most of the low light, his eyes difficult to see. But she felt them burning into her, impossible to escape. "Did you, now?"

"Don't take that the wrong way," Chloe told him quickly.

Red would love to take it the *right* way. The same way he suddenly wanted to take her: all the way to bed. A sparkling energy had hummed between them all night, too powerful to ignore— lust and chemistry turned intoxicating by delicate, newborn trust.

He was almost positive Chloe wanted him the way he wanted her, but that didn't mean she intended to do a damned thing about it. In fact, she definitely didn't; she kept making that clear. And he wouldn't push. He couldn't be that guy. So he let her comment pass, changing the subject, resisting the bait she hadn't meant to throw out.

He cleared his throat and asked, "Are you drunk?" because she wasn't wobbling anymore, and because it was as unsexy a subject as he could think of.

She flashed him a smile that was both grateful and embarrassed, then cocked her head as if testing herself. "I don't think so."

"Good." When they emerged from the alley, he pulled her

toward the Day Cross, a random stone monument to no-one-knew-what, tucked beside the old cathedral. "You want to sit down before we walk back?" He had no idea how long she could comfortably stand, but he wanted to talk for a while, and he kept remembering the little chair in her kitchen. She seemed fine, but then, she seemed fine all the time . . . and yet she was in pain all the time, too. When it came to looking after Chloe, that pretty face of hers couldn't be trusted.

She was suspicious, as if his offering a seat on a local monument was all part of some evil plan. "On the steps?"

"Oh, sorry. For a second there, I forgot you were classy as fuck." He wasn't being sarcastic.

"Actually, I got over my aversion to sitting on the ground a couple of years after I got sick. Needs must, and all that. But, er . . . you don't mind?"

He fought a frown that wasn't for her, but for whoever had made her feel like sitting in the street with a friend was some big sacrifice rather than just another thing people did. "No, Chloe. I don't mind." But he did remember, now, how shitty her old friends had been. How shitty a lot of people must be to her, the way she acted sometimes. He'd seen how people treated his mum, after all, because she was diabetic. Like being unwell was a crime or a scam or a self-indulgence.

Whether she admitted it or not, what Chloe really needed was a decent fucking friend. And what Red really wanted, badly enough to surprise himself, was to give her that. To show her every kindness she should take for granted. To make her smile and laugh and feel like herself.

The way she did for him.

They sat down, and everything around them seemed to slow, grow quiet, fade away. This side of the monument faced another narrow, cobbled street, not quite an alley but as poorly lit as one. The churchyard was behind them, and farther up were the old Galleries of Justice. In the day, this street would be full of schoolkids on trips and historically minded tourists, but right now it was deserted. They were alone in the center of the city, like a heart that didn't know who it beat for.

Quietly, Chloe said, "I think Julian would exhibit your work."

He shrugged. Pushed his hair out of his eyes. Drummed his fingers against his thigh. The knee of his jeans was wearing out again.

"Do you disagree?" she asked.

"Nope." The *p* popped like a gunshot. He sighed at himself and tried to sound like less of a miserable, defensive fuck. "I just . . . don't think I want that."

Her shiny shoes had ties that wrapped around her ankles. He watched the bows float up and down as she tapped her feet thoughtfully, her words coming slow but certain. "You don't want anyone to exhibit you. You don't want to be in galleries or museums at all, do you?"

It was a relief, like exhaling after months of holding his breath, to hear the way she said that. No incredulity in her voice, like he couldn't possibly manage it. Just quiet interest, like she trusted him to do shit his own way.

He trusted himself to do shit his own way, too. That was a dizzying realization.

"I'm an independent artist," he said with a faint smile. "You're making me an online shop. I'll work with collectives and all that. I don't need places like Julian's."

"Anymore," she finished.

If she asked about the past right now, he would tell her everything. It was on the tip of his tongue. She'd shown him hers, with the list and the fiancé and the filtering. Now it was his turn. And he didn't even mind, because she felt like the kind of person you could say anything to.

He wished she didn't think she was boring.

"You disappeared," she murmured. "You disappeared, and your work changed, and you don't want the same things anymore."

He nodded.

"And you only ever seem to paint at night."

He stiffened before she did. Realized what she'd just admitted before she did. It took her a moment to freeze, to flick a nervous glance at him, to stutter, "Um . . . ah . . ."

This was the part where he said, *How do you know I only paint at night?* After all, he'd just been perilously close to revealing every one of his secret scars. He should be dying for a subject change. Instead, he was dying for . . .

She took a breath, sat up straight, and said, "I have a confession to make."

Her voice was soft and wavering. He found her hand, flat on the cold stone, and laced their fingers together. Hand-holding had never been his thing, exactly, but it felt natural—or necessary—with Chloe. Like an anchor.

"All right," he said, as if he didn't already know. "So confess."

"I don't know if I should. No, no—I have to. Especially because we're friends. You said that, didn't you, Red?"

"Yeah. We're friends." Although he'd never wanted to kiss his other friends' wrists just to feel their pulse racing under his lips. For example. But still, friends.

"All right." She smiled, but it was a nervous sort of smile. "Well, you know the list I showed you is . . . censored, I suppose. And there's an item you haven't seen that, um, that you've already helped me cross off."

His eyebrows rose. This wasn't going where he'd expected it to. "Okay?"

"I wanted to do something bad." She sounded tortured.

He found himself smiling. "Uh-huh?"

"So I . . . well, I . . . Oh God."

"Just spit it out, Chlo. You're killing me."

She spat it out, all right. "Imighthavemaybekindofspiedonyou-alittlebitlikethroughthewindow?"

He blinked. "What?"

"I *spied* on you." Her voice was clearer this time, since it was a banshee-level wail. "Like a *weirdo*. I mean, the first time was an accident, and I only did it twice after that, but that's twice too many, and you were *basically* naked—which is not why I did it—"

"So why did you do it?"

She bit her lip, her eyes widening slightly. Probably because he'd asked like it was fucking life or death. He held his breath, wondering if her answer would ruin this. Ruin everything.

It didn't.

"I watched because . . . when you paint," she said softly, "you seem so vital. It was addictive. It felt like coming to life."

Something in his chest, sort of . . . skipped. Pleasure rolled through him the way fire warmed cold hands: slow and intense and so sharp you weren't quite sure if it hurt, but didn't mind either way. He didn't realize he'd been staring at her in silence until she begged, "Oh my God, say something."

The nerves in her voice squeezed at his heart. "It's okay," he said quickly. "I already knew."

Her jaw dropped. "I beg your pardon?"

"About the spying, I mean," he clarified. "Not about the, er . . . coming to life part." He was grinning as he said it.

She set her jaw and stared at her knees. "I shouldn't have said that. And how did you already know?" She had the nerve to sound irritated with him, which, for some reason, he liked. He liked a lot of things about her, in fact, with a summer-sky-blue intensity that almost made him want to look away.

"Rule of thumb," he told her. "If you can see someone, they'll probably see you."

"But . . ." She spluttered helplessly. "It was dark outside!"

"Your lights were on. My lights were on. Do you know how windows work?"

"Oh, shut up." All at once, her indignation faded. "I'm sorry. I'm really, *really* sorry. You should hate me."

He'd expected to. He'd thought her reasons would drag him back to dark places—that she'd been consuming him for her own amusement, that maybe she'd been watching him the way she'd watch animals at the zoo. But she hadn't been. Her explanation was nothing like he'd once expected. It was . . . sweet, as if she'd put a hand on his heart for a moment. And really, he didn't actually care who saw him painting—hence why he did it in front of a bloody window.

But, all things considered, he thought she was bullshitting just a little bit. "Not that I don't believe your flattering explanation, but are you sure you didn't watch *partly* because I was half naked?"

She gasped. "Of course not. Outrageous. As if I would ever. I'm not a pervert, you know!"

"Then why'd you feel guilty?"

Her pretty, pillow mouth formed a perfect *O*. It was getting so dark he could barely see her, but strips of orange streetlight sliced over her jaw, glinted off her glasses, illuminated her sparkly, skirt-covered lap. Maybe he should take that as some kind of sign. Maybe the universe was telling him to kiss her, take off her glasses, and push up her skirt.

Yeah, right. What had they *just* said? They were friends. F R I E N D S.

But then she pursed her lips, and sighed, and said with an air of confession, "I suppose you're right."

He stilled. Cleared his throat, because it suddenly felt rougher than sandpaper. "Right about what?"

She glared, as if he was being difficult. "You know what you look like."

You know what you look like. Coming from Chloe, that might as well have been a fucking ode to his attractiveness. And now she narrowed her eyes at him, chin up, as if daring him to have a problem with that.

There was only one problem, really: the fact that they weren't touching. So he stopped holding back, and his free hand cupped her cheek, cradling that beautiful fucking face. She breathed in sharply, caught her lower lip between her teeth, and he teetered on the edge of a possible mistake. Would she regret him, after tonight? Would she see him as a failed plan, a thing she couldn't control and wanted nothing to do with? Would she leave him, and everything wonderful growing between them, behind?

He couldn't let that happen. But he couldn't let this moment pass, either.

"I'm going to ask you something," he said softly, studying her face—the V between her eyebrows, the heat in her eyes, the vulnerable flash of pink inside her mouth, revealed by her parted lips. He wanted that mouth. He wanted that vulnerability. "I'm going to ask you, and I don't want you to worry about anything. Not a fucking thing, Chlo. We're friends. This doesn't have to be complicated. I'm not going to make it complicated. Okay?"

He heard her breath hitch slightly as she nodded. "Okay," she said softly. "Okay. So ask."

"Should I make you moan again?"

Her answer was so fucking sweet. "Please."

CHAPTER FOURTEEN

She'd thought he would kiss her. He bit her instead.

The tip of his nose bumped hers, his big hand cradled her jaw, and his teeth grazed her lower lip. Soft and slow. Tugging slightly. She felt that tug right between her thighs, a molten rush. He bit again, harder, and arousal shivered over her skin. Her nipples tightened, as if they were trying to catch his attention like a pair of shameless hussies. She approved. More bites, everywhere. Clearly telepathy wasn't his strong suit because he didn't rip off her clothes and devour her, one breast at a time; he licked her lip instead. His tongue swept out to soothe the tingle left behind by those bites, except it didn't work. That wet slide turned the tingle into a spark, a current, a bolt of lightning. She moaned.

He pulled back, slowly, slowly. "There," he whispered.

"More," she told him.

"Know what I'd do with you, if you were in my bed?" His voice was gravel and bittersweet longing. "Kiss you until I couldn't taste myself anymore. Just fruit tea and too much mouth. Put my hands on every inch of you. So soft, Chlo." He swept his thumb over her skin. "How do you do that?" His voice cracked as if she'd ruined his life by moisturizing after she showered. He shook his head and laughed, apparently at himself. "I want to make you cry. I bet you get like that, don't you? When it's too much. When it feels too good."

She'd been wrong about his lack of telepathy. He was an excellent mind reader. "Maybe. Sometimes."

He groaned. The thumb stroking her cheek moved lower, parting her lips. She bit him back. He swallowed so hard she heard it. She sucked his thumb into her mouth. He groaned again. Then he ruined everything. "Tell me why you stopped me. Before."

She hesitated, uncertainty draining most of her pleasure. She couldn't tell him, not without revealing too much of herself. What was she supposed to say? That she already liked him far too much? That he made it too easy to be intimate, to be honest, to be weak in a way that felt so good but also left her open to so much hurt?

She didn't want to have that conversation, to admit how she'd worried then, or how she wanted him too badly to worry now. She could see how easy it would be to fall for this man. She could see the phantoms of all the feelings she could develop for him, like premonitions. And she could see him throwing those feelings in her face, the way people always did.

Her body was vulnerable enough without her heart following suit.

So she reminded him gently, "You said you wouldn't make this complicated." *Please don't make this complicated. I really want to put my mouth on you.*

He gave her a rueful smile and murmured, "I did, didn't I?"

"Your rules, Mr. Morgan. Please abide by them."

As she'd hoped, her crisp, mocking tones widened his smile. "Shut up. Come here." Her stomach dipped as he lifted her, then put her between his spread thighs. Her back was against his chest. He leaned against the stone pillar of the monument they were absolutely not about to defile. From his position behind her, he murmured in her ear, "Comfortable?" His breath shivered over her skin. She felt his voice rumble in his chest, pleasure zipping down her spine.

"Yes," she breathed.

"Are you cold?"

"No." Because he'd wrapped his arms around her, shielding her from the night air with his big, warm body. And because all she could feel at this moment was a painful mix of pleasure and frustration.

"Good," he said. His lips brushed her frantic pulse. "Let's play *I want.*"

She settled against him, put her hands on his thick forearms as if she could stop him from letting go. "*I want?* As in, I want to trace the tattoos on your chest with my tongue?"

A long breath shuddered out of him. "Yeah. Like that."

The fact that he was turned on by something as simple as her words made her brave. Reckless. Wild, for a woman like her. "As in . . ." She thought for a moment, flicking through fantasies she'd never let herself fully acknowledge. "I want to lie naked with you just to know what your skin feels like against mine?"

"You're good at this." He shifted behind her. The hard jut of his erection hit the base of her spine.

"I want to see your cock," she blurted, then bit her lip.

He groaned. Pressed his face against the back of her neck. "My turn."

"Tell me."

"I want to see *you*. Right now, in the light. I want to see how you look when you're so turned on it's making you shake."

He was right, she realized; she was shaking. "Oh."

"I want to put my hand under your skirt and feel how hot your pretty cunt is. But I bet you wouldn't let me do that in public."

She sucked down a gulp of cold air to stop herself from burning up inside. "Certainly not," she lied.

"I want to know how wet you are right now."

"Very," she whispered.

He put a hand on top of hers, laced their fingers together. "Touch yourself, if I can't. Will you do *that* in public?"

When she slid her hand under her skirt, his came along for the ride. But she didn't lead for long. He took over, as if he couldn't help himself, all firm, easy strength. Slowly, he trailed their interwoven fingertips over her inner thigh. Chloe swallowed a gasp. "This is cheating," she breathed.

"Nope," he said softly. "Ain't this what they call creative problem solving?"

She couldn't speak. She had no oxygen left; the hypnotic circles he made, the sensations he sent dancing over her skin, had stolen every last breath from her lungs. There was too much blood in her veins, too much need pulsing through her clit. Her belly was tense and trembling, her body rigid, every muscle taut. She was on the verge of overloading in the best way possible.

The uneven click of stumbling heels floated to her ears. Happy shrieks, too-loud chatter: a group of drunken women walking by, just up the street. Friends, probably, out having fun. On any other day she'd feel a pang of jealousy; irritation at herself for holding back from that; annoyance at the world for flinching away from her. Today, though, all she felt was frustration because Red's slow, addictive circles over her thigh had stopped.

She tried to tug his hand back into motion, and he laughed. "You always surprise me, Chloe."

"They can't see us."

"You're bad tonight." His voice was all gravel. "Don't know why I'm trying to behave."

"Feel free to stop trying." She was done pretending to be demure.

He caught her earlobe between his teeth and an arrow of sensation flashed through her. "All right." Rough, wicked words. A switch had been flicked. Beneath her skirt, his hand disentangled from hers. He was bolder without her. He squeezed her thigh and whispered hot against her cheek, "I want to hold you open like this when you take my cock."

When she closed her eyes she could see it: him kneeling over her, forcing her legs apart, fucking deeper and deeper. She whimpered and the sound seemed to spur him on. He pressed his palm against her pussy, cupping her possessively over her underwear, and the same moan shuddered through both of them at once.

"You're soaked. You're fucking—Chloe—"

"Please," she gasped, her hips jerking forward. "Please." The heel of his hand was a delicious pressure against her swollen clit. How did he know where to touch, how to touch? He was some kind of vaginal magician. When he hooked one thick finger under the edge of her knickers she wanted to scream. Bit her lip hard. Shook with the effort of keeping quiet.

Supposedly, Chloe felt more than other people did. Chronic pain literally rewired brain pathways until you were more conscious of your own body than you should be, until you hurt more intensely than was healthy. An inescapable cycle. Only now did she see a potential upside: she must feel more pleasure than normal, too. She *must*. Because surely this wasn't ordinary. Lungs tight, ears ringing, heart shaking instead of beating, and her pussy slick and swollen—this couldn't be ordinary.

But he was shaking, too, his breaths heavy, his body tense behind her. So maybe it was ordinary with Red. Maybe this was just the way things were between them.

He tightened one strong arm around her as if he could hold her steady, keep her safe from the surge of desire threatening to short-circuit her system. But he couldn't, because he was the cause. His fingers parted her folds with heart-stopping certainty, spreading her open like she belonged to him. He delved into her wetness and growled, "God, I'm losing my fucking mind. Kiss me. No. Don't. I'll lose it."

She twisted, tipped her head back, and sucked his bottom lip into her mouth. She wanted to consume him. This wasn't quite a kiss, was it? He groaned and found her aching clit, his fingers slick with her arousal. His touch was an easy glide, barely any pressure, just electric sensation. She jerked her hips toward him but he resisted, lightly circling that swollen nub until she felt drugged with pleasure, breathless with need.

He dragged his mouth away from hers and sucked at her jaw, her throat. His usual calm had been shattered, the jagged edges glinting dangerously in the low light. "Turn around. Show me your tits. Please."

She wanted to. So badly. Who *was* she? Apparently, the kind of woman who thrilled at coarse orders like that, and broke a little bit when they were followed with hoarse manners. She turned, rose up on her knees between his legs. Somehow, he kept stroking her, kept up his beautiful torture. Her hands trembled as she tore open his borrowed jacket and shoved down the front of her dress. He growled, then bent his head and used his teeth to drag down one side of her flimsy bra.

She felt cold air against her tight nipple for a moment before his warm, wet mouth enveloped her, the change a sweet shock, an almost-pain that she craved more of. Wasn't that strange, craving pain? But this pain was different. This pain was good.

And then it was gone, replaced by tendrils of pure pleasure that coiled around her limbs, tightening with each lazy lick. He suckled her breast and circled her clit and she felt that frantic fluttering deep inside that meant she was going to come. She sank her fingers into his hair, hair that looked like fire but felt like cool silk. "Keep . . ." She couldn't get the words out, but she didn't need to. He kept. And kept.

Luckily for both of them, Chloe always came quietly. She

didn't have enough oxygen to cry out; the screams building in her chest came out as desperate gasps. Her head fell back as pure satisfaction flooded her body. Red bit her nipple gently and nudged her clit one last time, then chuckled at the strangled sound of protest she made. By the time her heart stopped ramming against her ribs, he was putting her knickers in place and tugging her bra over her breast.

"Come on," he said softly, rearranging her dress. "You're cold." He zipped up the jacket for her, tapped her nose, helped her to her feet.

Was she cold? She hadn't noticed, but she supposed she must be. She wasn't wearing gloves. It wasn't good for her fingers to get stiff.

As they stepped off the monument and into the light, her gaze flitted down to the hard shape ruining the line of his jeans. That didn't look good for him, either. Pre-orgasm, her arousal had made her brave, but now she had to force her words out. "Um, Red . . . I don't suppose—well, I mean, obviously you haven't— and if you—"

"Chloe, love. Please don't say you'll finish me off. I'm trying really hard not to fuck you in a back alley, here."

She bit her lip and let him take her hand, leading her toward the nearest taxi rank. The mist in the air cooled her fevered cheeks and spotted the lenses of her glasses. His strides were long, and she was starting to get exhausted, but she didn't say anything because she was too busy overthinking. Remembering. Feeling a pulse of pleasure inside her, like an echo. Worrying, as always, because she felt so achingly close to him, but she didn't think he felt the same. He was the one who'd said, after all, that he wouldn't make things complicated.

When he'd whispered those words, she'd honestly thought she was okay with it. But that, obviously, had been the horny demon inside her telling lies to get what it wanted. Because now she'd come, and suddenly she was complicated again—complicated and getting dangerously attached.

Tut, tut, horny demon. Unfair.

They were almost there when Red realized she was lagging behind. Instantly, he stopped, squeezing her hand. "Sorry."

"It's okay."

"Are you tired? I can—"

"I'm *fine*," she snapped. She was not fine, but it had nothing to do with his walking too fast.

He shot her a suspicious look. He was beautiful. She wanted to kiss him. They hadn't actually done that, and she knew why she'd avoided it: because she was afraid he might taste her feelings on her tongue. Because she was tumbling headfirst into a connection that probably wasn't as deep on his end.

She wondered why he hadn't kissed her.

He stepped closer, cradled her jaw in his hands. "Hey, Button," he said softly. "What's wrong?"

Her breath hitched like she might cry, which she absolutely would not do. Instead she would take a deep breath and tell him calmly that they should forget about tonight because it was already messing with her head. That he should stop holding her like something precious. That he was absolutely wonderful, honestly, he was, and that was exactly why he must never touch her again, or call her Button, or even smile at her. His smile was very handsome, handsome enough to trick her into ill-advised feelings that could not end well; better safe than sorry.

Always, she was better safe than sorry. And better left alone than left behind.

But, before she could say any of that, everything went to hell in a handbasket.

"Is that my Chloe?" The question rang through the air, slightly slurred and more than a little incredulous.

She froze. Oh, for heaven's sake, no.

"*Chloe!*" the voice repeated, unmistakable now.

Disaster had struck. The end days were nigh. She already wanted to sink into the floor. She jerked back from Red until his hands fell from her cheeks, but that did absolutely nothing to help the situation. The man who seemed to be attempting a no-strings-attached affair with her was about to be subjected to one of her bonkers family members. Because men loved to meet the relatives of the women they got off on public monuments. They *loved* that. It was well-known.

"Darling! It's me!"

Chloe turned. "Yes, Aunt Mary. I know."

"Don't be so *dour!*" Aunt Mary beamed. "I'm thrilled to see you out and about, my darling, I'm absolutely thrilled."

If it weren't for the purple lipstick, the spiky heels, and the, er, volume, Chloe might think she was standing face-to-face with her mother. Mary was Joy Matalon-Brown's twin, and also, possibly, the reason Chloe had been born. Chloe held a private theory that her parents had bonded over the surreal experience of growing up with a mother like Gigi and a sister like Mary. Her poor, ordinary dad and sensible, highly strung mum had been thrown together by a shared experience in stress and long-suffering sighs.

"I'm pleased to see you, too, Aunt Mary." It wasn't exactly a lie: Chloe loved to spend time with her aunt. In a controlled environment. Under very particular circumstances. "You look nice."

Aunt Mary lifted one fuchsia-booted foot. "Imitation croc skin, darling. Aren't they absolutely hideous?" She was beautiful, intelligent, a successful partner in the Matalon family law firm, and therefore took great pleasure in dressing however she wished.

"Very striking," Chloe nodded.

"You're a doll. Now, who is this, darling? He's very quiet. I so adore quiet men."

Oh, God. The twinkle in Aunt Mary's hazel eyes did not bode well. Surely the last thing Red wanted was to face the full, inquisitive force of that twinkle and all that it threatened. What could she say to avoid it? *He's my friend?* That sounded like a euphemism. *He's a man I love spending time with and also want to lick, and I'd like to care for him, but I don't really dare?* That sounded like an inappropriate and inconvenient truth.

"He's no one," Chloe said quickly.

Aunt Mary cocked one perfectly threaded eyebrow. "What an interesting name."

This situation, Chloe realized with a spike of panic, was rapidly getting out of control.

She could feel Red beside her, slightly behind her, and usually that might be reassuring. But after what they'd done tonight, and how uncertain it made her feel, and how awkward this was—well, his presence didn't seem quite as soothing as usual. She couldn't even bear to look at him. Her frantic gaze wandered over Mary's shoulder, where she spotted a gaggle of exuberant fifty-somethings teetering about in high heels. "Don't let me hold you up, Aunty. Your friends are waiting."

Mary rolled her eyes. "Oh, please. They're so drunk, time has become an alien concept." She raised her voice from foghorn to rushing train. "I'm talking about you, Sheila! You gin fiend!"

"Aunt Mary—"

"Sorry darling, sorry, back to your friend. Do introduce us."

"He's the superintendent of my building." Chloe was running out of options. Hopefully the mention of her living arrangements would prove a solid distraction.

"Oh," Aunt Mary said, wrinkling her nose. "Your little . . . look, darling, I completely understand wanting to leave the family home. I told your mother many a time that they were suffocating you. But really, this communal situation—"

"It's a life experience," Chloe interjected. "Anyway, so sorry, but we're late for a building-type meeting, so we must dash."

Aunt Mary looked suspicious. "A building-type . . . ?"

"It's something you do," Chloe said wisely, "when you live in flats." Aunt Mary had lived in mini mansions her entire life, both in England and as an infant in Jamaica. Hopefully, she'd have not a clue what people did when they lived in flats.

"How awful," she said faintly. "I'll let you get on, my

darling." She leaned in to kiss Chloe's cheek and whispered, "I do hope you've asked your new friend for test results. Your immune system is very weak, and accidents do happen no matter the precautions—"

"*Aunt Mary!*" Chloe snapped. "Go away!"

"I'm off! I'm going!"

As her aunt hurried back to her friends, Chloe eased out a sigh of relief. "Well. That was relatively painless." She turned, finally, to Red.

His hands were in his pockets, his eyes fixed somewhere over her head. He nodded slowly.

She swallowed. "Sorry. Aunt Mary can be overwhelming."

"That what that was?" he asked mildly. "You being over-whelmed?"

Chloe twisted her fingers in the material of his jacket, zipped up over her dress. She had this awful, doomed feeling in her stomach. This disturbing certainty that he was upset. But she'd done the right thing, keeping him at arm's length there, pro-tecting him from misunderstandings that would only embar-rass them both. Hadn't she? "Mary, she just, she gets overexcited about things, and I didn't want to give her the wrong idea. She's my mother's twin. They tell each other . . . things."

He turned, started walking again. His pace was easy to keep up with this time, but he didn't take her hand. "Right. And what would the wrong idea be? That we even know each other?"

He *was* upset. He'd misunderstood her reasons. The impulse to apologize tugged at her gut, so strong it felt like the urge to vomit. She swallowed acid and knew, all of a sudden, that she should've introduced him politely and dealt with wrong assumptions later. But she'd panicked. How long had it been since she'd let herself care about someone new, even the tiniest bit? She had no idea how to handle things like this, no idea what the parameters were—she barely even understood what *uncomplicated* meant when it came to two people touching each other.

She had to fix this, without slipping up and saying too much, revealing too much. Her mind raced. Her throat tightened.

In silence, they reached the line of taxis, waiting under harsh streetlights that ruthlessly illuminated his brilliance, her mistakes, and probably every pore in her T-zone. Before he could grab a car, she blurted out, "What should I have said?" She tried to make her voice light, teasing. "That you're helping me get a life in return for a website?"

He softened slightly, laughed gently. "No. No, I guess you couldn't tell her that."

She laughed, too, or tried to, but it sounded off. Her breaths were strange, sucking in air when her lungs already felt full, exhaling harder than was comfortable. "You're my . . . my bad-boy tutor," she quipped. Ridiculous. She was being ridiculous. He would hate that.

His smile tightened. "I wouldn't say I'm—"

"Services including but not limited to illicit orgasms." *Services?* Why did she say that? Why, why, *why* did she say that?

He looked like she'd just punched him in the stomach. But only for a second. His mouth was a thin, flat line when he turned away from her. "Right. Yeah."

It was guilt that burned away her panic. She felt as if she'd been body snatched for the last ten minutes. She blinked hard and smoothed her hands uselessly over her hair. "Oh, Red, I didn't mean—"

"No, don't take it back now," he said calmly. "You're already confusing the fuck out of me."

"I'm sorry."

"And I'm pissed. Good talk." He strode away from her toward a taxi, bending to talk with the driver, his voice low and tight. His anger seemed to surround him like jagged spikes. Or like knives she'd shoved into his back. She was a sad little mess and an absolute traitor. He would never stand beside her and call her no one, no matter how awkward the situation was. Self-imposed isolation had eroded many of her social skills, but for heaven's sake, could she be any more of a . . . a twat?

Apparently, she could. Because she knew she needed to say something, anything, that would fix the mess she'd made and erase the new, stiff way he held himself. But all through the drive home, she remained painfully silent.

And then they were back, and he walked her to her door, and she gave him his jacket. He nodded, he left.

And she hadn't said a word.

CHAPTER FIFTEEN

Red sat on the floor of his studio, the afternoon sunlight glinting off the silver buttons of his overalls. It was Monday and he was on duty, but he hadn't been able to focus since yesterday morning—when he'd woken up to an apology text from Chloe that he didn't know how to answer. Ever since, two very different cards had been burning a hole in his wallet.

Julian's, of course. And Dr. Maddox's.

The one in his hand right now, crisp and white and heavy as a brick, was the doctor's.

His mother had given him this card six months ago and asked him to get therapy. He'd promised he would, but he hadn't said *when,* and Maddox's details had peeked out from behind his library card ever since, whispering that Red was a coward and a big baby and for God's sake he needed to talk to someone. But he'd been coping fine without. Painting was his therapy and it always had been.

He looked to his right and his gaze fell on the canvas he'd

essentially destroyed last night, vicious yellow-green worked into its surface so hard that it had ripped.

Maybe painting wasn't doing the job anymore.

He raked his hands through his hair and laughed bitterly. All this, days of confusion and angry acrylic shades, because he couldn't decide what to do about Chloe fucking Brown. He was supposed to see her this week, to check the progress on his website. They'd arranged the meeting last week, before everything had gone to shit. But then . . . well, everything had gone to shit. And now he was trapped in a familiar whirlpool of past and present, one he was starting to get really fucking bored with.

It went like this: first, he'd remember what Chloe had done. How she'd treated him like a dirty secret, like a giver of illicit orgasms—might as well borrow her words, since she'd put it so perfectly. And he'd feel sick.

But then he'd remember that she hadn't looked pleased with her own knifelike phrase. She'd looked guilty. She'd looked miserable. She'd said instantly, unreservedly, *I'm sorry,* and when he thought about that, he was filled with the urge to give her a chance to explain.

Until Pippa forced her way into his head, with her tears and her clever words and her own gasping, weepy *I'm sorry*s, the ones that somehow turned him into the brute who'd started it all. The ones that always made him apologize for everything she'd done. His rational mind would say, *It's not the same. They're not the same. That's not even close to what Chloe was doing.* But his chest would still feel tight and his hands would freeze when he tried to pick up the phone and call her.

All of which suggested it was time to pick up the phone and call Dr. Maddox instead.

He eyed the card suspiciously. Dr. Maddox's first name was Lucinda. He used to live on the same street as a lady with a one-eyed mongrel called Lucinda. He'd really liked that dog. Maybe that was what people called a sign, or maybe he was being a twat.

He heaved out a sigh and put down the card, reaching for the canvas he'd ruined, running his fingers over the tear. He was overthinking again, and pissing himself off. Time to change tack. He had another problem to agonize over, one he hadn't let himself acknowledge yet: Vik might let Red have dinner with old ladies, but he would *not* approve of Red fingering a tenant in the street. Or anywhere, really. A bed wouldn't have made it more professional. He should be at Vik's right now, confessing all and tendering his resignation.

For some reason, the thought didn't disturb him as much as it should.

Red paused for a moment, staring blankly at the canvas in his hand. He thought again, deliberately, about quitting. About leaving the safe little hiding place Vik had given him. No clanging, panicked alarm sounded in his head.

All right. That was interesting. That was good. He worked at the discovery like a loose tooth.

This job was supposed to be temporary, but the two-year mark crept closer, and he knew Vik was worried. So was Mum. Maybe when that milestone finally hit, instead of feeling guilty and pressured and trapped by his own insecurities, Red could be leaving. Suddenly, it didn't feel impossible. He was more confident now, ready to display his work, and he'd been researching sales tactics, marketing, and whatever. He should try. He'd get a part-time job, too, if he couldn't make enough money. Whatever it took, he'd claw his way back to his dreams. The only question was whether his new stuff was good enough to sell—but he'd find out soon enough, when Chloe finished his website.

And here he was, back at Chloe again—thinking, without a moment's hesitation, that she'd hold up her end of the deal. He sat with that for a second. It wasn't the kind of assumption he'd have made about Pippa; no, if this were Pippa, she'd take away what he wanted most, to punish him for being angry, or to manipulate him into forgiving her. But Chloe wasn't going to do that. Of course she wasn't. She never would.

He put down the canvas and picked up the card. Took out his phone. Dialed the number. After three long rings and three thousand rapid heartbeats, a cool voice said in his ear, "Dr. Maddox's office, this is Jonathon speaking. Can I help?"

"Yeah," Red said, then cleared his rough throat awkwardly. "Hi. Uh . . . I think I'd like to make an appointment?"

For her own peace of mind, Chloe had decided to stop thinking about Redford Morgan. Which was, admittedly, difficult, since her sisters were devoting their every waking moment to bothering her about Redford Morgan.

He was definitely avoiding her. She'd never gone more than a day without glimpsing him around the courtyard or the corridors before, and their email thread was conspicuously silent. He'd answered her apology text two days ago, but only to say, It's fine. It clearly wasn't fine. She didn't know how to reply. He knew that she was sorry, so she should give him space, as much as he needed, even if what he needed was space that lasted forever. Even if the thought made her stomach twist.

She was a mess, and her family's meddling wasn't helping the situation.

True to form, Aunt Mary had informed her twin that Chloe had been *seen* with a *man*. Mum had, of course, told Dad, and Dad had grumbled at Gigi, who had promptly called to recommend La Perla lingerie because "I know you like to budget, darling." She'd also passed on the gossip to Dani and Eve, both of whom had proceeded to blow up the sisterly group chat with encouraging, if inappropriate, GIFs and profoundly annoying questions. It hadn't taken them long to realize that Chloe's *"mysterious gentleman, rather large, gorgeous hair"* was Red.

Chloe had muted her chat app after two days of nonsense. Her sisters had begun sending emails. She didn't open them, of course, but the subject lines were depressing enough. Dani's latest had been entitled LOVE POTION RECIPE: REQUIRES ONE (1) LOCK OF GINGER HAIR.

But, today, annoying sisters were the least of Chloe's worries. Because today was the day she was to give Smudge back.

She stood in front of the apartment building, pet carrier in hand, knowing Red would be here for moral support if she hadn't horribly insulted him. Not that she was self-flagellating. She'd received communication from the footloose, fancy-free, and clearly irresponsible *Annie* yesterday, and now the woman wanted "her" cat back. Hah. Hers indeed. Just because she'd purchased him, raised him, and fed him for quite some time, didn't necessarily make Smudge Annie's. Chloe had snuggled with him for many hours and also rescued him from a tree. Hers was definitely the greater claim.

And yet . . . she couldn't steal, especially not a pet, so she found herself standing by the building's front doors, waiting for Annie to arrive. Chloe had suggested this location because her flat might be difficult to find, and also because she didn't want to have to invite this woman in and engage in pleasant chitchat. It was difficult enough standing here, ignoring Smudge's questioning miaows. She knew exactly what he was asking, of course: *Why on earth have you put me in a box, you baffling woman?*

She couldn't bring herself to reply.

The woman was three minutes late, which only reinforced Chloe's poor opinion of her. But then, at 11:04, she heard the slap of flat shoes against pavement and the jingle of what sounded like a large bunch of keys. A moment later, a tall, slim woman with honey-colored curls came into view, covered neck to shin by an oversized camo coat. Despite the odd outfit, she was pretty, with soft features, skin a few shades deeper than her hair, and eyes so bright, Chloe could see them from meters away.

"Hi," the woman said, hurrying over. "Chloe, right? Nightmare parking around here. Annie, by the way, I'm Annie. Oh, is that Perdy? Yeah, that's Perdy. Hey, Perdy! Hi! Hi, baby!" She bent to poke a finger into the cat carrier, then straightened. "You are Chloe, right? I'm not getting your name wrong, am I? I forget names. I like your glasses."

Chloe intended to say, *Yes, that's me, hello, and thank you.* What came out of her mouth, in clearly scornful tones, was "Perdy?"

"Short for Perdita," Annie said fondly. "You know, from *101 Dalmatians.*"

"But he's not a dalmatian."

"She," Annie said, and reached for the cat carrier. For one tense moment, Chloe worried her fingers wouldn't release the plastic handle. But her subconscious behaved itself—for once—and she didn't start a fight over a cat in the middle of the street.

Of course, if she had, it wouldn't be the most scandalous thing she'd done in the street recently.

"He's not even spotty," Chloe insisted, ignoring the wild and unfounded claim that Smudge was, of all things, a girl.

Annie gave her a strange look and said, "You're funny. Want to go for a coffee?"

"I . . . er . . . sorry?"

"You're funny. Bit strange. Want to go for a coffee? You are Chloe, aren't you? Thanks for finding Perdy. My great-aunt Amy was supposed to be watching the girls while I was in Malmö— I've been in Malmö by the way, fabulous place, have you been?— but she got confused—my great-aunt—because I have quite a few cats and I suppose she is quite old. Also, there's that one fox. Yes, in hindsight, it is quite confusing."

Somehow, through a haze of bafflement so thick it might as well have been a brick wall, Chloe managed to croak, "Pardon?"

Annie gave her an indulgent smile, as if she was being an absolute ninny, and shoved a hand into a cavernous coat pocket. "Hmm, now, where is my . . . oh." She produced a handful of debris. There was an empty Lindor wrapper, an enormous set of keys, what looked like a few foreign coins, a faded receipt, and . . . "Take my card. There. See it?"

It really couldn't be missed. It was hot pink and glittery. Chloe took it gingerly by the corner.

"Give me a ring and we'll go for a coffee. My treat! Because you found Perdy."

"I don't drink coffee," Chloe murmured, honestly enough, as she studied the card. It read: ANNIE AMANDE, KNICKER WHISPERER.

What in the bloody hell?

"Tea, then," Annie said brightly. "Got to dash. I'm late. Come on, Perdy, let's be having you, you great big wandering nitwit. Off we go, off we go, off we go." She turned and hurried up the street again.

Chloe stared after her, feeling slightly dazed. When Annie's tall figure disappeared around a corner, Chloe looked at the card in her hand again: KNICKER WHISPERER? What could that possibly mean? There was a website, along with several social media links that would probably reveal all, but she didn't want to go searching. Didn't want to spend any more time dwelling on that odd woman and her strange invitation, because it would only remind her of one fact: Smudge was gone.

She shoved the card into her pocket and strode back into the building, driven by an urgent need to get home. It took her a moment to realize that the odd wetness sliding down her cheek was a tear. Oh, how mortifying. She was crying over a cat she'd had for only a couple of weeks, and in public, too. Worse than that, she actually felt . . . sad. More than sad. Devastated. As if someone had ripped a hole in her chest.

The only thing that could possibly make this situation worse would be bumping into Red. She would hate that. It would be awful, horrible, the end of the world, so she was glad when she made it to her flat without seeing him.

Very glad indeed.

When someone knocked on Chloe's door the next day, it never occurred to her that it might be Red. She had gotten used to the weight of his absence. She'd closed her curtains because she refused to accidentally spy on him. She was giving him space, damn it.

But there he was, on her doorstep, only four days after she'd ruined everything.

"Hey," he said.

She swallowed, which hurt. Right now, everything hurt. He couldn't have shown up at a worse time if he'd tried. She felt like bird poop and she looked *under the weather,* which was a phrase her cognitive therapist had told her to use instead of calling herself hideous. But really, sometimes, human beings just looked hideous. There was no shame in it. Or at least there wouldn't be if Red weren't standing there on her doorstep looking delicious.

She opened her mouth to croak a startled *hello,* but he held up a hand to cut her off. He was unusually smile free, severe and serious in a way that made her nervous—not because he was upset with her, but because he was upset at all.

Redford Morgan should always be smiling.

He raked a hand through his hair and said, "I just want to make it clear that I'm incredibly pissed at you. But . . ." He cleared his throat, looking slightly unsure. "But I don't think you meant to—to say what you said. I'm still pissed, though. And I'll be pissed until I'm ready to stop."

She nodded slowly, not entirely sure why he was explaining the mechanics of human anger, but quite certain that it was important to him. "Okay."

For a moment, he seemed almost painfully relieved. Then his eyes narrowed at her faint, raspy voice, and he said accusingly, "You're sick."

She supposed she should be flattered he couldn't tell by sight alone. But something about that speech he'd just made, and the look on his face, was nagging at her brain. "It's nothing. You know you're allowed to be angry, don't you? In general, I mean. And at me. You are allowed to be angry at me."

He faltered for a moment. "Of course I know. I just said all that, didn't I?"

Suddenly, she realized what was bothering her. He *had* just said as much—but he'd spoken as if he was trying something new and he wasn't entirely sure that it would work.

"You need to lie down," he said, interrupting her thoughts.

"Don't be silly. This happens all the time." Although, she *would* love to lie back down. In fact, she might just . . . sit. Red wouldn't make her feel like some kind of freak because her body was giving out on her and spoons were a distant memory. She leaned against the wall, then started to slide down it, just a little.

He frowned. "Are you passing out right now?"

"That's usually much more sudden," she said absently. "I'm just going to sit right here . . ."

"Or we could do this." He stepped into the flat and picked her up.

"Oh. Um. What are you doing?"

"Carrying you. Work with me, here." Presumably, he meant that she should stop kicking her legs around awkwardly. Since she was very, very tired, and since walking felt like being stabbed in the lower back, she did. He nudged the door shut and said, "Where d'you wanna go?"

"I've been in the living room. Red, I'm really, really, super, eternally sorry about—"

"You should stop talking. You got tonsillitis or something?"

"Or something. But it'll pass soon. This is just what happens when I get too tired or I don't eat right—"

"Or you step on the cracks in the pavement." He put her down gently in the little nest she'd made on the sofa, then knelt on the floor beside her. "You know, for such a funny-sounding word, fibromyalgia is—"

"A motherfucker."

"*Chloe!* Did you just swear? You never swear." He paused. "That was fun. Do it again."

"No," she said primly.

He chuckled, shook his head, and she'd missed him so much her heart cracked open like an egg. Sticky emotion spilled out. The remnants of her protective shell were scattered around in tiny shards.

"I'm sorry," she whispered. An explanation, a real one, was necessary, but she couldn't bear to look at him as she did it. If she focused on her knees, Chloe decided sensibly, Red wouldn't be able to see the truth of her feelings in her eyes. "That night," she sighed. "I know you said it wasn't complicated, but it complicated things for me. I suppose that's just how I am. As soon as you stopped touching me, reality kicked in, and I started panicking about what it meant and what you wanted, or didn't want, and—well. In short, I overthought everything and made several colossal mistakes, and I'm sorry."

"Chloe. Look at me."

Her first instinct was to refuse, like a toddler rejecting vegetables. But that wouldn't be very mature, and immaturity had gotten her into a mess just last weekend, so she made herself face him.

He was running his knuckles over his lips thoughtfully, studying her with those three little lines between his eyebrows. Like he didn't know what to make of her. Finally, he said, "So it complicated things, huh?"

She swallowed hard, his pale gaze freezing her in place. He was endlessly hypnotic. Her voice a thready whisper, she confirmed, "Yes."

Quietly, he said, "Complicated things for me, too. It's funny— you're so smart. And I feel so fucking obvious. But you don't seem to know what I want from you."

She shook her head. "No. I don't." *Or maybe I do and I'm too afraid to face it.*

As if he'd heard the echo of her thoughts, he leaned closer, raising a hand to her cheek. "I should show you." His fingertips traced the curves of her face, her jaw, her throat, his eyes following the movement as if he were mapping her out. His focus was so formidable, it stilled the earth and stopped time. It made her feel . . .

But that was it. That was all. Red's focus simply made her *feel.*

She released a shuddering breath. Her heart thudded a bruising rhythm against her chest. She supposed he'd kiss her now, and she'd succumb to his sexual onslaught, or something along those lines—only, she realized with a wince, she didn't quite feel up to it. Sitting this close to him made her skin feel like shivering silk, but arousal was a whimper beneath the scream of her body's aches, pains, and sheer exhaustion. Abruptly, she remembered nights with Henry, nights when he'd turned away from her with disgusted mutters after failed seductions that only embarrassed them both. *If you didn't want to, you should've just said.*

She *had* said. She'd said, *Henry, I'm sick,* and he'd thought the power of his bloody penis would make it all better.

Well, she wasn't about to go through that again—not even

with Red, no matter how much she liked him. Chloe stiffened under his featherlight touch, and he faltered, concern softening his gaze. Not anger. Just worry. Good. Perhaps he wouldn't react badly at all. Her breaths came a little bit easier.

Firmly, she told him, "You should know that I want you, but tonight I don't feel particularly—"

"Chloe," he interrupted softly, his frown back in place. "Sweetheart. You really *don't* know what I want, do you?" He caught her hand, pressing his lips to the slice of her palm framed by her wrist support's Velcro straps. After a moment, he said carefully, "I'd like to stick around tonight. Just to hang out. That okay?"

She felt dizzy with relief. He wouldn't make things difficult and he wouldn't make her push him away. Thank goodness, because, for once, Chloe really didn't feel like pushing anyone away. "Oh. Right. Yes. That's fine." Apparently, she'd lost the ability to form complex sentences.

His eyes crinkled at the corners as he smiled. "Nice to know you want me, though."

"Oh, God." Heat flooded her cheeks even as a rueful smile curved her own lips. "Don't be awful."

"Can't help it. And, just so you know, it's mutual." His gaze darkened. "But we'll talk about that another time."

For a second, the promise of that other time—of that conversation and all it might mean—hung hot and heavy between them. Rather how she imagined his body might feel covering hers.

But then she remembered why a conversation like that could be difficult—because if Red wanted more than just touches in the dark, if he wanted what she wanted . . . Chloe might be too afraid to reach out and take it. The promise of more with him glittered like broken glass, beautiful but potentially deadly. Good things usually hurt in the end.

But she was being maudlin and getting ahead of herself and overthinking—which hadn't served her well the last time. Brushing the ghost of her mistakes aside, Chloe sat up straighter—ignoring the stabs of pain sliding between her vertebrae—and asked, "You do forgive me, don't you?"

"I do." He reached for her again, and her heart practically stopped beating. She remembered the warmth of his touch and the cold of those silver rings with hazy desperation, as if the last time had been a fever dream. But all he did was tap one of the buttons on the front of her pajamas and say, "You do know how to apologize, Button. I forgive you just fine."

Well, that was a relief, at least.

CHAPTER SIXTEEN

Chloe wanted him. That's what she'd said, loud and clear, in a way he'd never expected to hear—at least, not outside the bedroom. She struck Red as the sort of woman who'd only share her desires when she was already halfway to orgasm. Who'd whisper hot commands and sweet confessions in the dark. But she wanted him, and she'd said it out loud.

She also didn't know what he wanted—which, he supposed, was understandable. Because it was only here and now that his purest want—his *need*—had become fully clear to him. When it came to Chloe, it turned out Red's ultimate goal was to make her happy. That was it. That was all. The realization jolted him like a thousand volts to the heart. He felt . . .

He felt something she might not want him to feel. Something she seemed almost afraid of. Her gaze flickered away whenever his words were too intense or his voice too tender—he knew that. He'd noticed that. So he shoved the soft warmth in his chest aside; he'd examine it later.

Chloe's eyes fluttered shut for a moment, and he drank in

the sight of her. She was wearing pink, pinstriped pajamas with buttons down the front, the kind grumpy old men wore. She had a lot in common with grumpy old men, actually, except for the part where he was desperate to kiss her.

Instead of her hair's usual neat, shiny bun, it looked like she'd grabbed the dark waves with a fist, shoved a hair tie over them, and hoped for the best. It was what Red did with his own hair when he was working out. Judging by her small mountain of blankets and the mess strewn across her coffee table, it was what *she* did when she felt like shit. He was probably the worst kind of monster because Chloe was sick, but he still thought she was unbelievably sexy. Then he remembered that she was always sick, so maybe poor health wasn't something that should de-sex a person.

Definitely couldn't de-sex Chloe.

He cleared his throat and stood, looking around the room. The empty water bottles and cardboard boxes she left by her front door had reproduced like bunnies, creeping down the hall until they were visible from here. "You should call me when you need things recycled."

"Maybe," she mumbled, snuggling deeper into her blankets.

"Definitely. It's my job." Although a cautiously excited voice in his head whispered, *Not for long.* This idea he'd had about finding his own place, about trying again with his art . . . it wouldn't let go. He rolled it around his mind like whiskey in his mouth while he gathered Chloe's empty teacups and glasses of juice.

"Don't clean up," she told him. "I can cope, you know."

"And I could cope without electricity, but why the fuck should I?"

She tutted. "Surely you have better things to do with your evening."

Nothing I'd enjoy more than being here with you. The words flashed up in his mind without permission, but thankfully he controlled his mouth more easily than his thoughts. "You can't get rid of me, Button. You're mine tonight. I booked you."

"You booked . . . ?" Her eyes flew open. "Oh, my goodness. I completely forgot. Your website."

His lips quirked. "You forgot? You mean your brain is actually a squidgy gray thing and not a computer? I've been wondering."

She didn't smile back. "I have done something, you know. I have the home-page design to show you, and I wanted to go through the shop's functionalities, but we'll have to move to my desk—" She sat up and winced. Just a tiny tightening of her features, but he felt like someone had ripped out his heart.

"Sit your arse down. Relax. It's not a big deal."

"Don't you want—"

"No," he said firmly. Then, when she looked genuinely disappointed, he added, "Send me a link tomorrow. I'm—"

She leapt on his hesitation, her eyebrows raised. "You're . . . ?"

Eager. "I'm starting to get excited about work again. That's all." He shrugged, as if it didn't make him feel electrified. "So I'll look tomorrow. If you're feeling better."

She gave him a delighted, if faintly exhausted, smile. "That's wonderful. That's fantastic."

"Uh, thanks. So, do you want more juice, or not?"

The smile became a narrow glare. "I can get my own juice."

"But why would you do that when you have a willing servant?"

She rolled her eyes. He knew why she hesitated. Considering the way her so-called friends and fiancé had dropped her, she was sensitive about letting people get close. When she finally closed her eyes and said, "Continue, if you must," he felt like he'd climbed a fucking mountain.

When he returned to the living room, she sat up for the juice without wincing and he said, "Is it me, or do you seem better than you were ten minutes ago?"

"You're right." She took a sip. "The power of your company has cured me. The doctors were right about natural endorphins all along."

"Uh . . ."

"It's because the buprenorphine patch I put on finally started pulling its weight. I am drugged to high heaven. It's delightful."

"Oh. Good."

"I should have powered through," she told him, "since it's my strongest painkiller and I'm not supposed to build up an immunity to opiates in my thirties, but I was fed up with feeling my joints scrape together inside me like knives, so I have no regrets."

He stared. "You really are a badass."

She waggled her bunny slippers. "Yes."

"Have you eaten?"

She shrugged, sipped her juice some more, and said in a suspiciously casual tone, "Not yet."

Ah. She was one of those. He should've known. "I'll put that another way: When did you last eat?"

Chloe's face took on the shiftiest expression ever made by a human being in the history of the world. She hid guilt about as well as the average family dog. "I'm not sure." As if on cue, her stomach rumbled. She looked down irritably and muttered, "*Et tu?*"

"Today?" he nudged.

She shrugged.

Oh, for God's sake. "You haven't eaten today? Are you serious?"

"I couldn't be *bothered*," she snapped.

"Right, sure. You're too lazy to feed yourself. It's not because you feel like shit or anything."

"Oh, be quiet."

He stood, and she looked up at him, something bleak and resigned in her gaze. In the second before she schooled her expression, he realized that she thought he was leaving. His heart constricted. He wanted to find every friend who'd ever ditched her, and especially her fucking fiancé, and force them all to walk barefoot across a room full of Legos for the rest of their lives. Not that he'd been thinking much about punishments.

"What do you want to eat?" he asked briskly, hoping she wouldn't hear the emotion rumbling beneath his voice.

Her mouth opened, closed, opened again. "You—I don't—"

"You like stir-fry?"

She shot him a mutinous glare, like he'd offered to piss on her PlayStation or something. "Red—"

"I mean, who doesn't like stir-fry? Weirdos, that's who." He headed for the kitchen.

It took a second or two, but she stumbled after him, her blanket wrapped around her like a cape. Cutest, prissiest Batman he'd ever seen. When she said, "Red, you're *not* cooking for me," he smiled to himself, just a bit.

The flat's little kitchen, all tiles and steel, always seemed cold to Chloe—but today, the air vibrated with sultry heat even before the stove was turned on. That was Red's fault. He stood in front of the fridge looking horribly sexy in his usual T-shirt and jeans, bending over at an angle that should be illegal for men who had backsides like his. She sat in her comfortable little kitchen chair and fiddled with the neckline of her pajamas. Maybe her current haze, partly feverish fatigue and partly the patch on her back pumping drugs through her skin, was a blessing in disguise. If she weren't feeling so rubbish it would be much, much harder to ignore how pretty he was.

"Who does all this food prep?" he asked, popping up from the fridge door with far too many boxes balanced in his arms. What was he making, gourmet chow mein?

"Eve."

"The rainbow girl? Really? She's . . ." He put the boxes down and waved his hand in a way that conveyed Eve's chaotic vibe perfectly. "If I'd had to guess one of your sisters, I would've said—what's her name, Danielle?"

"Danika," she corrected automatically. Being around him was so incredibly easy, she forgot how strange their relationship was sometimes. How he didn't know basic things about her, like her sister's full name, but he knew she loved Smudge and didn't trust and wanted to be brave.

She wished he knew more. Wished he knew everything. Wished she could share it all with him. That wasn't a desire Chloe felt often, or at all, but he made everything . . .

Safe.

"Christ, woman," he spluttered, interrupting her thoughts and bringing a smile to her lips. "Why do you have a kitchen drawer full of fancy pens?" He shut the offending drawer in disgust and turned toward another. "Where are your spoons?"

"Red. Don't. I don't want you to cook for me. And that's not—"

Too late. He'd opened the next drawer, which was full of her spare medication. But he didn't gawk at the countless colorful boxes, old painkillers she'd abandoned because they made her mouth too dry to talk, or because she'd gotten used to them and upgraded like an addict grown accustomed to the hit. He didn't ask about them, either, or slam the drawer shut and give her a part-pitying, part-worried look like her mother would. Instead he shook his head and said, "You got everything in this kitchen but cutlery, Chlo." Then he turned to the next drawer, discovered the spoons, and carried on as if nothing had happened.

Funny. Chloe was used to seeing her life and her illness as normal, but she wasn't used to other people acting the same way.

"Now," he said, popping the lid off one of the boxes and grabbing pre-sliced peppers. "If you really don't want stir-fry—

because, let's face it, you are a weirdo—this is your last chance to tell me."

"You are not cooking for me." There; that sounded firm, reasonable, and mature. Kind of.

"Why not?" he asked just as reasonably while he rifled through her cupboards.

"Because you're not a bloody home helper!"

He turned to look at her. "Chloe. *Language.*"

"Oh, for—"

He interrupted, his tone serious, his words quiet. "Stop worrying, okay?" His search of the cupboards abandoned, he crossed his arms over his broad chest. Her gaze absolutely did not catch on the shift of his biceps or the raised veins on his strong forearms. Well, it did, but only for a second. "You think this is a big deal because, no offense, you've had a lot of people in your life who claimed to care about you but didn't act like it. That's not me. I can cook, and right now, you can't. So I'm doing it for you because that's how people should behave; they should fill in each other's gaps. Don't think about it too hard."

She nodded slowly, staring at her clasped hands for a minute as inconvenient, mushy emotions flooded her. Then she released a slow, shaky breath and finally said what she'd wanted to say for a while, but hadn't been able to force past her clenched teeth. "Thank you."

"No worries," he said easily. And she didn't even wonder if he meant it. There was no doubt in her mind that he did.

Red found a wok and opened more boxes; poured oil into

the pan and yanked out what seemed to be every seasoning she owned. Then he ran a hand through his hair, rolled his eyes as if at himself, and said, "You got a hair tie?"

"I never know where they are," she admitted. Except for the one currently in her hair, which she tugged free and handed to him.

"Thanks." Bright blue paint stained some of his nails. His fingertips grazed hers. Her body lit up inside, reacting as if he'd offered to rip off her clothes and do her on the counter—not that she wanted him to, because she really wasn't feeling very well, and it would be murder on her lower back. She sternly informed her nipples of these pertinent facts, but they gestured rudely at her and continued to tingle like a pair of slutty batteries.

Meanwhile, Red somehow managed to remain gorgeous while wearing a man bun.

When the kitchen filled with the sharp sizzle of cooking food, she spoke again. "So, you like to cook?"

"I like to cook for other people," he said. "Cooking for myself is okay, but it's not exactly the same."

Something about that revelation filled her with equal parts relief and disappointment. "I see."

Though his focus was on the food, he arched an eyebrow, amusement dancing over his expression. "What do you see, Button?"

"You run around making dinner for everyone." She'd meant that to sound teasing, but it came out a little bit . . . not.

His smile widened as he shot her a look. "Jealous?"

She snorted. "Pardon me? Of course I'm not jealous." When had she become such a shameless liar? Her dad would be so disappointed in her new habit of casual deceit.

"That's good. Be weird if you were jealous of my mother."

And now she was mortified. She wrapped her blanket tighter around herself, as if she could disappear inside it. This was what came of *liking* men: rampant idiocy. She opened her mouth and searched for a way to dig herself out of that particular hole.

But Red didn't seem to think it was necessary. When he looked at her again, his obvious amusement was replaced by curiosity. "Hey," he asked, as though it had just occurred to him. "Where's Smudge?"

Her heart lurched. She'd been hoping he wouldn't notice. "Gone."

Red stilled. "Gone?"

"Annie came back a few days ago. She was in Malmö." Chloe narrowed her eyes. "She calls Smudge *Perdita,* which would be an excellent name—I love *101 Dalmatians*—except that Smudge isn't a dalmatian, so it's ludicrous."

For some reason, Red didn't agree with her on the name. He didn't comment on the name at all. He abandoned his post at the stove and before she knew it, he was standing in front of her. He sank his hands into the tangled mess of her hair. He kissed her head and she almost fainted dead away. He said gravely, "I'm sorry, Button."

"I don't care," she mumbled, breathing deep. Not because he smelled like fresh sheets and warmth and blueberry shampoo; she was just breathing. "Smudge wasn't even my cat."

"I'd get you a new one, but you know the rules."

"I don't *want* a new one."

He smiled down at her. "Did you cry?"

"I . . ." *Say no. Say no. Say no.* "Only a little bit."

Red seemed satisfied. "As long as you cried, you'll be okay. That's what my mum always says." He went back to the wok and her head felt cold without his hands cradling it.

Since she was saying things she shouldn't tonight, she murmured, "I'd quite like to meet your mother. I mean," she added quickly, "I'd be interested to see what she's like, because you're so . . ."

He arched an eyebrow. "I'm so?"

"Infuriating."

"Right. Don't know how you put up with me." He chuckled. Shot her a knowing look that made her cheeks burn hotter than the sun.

"She gave me her card," Chloe blurted. "Annie, I mean. And do you know what it says?"

"Something shit," he guessed, "because we hate her."

"It says 'Knicker Whisperer.'"

Red's lips twitched. "That's . . . interesting. I mean—weird. Very weird."

"I know it's funny," Chloe sighed. "It's brilliant. Unique and intriguing and catchy, and the card is beautifully designed, and I bet if I go to her mysterious knicker-whispering website, that'll be great too." She huffed and glared at nothing in particular. "What is that woman's *game*? What is her *angle*?"

"Why'd she give you the card?"

"She says we should have coffee. I don't believe it. I'll turn up and she'll text and say, so sorry, she's in Venice."

Red ignored almost everything she'd said, which was both irritating and hilarious. "So she wants to be friends?"

Chloe stared at him. "I don't see why she would. We spoke for all of five minutes."

"But she made a big impression."

"She *took* my *cat*." The man had lost his marbles, clearly.

He went on as if she hadn't spoken. "Maybe you made an impression on her, too."

"What about me could possibly make an impression?" Chloe demanded.

Red stared at her for a little too long. She bit her lip. He smiled. "Look, all I'm saying is, Annie might like you. And you might like her, if you gave it a chance. You have similar taste in cats."

"You are not funny."

"I want you to make a friend."

"You're my friend," she snapped. "New topic. When are you setting up that Instagram account?"

"I don't know." He tried to run a hand through his hair, failed because it was tied up, and tutted.

Now a slow smile curved *her* lips. "I can do it for you, if you're busy." In all fairness, he *was* often busy, tending to old ladies and feeding street urchins and painting magical masterpieces like a patron saint of goodness and art. But she didn't think that was the problem.

"You don't need to do that," he said. "I'll . . ." She'd bet money that he was trying to say, *I'll do it*, but couldn't quite make himself.

"Funny," she murmured. "I didn't notice before."

He gave her a suspicious look. "Notice what?"

"That you're scared of social media."

"*Scared?*" He scowled, turning to face her. "Chloe. I'm not—it's—you're winding me up again, aren't you?"

"I'm simply acknowledging your obvious aversion to—"

He pointed a stern finger at her. "Stop trying to confuse me. I'm not saying shit." He was blushing, slashes of pink high on his cheekbones. His ears, too, which she'd never seen before, since his hair was usually down.

Something in her chest softened like a marshmallow, which couldn't be healthy. "I'm serious," she said. "I'll do it for you. I'll manage it for you. You wouldn't even have to look at it unless you wanted to." She didn't know why he felt this way, when once upon a time his work had been everywhere. But she didn't need to know. She'd take care of this, to give him space to take care of himself.

He looked at her for a long moment before taking his phone out of his pocket. She watched with a frown as he tapped at the screen, his embarrassed flush barely fading, his lower lip caught between his teeth. Then, just as her understanding dawned, he came over and held out the phone.

"There," he said, showing her the log-in screen. "I downloaded Instagram."

She stared. "I—Red—I didn't mean to pressure you."

"You didn't. I said I was going to do it, and I meant it. I'm serious about this. So, if your professional opinion is that I need one . . ."

"I'm not an expert," she said quickly, suddenly self-conscious.

His gaze snared hers, so simply trusting, it burned all her hesitation away. "You're a successful small business owner," he said, "and you know computer shit."

She snorted. "'Computer shit'?"

"Be quiet. I'm concentrating." He tapped some more, and before she knew it, he was showing her yet another screen—a blank account with his name on it. "That's that," he said, looking slightly surprised by himself. Then he blinked, cleared his throat, and his blush deepened. "Thing is, I really don't know much about this stuff. So maybe, you could, uh . . . maybe you could help me?"

He was so sweet, she was in danger of losing a tooth. Soft warmth flooded her at the sight of this huge man with his pink cheeks and hard jaw. Then came admiration, because he'd smashed through the brick wall of self-doubt like it was nothing. The same wall she often struggled to even approach.

"Whatever you want," she told him, and she'd never meant anything more.

"Thanks," he said gruffly. He caught her hand for one heart-stopping moment, and squeezed. Then he turned away, back to the wok. "Let's get some food in you."

Apparently, feeding Chloe made her sleepy. Very, very sleepy. Red washed up while she dozed on the sofa, then checked her biscuit tin for more of those homemade gingersnaps. He scored big time and munched on them while he made tea. Did Eve bake these as well as prepping all the food? Because if so, next time she flirted with him, maybe he should flirt back. It would be an amazing plan if he wasn't completely hooked on her sister.

But he was.

He returned to the living room and sat beside Chloe as gently as he could. Since he was overgrown, his weight shifted the cushions a little too much, and she stirred.

Her lashes fluttered. Eyes opened. She'd taken off her glasses, so she looked at him without focusing and gave him a soft little smile. Maybe every single atom in his body imploded, re-formed, and *ex*ploded at the sight of that smile. Maybe. But he tried to keep that to himself.

"You should go to bed," he told her.

"I won't sleep. I can already tell."

"Weren't you just sleeping?"

"Nothing so satisfying as that, I assure you," she muttered, and cradled the tea in both hands. "I don't suppose you'd like to watch something over-the-top and faintly ridiculous. I feel like cowboys. Oh—space cowboys. Do you like space cowboys? You probably don't." The tangled waves of her hair were a dark cloud around her face. She gave him a sideways look through the wild chestnut strands, eyebrows raised, lips pursed at the edge of the mug.

He told her truthfully, "I love space cowboys."

But they only got twenty minutes through an episode of *Killjoys* before Chloe's eyelids drooped. Red turned off the TV, put her glasses safely on his head, and scooped her up in his arms.

His heart beat brighter than it had before. She turned everything pink—pink like poofy skirts and pinstriped pajamas and the tip of her tongue when she tapped it against her teeth. Pink like he was fucking gone for her. Pink like the little decorative pillows on her bed. He nudged them off and laid her down, and she mumbled, "Red?"

"Yeah, Button?"

"C'mere. You smell like sleep."

He didn't know what that meant, but he decided it was a good thing. After a moment's hesitation, he tucked the covers over her, then crossed to the other side of the bed and lay on top of them.

He'd just stay here for a while until she fell asleep again. He'd practice some of the techniques Dr. Maddox had mentioned at their first appointment today—taking the time to arrange his thoughts and feelings, sinking into positive moments. He was supposed to write shit down, but he preferred to visualize, and the doc had said that was okay, too.

So Red lay back, closed his eyes, and thought about Chloe's smile. About stir-fry and space cowboys. About feeling like himself. He counted the moments of clarity he'd teased from his messy mind today, and he was proud. He let himself feel good, good, good.

It was surprisingly easy.

CHAPTER SEVENTEEN

When he woke, the bedroom was bright. Birdsong and cold air floated through the open window, and Chloe was standing by her dresser in a towel.

This was an excellent way to wake up. "Hey, Chlo."

She screeched, then clapped a hand over her mouth. "You're awake!"

Her hair was dripping wet, her skin glistened with little water droplets, and the towel wrapped around her only hit midthigh. "Yeah," he said roughly. "I'm awake."

She made a strangled sort of noise and grabbed some stuff from the dresser. He looked away from her thighs long enough to notice she was holding a pile of clothes. Then he looked back at her thighs.

"Be a gentleman and close your eyes," she sniffed.

"Do I have to?"

"Not anymore, because I am leaving." She clutched her clothes to her towel-clad chest and rushed off toward the bathroom. Under the slick strands of her hair, he caught sight of something on her upper back, a pale rectangle that looked kind of like a bandage. No, he realized, it was like a giant nicotine patch. Maybe some kind of medication. Then she slammed the door shut.

He stood, ran a hand through his hair, and wondered how the hell he'd managed to fall asleep.

Abruptly, the bathroom door opened again, just a crack. Chloe called, "Do you still have my hair tie? I can't find any of the others."

He tugged it off his wrist and handed it through the slight gap in the door. "You feeling better?"

"Quite."

"Details," he ordered, though he expected she'd tell him to piss off.

Instead, after a pause, she said, "I'm still exhausted. But I'm not *tired*. That helps." She shut the door. Her next words were muffled through the wood. "Thank you."

You smell like sleep. "Anytime."

When she came out again, he was sitting on the bed, trying not to look like a man who'd barely resisted the urge to snoop through everything she owned. It had been hard because this room was so Chloe, from the sci-fi-looking computer with two screens on her desk, to the pretty row of shoes tucked just under her bed. There was stuff everywhere: candles she'd never lit, fancy bottles of perfume she'd clearly never used, notebooks stacked in piles so high she'd surely never use those, either, and a thousand pictures of her family. It was adorable.

"Sorry about that," she said, smoothing her hands over her

skirt. It was sunshine yellow, with a thick white stripe at the bottom. Made her skin glow. Made him want to go over there on his knees. Her hair was up and sleek as glass, her glasses perfectly polished. "I meant to take my clothes into the bathroom with me, but I forgot."

"I didn't mind." Understatement of the year.

She gave him a look. "I have a spare toothbrush, if you want it. You could also just go home. However, I thought I might make you breakfast, to say thank you for dinner."

That took his attention away from her legs, which was no mean feat. "You want to make me breakfast?"

"Don't sound so surprised. If you like eggs and toast, I am more than capable."

"No, I just—" He just wasn't used to women doing things for him. He did things for them, and that was it. That was how it worked. He ran a hand through his hair and realized that, apparently, that wasn't how it worked anymore. "All right. I like eggs. Thanks."

He found the spare toothbrush. Her bathroom shelf was full of products that matched: she bought the same brand and scent of shampoo and conditioner, body wash and moisturizer, because of course she did. She liked flowers, and strawberries. He added that carefully to the list of things he knew about Chloe Brown, a list that was longer than he'd ever expected it to be, but still not long enough. Maybe it would never be long enough.

Still, it was satisfying, as the morning went on, to add to that list again and again. First, it was *Chloe makes great scrambled eggs.* Then it was *It feels good to wash dishes while Chloe dries.*

Finally he realized: *Starting my day with Chloe feels like starting my day in front of a canvas.*

When they finished washing up, Red had a smile on his face that he already knew would last until he went to bed that night. Then, all at once, he turned left, Chloe turned right, and they both moved at exactly the wrong time. Or maybe it was exactly the right time. It felt right, when she stumbled into him. It felt right, gripping her waist to steady her. It felt right, her hands pressing against his chest.

So right he didn't move away.

She must be able to feel his heart pounding. He was surprised it wasn't visible through his clothes. She tilted her head back to look at him, her lips parted. Was this how she'd look, just before he kissed her? He wanted to add that knowledge to the list.

She said, her voice still a little hoarse, "Sorry. Gosh, sorry. I wasn't looking where I was going." But she didn't move, either.

His hands tightened at her waist for a moment before he forced himself to relax. It was a long, slow process, loosening every tense muscle in his body, reminding the unthinking part of himself that he couldn't just put his mouth on hers. He meant to let go of her completely, meant to step back, meant to say something.

He only managed the last of those goals. And what he said wasn't exactly sensible. In fact, he didn't know how it sneaked past security to roll off his tongue. "Do you know what I want yet, Chlo?"

At his rough whisper, she froze. She hadn't exactly been moving before, but now everything about her was unnaturally still, as if she wasn't even breathing.

He closed his eyes and cursed himself. Too much. Too—

"Yes," she said softly. "I do. And I think I'm scared."

When he opened his eyes, she was dragging her teeth over her lower lip, her frown agonized. The expression on her face practically ripped his heart open. He swallowed. Kept pushing, because screw it. "Why? Do you think I'd hurt you?" He didn't add, *Like everyone else.*

She seemed to hear the words anyway. "Maybe." Her frown deepened and she shook her head irritably. Against his chest, her hands curled into fists, fingers tangling in his T-shirt. "No. Yes. I just—I'm always afraid that . . ." She looked up at him, realization dawning on her face. "Red. I think I'm being a coward."

"There's a big difference between being a coward and putting your emotional safety first," he said. He knew all about that.

Then again, so did she. She was nodding slowly, but her eyes narrowed behind her glasses. "There is a difference. I look out for my own safety all the time. Constantly. That's not what this is. The urge I have to avoid this," she murmured, almost to herself, "it's like . . . it's like going to bed at nine sharp every night. Like refusing to make plans, even with my sisters. Like staying inside for a year because I don't think I can handle catching a cold."

He blinked, distracted for a second. "You did that?"

Her smile was a quicksilver flash. "The first few years were not good, Red. I was not good. This list isn't the first challenge I've had to set myself." She wet her lips, her eyes drifting away from his face as she sank into her thoughts. "But I always succeed. One way or another. I always take the next step, no matter how long it takes."

"Of course you do," he whispered. "You're a tough mother-fucker, remember?"

She looked up at him again, her smile wider this time, more certain, like it was going nowhere. Her eyes glittered with something that made his heart feel light in his chest. "That's true. I am. And I want . . . you. All of you. I haven't done this sort of thing in a while, you know. But I'd like to try. Would you?" Her gaze, dark and serious, felt like a weight—the satisfying kind, the weight of expectation that meant someone might, almost, trust you not to fuck up. His whole body went rigid with anticipation, the kind of oh-shit giddy nervousness he usually felt before an exhibit.

"Yeah," he breathed. "Chloe. Yes."

She smiled. And then she kissed him.

It was the slightest brush of her lips over his, once, twice, three times. So soft, so gentle, his heart ached. He held his breath and closed his eyes and bent down for her, so she wouldn't hurt herself. His fingers sank into the lush curves of her hips for one desperate moment before he forced himself to relax, to not maul her like a caveman. At least, not until she asked him to.

Her fingers fluttered at his jaw, like she wanted to touch him but wasn't sure how to do it right. He wanted to tell her that any way she touched him would be right, but he'd rather step on a rusty fucking nail than break this barely-there kiss. Her lips brushed his again and the sensation seared through him like a shooting star, the kind that streaked the sky for long moments after it had passed. She tasted like minty toothpaste, sharp-tongued sarcasm, surprising hesitance. She was killing him. She was absolutely killing him.

Red slid a hand over her jaw and tipped her head back. She sighed as he slanted his mouth over hers and gave her the sweetest kiss he was capable of, because that's what she'd just given him. Slowly, carefully, he sank into the mouth he'd dreamed about. When he felt the edge of her glasses against his cheek, he pulled away to let her take them off—but she followed with a sound of protest. That indecisive hand of hers finally stopped hesitating; she threaded her fingers into his hair and tugged, pulling him closer, trapping him. Apparently, she didn't care about her glasses.

His hand slid down from her jaw to her throat, just because he wanted to feel more of her skin. She hummed low and pulled his hair again, setting off flashes of pleasure like camera pops behind his eyelids. Her tongue licked shyly at his and arousal shot up his spine, bright white and urgent scarlet. She pressed herself against him, full breasts and soft belly and breathless pants into his mouth. One of her hands tugged at his T-shirt before slipping beneath. The glide of her fingertips over his abdomen made him moan like she was sucking him off. *Touch me. Want me. Be mine.*

He liked to let her lead, but God, someday soon, he'd touch her, too. Anywhere. Everywhere. He wanted to feel her stomach tremble under his lips when she sucked in a breath, wanted to hear her beg for more as he palmed her tits, wanted to taste her hot pussy melting under his tongue. But he had no idea if she was there yet, and the last thing he wanted to do was lose it and rush her. She'd only just decided, officially, to do this at all.

He pulled back slightly, just enough to breathe, "Slow down, Chlo."

She stopped completely, let go, and stepped away, her gaze awkwardly avoiding his. In an instant, she was stiff and self-conscious. *Not* what he'd wanted. It was so not what he'd wanted that he had to resist the urge to whine like a dog. Instead, he caught her hand and dragged her back into his arms. "Don't do that," he said against her hair. "This is your spot now. Okay?"

Chloe hadn't known it was possible to go from mildly embarrassed to melting like goo, but apparently all it took was five short words. *This is your spot now.*

Her voice muffled, since she was currently plastered against Red's wonderful chest, she said simply, "Oh."

"And when I said *Slow down,* I meant, *Give me a second before I come.* Not *Go away.*"

"Oh." She looked up.

He straightened her glasses and tapped her on the nose. "Yeah. This is me checking in. I know you're still not feeling great."

She wasn't sure how he noticed things like that. She was up, she was dressed, she was medicated and smiling. He should've had no idea about her slight, lingering headache, or the thrum of pain that her patch couldn't quite touch, insistent enough that she was already frustrated.

She supposed whatever it was about him that made him notice might be the same thing that made her trust him.

"I don't feel that bad," she muttered, honestly enough. On her personal scale of one—*wonderful*—to ten—*excruciating*—this was a smooth six. Six was fine. One point above average. On the rare occasions she got down to a four, she often wondered how one found the universe's feet in order to kiss them.

Apparently, though, Red wasn't impressed by Chloe at a Six, because he just snorted. But he didn't let her go. And, when she burrowed deeper into his arms, she felt his hardness through his jeans, pressing into her belly and singing through her blood. Well now. She wasn't letting *that* go. Not when she'd decided to be brave.

"I think you should kiss me again," she said, "and this time, don't do anything silly. Like stop."

He smiled, but his eyes were serious. "You aren't well."

"I'm never well. And my consultant does like to go on about endorphins being natural painkillers, and—"

"Really? Your *doctor* tells you that?"

"Well, yes, but usually in a *Chloe, you should go out and have fun* sort of way." Not a *Chloe, you should clumsily seduce someone by discussing pain management* sort of way.

He wrapped an arm around her waist, hugging her tighter against him. No avoiding that erection now. She tried to maintain some dignity, succeeded for half a second, then crumbled like feta and rocked her hips into his. The choked groan he gave was . . . pleasing. The way he screwed his eyes shut and let his head fall back, exposing the vulnerable line of his throat, was intoxicating.

Sounding pained, he asked, "Orgasms cause endorphins, right?"

"They do."

"Want one?"

She blinked at his lovely, flushing throat for a moment. Was this actually working? It seemed so, but she wasn't sure, because she suddenly couldn't think straight. Then her backup brain kicked in—the smaller section of her mind that took over like a generator whenever something wiped out her general brain's power. "Something" such as the casual offer of an orgasm.

The backup brain told him, "I'm still wearing my buprenorphine patch. Which makes it more difficult for me to do, um, that."

"Want to try?"

She exhaled sharply. "Yes, please."

Chloe could not be held responsible for the actions of the backup brain.

He opened his eyes and she saw the naked lust there, as if someone had switched on floodlights in the dark. That sharp green gaze settled on her like a ton of bricks. A ton of sexy bricks. Apparently, bricks could be sexy when they were shooting from Red Morgan's eyes like lasers. She may or may not be delirious with lust. The backup brain was still in control. Never mind.

He cupped her face in his hands like she was something delicate and kissed her like he'd missed her for a lifetime. His callused thumbs swept over her cheeks while their bodies pressed together from chest to thigh, his erection rigid against her belly. His lips claimed hers hungrily, every slick, hot glide of his tongue tugging at something delicious between her thighs. She moaned, and he pulled back as if that was what he'd been waiting for. The size of his jet-black pupils made his pale eyes seem strange, otherworldly.

"Bedroom," he said.

She ended up sitting primly on the edge of her bed with a tightly leashed storm of a man kneeling between her thighs. He wrapped his big hands around her bare ankles and muttered, "You always wear those fucking shoes . . . and these skirts. You drive me out of my mind." He let go, flicked one of the buttons on her jumper, then frowned. Fiddled with it for a moment. "Chloe . . . are these buttons fake?"

"Of course they are," she said. "Actual buttons would be an inefficient use of limited dexterity."

He laughed like she was a headline act at the Apollo.

Laughing wasn't exactly what she wanted from him right now, but it was so adorable she let it slide. He rested his head in her lap as he chuckled, and she slid her fingers through the golden fire of his hair until he calmed down. When he looked up at her again, his smile was even brighter than his eyes. "You and your fucking cardigans. Your fake fucking cardigans."

"Do you like cardigans?" she asked pertly.

The last of his amusement faded away, replaced by something raw and animal. "I like yours."

She'd never been happier about her own strange obsession with buttons she couldn't use. Before she could lose her nerve, she pulled the jumper off over her head. "See? Efficient."

He didn't answer. Apparently, he was too busy staring at her chest. His brow furrowed as if in pain and his eyes fluttered shut for a second before he forced them open again, like he didn't want to miss anything. And then, good Lord, he bit his lip. As if he wanted to bite her. As if she made him hungry.

Well, the feeling was mutual.

She slid her bra straps off her shoulders, but he finally found his voice. "Woman. Don't take that thing off unless you want me to die here."

She rolled her eyes. "So dramatic."

"You don't know how much I want you," he whispered, his gaze devouring her bare skin. "I can't fucking tell you. I don't know how."

Maybe that was true, but right now, she thought she heard it in his voice and saw it in his eyes—and felt it, when he ran his hand from her skirt-covered hip, to her waist, to her ribs. He toyed with the lace at the edge of her bra, then leaned forward and kissed her belly. She sucked in a gasp at the rasp of his stubble, the heat of his tongue. Languid need turned the blood in her veins to wine.

She tipped her head back and murmured, "I don't suppose you'd take your shirt off for me, would you?"

"I think that can be arranged." He dragged his shirt over his head. The ache between her thighs only worsened at the sight of him. He was so divine. This close, she finally realized that the tattoos covering his shoulders, his chest, his right side, were the old-fashioned, classic kind that usually came in color, but his were black and gray. An eagle, a stag, a crying woman with roses in her hair—her gaze traced over every intricately shaded piece.

He pushed her skirt up her thighs and said, his voice rough, "I like the way you look at me."

"I—"

His phone beeped, not a call but an alarm or reminder. He took it out of his back pocket, pressed a button, then threw it— actually *threw* it—out of the open bedroom door.

She blinked. She'd been rather thoughtless this morning. "Oh, Red. You have work—"

"I'm busy. Be quiet."

"I don't think you want me to be quiet." She said it without thinking and was rewarded with a wicked smile.

"No. I don't." He rose up on his knees and kissed her again, licking into her mouth, hungry and filthy in a way that got her really wet, really fast. He hiked up her skirt, but instead of touching her desperate pussy he splayed his hands over her ribs again. Slid higher. Reached into her bra and cupped the weight of her breasts, squeezing, kneading, shamelessly enjoying. She shuddered against him, moaning into his mouth. He bit her lower lip, then sucked away the sting. Each slow pull sparked electric pleasure in her clit. If he didn't get a move on, she was going to start touching herself.

"Here's something I haven't told you," he murmured against her lips. "I love your tits." His thumbs swept over her nipples, circled her sensitive areolas, and when she whimpered, he kissed her again, fast and hard, as if he wanted to take her pleasure into his body. Then he continued. "I love your tits, but not as much as I love your legs. Don't ask me why. I've been fantasizing about your thighs." His hands skimmed back down her body, over her hips and belly, until he squeezed the aforementioned thighs. "All soft and thick and lush." He groaned and pressed hot, openmouthed kisses to her jaw, her throat, her collarbone.

She sucked in a breath when his mouth reached her cleavage and kept going. He'd told her to keep the bra on, but now he muttered, "Fuck it," and pulled down a cup until she spilled out. Then the tip of his tongue, impossibly light and achingly delicate, nudged her nipple. At the contact, a moan shot from her lips. Her body arched without permission, her hips rocking forward. He took her nipple into his mouth, sucking hard, and she lost the very last of her control. It was as if she'd been on the edge of consciousness, clinging to lucidity by her fingertips, but now she was tumbling into a dream world. She was lust.

"Red," she gasped, her fingers sinking into his hair. "Oh, my God, Red. More." She grabbed one of his hands and shoved it between her thighs, rocking her swollen clit into his palm. He released her nipple with one last, sweet lick and her sensitive skin tingled from the rasp of his stubble. She wondered how that same sensation would translate against her inner thighs.

God, she wanted that.

"You want to know what I like best?" he asked conversationally, as if this was a perfectly ordinary interaction. As if she wasn't frantically grinding against his hand.

"What?" she gasped, barely caring, barely hearing.

"This," he murmured. "You. My desperate little angel. Losing it for me." He took his hand away and she whimpered. The sound turned into a moan when he finally pulled down her underwear. "Oh," he said. "And this." Without warning, his thick fingers slid through her folds. Her gasp was ragged, torn from somewhere deep inside her. The way he parted her was so intimate, it should've been obscene. He spread her open and said, "Your soft, wet cunt. Oh, Chloe." His thumb circled her clit just right, so right she thought she'd fall to pieces, disappear in a shower of sparks, a fleeting surge of dangerous power. "You're all swollen and slippery and I . . ." He broke off, shut his eyes, his expression agonized, and bit his fist. "No," he muttered. "Not today."

"Yes, today," she ordered, spreading her thighs wider, arching her back, showing him everything he claimed to love so much.

He held her gaze, his thumb still teasing her clit. "I'm not rushing this. Also, I don't think you have condoms."

Oh. Yes. That was a rather intelligent point. "Don't you have one in your wallet, or something?"

He snorted. "You're confused about the state of my sex life. No, there's not a condom in my wallet. And even if there was, I wouldn't give you what you want. I'd need to take my time. And I like hearing you beg."

"You're evil."

"You like it." He cupped her jaw, kissed her gently. He always touched her so carefully, but she didn't feel like he was afraid of breaking her. More like he worshipped her even as he debauched her. More like she was his, and precious, but he planned to come all over her anyway.

Mmm. Please.

He eased his tongue into her mouth and pushed two fingers inside her—not deep, not hard, just teasing. Stroking. Exploring. When he glided over her G-spot she stopped breathing for a moment. Then she started again, and her next exhalation was a rush of "*Oh, that, stay there, stay there.*"

"Yeah?" he whispered against her lips. "Sure you don't want me to—?" He pulled out and she sobbed. Then he circled her clit, fingers wet with her arousal, his touch so certain, she screamed.

And then he went back to her G-spot.

She clutched his shoulders because she felt like she might faint. "Red, please, please—"

"All right, love," he murmured, his fingers moving faster, his warmth fading as he moved away. His next words were a hot breath against her thigh. "You're so beautiful. So beautiful, and the longer I look, the better it gets."

How he could say that, when he was shirtless and stunning on his knees before her, *torturing* her, she had no idea. Then he lowered his head and flicked his tongue over her swollen flesh, and it didn't matter, because nothing mattered except feeling. Feeling this. Feeling him. His mouth was hot and wet and slow, so slow, as he licked and sucked her clit. His tongue rubbed every inch of her with shameless intensity, slick and thorough and dizzyingly good. She moaned, choked out his name, pulled his hair, but none of that released the divine, impossible pressure building just beneath her skin. He did that. He loved her steadily, thoroughly, his fingers thrusting deep inside her while he lapped, sucked, pressed deep kisses to her labia the same way he'd owned her mouth. She melted, and he licked up her wetness like nectar.

Her orgasm was so powerful she thought she might black out. She released a high, desperate, gasping sound that might've been his name, might've been nonsense, might've been "Oh-my-goodness-this-is-fantastic-thank-you-so-much." Who knew? Certainly not

Chloe, because sheer pleasure took up so much of her body that it shoved awareness out of the way to make room. She came until she was nothing but a limp, worn-out mess of a woman with hot tears spilling over her cheeks.

Red held her tight and kissed her hard, and she sucked her own taste from his tongue. Then he brushed his lips over her tears and murmured, "I knew you'd cry."

She wasn't sure how her voice still worked, but she managed to ask, "How?"

"You feel so much," he said simply.

Oh, if he only knew. If he only knew how very much she felt for him.

CHAPTER EIGHTEEN

Chloe didn't think it was unreasonable to say that an orgasm courtesy of Red's wicked mouth was now her favorite way to start the day. And, speaking of: an orgasm courtesy of Red's wicked hands was her favorite way to float into sleep. She could say that with certainty, because on Thursday night, he came back after work and made her dinner, and approved the work she'd done on his website so far. Then he took her to bed and stroked her until she fell apart for him.

He wasn't there when she woke up on Friday morning, but he'd left something behind on her desk, right beside her computer: a message scrawled in his familiar handwriting on one of her pink sticky notes.

> **Call if you need me. I'll see you tomorrow.**
> **(FOR CAMPING.)**

Underneath, he'd scribbled a cute little picture of a tree. What, exactly, made the picture cute? She couldn't say, except for the fact that it came from Red.

So, he'd be busy until tomorrow, would he? She found herself smiling at the thought of all the things he might be getting up to. For someone who'd once seemed like her antithesis, he had a secret fondness for plans that made her want to kiss his lovely, blushing cheeks. She ran a finger over his cartoon tree and sighed. Camping. Ick. Not exactly her forte, but she had the oddest feeling that she'd enjoy it anyway. There was a warm, jittery thrill in her stomach, like the screaming smile of someone on a roller coaster.

This, she decided, was how an adventure should feel. Not like an ordeal, the way drinking and dancing had, but like a welcome risk. When she and Red had left that awful nightclub, a seed of possibility had started growing in Chloe, daring and electric: maybe the list should be more than a box-ticking exercise. Maybe it should *mean* more. Maybe changing it wasn't the end of the world.

Now, that seed had become a sapling, and Chloe was ready to make changes. A little apprehensive, but ready all the same.

She found her glittery blue notebook and sat at her desk, Red's sticky note beside her, a momentous weight in the air. After a moment's hesitation, she crossed out item 2, *Enjoy a drunken night out,* with quick, sharp lines of her pen. Beside the crossed-out entry, she wrote simply, awkwardly, with a what-am-I-doing wince: *Call Annie. Be nice. Make friends.*

Dani often said that writing down one's desires, even in the slightest way possible, was a vital step in manifesting one's ideal future. Chloe often replied that that was nonsense, but the truth was, she believed in it. She stared down at the altered list with growing satisfaction, like a streetlight slowly switching on as the sun set behind it. She crossed out item 5, meaningless sex, with relish.

And then she wrote something else: an entirely new entry, because he made her feel entirely new things. Another wish, another manifestation, a stepping stone to an ideal future she only dared to peek at through splayed fingers. One she was determined to reach out and grab.

8. *Keep Red.*

Contacting Annie proved to be the easiest list item Chloe had ever completed. When she forced herself to find the mysterious hot pink card and type its number into her phone, she was still on a list-editing high, utterly dauntless. Perhaps that was why, when Annie suggested coffee that very afternoon, Chloe agreed without even checking her schedule.

She was spontaneous, after all. She was flexible. She was committed to her new and improved list.

Hours later, she was also nervous. She sat at a table in a busy, overloud, and likely unhygienic coffee shop in Harebell, which could only be described as the hipster quarter of the city. Of course Annie, with her strange outfits and excellent business cards, had wanted to meet here. And yet, she *wasn't* here, leaving Chloe to sit by the cold window like a shivering loner.

Wonderful.

But waiting wasn't all bad. It gave her time to text her new favorite contact.

CHLOE: Guess where I am?

RED: Climbing Mount Kilimanjaro?

CHLOE: Not yet.

RED: I hope you haven't gone to New York without me.

She stared at that message for long, happy heartbeats, a thousand wonderful implications threading through her mind like a never-ending daisy chain. Perhaps they'd go to New York together. Because *they* were together. And they shared goals and future plans. And things.

CHLOE: I'd never go without you. I'm at a coffee shop waiting for Annie.

RED: What?

RED: ANNIE Annie?

RED: Actually, I don't care which Annie it is. You're waiting for someone? To have coffee? Not to throw the coffee at them, or anything, but to actually have coffee?

She snorted, clapping a hand over her mouth.

CHLOE: YES. Honestly, what on earth do you think of me?

RED: That you're short-tempered and always interesting.

CHLOE: You are a very difficult man.

RED: That must make me perfect for you. ☺

She was still smiling when Annie arrived.

"Chloe!" Annie plonked herself down in the seat across the table with a sound like a bubble bursting. "There you are!"

Chloe stared. *There she was?* She'd been *here* for the last thirty minutes, for Christ's sake. "Yes," she said dryly. "Here I am."

"So sorry I'm late. I've had a Marmite disaster."

"Oh. That sounds . . ."

"Vitamin rich? Very." Annie's golden curls were pinned almost flat to her head with what appeared to be a thousand black hair slides. She was wearing her enormous camo coat again, but she unzipped it to reveal a surprisingly ordinary outfit that consisted of jeans and a raspberry-colored jumper. "Coffee?" she asked brightly.

Since Chloe had been politely waiting before ordering, and ignoring the death glares of the lady behind the counter, for half an hour, she nodded eagerly before realizing what she was agreeing to. "Oh—no coffee for me, but I'll get tea."

"My treat!" Annie was up and off before Chloe could say another word. She was so . . . *springy*. Energetic. Possibly earnest, potentially a master of sarcasm. Chloe wasn't sure which, but she suspected her own prickliness stemmed from an urgent desire to find out, and a worry that she never would. How long had it been since she'd made and kept a friend? So long she must have lost the ability, rather like a wasted muscle. She should've been doing social exercises alongside her physiotherapy all these years. She found her own distorted reflection in the shiny metal sugar cup at the center of the table and gave herself a stern look. "Pull yourself together," she told the metallic Chloe with the aubergine-shaped head. "Think victorious thoughts. Triumphant thoughts. The thoughts of a woman who succeeds in all endeavors."

"An excellent philosophy!" Annie said.

Oops. Chloe slapped on a smile and tried to look less like someone who encouraged their own reflection in the middle of cool coffee shops.

Annie set down a tray of hot drinks, took her seat again, and said, "So! Are you still cross with me about Perdita?"

"I—erm—oh, gosh, I wasn't *cross* with you—"

"I know you were. I would be, too, if it were me. Perdy's a *doll*." Annie paused. "Well, as far as cats go. I don't actually like them that much."

Chloe stared. "You don't?"

"Gosh, no. I'm more of a dog person. But the thing is, I have to look after them. It's part of the deal."

"The deal?"

Annie's voice dropped. "With the goddess of the underworld."

Oh dear.

Annie's voice dropped further as she went on, "My *mother*."

Ah. That was quite a bit less bonkers.

"You made some sort of deal with your mother that involves looking after cats?"

"Eleven cats. Thankfully, most are outdoors. I have to keep

them all safe and tend to their needs with my own fair hand as much as is possible."

Chloe stared, aghast. "And what on earth do you get out of the bargain?"

"I get to live in my mother's house while she sails the world on a piddling little boat with her third husband, Lee. Now, I know what you're thinking—only three husbands? But my mother was quite young when she had me, so she's not as mature as you'd assume. Hopefully, by the time she hits her sixties she'll have found a rhythm and will be on her fifth husband at least."

"I'm sure," Chloe agreed. "There is nothing wrong with being a late bloomer."

"Certainly not. I myself, however, am a lost cause," Annie said. "Thirty-four years old and not a single husband, divorced, deceased, or otherwise disposed of."

"Me neither. I blame the modern age for an outrageous gap in my education. Schools simply aren't providing their girls with the skills needed to acquire and eliminate spouses."

"Hear, hear. So, since you, like myself, suffer from a lack of life insurance checks and/or alimony, what is it you do to keep yourself in chocolate biscuits and such?"

"I'm a web designer," Chloe said. "I ought to give you my card. It's not as good as yours."

"Flatterer." But Annie looked pleased. She had a Julia Roberts sort of mouth, so it was impossible to miss the smile she tried to hide.

Chloe found herself smiling wider in return. "And what do

you do?" Because really, she'd been dying to know, and she still hadn't allowed herself to look.

"I'm a lingerie designer," Annie said.

"Goodness. That's . . ."

"Your bra doesn't fit, by the way."

Chloe blinked and looked down at her own chest. "It—?"

"Sorry. Auntie always tells me not to say things like that. But you seem the type who likes to know what's what."

"I am. How can you tell it doesn't fit?"

"Oh, please don't worry, you look lovely. But I can tell."

Chloe nodded. "So I don't look as if I have one giant, central boob or anything?"

"Certainly not," Annie said immediately. "Not at all."

"Oh, good. Well, I suppose I need to go bra shopping, then." An idea struck her, the sort she'd usually dismiss out of hand. The sort she'd be too afraid to say out loud, in case she was struck down and embarrassed. But Chloe was being brave, these days, so she pulled herself together and blurted it out: "Perhaps, at some point, you'd, er, be interested in advising me on . . ."

"I'll come with you," Annie said immediately. "Shopping. We'll make a day of it."

Chloe beamed. That had been easy. That had been beyond easy. "Wonderful. Yes. Let's."

Spending the day without Chloe had felt kind of like shaving off his hair. Or maybe Red's appointment with Dr. Maddox was to blame for that. After two sessions in relatively quick succession, he wasn't exactly enjoying therapy, but he was enjoying how much more he understood his own head. And, kind of like Chloe ticking shit off her list, he felt better every time he went.

He could say the same about the phone call he'd had with Vik, even though it had been about as easy as therapy. Telling his best friend he was ready to move on, to leap back into the real world independently and leave this safety net behind? That was one thing. Admitting to his boss that he'd been literally sleeping with a tenant? Not quite the same moment of brotherly love. But at least Vik hadn't driven over to kick him in the nuts. That would've made Red's plans for the weekend a hell of a lot more difficult to accomplish.

Now it was Saturday afternoon and he was standing on Chloe's doorstep with two duffle bags, already smiling. He'd knocked, which meant he was five seconds closer to seeing her again. To hearing her voice, instead of imagining it as he read her texts. To touching her . . .

She opened the door.

The first thing he noticed was her eyes, bright and excited behind her glasses. Maybe because she wanted to see him, too. Or maybe she was unexpectedly buzzed about camping. She certainly looked prepared: her hair was in one of those fancy-looking braids he didn't know the name of, and she was dressed in color-coordinated walking gear. Usually he'd miss her pretty skirts, but the leggings clinging to her thick thighs suited him fine.

"Stop staring at me, you pervert," she said.

He looked up just as she launched herself at him. Between the force of Chloe flinging her arms around him, and the weight of the bags on his shoulders, it was a miracle he didn't collapse. But he managed to stay upright, and his reward was her mouth: she kissed the hell out of him.

Reality shifted, shrinking to a fine point that consisted of nothing but her hands tangling in his hoodie and her tongue easing tentatively over his. She smelled like rain-scattered flowers and warmth and comfort and mindless fucking lust. He couldn't hold her the way he wanted to, so he let his mouth speak for his occupied hands. He tasted her like sweet nectar, bit her lower lip, swallowed her soft little moans greedily. Then, after the shortest forever on earth, she pulled away. Broke the kiss. Rested her forehead against his and closed her eyes, breathing heavily for a moment. The sound of her panting made him smile.

She opened her eyes and murmured, "Hi."

"Hi," he replied, his voice rough. "I take it you're excited to camp?"

She laughed and pulled him inside, shutting the door behind them. "Gosh, yes."

He followed her into the living room, noticing happily that the flat was just tidy enough to suggest that she was feeling okay. "Really?"

"Of course," she drawled. She was kneeling on the floor by a single enormous rucksack, fiddling with the straps and sliding a pink water bottle into a side pocket. "I'm like a child going to Disneyland. I can't wait to be trampled by moose in the night, or perhaps eaten by a bear, or chopped up by a serial killer, wrapped up in pieces of the tent and kept in a freezer for the next five years."

He pinched the bridge of his nose, shaking his head. "Button. We don't have to do this. You know that, right?"

"Of course I know it. I want to do something that scares me."

"Camping," he said. "Camping scares you."

"No comment." She gave him a sphinxlike smile. He wanted to kiss it off her face.

"Well, you don't need to worry," he said, finally putting down his massive bags. "I'm not going to let anyone chop you up."

"Right. Because you're a big strong man who can fight off seasoned machete murderers with the power of your mighty masculinity."

He would not laugh. "And we don't have moose, Chlo. Or bears."

She turned to look at him. "I'm quite certain that we do."

"We don't."

"We definitely have bears."

"We don't. If we had bears it'd be in the news all the time. You know, *Fine upstanding British man attacked by a bear, EU to blame, Brexit now.*"

"I'm quite certain I saw that headline on a copy of the *Daily Mail* the other week."

"You didn't, love."

She tutted as if he was being unreasonable. "We'll see. Do you have bug repellent, by the way? I do."

Bug repellent? Where did she think they were going, a swamp? "Are you offering to share?"

She sniffed. "You really should've brought your own. Two bags, and you didn't bring your own?"

"I've got other stuff in my bags," he said, sitting on the floor beside her.

"Such as?"

He unzipped his duffel and pulled out a packet of marshmallows that was the size of a child. "We're gonna make s'mores and shit."

She dropped the bug repellent and jumped him again. Literally threw herself into his lap. He barely caught her, and then she was kissing him, kissing him, kissing him with the kind of hot, dark determination he felt for her, and it was wonderful. Her hands slid into his hair, her body rocked against his, and he felt as if she'd reached into his chest and squeezed his heart because it was suddenly, blatantly obvious that it belonged to her. He belonged to her.

He blinked, dazed, unsure of what to do with all these intense, impossible feelings. She pulled away, her laughter bright and infectious. "S'mores! I do love a man with a food-related plan. I hope you know we're going to finish that bag."

He smiled, but he couldn't even speak. That divine, Rococo face had turned him on and pissed him off from the very beginning, but now when he looked at her he didn't see her untouchable beauty so much as he saw *Chloe,* his Chloe, with that sardonic tilt to her lips and that superior gleam in her eyes. His heart shook. He ran his hands over her body just to remind himself that he could, that she was real and there and his. She felt soft and lush beneath what seemed to be three or four layers of clothing. He grabbed a handful of her arse and finally managed to say, "That's my girl."

"Shut up, you misogynistic pig." She kissed his right cheek, then his left. "I didn't see you yesterday."

"No, you didn't. Did you miss me?"

"Choke, Redford. Just choke."

He seemed to adore her more every second. This could be a problem. "Come here." He kissed her again because she was addictive. But then he reminded himself that he had specific and important plans, none of which included fucking Chloe on her living room floor. With a sigh, he nudged her off his lap. "All right. Stop distracting me. We gotta go."

"*Distracting* you?" she said, then grabbed her rucksack and stood, hands on her hips. She was moving faster, more easily than usual, even for a good day. "Honestly, I can't stand you sometimes." But she was smiling, big and uncontained, just like him.

Red made fun of Chloe's driving all the way to the campsite and she couldn't even bring herself to mind. When he'd learned she actually had a car, he'd feigned deathly shock, which was ridiculous because he must have known already.

"Who did you think was parking in my designated space?" she demanded.

"I had no idea," he said cheerfully. "Drug dealers. Aliens, maybe."

On the way to the site he'd chosen for them, a place named Tyburn's Wood, they got lost three times in a maze of sweet little villages with houses built of stone. After the third time, Red turned off her sat nav and pulled out a bright yellow booklet. She snorted as he opened it on his lap, revealing the kind of massive, multicolored map that made her eyes blur far worse than any line of code ever had. "What on earth is that monstrosity?"

"It's what human beings used to get around for the last couple thousand years. You know, instead of relying on fancy sky computers."

It was all she could do not to veer off the road. "*Fancy sky computers?* Why, Redford, I had no idea you were such a technophobe."

"Not a technophobe," he said in his lying voice. "Second left up there. No, Chlo, *left*. You really don't know your left and right, do you? Maybe I shouldn't blame the sat nav."

"The sat nav? Don't you mean the fancy sky computer?"

"Fuck off," he grinned.

And so it continued, until they finally reached the campsite.

Tyburn's Wood was, once you got past the vast open field of expensive motor homes, a literal wood. Behind a series of huge log cabins and the neatly organized holiday park, a dense sea of tall, spindly evergreens stabbed the sky, upright and tightly packed like centurions. There were a few clear paths in and out with big, colorful signs depicting various trails and pitch-ready locations. As they unloaded the car—or rather, as Red unloaded the car while Chloe leaned against a nearby wooden fence—he pointed at one of the signs and said, as if he were talking to a toddler, "Look, baby, a map. You remember maps, right? Nice pictures with lines that show you where to go!"

She bent, scooped up a handful of bark chips, and threw them at him.

"Excuse me!" a brusque voice cut in. "Please don't throw the bark!"

Chloe looked over, cheeks warm, expecting to see some campsite staff member glaring at them. Instead she found a pair of yummy mummies with about fifty-eight kids between them, some shoved into sporty-looking strollers, some perched on the women's Lululemon-clad hips, most running around throwing bark at each other and having a fabulous time.

"Erm, sorry," Chloe said.

One of the mums sniffed as if to say, *You ought to know better.*

The other mum pursed her lips as if to say, *Setting a bad example for the children!*

The sniff and the lip-pursing were very effective. Clearly, they were excellent mums. As they herded their broods away, Red wandered over to her and murmured, "How come you're never so well-behaved with me?"

"You're not a mum," she said pertly, ignoring how close he was, how rough his voice was, how his body gave off sheer heat and she wanted to wrap up in him like he was a blanket. "You don't get to boss me around."

He dragged his gaze over her from head to toe, slow and sweet and sticky like honey. She wanted him to lick her just like that: thoroughly, everywhere.

He probably would if she asked.

His hands came to rest on either side of her on the fence, so that his arms caged her in, his body crowding hers. His lips hovered over her ear and he whispered, "You'd let me boss you around."

"I would not," she drawled, as if the ghost of his mouth over her skin didn't send delicious little shocks down her spine.

"You sure? Not even if I think you'd like it?" His lips moved from her ear to her throat. He kissed her there, the sweet, subtle glide of his tongue making her body hum with erotic energy. Then he stopped for long enough to ask in a low, rough voice, "Would you let me boss you around if I made it good?"

"Maybe," she admitted, her voice alarmingly breathy.

He kissed her throat again, hotter and wetter this time. "Just maybe?"

"*Yes*." She bent her head, exposed more of her throat to him, her pulse racing.

"Good. Now, listen carefully . . ." His hand caught hers, but he didn't lace their fingers together like usual. Instead, he gave her something that felt like paper and said seriously, "I want you to read the map."

He stepped away, his slight smile coming into focus as her dizzying lust disappeared. She looked at her hand and found she was holding a printed-out Tyburn's Wood leaflet that, according to the chirpy front cover, included a map of the campsites. Caught between outrage and laughter, she bit her lip, sucked in a breath, and said, "Redford Morgan—"

"Don't worry. I'll help you with your left and right."

"I know my left and right!" she spluttered, shoving at his big, annoying, handsome chest.

"Sure you do, Button," he soothed. Then he wrapped an arm around her waist, dragged her close, and laughed into her hair.

There were sites spread far and wide, but Red insisted they stay close to the edge of the woods. They chose a little clearing where the light filtered through the slender tree trunks like something out of a painting, and Chloe took a minute to fill her lungs with fresh, frosty air, the kind that was just cold enough to seem wet even though it was dry. The setting sun's honeyed rays were so warm, golden fire just like Red's hair, but they couldn't touch the forest's crisp autumn chill. She liked that. In fact, despite her last-minute misgivings, she liked a lot about this particular list item so far.

But she especially liked her companion. She turned to find him already grappling with the tent and said, "Did you choose this spot because of me?" She knew the answer. Just like she'd known she wouldn't need to remind him of how far—or not— she could walk.

He gave her a wary look, then returned to fiddling with tent poles. "You don't know how you'll feel tomorrow morning. Seemed smart to stay near the car."

There was no fighting the smile that crept across her face. She wandered over to him and grabbed a few tent poles of her own. "You're very thoughtful."

"Yeah. I thought long and hard about all the ways I want to defile this tent tonight, and I decided to factor that into our plans." He shot her a grin that only widened when he caught sight of her face. "Aw, Chlo. Am I embarrassing you?"

A blush crept up her throat. She felt like she'd swallowed a star: hot, hot, hot, burning and bright and fundamentally unstable inside. "Does that mean—are you finally going to let me—"

"Screw my brains out?" he offered cheerfully.

She choked on fresh air.

"I *am* embarrassing you," he said, clearly pleased. "Wait until you see the air mattress."

"The *what*?" she almost shrieked.

He gave her an odd look. "Well, you didn't think I was going to fuck you on the ground, did you? I'm not a *complete* animal."

"You, sir, are a menace. A menace to good and decent society, and to noble, chaste women such as myself—"

She might have been insulted at how hard he laughed if she wasn't giggling too.

Red put the tent up with disturbing speed, produced both the famous air mattress and a foot pump from his magical duffel bag—"I *told* you I had more important things than bug spray"—and slipped inside the tent to "arrange" things, whatever that meant. Then he came out and showed her a mysterious tin. Eyes bright in the growing darkness, told her, "Time for the campfire."

She sat in the dirt outside the tent and was very proud of herself for not thinking about wolf poop or grass snakes or possessive, murderous wood fae. "Actually, Red, I've been researching, and campfires are illeg—"

He popped open the weird tin and said, "Chlo?"

"Yes?"

"Shhh." He put the tin into a little well of dirt he'd created and took a silver Zippo from the pocket of his ever-present leather jacket. "No, I don't smoke," he said, just as she opened her mouth. She closed her mouth again. Was she predictable, or did he just know her that well? Possibly a bit of both. She watched in confusion, then something like awe, as he lit whatever was in the tin. He sat back beside her, and they let the flames grow.

"What on earth is that thing?" she asked.

"It's a portable, reusable, relatively safe and eco-friendly"—he valiantly ignored her snort—"campfire. If we want to put it out, we can just put the lid on again."

"Seriously? And that works?"

"Sure. It's science, or whatever. Want to toast some marshmallows?"

It was a juvenile, still probably illegal, and definitely unhygienic activity that belonged to the world of silly American films. "Yes please," she said.

"Good. I lied about the s'mores thing, though. I don't know what the fuck s'mores are."

She snorted. "Neither do I."

Reaching for his bag, he said, "I'll open the marshmallows, you go and collect twigs to stick 'em on."

She stared.

He stared back at her with a stressfully serious expression for two long seconds before he cracked, those catlike eyes creasing at the corners as he threw back his head and laughed. "Oh my God, Chloe. Relax. Look, I bought skewers."

"Oh." She pressed a hand to her chest. "I was really reconsidering this entire thing."

"Camping?"

"Letting you put your tongue in my mouth again."

"Shut up," he grinned. "You'd always let me put my tongue in your mouth."

"Maybe in secret moments of weakness," she admitted. "Give me that. I want to put my own marshmallows on."

"You sure? You don't want the assistance of a marshmallow-skewering expert?"

She rolled her eyes and took the bag of marshmallows from him. "No. But speaking of that expertise—"

"This feels like a great time to make a joke about penetrating soft, sweet things."

She ignored him. "—why are you so good at camping-type stuff?"

"Ah. Well." He stared thoughtfully at the skewer in his hand, his hair falling over his face for a moment. The fingers of his free hand began to drum against his thigh and she wondered, with more than a little regret, how she'd managed to turn camping into a topic that made him nervous or unsettled or whatever it meant, precisely, when he got this way.

Biting her lip, she said hurriedly, "You don't have to—"

"No, it's okay." He looked up at her with a smile, but it was a sad sort of smile. "Honestly, Chlo, it's fine." And then those drumming fingers stopped, and found hers, and now he was holding her hand instead. "I just got a little bit . . . ah, you know how I told you about my granddad who died?"

She nodded, feeling those silver rings against her skin.

"He used to take me places like this. All over. Not that often—maybe once or twice a year, when he had time off—but it adds up, yeah? We lived in the city and he was paranoid about air pollution and all that. He had this idea that spending time in nature every so often could . . . I don't know, clean you out." Red chuckled.

Chloe squeezed his hand, her marshmallows forgotten. "What was his name?"

"Leo." Just the word curved Red's mouth into a smile, and she was struck by an odd, sudden certainty that Redford Morgan's near-constant cheer had come from one man in particular. *Leo.*

"He sounds wonderful," she murmured.

"Yeah. He was. Sometimes I wonder . . ."

He trailed off, but she thought she knew what he was going to say. She knew, because she knew him—not just the achingly cool, charming, handsome man who was quick to joke and quicker to help, but the not-so-shiny parts beneath that formed the foundation of who he was. The parts that some people might look away from because they were a little less easy to swallow. The parts that called to her just as much as his sweet smiles. "You wonder if he'd be disappointed in you." The way Red, as she'd realized over these past weeks, was disappointed in himself. "Because of whatever it was that happened to you in London."

He turned to look at her so fast, his hair flew around his face like a flame. "I—London was—" He sighed, his grip on her hand tightening. "Yeah." He cleared his throat. "Sorry. I don't know why I brought this up. Did I bring this up? Look, have a marshmallow."

"Red," she whispered. "You don't always have to be okay." She leaned closer and pressed a kiss to his cheek. He was still for a moment.

But then he looked at her, and smiled, and murmured, "I know. But I am okay, with you." The moment shimmered with something beautiful and delicate, and it wasn't broken when he turned away. It lingered, fine and lovely, under the surface. He pushed a marshmallow onto her skewer, and when she complained, he popped one into her mouth, too. Then he loaded up his own and showed her exactly how close to hold them to the fire, and for how long.

Then, when her mouth was full of the first hot, sticky, melting bite, he caught her gaze and said in the gravelly voice that rolled right over her clit, "Now, in the name of camping, bad decisions, and your list, you and me are gonna play a game."

CHAPTER NINETEEN

Red watched as the sympathy left Chloe's dark gaze, replaced by something hotter than the campfire. Her lips curled, that familiar, uneven smile so sexy he felt it in his chest—and his balls.

"What kind of game?" she asked. Her tongue snaked out to catch a dripping blob of marshmallow, and every inch of his body snapped to attention. He hadn't thought this whole "toasted marshmallow" thing through. He hadn't considered how fucking irresistible she'd look licking up gooey, white dessert, or how the light of the fire would make her skin glow like polished mahogany and her eyes light up like smoky amber. He hadn't imagined something this innocent could make him want to suck sugar off her tongue and drag her into the tent.

He should've, though. He always wanted Chloe. In every possible way.

She was still waiting for a response, arching those winged eyebrows at him, so he cleared his throat and finally answered, "Twenty-one questions. It's a time-honored camp tradition amongst people who're trying to get into each other's sleeping bags."

She crossed her ankles and leaned closer, her shoulder bumping his. The simple touch shimmered through his core like a shot of molten gold. "I'm assuming you didn't learn that from your granddad."

He swallowed to clear the roughness in his throat. This whole experience was for her, and she seemed to be enjoying it, so he wasn't going to grab her and make it all about his lust—at least, not yet. "I learned it the same place I learned about s'mores, smart-arse. You can't deny, this game looks fun in films."

"Oh, I don't know about that. Isn't it the game where a girl asks something useful like, *What's your favorite animal?* and then a horny little monster—ahem, I mean a *boy,* uses his turn to ask if she's ever had anal sex?"

Red's lips twitched. "Maybe. Luckily I'm not a horny little monster"—*lie*—"so I'll only be asking you very meaningful questions. But you can go first."

She tapped her fingers against her lower lip. "I need more marshmallows to help me think."

"Don't start." He nudged her shoulder. Must have caught her by surprise, because she almost toppled over in response, saved only by his hand on her arm.

"An attack!" she cried, all dramatic as if they were in a film.

"It's not my fault your balance sucks." He pulled her up again. Actually, he sort of . . . *picked* her up a bit, and settled her between his legs. Now his thighs bracketed hers, her back resting against his chest. She was close enough that he could smell the floral stuff she put in her hair over the smoky sweetness of toasted marshmallows, close enough that her body heat seared into him like a brand.

Perfect.

"All right," he said, trying to sound authoritative. "Now, you start."

She didn't hesitate. "Were you teased at school about your name? And, you know, your hair and everything?"

"Yeah." He wrapped his arms around her like he was a fucking koala and she was his forever tree. "I got some shit at school—who didn't?—but it never bothered me. My mum gave me this name. She told me it's a good one. And her hair's a hell of a lot redder than mine, but I always thought she was the prettiest lady in the world, so I didn't care what people said about the color."

The crackling of the fire and the rustles of the forest reigned for a second; they even heard someone whooping in the distance. Then Chloe said with a smile in her voice, "Well, that's incredibly sweet. I mean, I already knew you were a mama's boy—"

"Whoa, now. I'm a what?"

"Red," she said patiently, "you have the word *MUM* tattooed on your *hand*."

He grinned and ran that hand through his hair. "Yeah, well. You don't have any questionable tattoos? No, of course you don't."

"I don't like pain, remember?"

"And you don't make fucked-up decisions like me." When she twisted her head to frown up at him, he winked and kissed her cheek.

It didn't change the frown. "You don't make messed-up decisions," she told him sternly.

"Chlo, we just went over this." He waggled his tattooed fingers and raised his eyebrows. When she laughed, the sudden tightness in his chest faded. He was all light again. "Okay, now it's my turn. What do I want to ask?" he murmured thoughtfully, as if he wasn't fucking bursting with questions about this woman. As if he couldn't spend hours lost in a Chloe rabbit hole of wondering. "Since we're talking about awkward childhood moments . . . when was your first kiss?"

She laughed. "Who says I was a child? Maybe my first kiss was at twenty."

"Was it?"

"No." Her voice was bright and glittering now. He could hear her smile even if he couldn't see it, his gaze too busy alternating between marshmallow watch and the electric-soft texture of her hair. Then her head dropped back against his shoulder, and he got a front-seat view of her carefree smile and the sparkle in her eyes. Everything turned Button-pink like Cupid had just shot him in the arse. "I was sixteen, at a house party with one of my friends. We played truth or dare and someone was dared to kiss me. It went quite well, I suppose, because I spent the rest of the night with my tongue down his throat."

"See, this is where I'm going wrong. I've got you answering questions when I should've been offering dares."

She slapped his thigh. "You don't need to dare me to kiss you."

"Well, in that case," he murmured. He put his hand on her belly for no reason other than he liked its warmth and its curve and the fact that it was Chloe. He bent his head, brushed his lips over her cheek, and the feel of her was like the sweetest possible punch to the gut. This was all it took; one taste, and his hard-on was probably jabbing her lower back. But she didn't seem to mind, because she tangled her fingers in his hair, yanked him closer, and pressed her lips to his. For precious, perfect seconds, her tongue slid, tentative but demanding, into his mouth. Everything was as intense as her midnight eyes, delicious as her thighs, urgent as the way he needed her.

Then she pulled away, and said, "My turn."

Slightly dazed, he murmured, "Uh. Right. Yeah."

"Do you like your website?"

He blinked, then burst out laughing. "What do you mean, do I like it? Didn't you see my seventy fucking texts?"

She'd sent him a link to preview the current design just yesterday, during their day-long virtual conversation. And, even though there was apparently still technical shit for her to do, he thought everything looked perfect. Just . . . perfect. So much so that if he thought about it for too long, his chest got tight and all his hope and gratitude made a lump of not-so-impossible dreams in his throat.

"There weren't *seventy* texts," she said. "More like five. But I know you'd hate to hurt my feelings, and texts are easy to lie over, so—"

"Hey." He held her tight, gathering her closer against his chest, nudging her chin until she met his gaze. "I don't lie to you. Okay? I just don't."

She rolled her lips inward, but that couldn't hide her smile. "Okay."

"I love it."

"Okay. Can I ask another question?"

He arched an eyebrow. "I thought we were taking turns?"

Her expression turned pensive. "Maybe this question isn't part of the game. I wanted to know . . ." She seemed to gather up her courage in a single breath. "I wanted to know what happened to you in London. What happened to your career."

Ah. He looked up at the canopy of trees and the night being born above them, stars glowing into view like a thousand bright-white candles.

"Marshmallow's burning," she said softly.

"Oh, shit." He came back down to earth, yanked the latest marshmallow out of the fire and stared at the smoldering blob. "Uh—"

"It's fine. I'll still eat it. Will you answer me? You don't have to."

But he would, because he loved her.

The thought froze him for a second before he sank into it like a feather bed. Before it became the comfort that helped him figure out how to speak. He loved Chloe. He loved Chloe like a blank canvas and a finished piece and all the exhilarating, painful, stop-and-start moments in between. He loved Chloe like tearing through the night on his Triumph, feeling alive in motion when he couldn't feel alive inside. He loved Chloe like every glare she shot him was a kiss and every kiss she gave him was a breadcrumb-sized piece of her heart in his hands.

He pushed the length of her braid aside and kissed the back of her neck, soft and vulnerable. The last time he'd put his mouth on her, all of five minutes ago, he hadn't known he was in love. He wondered if she'd feel the difference. Probably not. Because he had a feeling he'd been kissing her with love for a while, even if he hadn't noticed until now.

"Red," she murmured, regret chiming sharp, because she thought she'd hurt him.

"It's fine," he said. "It's fine." And it was. If he ripped off the bandage like a big boy, it would be done, and he'd be able to enjoy the fact that she'd asked, that she wanted to know about the hidden parts of him, the parts that didn't help anyone or make people smile. The parts that weren't fit for exhibition.

"I went to London because I thought I had to. I spent years there, trying to break into a world that wasn't exactly welcoming. I worked as a laborer to support myself and at night I'd run around crashing galleries and handing out my card, which was actually made of paper because—" He laughed, because this was funny, though at the time he'd been embarrassed. "Because I made them myself on the library computer, you know, using Word? And I'd print eight on a page, then cut them out." He shook his head. "I never could wrap my head around online networking, but it would've made life a lot easier."

"You *are* a technophobe," she said triumphantly. "I knew it!"

"Maybe," he admitted. "Maybe just a little bit."

"Well, you're lucky you have me to keep your website

updated," she said smugly. And he was struck by happiness like a bolt of lightning because he was pretty sure—pretty fucking sure—that she didn't just mean that in an *I look after all my clients long-term* sort of way. His mind focused on three words, blew them up, and made them flash a thousand different colors: *you have me.*

Did she know that she had him, too, no matter what? She was skittish about things like this. If he told her just how much feeling burned inside his chest, it might freak her out.

He'd have to show her first. Get her used to the idea. He wanted to squeeze her to him and tell her that she had him, and that she could drag him along on all her wild schemes forever and ever, amen. Instead, he kissed her temple and went on with the story.

"My old-fashioned ways did work, in the end—or at least I thought they did. One night, I met a woman on her way out of some glamorous party. Her name was Pippa. She wanted to look at my stuff. I asked where she worked, and she laughed and told me she *didn't* work. But I let her look anyway because she was confident and I was desperate."

He felt Chloe tense as if she was worried about what came next. God, he wanted to kiss her again. But it was too easy to hide in the comfort she offered, so he squashed the urge and kept talking.

"Long story short, me and her got together. Turned out, her dad was an art dealer, and he liked my stuff. She took me places, and instead of sneering at me or throwing me out, people listened when I talked. I finally started making money, enough that I could quit laboring and focus on my work. Everything was great. Everything was perfect. Except Pippa. She was . . . well, she was abusive."

Chloe twisted round to look at him. "What?"

"She was abusive," he said simply. "Not that I realized at the time. I thought she was just bratty. I mean, she was so little; it's not like it hurt when she hit me. And when she treated me like shit or fucked with my head . . . somehow she always managed to convince me it was just a disagreement, and I was being sensitive. But after a while, that got old. I remember she tried to stop me going home to see Mum. I used to visit once a month, then once a fortnight when I got more money. I brought Pippa once, but, ah, Mum didn't like her."

Understatement of the fucking century.

"She told me Pippa wasn't treating me right. Hearing it from someone else made it easier to hold on to. And then when Pippa tried to stop me visiting again, I started to realize what was going on. Maybe it would've taken me longer to leave her, only she got pissed and stabbed me with a fork."

"She did *what*?" Chloe thundered, and he realized he'd never seen her angry before. She was angry now. She scrambled onto her knees and looked down at him like an avenging god. Her voice came out like thick, choking smoke just before a volcanic eruption. "What the *fuck*?"

He held up his right hand and wondered if she'd see the four tiny scars under his knuckles. "Lucky I'm a lefty."

She grabbed the hand and studied it for a second before pressing a kiss to the marks. "Wow. *Wow.* So this is what murderous intent feels like."

He smiled despite himself. "It's fine. I'm over it. Healed fast."

"You might be over it, but it is *not* fine." The words were sharp, but her voice cracked and her breath hitched.

"Hey, no, Chloe." Heart breaking, he cupped her face, met her shining eyes. "Don't cry, love. It's okay."

"It most certainly is not! It is not. *You're* not. You can't even talk about London, and—"

"That's not why I don't talk about London," he said.

She blinked up at him. "What?"

"I mean, the whole relationship was a fucking nightmare, and I'm still . . ." He grimaced. "Well, you know. But I haven't finished."

She looked horrified. "What *else* happened?"

"Sit down, and I'll tell you."

Slowly, reluctantly, she turned and sat again. Back where she belonged, in his arms. He kissed the top of her head and kept going. "So I broke up with Pippa, and kind of lost it. She told me . . . well, she told me I was nothing without her anyway and she'd been slumming it, and blah blah blah. She said that her dad had only promoted my work because I was with her. And that people only bought it because she'd made me someone. I think she said she created a, uh, *cultural moment* around me. She was always saying shit like that."

Chloe's hand came to rest over his, and the soft, warm pressure jolted him out of the cold, hard place his words had dragged him into. He blinked at the realization that he'd been drifting away as he spoke, back into years of imposter syndrome and paranoia and constant, toxic whispers chipping away at him. Grateful for the touch, he squeezed her hand. She squeezed back.

He cleared his throat and said, "I think the success coming all at once after so many years of trying so hard, it fucked with my head. I didn't think I deserved anything, so I believed her. I yanked my work from just about everywhere, shut down the website and social media I'd finally gotten set up. I cut off the friends I'd made in the art world—before and after her. Anyone. Everyone. Like Joanie, like Julian. I burned bridges and disappeared in a blaze of glory. 'Course, it didn't feel so glorious when I finally stepped back enough to realize what I'd done, but . . . It was too late. I *almost* got somewhere, and then I took myself back to square one. And when I thought about trying to fix it, I just . . . froze. I spent over a year frozen." He shrugged. "Bad choices and fucked-up decisions. That's me."

She stiffened. "You were hurt, and you reacted. You were in an unhealthy situation in more ways than one, and you panicked and cleansed everything with fire. Don't dismiss your emotions and your self-protection as just a fucked-up decision. Don't reduce something so complex and real and important to nothing."

That sudden, unexpected stream of words was delivered with Chloe's typical crisp precision and calm certainty, as if she couldn't possibly be wrong. Maybe that was why the words didn't *feel* wrong. They weren't what he'd believed for so long, and yet, somehow they sounded just right. Like he was only human and his mistakes could be excused. Like a few fuck-ups didn't make *him* a fuck-up.

Like maybe he should forgive himself for everything. And maybe he should trust himself again. He'd really like to trust himself again.

"Have you ever had any therapy?" she asked.

He cleared his throat, tried to focus on the conversation instead of his tangled thoughts. "I just started, actually."

"Good. Gigi says therapy is the most important medical service there is."

"Really?" he asked dryly. "So it's just, *Fuck antibiotics,* huh?"

"I didn't say she was right. Or wrong, for that matter." Chloe wriggled around until their eyes met, her hands rising to his shoulders. "I'm just emphasizing its importance. Now, here are some more things I'd like to emphasize." She leaned closer until their noses touched. "First of all: that fucker did not *make* you. She spotted you before anyone else, which was smart, and she sank her fangs into all your loveliness like a leech, which was disgusting. Second: I know you regret leaving everything behind, but that doesn't mean it was wrong, and that doesn't mean it can't be fixed. *You* can fix it. You will."

The way she said it, the sentiment came out as strong and natural as the forest around them. She stared at him so hard he was surprised she hadn't burned through her glasses. She seemed to think she could get the message into his skull through sheer force of will, and her will was pretty impressive.

He cleared his throat, tried to sound unaffected and missed the mark. "Anything else?"

Her expression became gentle, almost tender. "So much else. You always say such lovely things to me, Red. Do you say them to yourself?"

No. No, he didn't. It had never occurred to him that he should, not until recently.

"I'll say them," she murmured. "I'll tell you how incredibly clever you are, and how you're funny, and kind, and sweet, and a damned good artist. I don't understand how things work in creative circles, and I don't know how much *Pippa* actually did." She screwed up her face and spat out the name like it tasted nasty, which he enjoyed way more than he should have. "But no matter what she did or did not do for your career, no one can change the fact that you're talented. You're skilled. You're *good*."

He hadn't been sure about that for a long, long time, but things had changed these last weeks. He'd known they were changing. And now, when she said that out loud and he believed her without question, he realized things really had changed. It was done. Something in him had been knocked loose, back then, but somehow it had clicked back into place without him looking.

He was good.

His grin started in his toes. It was a warmth that rushed through every inch of him, a warmth he wanted to share with her because it was pure and so was she. He couldn't think of anything to say, of a way to explain what he felt right now—how free he was all of a sudden. So he showed her.

He sank his fingers into her hair, pulled her closer, and kissed her. She came to him so easily, like she knew this was where she belonged and how they should be: the two of them kissing in the cold, their bodies creating more heat between them than the fire just a few feet away. Above them the sky had long since tumbled into star-spotted night, and below them the earth was fresh and real like the way Chloe made him feel. Her cool hands pressed against his flushed cheeks and her lush mouth joined with his, and he loved her so much his heart felt too big for his body.

So this was bone-deep contentment. He'd almost forgotten, for a while.

CHAPTER TWENTY

Around Red, Chloe tended to talk a lot. But there was something about this kiss, this hungry, hopeful, heart-filled kiss, that pushed her gently into silence, like sliding underwater and blocking out all sounds from the outside world. He surrounded her now. He held her tight. Even when their lips parted, when his hands left her so he could put out the fire, when he unzipped the tent flap and sat back on his knees so she could crawl in first, he was still holding her somehow, deep inside in a way that soothed her. So she didn't speak. She couldn't. She was drowning in long-coming lust, and soon she'd be under him.

Lord, she couldn't wait to be under him.

Red crawled in after her, zipped up the tent's flap, and they were plunged into an odd almost-darkness that seemed other-worldly. She could make out the vague shape of him, those broad shoulders and the fall of his hair unmistakable even as shadowy outlines. And she had the oddest, deliciously heavy feeling that he was looking right at her.

But the feeling faded as he turned away, fiddling with something she couldn't see. After a moment, she heard a *click*—and then there was light. Chloe blinked as her eyes adjusted, then gawked as reality filtered in. Somehow, he'd wreathed strings of fairy lights all around the tent, glowing pinpricks that illuminated the small mountain of blankets and cushions.

She stared, awed. "Oh my goodness. This is what you were messing around with earlier?"

"When you were shouting at me to hurry up and feed you? Yeah." He winked. "Honestly, the things I put up with."

Her heart was a burning, brilliant thing lodged against her ribs. "Red, why did you do all this?"

"For you," he said, as though it was obvious. "It's always for you."

Camping had been on her list because it seemed gritty and normal and slightly scary and more than a bit of a challenge, but truthfully, she'd barely wanted to do it. Now, in this moment, she realized just how magical Red had made it. Not only by arranging everything, by making her laugh all day, by remembering her limitations so she didn't have to constantly point them out—but with things like this. Things like the marshmallows. The extra effort he put in to make this a wonderful experience instead of a checked box.

She looked up at him, his hair gleaming like silken flames, his beautiful face still flushed and his lower lip caught between his teeth, and she realized that his sharp eyes studied her with something like trepidation. As if he was nervous. As if he wanted to know that she liked it.

How could he doubt that she loved it? How could he doubt

that she loved *him*, that she wanted him and trusted him and hungered to do everything with him just for the joy of experiencing his reactions?

She was in love with Redford Morgan, and quite horribly, too. It smacked her over the head so hard she felt dizzy. She should be afraid, should want to hide it, but the knowledge lit her up until she felt just like the fairy lights, and hiding that would be something close to a sin.

But the feeling had come on too fast, surely, for him to feel the same, so she wouldn't blurt it out yet. Instead, she told him, "I adore you," and it was truer than her heartbeat.

He smiled, his worry easing in an instant as he crawled toward her, his proximity shrinking the already-cramped space. "Oh, do you?"

She couldn't believe she'd said something so emotional, so honest, but she also didn't want to take it back. She'd started all of this in order to be brave, and now, for the first time in a long time, she felt it. If she were to die tomorrow, she wouldn't have regrets anymore. "I do. I really, really do."

"You're not so bad yourself, Button." He pushed her back against the cushions and she laughed as she bounced a little on the blow-up mattress. But the laughter faded in her throat when Red lowered his body over hers, pressing her firmly into the blankets, grounding her and whipping her into a frenzy all at once. Her lips—and her legs—parted on a gasp. He kissed her jaw and whispered against her skin, "So. You gonna let me slide inside that pretty pussy tonight, Chlo?"

"Yes," she breathed, trying to arch up against him. But she

couldn't because there was no space between them in the first place, the hard planes of his body forced intimately against hers, her legs wrapping around his waist as if they were puzzle pieces slotted perfectly together.

"Good." He kissed, then licked, then sucked the base of her throat. She shivered at the hot, wet love, at the lust it stirred between her thighs, and wondered if he could tell her pulse was racing. He must be able to hear the way her breaths sped up and grew ragged, must feel her hips trying their best to rock against his. Her clit was already swollen and needy and desperate for a little more pressure, for sweet friction. He didn't provide it. Instead, both of his hands found both of hers and he twined their fingers together. Through their clothes, she could feel his hard cock wedged tight against her cleft—and yet, all he did was hold her hands.

"Red," she whispered.

He kissed her cheek, her temple, her nose. "Chloe."

"Not to ruin this very romantic moment, but would you possibly consider fucking me now?"

His laughter rumbled through his chest. "I've already considered it. Frequently."

"In that case, would you hurry up and *do* it?"

"Demanding, aren't you?" But without warning, he thrust his hips. The thick jut of his erection nudged her clit so beautifully that even with all the clothes separating them, pleasure ripped through her. She was gasping, her sight unfocused, her body already reaching a tipping point. That easily.

Oh, God.

"Baby," Red murmured with a smile in his voice. "You should've told me you were desperate."

She gritted her teeth. "Shut up."

"Are you sure that's what you want?" His lips brushed her ear, the glide of skin on skin hot and sensual. "You seem to come much faster when I remind you of how bad you want it."

"Red!"

"Chloe. Will you take your hair down for me?"

Even though it would wind up a mess in the morning? "Yes. Whatever. Just—"

"I know, I know. Just hurry up and fuck you. Come here." He rose up on his knees and she felt so suddenly cold and alone, she actually whined out loud. But then he pulled her up into a sitting position and said, "Hair."

Her hands rose obediently to undo her braid. But they froze when he yanked off his hoodie and T-shirt, her mind skittering to a stop at the sight of his bare torso. In the low, warm light, his fair skin was burnished pale gold. Shadows played over the lean lines of his body, the ridges of muscle. He flashed her that confident smile as he removed the rest of his clothes. "Now, Chloe. I know you're wearing twenty thousand layers of clothing and I'm pretty eager to get it all off, so if you could—"

"Okay," she blurted out, because when he spoke his hands stopped moving, which meant that the fabric covering his body stayed in place, which meant that she still couldn't see his cock. And she really, really wanted to see his cock, now, immediately, for what she abruptly realized would be the very first time. She unraveled her braid with suddenly rapid fingers, then started dragging her hoodie over her head. Next was her T-shirt, her undervest, her sports bra—God, that was a nightmare—

Holy shit, Red was naked.

She'd been yanking off her clothes, putting her glasses away, and cataloging everything she had to remove, and then she looked up, and there he was, just fucking naked. And glorious. Her mouth practically watered as her gaze dipped lower, taking in all of him, blurry as he was. His thighs were thick and muscular and dusted with fine golden hair, and as a definite leg girl she'd usually take her time enjoying them—except she could barely spare them a glance when his dick was right there, curving proudly up against his taut stomach. It was rigid, heavy, the swollen head flushed and glistening. She reached for it as if hypnotized, but he caught her wrist, holding her off with ease.

His voice more urgent than she'd ever heard it, he gritted out, "You. Clothes. Off." Then he grabbed the waistband of her tracksuit bottoms, the leggings underneath, and her underwear all in one go. How had he managed that? Was he a witch? The question flew out of her head when he pulled, easing the clinging layers of fabric off her. In the name of teamwork, she dealt with the vest she was still wearing, then started wrestling with her sports bra. Which, unfortunately, was not the most graceful thing she'd ever done.

But Red didn't seem to mind, possibly because it involved a lot of jiggling and bouncing around. In fact, by the time she yanked the bra off over her head, his labored breaths sounded more like growls and his eyes were glued to her like a tongue to treacle. He dragged the last of her clothes off of her ankles and then they were just two people sitting in a tiny, pillow-strewn, fairy-lit tent, staring at each others' naked bodies.

She liked what she saw.

He liked what he saw, too. She knew because she could see the frantic rise and fall of his chest, and because his high cheekbones were stained scarlet. His eyebrows were drawn in a fierce expression that sent a spiral of jittery desire through her nerve endings. He wrapped one big hand around the base of his dick and squeezed. "Chloe?"

"Yes?"

"I have this idea. I think—just hear me out, yeah?—I think that you should maybe consider being naked all the time. I mean, just, always. Think about it, okay?"

"I will," she said, and then, just to see what would happen, she ran her fingertips over her own chest, circling her nipples. "I'll definitely—"

She never managed to finish that sentence, because when she touched herself it was as if something in Red snapped. He lunged for her, but when he pushed her back onto the cushions he was gentle despite the wound-up tension she could feel vibrating through his body. And then his mouth was all over her, sucking at her breasts, licking at her throat, while his fingers went straight to her wet, aching pussy. He moaned when he felt how slick she was, the sound muffled against her breast. Then he shoved those wonderfully thick fingers inside her and she let out a moan of her own, a sharp, broken thing that was closer to a scream.

"Oh my God, Chloe." He said it again and again, rasping out

her name as he rubbed her swollen, sensitive depths. "Oh my fucking God, you feel so good. Fuck, I can't wait to be inside you."

"Hurry up then," she gasped, her hips jerking as he stroked that secret spot in her, the one that scattered stars across her vision and made her feel more limp and languorous with pleasure than any drug. "Oh, please, just hurry up."

"I want you to come first."

"Oh, for—"

He kissed her again, softly, until she released her lower lip from the cage of her teeth. And then he kissed her harder, hotter, wetter, his tongue thrusting in a bold, steady way that made her breathless. When his fingers started moving inside her again, they matched the rhythm of his tongue, fucking her in that deep, consuming, almost obscene way that drove her so damn wild.

He broke the kiss even as his thumb nudged her clit. When she moaned and arched into him, her body demanding more, he smiled. "Relax. We have all night."

"O-okay," she gasped out, her voice shaking. Her whole body was shaking, in fact, vibrating as coils of energy lashed around her, holding her hostage, driving her toward what felt like an explosion. "Sounds good."

He laughed darkly. "Yeah, baby. Sounds good. Good like these little moans you're giving me." He kissed her again, quick and hard and so hot she felt seared down to her soul. The thumb that had brushed her clit so delicately touched her again, firmer now, *deliciously* so. He circled the swollen bud and her whole body jerked as if electrocuted. So he did it again. And again.

Even when she dug her nails into the curve of his arse. Even when her breathy sighs turned into something like sobs. Even when she sank her teeth into his shoulder because she was just so fucking beside herself, didn't know what to do with all this swirling, swelling, pent-up sensation.

He didn't stop. He didn't even falter. Instead he told her she was gorgeous, falling apart for him, and that her pussy was going to kill him, and that she was so wet he could feel it dripping into his palm, and that he could do this forever just to feel her shaking under him—

And then she came so hard she couldn't hear him anymore, couldn't see him anymore, for a moment couldn't even feel him anymore. But God, she still knew he was there.

By the time Chloe's eyes opened and refocused on him, Red was about ten seconds and one touch away from coming. How could he not be? Jesus, just the sounds she made were enough to push him over the edge. He'd regret bringing all these damn lights if they hadn't made her so happy, because seeing her laid out naked in front of him was doing absolutely zero for his stamina.

She was gorgeous. She was just fucking gorgeous. The midnight storm of her thick, wavy hair spread around her face like a halo. Her naked skin looked so vulnerable in the low light, completely bare to him for the first time, and so delicate. She was soft, soft all over, from the gentle weight of her full breasts to the lush roundness of her belly to the sheer decadence of her hips, her thighs, her—fuck. He dug his short nails into the palms of his hand and dragged his gaze away from the plump, pouting lips of her cunt, but it didn't help. Without permission, his fingers rose to his lips and he sucked off her honey, groaning at the taste. So fucking good. Even better than he remembered.

"Oh, gosh," she said suddenly. She sounded worried. Why the fuck did she sound worried? "I bit you!"

Ah. He smiled and bent to kiss her little frown, his shoulder still stinging from her teeth. "I liked it."

"Really? Well, that's okay then. But still. I should've asked."

"You were busy." He kissed her again. *Busy coming on my fingers.* "But now you know. I like it."

She gave him an impish smile. "Hmm. Well, Red, you made me come, so if you're a man of your word you will now fuck me into oblivion."

He almost choked on his own tongue. The pressure building at the base of his spine got even worse. "Into oblivion, huh?"

"That's what I said. Get on with it."

Well, that was him told. He found the strip of condoms he'd packed, ripped one open, managed to roll it on with gritted teeth. Maybe she would've done it for him, and maybe that would've been hot as hell, but since he wanted to actually get inside her before he went off like a gunshot, he needed to keep touching to a minimum.

Of course, as soon as he thought that, she grabbed his hair and dragged him down, pressing all her soft, lush curves against his body. Her skin was hot and damp from the exertion of her orgasm. Her pussy was wet and open, ready for him, begging for

him as she spread her legs and reached down to grasp his erection. In his ear, she whispered, "Hard, please."

Oh, holy fucking fuck. "Chloe—"

"I mean it." She squeezed him, then positioned his shaft at
her entrance. His eyes rolled back into his head. He felt as if he'd
been burned in the best way, *branded*. Jesus. He grunted something that barely sounded human and thrust, the need uncontrollable, his body reduced to its most basic instincts. She was
so slick, she took him all at once, releasing a low moan that sent
shivers through his body.

When he was buried inside her, he held still for a moment,
sucking down air because he felt almost dizzy with pleasure,
running his hands over her thighs because he couldn't quite believe that he had her. He had Chloe Sophia Brown. And she was
fucking glorious.

She rolled her hips beneath him, and he gasped out her name.
She bit him again, at the base of his throat this time, and he
almost came on the spot. Then she slid her fingers into his hair
and dragged him down for a kiss that stripped him to the bone,
that destroyed him from the inside out, her sweet little tongue
tasting him with shameless greed, her lush mouth frantic. And
she whispered, "Please."

He grasped her soft hips, buried his face against her shoulder,
and fucked her. Each thrust was slow, hard, deliberate, wringing
gasps and then whimpers and then long, rolling moans from
her. He gritted his teeth as his orgasm came barreling at him like
a freight train. It would be so fucking good, but he didn't want
this to end. It couldn't end. Being inside her was undoing him,

taking him apart and putting him back together differently, better, more himself than he'd ever been before. So he forced himself to hold off and gave her what she wanted, what she begged for: more of his dick, more of him.

But when she came again, shuddering beneath him, her hot pussy fluttering around him, he couldn't stop his release. With a growl, he thrust wildly, once, twice—and then everything around him shattered until it was all just colors and light, colors and light.

Neither of them moved for a good, long while, but eventually he had to get up. Had to do something with the condom. Luckily, he'd planned for that, too. When he finished and was relatively cleaned up, he lay back down beside her and gathered her against him, pressing a kiss to her head.

"Would you do something for me?" he asked.

She said, her voice sleepy, "I would do anything for you."

The words struck him like an arrow to the chest. Like she'd just loved him out loud. Like she wanted him the way he wanted her: completely and impossibly and with ill-advised devotion. Happiness bloomed inside him like a garden. He held her tighter and continued, "If you can't sleep tonight, I want you to wake me up. Okay?"

She didn't reply. She was already asleep.

Red packed up the next day with a silly smile on his face—one he was happy to see reflected on Chloe's. Those smiles somehow remained throughout the day, despite Chloe's morning joint pain, and the argument they had over which road was the A46 on the way home. Her sense of direction—or lack of—was the ninth wonder of the world, after King Kong. He understood now why she rarely used her car.

"You really do need me around," he said with barely hidden satisfaction, his urge to be useful fulfilled. "For camping and map reading and all that shit."

"I don't need you around," she said pertly. "Not for directions, and not even for the list, as I've come to realize." But then her gaze flitted to his and her lips tilted a little. "I just really, really *want* you around."

His grin was a mile wide.

They got home at lunchtime, and he knew he was supposed to go to his own flat and give her space and all that crap, but she was a bit wobbly and sleepy-eyed. He wanted to feed her and put her to bed, so he bullied his way into her flat. He cooked. He made her eat. He supervised her shower much more closely than usual, and found another use for the cute little plastic seat she had in there.

But eventually, *finally,* the heady mix of love and lust that was powering his cock like the greatest battery on earth calmed down, and Chloe's energy levels dipped at around the same time. So they found themselves back in bed, still slightly damp, in a cocoon of warm, naked skin and pounding hearts and soft, searching mouths, and he thought he'd never felt so purely, completely *good* in his whole damn life.

She trailed a finger over his chest, then pressed a kiss to his heart. "I rather like you, Redford."

He tried to turn his grin into a groan. "No one says my full name as much as you do, you know. You throw it around like rice at a wedding."

"Weddings on the mind, hm?" she asked in that familiar, mocking tone. "Clearly I am excellent in bed."

Usually, he'd snicker and shoot something back and they'd snipe at each other for a while. But the truth was, he did have weddings on the mind, if that meant that he absolutely planned to marry her arse at some point in the not-too-distant future. And the fact that he even knew that made him feel so weirdly vulnerable, all he could do was mutter something vaguely belligerent and curse his heating skin.

She pulled back, looking delighted and also ready to rib him until the day they died. "Red! You're *blushing*. Why are you blushing? Oh, *do* tell me—"

"Shut up, woman." He sat up and kissed her pretty mouth quiet, and she leaned into him with a sweet little hum.

Then came a knock at the door that had them both jumping out of their skin. Their bare skin. Which was a problem because, a second later, they heard the rattle of a key in the lock.

"Ack," Chloe yelped, and leapt off the bed with an agility he had literally never, ever seen from her. She winced at the movement—he didn't care what she said or what fancy medicine patches she put on, she was definitely hurting after yesterday— then grabbed frantically for some clothes.

"Who is it?" he whispered, sitting up and looking around for—oh, hell. His dirty clothes were stuffed in Chloe's washing machine, which she seemed to use as a wash basket. His bags were in the living room, which he couldn't get to without running through the hall, balls swaying in the breeze for whoever just came in to see. Looked like he was stuck in here with his own bare backside and Chloe's several thousand notebooks. Maybe he could use those to cover his junk if anyone burst into the room.

Or you could use the fucking sheets, genius.

Oh yeah. Chloe's panic was catching.

"I don't know who it is," she told him, hopping around as she stabbed her legs into a pair of pajama pants. "But the options are either my parents—"

Crap.

"Or my sisters."

Fingers crossed for that option. This wasn't quite how he wanted to meet Chloe's mum and dad. Ideally, he'd be, at a bare minimum, *clothed* for that introduction.

"Chlo!" a cheery voice hollered from the hallway. "It's us! Hope you're not dead!"

Everything about Chloe relaxed as she shoved on a pajama top. "Eve," she said with obvious relief. "And—"

"I *know* you're not dead," called another, eerily similar voice. He realized with a jolt that all three of the sisters sounded almost identical. He'd never noticed before. "I'd feel it if you died, darling. Which means you're ignoring us, you bitch."

"Annnnd Dani," Chloe finished, rolling her eyes. But then

she looked a little shamefaced. "Gosh, I was so distracted preparing for our, um, trip, I haven't texted them in two days. Maybe three." She frowned, grabbed her glasses from the bedside table, and told him, "I won't be a moment." But then she hesitated, turned back to face him, bit her lip. Raising her voice, she called to her sisters, "I'm fine! Just . . . give me a minute!" And then, to Red, she whispered, "Would you like to come?"

He looked down at himself. "I'm naked."

"Oh, yes." She blinked.

"But thanks, love. Really." He knew what she was doing. The last time she'd tried to ignore his existence in front of a family member, he *may* have been mildly offended. But this was different. He already knew Chloe would hate to even hint at the fact that she now had a sex life, no matter who it was with.

"All right," she said softly. "In that case, stay quiet!"

Before he could reply, she hurried out, pulling the door almost shut behind her. Because, he realized with a quiet laugh, his awkward, uptight Button was going to try and keep his presence a secret. Even though his shit was lying all over her flat for anyone to see.

She was adorable.

Shaking his head, he got out of bed and stretched his tired muscles. He was just wondering how to occupy himself in the bedroom of a woman who regularly used phrases like *sleep hygiene* when a voice drifted in from the hall. Even though it was technically indistinguishable from Chloe's, he knew it didn't belong to her. If he had to guess, he'd say it was Dani. ". . . isn't a particularly believable explanation, sister mine. I do believe you're up to something." She managed to make the phrase as darkly ominous as Professor Snape.

"What could I possibly be up to?" Chloe asked, sounding almost bored, but not quite pulling it off. The fact that she was even trying made a laugh bubble up in his throat.

A third voice piped up. "I really couldn't say, but I will point out that it's catatonically impossible to believe—"

"*Categorically,* darling."

"—that you went camping alone. Not even because of your fibro; we simply weren't made for the outdoors. And you don't look traumatized enough to have spent the night in a tent."

Chloe replied with a thread of fondness in her voice that wrapped around him like silk. "It was a very, *very* nice tent. A wonderful tent. I will be leaving a five-star review online."

Oh, he bet she would.

"Hmmm," someone murmured—he couldn't tell who. And then, "Do the tent's wonderful qualities have anything to do with the massive pair of men's boots by your front door?"

"Oh, those are—ah—I'm sorry, I don't see—"

He cracked a grin as Chloe spluttered.

"I knew it!" someone cried. "You—"

"Be quiet! He'll hear you!"

"He's *here*?"

"Shut up!"

The conversation dissolved into a chorus of whisper-shrieks. He tried not to eavesdrop, but the walls were bloody thin, and Chloe's voice was impossible to ignore. Still, he tried. But then he heard a murmur, sharp with amusement, that shattered all his good intentions.

"Maybe I'll owe you fifty pounds after all, Evie-bean. Meaningless sex and camping were the two items I didn't think she'd manage to cross off."

Red frowned. Meaningless sex? That wasn't on the list.

Then, slow as the blood draining from his face, he remembered: the list he'd seen was incomplete. But, clearly, Chloe had shown her sisters the real thing.

A strange ringing sound filled his ears. His stomach tightened, as if a pound of lead suddenly lined his gut. Was he—did Chloe—?

No. No. He wasn't going to assume the worst based on an overheard, throwaway comment. How could he? Chloe wasn't like that. He loved her. And she might not love him yet, but she couldn't treat him the way she did—couldn't be so sweet—if she secretly saw him as . . .

Nothing. No one. That's who you are.

Panic crept over Red's skin, slimy and cold. He dragged a hand roughly through his hair, searched for an anchor, and found one: the sticky note he'd left Chloe on Friday morning, now taped to her desk. *Taped*, like she loved it, like it was there to stay. He focused on that sight as he grabbed his crawling, anxious memories by the throat. He wasn't nothing, not to Chloe or anyone else who mattered, and definitely not to himself.

And then, as if to back him up, he heard her voice. "Meaningless sex is off the list."

"You mean you changed it?"

"I did."

His exhale was a rush of dizzy relief. He sagged against the bed as his numb limbs tingled back to life.

"I think that should affect the terms of the bet. She's making it easier for herself."

Chloe snorted. "I am not!"

"Fewer items is easier."

"I replaced it," Chloe said hotly. "I put Red on there."

Something strange happened then. His organs just . . . just up and rearranged themselves. Shifted around like they were trying to make room at a full table. His heart was in his stomach. His stomach was lodged in his throat. His skin was tight, like it wanted to turn inside out. His eyes burned. His limbs went numb again. The ringing sound was back. His right hand ached. He couldn't breathe.

That was a bad fucking sign, wasn't it? He forced himself to inhale, gulping down air, but he barely felt it in his lungs and his head was light. The kaleidoscope of color that had surrounded him since last night leeched away until his world was gray. He was panicking and he needed to stop but he couldn't. Fucking. Breathe. He clutched the bedsheets to remind himself of where he was, but all he felt was naked and ridiculous and fooled a-fucking-gain—

"It can't be what it sounds like," he murmured to himself, because his brain was rebelling but his mouth was still his.

Then his mind showed him a memory, like a convenient flashback in a badly made film: that first ride on his bike, with Chloe. Back when she'd mentioned her plan to get a life, and he'd assumed it was some kind of bad-girl bucket list. That she was chasing a thrill and trying to slum it, the same way Pippa would.

Only, Chloe was nothing like Pippa. *Nothing* like Pippa. There was no way she'd use him just to feel alive again. No way she'd see him as an item to cross off a list.

. . . Or a specimen to study through a window.

Fuck.

CHAPTER TWENTY-ONE

After far too long, Chloe's sisters took pity on her and left her to her "obvious sex fest." Her cheeks were still burning when she finally returned to the bedroom. "Sorry about that," she said. "They—Red, are you okay?"

He didn't look okay.

He was sitting on the edge of her bed, his fingers white-knuckling the sheets, his chest heaving with each breath. His eyes were flat and lifeless. He stared at the plain, gray carpet with a focus so intense, she wondered if he could see things she didn't.

That focus didn't waver when he replied, his voice rough and uneven. "Yeah."

The single word wrenched at something deep in her chest. He sounded wrong, wrong, wrong. "Are you sure? You seem—"

He stood, sharper than a knife. "I need some clothes."

Anxiety churned in Chloe's gut. Her skin prickled hot and cold all over. Something was going on, and she needed to find out what, but she couldn't ask right now—not when he strode to the living room as if it was an effort not to run. He was upset, and he wanted to get dressed so they could discuss the problem like reasonable adults. That was all. *Obviously* that was all. She told herself that to stave off the old, terrifying panic that rose as he dragged on his clothes. His movements were jerky and desperate and frantic.

As if he couldn't wait to leave.

No, she corrected herself. As if he couldn't wait to have a lovely, mature conversation with her.

But when he was dressed, he picked up his bags. Her heart lurched. Just like the night they'd bumped into Aunt Mary, he seemed to be surrounded by invisible spikes, warding off all tenderness with the set of his shoulders and the muscle ticking at his jaw. But she didn't care. She reached for him anyway. "Red—"

He jerked away from her outstretched hand as if she was toxic.

They stood in silence for a moment, wide-eyed and tense. Soaking in the aftermath of that near-automatic rejection. Then he blinked hard, seemed to pull himself together. Avoiding her gaze, he bit out, "Is it true? Am I on your list?"

Oh, God. He'd heard. That's what this was about. Mortification hit her like a bullet, ripping through flesh and blood and bone to decimate her composure. He knew how much the list meant to her. Maybe he thought she was pathetic, and clingy, and all the other things Henry had called her before he'd left. But that didn't sound right. That didn't sound like Red, so what could be the problem?

"Chloe," he said, tightly leashed anger singeing his words. "Answer me."

She might be confused, but she wasn't going to lie. "Yes." His face shut down like his power had been cut. Suddenly, he was a cold, distant stranger, and she didn't understand. "Why are you so upset?"

Just like that, he wasn't blank anymore. A sort of horrified rage filled him, clear in the flat blade of his mouth and his empty gaze. It even brimmed from his voice. "Are you seriously doing this?" he asked. "What, are you trying to say I'm overreacting?"

"No," she said immediately. "Absolutely not." Her mind raced. Things were becoming clearer, but she didn't know how to fix this tangle sensitively, so she went with plain facts. Obviously, he thought his presence on the list meant something awful. She could explain otherwise. She just had to be patient. "Just calm down, okay? Being on the list isn't a bad thing."

Disbelief joined his fury, like kerosene to a flame. He spoke rapidly, his whole body shaking. "*Calm down*? *It's not a bad thing*? I'm not an idiot, Chloe. This whole time, I was—and you were just using me for your fucking—ticking boxes and laughing with your sisters about—"

"I would never do that and you know it!" she snapped, panic sharpening her breaths. "Red, listen to me. I put you on the list because you're important."

He dragged his hands through his hair so hard she knew it must have hurt. "Important like doing something bad?" he rasped, his tone harsh and mocking. "Didn't you use me for that, too? And I thought it was fucking *cute*."

She stiffened. "You don't understand—"

His shout was ragged, ripped from his chest, a mix of anger

and pain that burned her like acid. "Don't tell me I don't fucking understand. You will *not* make a fool out of me!"

A strained silence fell. He looked as shocked by his outburst as she felt. But the hollow emptiness between them birthed a desperate idea: she couldn't make him trust her, not when he was so obviously spiraling, but she could *show* him the truth—if only he'd give her a chance. She'd find proof, find the list, and he'd come back to her and stop shaking, stop shouting, stop looking at her like she was someone else.

She'd never wanted to strangle anyone as much as she wanted to strangle a stranger named Pippa right now.

"Just wait," she said. "I'll show you." She bent over the coffee table, rifling through rubble and paper and countless notebooks, searching for *the* notebook, the one that would fix everything.

He heaved out a breath. Made a sound like cracking glass that might have been a laugh—a broken, broken laugh. "Yeah, I bet. You'll search for some kind of evidence that'll prove you aren't a manipulative, lying user, only you won't be able to find it. But oh, shit, if only you could. Right?" He didn't sound angry anymore. He sounded tired. Bone-deep, dog tired. "Just stop, Chlo. You got me. It's done. So tick me off the list and I'll pretend I never fucking met you. Good riddance." He turned and strode out of the room.

No, no, no.

She stood for a moment, stricken, unable to speak, or think properly, or even take a decent breath. Those words whipped at her heart and carved deeper lacerations than they should. She tried to remind herself that it was all a misunderstanding, that this was what Dani would call him being *triggered*.

But her demons howled louder: *He's leaving you.*

Once upon a time, Chloe had promised herself that she would never chase anyone who wanted to leave. She would never allow abandonment, desperation, *love* to make a fool of her. But her feet moved without permission, slowly at first, then faster, until she was stumbling over stray boxes and leaning against the walls for balance, righting herself with vicious determination. By the time she caught him, he was standing in the open doorway, his back to her. On the threshold.

Wasn't this always how it ended?

But he didn't move. He didn't take the last step. His muscles were tense, as if frozen. He seemed to vibrate with something that might have been rage or regret or indecision.

Hope flared inside her, sharp and dangerous and impossible to resist. "Trust me. Just trust me."

He didn't turn around. "I don't think I can."

She clamped her molars together so hard, she swore she heard one crack. A lump of painful pride, acid and sawdust and heavy concrete, formed at the back of her throat. Chloe tried to swallow it and failed. She tried to believe he wouldn't do this—wouldn't walk out on her just like that, wouldn't refuse to hear her out for even a second—and failed.

When she spoke again, her voice was panicked and fearful and she hated herself for it. No. *No.* She hated *him* for it, hated him for proving her every anxiety right. Surely he wouldn't prove them right. "Red. Don't."

Silence. Silence that burned.

"If you can leave this easily," she said, desperate, "don't fucking come back."

The slam of the door shook her bones.

She broke.

As soon as Red stepped out into the corridor, something forced his mind back into his body. For the last ten minutes he'd been distant, detached, floating above himself like a ghost. Watching himself lose it. Feeling the echo of his own pain as if it belonged to someone else. Now he felt it firsthand, as if God had just punched him in the gut.

The walls of Chloe's flat had been slowly closing in, her beautiful, heartbroken gaze had suffocated him, but now he was out and free and drained and weak. He leaned back against her door, unable to take another step, and sank slowly to the floor. His world was a haze of bright white melting into blood red, but when he pressed his palms flat against the cold linoleum, the shock of it helped him focus. His mouth was numb, as if it belonged to someone else. His tongue tasted coppery, like blood. His skin was sweat-soaked and clammy and he hadn't even noticed.

He was afraid. He realized it all at once, both surprised and resigned. He was afraid, and it made him angry, like a rabid fucking animal gnawing at its own trapped foot. But the thought was jarring, and he found himself frowning, correcting the negativity. *I am not an animal.* Then he said it aloud, because Dr. Maddox was always harping on about mindfulness and mantras. "I am not an animal," he whispered, his voice disappearing like smoke. "I am not an animal."

What came next? He told himself positive things, and he . . . he found something to focus on. That was it. Red chose the first thing his eyes fell on: the door to the flat opposite Chloe's, which had a scuff mark he'd need to paint over. Yeah. He stared at the black mark against the red wood and repeated his words like a prayer. That door better not fucking open, because he was in no shape to talk to tenants right now. Or to anyone. He sat with himself for a while.

"Okay," he finally murmured. "Okay, Red. What just happened?"

Chloe had manipulated him, that was what. She'd manipulated him just like Pippa had. Except the thought that had seemed so reasonable five minutes ago now felt absolutely ridiculous, because Chloe was nothing like Pippa. And he knew that belief was his own, because he'd thought it a thousand times before. This wasn't like his last relationship. No one was messing with his head.

The iron band around his chest eased a bit.

He cradled his right hand in his left and rubbed his aching scar. His head ached, too. Words settled in his mind like barbed wire, ripping into everything they touched. *I'll pretend I never fucking met you. Good riddance.*

He'd said that. It already felt like a dream, or a nightmare, but no—it had been him. The words had felt wrong in his mouth and they felt wrong in his memory. Then they swirled, twisted, transformed. He heard Chloe as if for the first time: *I put you on the list because you're important.*

When she'd told him that, it had sounded like bullshit. Like the kind of nonsensical excuse Pippa always managed to dredge up, except Chloe wasn't Pippa Chloe wasn't Pippa Chloe wasn't Pippa—and she'd told him it was a misunderstanding. Not like, *You're too stupid to understand,* even if he'd heard it that way at the time. No; she'd been begging him to give her a fucking chance. She'd told him to wait. She might have told him the truth. And he'd left. He'd treated her like shit and he'd left.

He let his head fall back to hit the door. Fuck, fuck, fuck. "Chloe?" he called, his voice hoarse, his hands twisting nervously together.

There was a pause that lasted a lifetime. Then her voice came through the door, thick with tears. "What do you want?"

His heart broke. It just fucking broke. How could he ever have thought that she would—? But he remembered exactly how. Remembered the desperate grip of panic that had choked his logical thoughts and dredged up remembered, toxic emotions. Now he just had to explain it to her, had to fix his monumental fuck-up.

Because whatever he'd overheard, whatever he'd believed, he knew Chloe wasn't using him. He knew.

"Shit," he said. Then, because it made him feel slightly better, he said it again. "Shit. I'm sorry, Button. I—I lost it."

He heard some faint sniffing, but her voice came back stronger this time, threaded with iron. "I noticed."

"Oh my God, Chlo. I'm a dick. I'm such a dick."

"Yes, you fucking are."

The fact that she was even talking to him filled him with hope. Golden and glowing, it sloshed uneasily in his stomach, mixing with the bitter aftertaste of his fear. He felt nauseous. Ignored it. "Can I come in? Can we talk?"

Her answer was immediate. "No."

He wasn't surprised. He remembered, vividly, what she'd said to him, muffled beneath the ringing in his ears. *If you can leave this easily, don't fucking come back.* He could tell her the truth—that it hadn't been easy at all, that it had been his only option, that he'd wanted to turn around and touch her but he'd been so fucking afraid—only he didn't think that would fix things. Because as far as Chloe was concerned, he'd just left.

The full impact of that fact hit him hard enough to rattle his teeth. He'd left.

"Chloe," he said, the word shaking with all his desperation, all his regret. He closed his eyes and threaded his hands through his hair. "I don't know what happened. No, I do. I fucked up, and I'm sorry. I panicked and I couldn't think but—"

"I know," she said, interrupting him. For a second, his heart gave a tentative little hop. But then she continued. "I know, Red. I understand. I really do. But . . . but I don't think we should see each other anymore."

Just like that, he truly understood the word *devastation*. He was the earth after a monumental asteroid, knocked off his axis, burned and choked and twisted into a wasteland. "Chloe, no. Please. I'm trying—"

"It's not because of you," she said firmly. Which couldn't

possibly be right, only . . . only, she sounded so sure. So calm. So in control, as if the tears he'd heard a moment ago had been imaginary. "It's me," she said. "I can't do this. Because we're only human, and I'll stumble, or you will, and it'll hurt just like this, and I can't. I *can't*. I should've known I wasn't ready for this. When you walked out . . ." She sucked in a breath so hard, he actually heard it. That breath painted a picture for him: Chloe, her lovely face streaked with tears he'd caused, her soft mouth rolled into a hard line to stop herself from sobbing. The thought caused him actual, physical pain. His hands ached, not because of his scar but because they needed to touch her.

But she didn't want his touch anymore.

"When you walked out," she said, composed now, "it felt like I was breaking."

Red officially knew the feeling. "Baby."

She kept going, the words marching out like well-trained soldiers. "No one should be able to make me feel like that. No one should have that power. It's not . . . safe."

A cold hand cradled the back of his skull, long, icy fingers flooding his nervous system until his whole body felt numb. She was shutting down again, because of him. He couldn't bear it. He refused to be the reason someone so brave went back into hibernation. "Chloe, listen to me. I've got issues coming out my arsehole but that has nothing to do with you. You did nothing wrong. Even if you don't—if you don't want me anymore, that doesn't mean you should give up on everyone. On feeling things for people. On risks."

Silence.

"Chloe, are you there?"

Nothing. Panic filled him like flames devouring a forest, an unstoppable destruction.

"Chloe, please. I'm sorry. I'm so fucking sorry. You can trust me. You can trust yourself. If you just give me time—I'm working on this. I can be better."

That, finally, garnered a response. Her voice was so gentle, but every word cut him deep. "You don't need to be better, Red, not for me. Never. *I* should be better for you. For *this*. It's been . . . perfect," she said, so softly he almost missed the word. "But now it's over. All right?"

For the first time, he turned around, abandoning the scuff mark that had anchored him. He faced the door he'd been leaning on, the door that hid Chloe, and said, "No." Because it wasn't all right at all.

"I'm going, all right?"

"No." And then, finally, his desperate mind settled on a solution. A possibility. A hope. "I can show you," he said. "I can show you that this is worth it. That you don't need to be afraid because even when I fuck up I'll make it better."

"Red—"

"You are *perfect* for me, Chloe," he said, determination stiffening his spine, strengthening his voice. Finally, his real self returned. He stepped into his confidence like a well-worn leather jacket. "I know you and I want you and I need you. We can do this. I'll prove it to you."

"You can't, Red." Her voice shook on his name. "This isn't . . . Relationships aren't supposed to hurt."

"Life hurts," he said fiercely. "It's unavoidable. But I know the difference between torture and growing pains."

She didn't reply. She'd probably walked away, fed up with him rambling like a fanatic, but that was okay. He was okay. He'd made his decision and he'd stick by it: she meant too much for him to let things end like this. Maybe they'd end anyway, no matter what he did, and he'd have to come to terms with that— but not before he'd tried to fix things. Not before he'd done everything he could to earn her trust. To prove that he was there to stay, to show her he was working on himself. For her. Whatever it took.

He stared at her door for a moment longer, pretending she was still on the other side. He told her absence a secret: "I love you."

Then he left. It was time to prove it.

CHAPTER TWENTY-TWO

Chloe wanted to believe that Red's whispered *I love you* had been simple desperation—another last-ditch attempt to change her mind, to fix everything that had just shattered between them. But the thing was, if she hadn't been pressed against the door, listening to him as her stung heart held her back, she wouldn't have heard it at all.

Had he meant it? Was it real? Maybe it didn't matter either way. Because no matter what he felt, no matter what *she* felt, he'd still ripped her open and shattered her insides just by walking out the door.

No one should be able to do that to her. Not like that. Not anymore.

So Chloe didn't allow herself to cry when he was gone. Instead, she got to work.

Her body stiff and robotic, her physical pain at the very back of her mind, she sat down at her desktop computer, grim-faced, to finish his website. She would tie up every loose end there was between them, and then . . . then, she would wait until the end of her lease and move out. She'd be the one to disappear on him. For the first time, she'd be Chloe Badass Brown who walked away from all the dangerous emotional tangles that threatened her.

The thought brought a vicious smile to her face, but it wasn't the kind of smile that made things better. If anything, it made her feel worse.

It took hours to finish the site. By the time she was done, her stomach cramped violently with hunger, her knuckles screamed with the agony of overuse, and her rigid, aching back brought tears to her eyes. She was hurting herself and she knew it, but she didn't have room to regret it. As she fired off her last email to Red, the only thing she could feel was relief.

She'd be so much better after this was done. After she brought all these messy feelings, this imperfect, uncontrollable connection, to an end.

She kept the email short.

Red,

Your website is complete and ready to go live. I've attached all the information and instructions needed. Please remember to change your administrative passwords in order to remove my access.

Chloe

There. She waited for the pain to fade. Instead, it doubled, a thought hitting her hard: What if Red hurt like this, too? What if he was lost and struggling, still shaken by his earlier loss of control? What if he needed her and she'd turned away?

Chloe shut down her computer with a sharp *click* of the mouse, and cut off each treacherous mental question just as firmly. It didn't matter. It didn't matter. This was for the best.

She hoped.

She saw the notice the next day, on the building's bulletin board. She almost dropped the post she'd come to pick up.

Superintendent Redford Morgan was leaving next month.

The words were like a fist to the gut. She'd been trying so hard not to remember his words through the door, promises she couldn't bring herself to believe. So much for that. But she was glad—definitely glad—that he'd decided to listen to her and move on. Good for him. Good for her. Good for them both.

Chloe was shaky and distracted all the way back to her flat. Her thoughts were so busy, she almost didn't notice the cardboard box waiting on her doorstep. She kicked it, in fact, the toe of her shoe bouncing off it as she went to put her key in the door. And somehow, the moment she saw it, she knew it was from Red.

After all, it couldn't be anything she'd ordered—in spite of her mild dependency on internet shopping—because it was sitting right outside her front door, rather than in the post room. It had no address, either: just a word scrawled on top in black. She told herself it was some kind of care package from her parents, because they'd been known to do things like this. She could imagine her dad chuckling to himself as he left it by the door.

But then she bent to pick it up and read the word scrawled on the box: *Button*.

She felt like a sack of useless bones after yesterday's exertions, so she dragged the box into the hall rather than trying to pick it up. Then, once safely inside, she sat on the floor and stared at it and tried not to feel anything at all. It didn't work. There was a hole in her chest the size of a lovestruck heart. This must be some sort of good-bye.

Good. The quicker he left, the quicker she'd never have to feel this way again.

Inside the box she found a notebook, its cover a beautiful iridescent gold. She opened it to the first page, saw lines and lines of Red's distinctive scrawl, and slammed it shut as if she'd come across the devil's Bible.

She should open it. Should read his good-bye, which doubtless included many apologies and would only confirm the very reasonable conclusion she'd drawn: that relationships were just too risky, and they'd both been fools to try. That she needed to be alone, because it was safer. After all, if she'd been alone these past weeks, she wouldn't have spent last night sobbing until she lost her voice. Wouldn't have had a reason to.

Chloe put a hand to her raw throat and reminded herself that he'd left, and he'd do it again, and it wasn't worth the risk, and she never should've bothered with a man anyway, not after she'd been so comfortable without one for years.

And yet, she still couldn't open the book.

She set it aside with the same care one might use to move a poisonous snake. There were more things in the box, hidden by a layer of tissue paper. She ripped it away to find he'd sent her favorite chocolate. Green & Black's sea salt. Not in a fancy hamper like the ones she knew they offered online, either—just slab after slab of the stuff, as if he'd walked into a shop and bought out all their stock like a loon. The bright blue bars tugged at her heart for precisely 0.002 seconds before she steeled herself against them. This was a good-bye present. Nothing that should make her wistful or hopeful or regretful.

She put the chocolate on her coffee table so it was within reach while she worked. No use wasting it.

The next day, another box arrived, significantly smaller than the first. This time, she was thoroughly confused. It was from Red, there was no doubt of that, but what else could he possibly need to give her? It turned out to be a jar, one with tiny gold stars embedded in the glass. They twinkled when she held it up to the light, and for a second all she could think about was that night in the woods, stars in the sky, little spots of light inside their tent.

And him. Red.

The jar contained a trio of the hair ties she liked, the soft fabric ones that didn't snag. She huffed out a laugh as she realized what he was trying to do; she never knew where her hair ties were, unless they were on her head. So he wanted her to keep them in a jar. But, she reminded herself, pushing the smile off her face, jars weren't any use to her. Between her fibromyalgia and the amount she used her hands for work, the strength in her wrists and fingers was usually zero. It was a rare and blessed day when Chloe Brown could open a jar.

She was about to put it back in the box when she realized that it didn't actually have a lid. Or rather, not a lid that resembled anything she'd ever seen. There was an odd, transparent-looking bubble thing around the opening, and she prodded it tentatively. It gave under her touch. She pushed just a little bit harder. And then her hand was in the jar.

She stared in amazement, her eyes catching up with what her nerve endings were trying to tell her. There was a circular band of cushioning around the jar's rim that ballooned up to "close" it, but shrank back under pressure to let her hand in.

Maybe chocolate and a letter she refused to read could be taken as a good-bye, but this, she didn't know how to take. This was something you gave someone to show them . . .

To show them you cared. Or that you loved.

Maybe she should read the note. Maybe it wouldn't be a good-bye after all. Maybe it would be sheer magic on a sheet of paper, and it would say exactly the right thing—the thing she couldn't even define, the thing she didn't know existed. The thing that would erase all the hurt she'd felt and make her brave enough to do this again.

And maybe she'd run a marathon tomorrow. But she wouldn't bet her life on that, now, would she? So she steeled herself against her heart's fanciful interpretations, and she put the jar beside the chocolate, and she absolutely refused to open the book.

Days passed and more gifts came.

Boxes of her favorite fruit and herbal teas. A little stuffed cat that looked so like Smudge, she might possibly have cried just the tiniest bit when she saw it. And maybe, perhaps, sometimes, she slept with it beside her. But that didn't matter, because there were no witnesses.

Next was a guide to New York City, light enough for her to carry, that gave directions using major landmarks and street signs instead of maps. Then there was a tiny, plastic pink chair, studded with little diamantés, that she realized on a bark of laughter was supposed to be Madame Chair. It was followed by a bag of marshmallows, accompanied by a handwritten recipe describing how to roast them with an oven. She could tell he'd tried to be neat with his rounded block capitals, but there was a smudge of sunset-orange paint on the back of the thick, creamy paper that made her smile. He'd drawn goofy little cartoon pictures next to each instruction.

She missed him. She missed him so much that she was starting to hate him.

She found the gold notebook and held it in her hands and tried to make herself open it. She knew it wasn't a good-bye. It was almost certainly an apology, an explanation that he'd panicked.

The problem was, Chloe had panicked that day, too, and she hadn't stopped ever since. Dragging herself out of this confusing, teary fog of fear didn't feel impossible, but it did feel daunting. As if she might not manage it alone. As if she might get lost in the dark. She could only think of one person who could shine a light on her murky thoughts.

She put the notebook down and grabbed her coat.

Gigi's attic yoga studio was warm enough to make Chloe slightly drowsy, as was the low, gentle music and the smooth hum of the instructor's voice. "Breathe in for me . . . and out. In . . . and out . . ."

Chloe found herself following those instructions as she waited awkwardly on a beanbag for the class of one to finish. She hadn't realized what a jittery mess she was until she'd gotten in the car to drive over here. She'd ended up calling a taxi instead.

"One more time . . ." the soothing voice said. It came from Shivani, a depressingly happy, confident, and glowing woman in her midfifties who swanned about in sports bras and leggings and did inhuman things with her spine. Not ripping-it-out-and-beating-aliens-with-it type inhuman things, though. More like particularly impressive bow poses. She stood at the front of the room, opposite Gigi, who was also wearing a sports bra and leggings and had, beneath her fine, crepey skin, better abs than any of her granddaughters. *Sigh.*

The class wound down. Gigi and Shivani chuckled softly to each other as if their mutual flexibility, fitness, and, presumably, inner peace were some sort of hilarious inside joke. Then they hugged for several long, sweaty moments, murmuring things in each other's ears. If Chloe allowed herself to think about it for more than five seconds at a time, she would have to accept that Gigi was 100 percent banging her yoga instructor and had been for about the last seven years, which was why Chloe did not allow herself to think about it for more than five seconds at a time.

"I'll see you later, Chloe, love!" Shivani called out as she left. She wasn't leaving the *house,* of course. No, she was just going downstairs to give Chloe and Gigi some privacy, and also to start Gigi's wheatgrass, chocolate, and Baileys smoothie, the perfect predinner tipple. Apparently.

"*So,* darling," Gigi purred, producing an electric blue silk wrap from thin air and slipping gracefully into it. She came over to the beanbags where Chloe had been waiting patiently for the past half hour. Or, to be truthful, where she'd been waiting sullenly and with a slightly frantic air. "To *what* do I owe the honor of this visit?"

"I just thought I'd pop by." Chloe attempted to say this airily, but the words hit the professionally distressed wood floor like six lumps of lead.

Gigi arched a brow. "You, a woman who has not driven voluntarily since 2003—"

"Slight exaggeration, Gigi."

"—were moved to get into your car, tootle out of your beloved, filthy, gray city—"

"I got a taxi for the safety of the public, actually."

"—and scurry through the house like a sneaky little mouse to avoid your parents and Eve—"

"I did *not,*" Chloe lied hotly.

"—because you felt the urge to *pop by*?" Gigi pursed glossy lips. When had they become glossy? Had she just applied makeup by psychic command? "Darling, as the children say, don't bullshit me."

"Ah," Chloe muttered, "my loving grandmother."

"Your impatient grandmother who wants her smoothie and her Shivani. I know how you get, Chloe, my love. Save us both the trouble and spit it out."

Perhaps those words were a spell rather than a suggestion, because they worked. Words tumbled from Chloe's lips before she could overthink them, convince herself to keep them inside, or even arrange them into something deceptively dry and apparently unimportant. "When you love someone, Gigi— someone who doesn't *have* to love you back—and they might hurt you, and you might hurt them, and anything could go wrong, and it already has, how do you know that it's, erm . . ."

"Real?" Gigi suggested. But, disturbingly, Chloe had no questions on that count. It hadn't even occurred to her to ask.

Her question was far more difficult. "How do you know that it's safe? How do you know that it's worth the risk?" *Please tell me it never is. Please tell me that I did the right thing. Please tell me I didn't abandon Red right back and that we're better off apart.*

No. Please don't.

Gigi regarded her for a long moment with those beautiful, maddening eyes, framed by smile lines that proved what Chloe already knew: despite her habit of telling her grandchildren not to frown, laugh, or otherwise emote for fear of wrinkles, Gigi had never let anything stop her from living life to the fullest.

Finally, the older woman said, "You've asked me two very different questions in one go, Chloe, and I hope you don't think they're at all the same. Love is certainly never safe, but it's absolutely worth it." She produced an unlit cigarette and twirled it between long, elegant fingers. Since Gigi wasn't wearing a head scarf this afternoon, her chic crop of white coils on display, Chloe had absolutely no idea where the Marlboro had been hidden. Her knickers? Up one nostril? In an alternate dimension she accessed at will? God only knew.

After a moment, Gigi spoke again. "I fell in love at sixteen with a scoundrel of a man who impregnated and abandoned me, which of course led to my parents kicking me out of the house because I'd set a poor example for my sisters. My caring for your—well, for your grandfather, I suppose—didn't do anything to fix the fact that he was a pathetic, nasty little man who wasn't worthy of the love I gave him. And his many flaws, unfortunately, didn't stop me from adoring him. After all, when it comes to love, it's not a person's flaws we're looking at, now is it?" She smiled wryly, but Chloe couldn't quite bring herself to smile back. "Love isn't safe, as that story proves. But is it worth it?" Gigi raised her arms in a typically grand gesture, and Chloe knew she wasn't indicating the mansion they currently sat in, so different from the tiny family home Gigi had been kicked out of, but the people who lived inside it. "I have your father. I have you girls. And, of course, I have my top-ten hit, 'Hey, Mr. Dick Junior,' which, if any lawyers or journalists happen to come sniffing around, has what, darling?"

"Absolutely nothing to do with one Richard F. Jameson, whom my poor, dear grandmother has never even heard of," Chloe recited obediently. "But, Gigi, I . . . Well, you might as well know that I'm talking about Red."

"Gasp," Gigi murmured.

Chloe glowered. "I suppose I've fallen in love with him," she said, which was the least embarrassing way she could phrase *I love Redford Morgan like a man-eating tiger loves soft and fleshy upper arms.* "And I think he might . . ." She cleared her throat and straightened her spine, accepting what she should've known from the start. From the moment he'd called her name through the door. "He loves me, too," Chloe said. Because she felt in her bones that it was true. "But we hurt each other, and now I feel trapped in this endless hesitation because, well—what if we keep doing it? What if we keep making messes? I've always felt like I'm the kind of person who . . ." She smiled, even though it wasn't funny. "I'm the kind of person who hurts. Too much."

"No," Gigi corrected calmly. "You are a woman who, in a life filled with pain, came here to ask about love."

Those words hit Chloe like a perfect, chiming chord, the kind that reverberated through her very soul. They were true in a way that spoke to her. True in a way that made her take another look at herself. "Yes," she murmured slowly. "I suppose I am."

Who else was she? Red always called her tough. He called her a badass. She agreed, because, physically, she was. But emotionally? She'd always been so afraid. And yet . . .

She was the woman who'd come here to ask about love.

She was the woman who'd decided to change her entire life with nothing but a list.

She was the woman who survived, every single day.

She was Chloe fucking Brown, and she was starting to wonder if she'd been brave from the beginning. If she'd just needed to love herself enough to realize it.

She supposed, as the knowledge dawned in her like a sunrise, that she must love herself right now. And it felt good.

She went home and opened the notebook.

It had been on her coffee table, shiny and golden, comforting and terrifying, for almost a week now. She grabbed her fake Smudge for moral support, then briefly wondered if she should call Annie for *real* moral support. But no—Annie was horrible at answering her phone, and while she would call back eventually, Chloe needed to do this now.

She needed *him*. And he, she rather thought, needed her. Time to find out.

She opened the book. His handwriting was careful not-quite-chaos, so very Red that she ran fond fingers over the letters. Then she told herself sternly to stop mooning and read.

Dear Chloe,

You might have heard that I'm quitting my job. That probably seems like I'm leaving you, but I'm not. I gave notice the day before our camping trip because being with you and being your superintendent seemed like a bad idea. This job was safe for me, but I want you more than I want that safety. And anyway, partly because of you, I don't think I need that safety anymore.

You've done a lot for me, and the fact that all I've done

in return is hurt you . . . well, it makes me feel like shit on a basic level, but then I feel *extra* shit, because oh my God, Chloe, I love you so fucking bad. I've been wondering if I should say it like this, after what happened. But this might be the only chance I get, and I need you to know because it's the truest thing about me. Chloe Sophia Brown, I am so in love with you. And I want to prove it, because that's what you deserve. I want you to trust me again. I want to make you smile until you forget how it feels to cry. I want you to know I'm not going anywhere.

And, since you're the expert planner, I decided to take a leaf out of your book. I made a list.

GET CHLOE BACK

1. Lure her with food and presents.

2. Wait outside Annie's house; nick Smudge.

3. Learn how to use a PlayStation. ✓

4. Paint in front of windows, shirtless. Maybe naked. Might traumatize residents/get arrested, but I think she'd like it.

5. Take charge of all buttons so she can wear real cardigans if she wants to.

6. Use my bloody Instagram account. ✓

7. Continue therapy. ✓

8. Love her, always, no matter what. ✓

I already started on some. I'm hoping if I work through the list, eventually I'll get you back. If it's all wrong or you want something else or you have this burning desire to tell me what a dick I am, feel free. Call me. Come over. Open your curtains and give me the bird. Please. I miss you.

We can do this. If you don't trust me on that, trust yourself. Because you must know you can do anything you set your mind to.

Yours,

Red

Chloe read the letter three times. Only when one of her tears plopped onto the page, drowning the *d* at the end of his name, did she rip herself away from the words. She looked up at her curtains, drawn tight as a shield, and her eyes narrowed. Bright, glittering power surged through her, and for the first time in a while, she felt alive. Impatient. Determined. *Demanding.* She stalked over, ripped them open, and winter darkness appeared before her.

Winter darkness and a stubborn square of light.

A familiar figure stood behind the window across the

courtyard, his sunset hair hanging over his face, his chest bare to reveal corded muscle, bold ink, vulnerable skin, and vitality. He was bent over a canvas, as always, but a second after she opened the curtains, he stilled. Then slowly, slowly, turned.

She didn't hide.

The distance between them made it difficult to see that feline, springtime gaze, but she felt the moment their eyes met. An electrifying shiver rushed through her body. He faced the window fully, put his hand against the glass, and she had the oddest feeling that this was one of those moments in life that could amount to everything or nothing. Could be a transformation or a regret. This was the sort of moment that reckless, exciting women experienced—

No. No. This was the sort of moment *she* experienced, lists, worries, razor-sharp shyness and all. Bravery wasn't an identity so much as a choice.

She chose him.

CHAPTER TWENTY-THREE

Red used to think that fucking up was his specialty—but after fucking up with Chloe, he hadn't let himself think that anymore. Because if it was true, he'd lost her forever. And if he'd lost her forever . . .

No. Not an option.

So Red had decided that his new specialty was fixing things. After all, he'd known from the moment love hit him like a truck that he couldn't shove it at her and hope for the best. He'd known she'd need more, that he'd have to make her understand everything in his heart, that he'd have to give her a reason to trust him. And so, he formulated his plan and he wrote his list. Then, since he'd handed in his notice to Vik and time was flying, he'd pulled himself together and gotten down to business.

Not just with Chloe. With everything.

Every morning he woke up, checked his window, and found her curtains shut tight. He let himself sit with sick, acidic fear for a few moments, breathing deep, wanting her, missing her. And then he got his shit together. He planned for next month, when he'd be leaving this building behind and plunging headfirst into the unknown again. He studied his savings in spreadsheets that would give Chloe a hard-on, checking and double-checking that he could afford the risk. He researched his business, reached out to old friends, and figured out his new website by reading Chloe's instructions, even if hearing her voice through the words twisted his heart.

He was going to be okay. He knew that. But he'd be so much better with Chloe. Only, the days passed, and her curtains remained closed, and each morning he lost a little bit of hope.

Or maybe a lot of hope. So much that when she did open the curtains—when he caught that flutter of movement and spill of light from the corner of his eye—he thought for a moment he was imagining things.

But then he turned, and he saw her, and he knew that not even his desperate memories could recreate that heavy, midnight gaze.

Red stared and stared and stared. Drank her in. Started to worry about his Grand Prix–worthy pulse and his painfully pounding heart. He might be dying of fucking euphoria at the sight of her. That might just be okay.

Then she was gone in a flash of turquoise glasses and a swirl of her pink-and-white skirt. He felt like he'd been knocked over the head. Stood there, transfixed, with his paintbrush in his hand, blue acrylic threatening to drip onto the floor, and thought, *Chloe, Chloe, Chloe* like a broken record . . . until a knock came at the door.

He'd heard that knock once in his entire life, but he knew

exactly who it belonged to. He dropped the paintbrush. Ran through the flat. Yanked the door open and there she was.

Chloe Brown. Beautiful with her hard stare and her hair contained by the polka-dot hair tie he'd bought her, and yes, he was looking that hard, and no, he would not stop. She sailed past him into the flat, and he forced his hands behind his back because dragging her into his arms and kissing the living daylights out of her would be *bad,* it would be very bloody *bad*—

"Here," she said, holding something out to him. Her voice was husky fucking music. He wanted to eat it. He could put his mouth over hers and—wait, no, that was just kissing. No kissing. Not when she might be here to give him a chance.

He took the thing she held—a notebook—his palms sweating and hope swelling. "Chloe."

"Red," she said softly. "Read that for me."

Heart in his mouth, he obeyed. He already knew what he'd find: Chloe's list. The real one, full and uncensored. He took a breath and finally read the goals that had started all this.

The list was so neat and orderly and utterly her. Every goal was printed carefully in black ink, painstakingly perfect. Some of the entries he recognized, others he didn't. Some were ticked off, some crossed out and replaced, all with so much care. His heart twisted. Why had he ever assumed that a spot on this list meant the worst? He should've known—he *had* known—that this was her path to the person she wanted to be.

Except he'd never really accepted that fact, because to him, she was already perfect.

He had the strongest fucking urge to throw this book across the room before he could find his own entry, except that would be a mistake, and he'd made enough of those already. He forced himself to look for his own name. Found it.

Keep Red.

He put the book down and looked at her. He wanted to say something. The right thing. He'd never managed it before, so he doubted he would now—but he tried. "I was wrong. I know I was wrong. I—"

"I read your letter," she interrupted.

She'd only just read it? Was that good or bad? She seemed edgy, nervous, her soft lips pressed tight, those hypnotic eyes avoiding his. Suddenly the room seemed darker and the moment took on all the dread and finality of a grave. She didn't want him. He'd failed. He'd lost her, really lost her.

But then she said, in a tone he couldn't decipher, "I liked my presents."

He laughed brokenly and ran a hand through his hair. Tried to make his fear a joke, because she wouldn't appreciate him scattering the pieces of his broken heart over her like confetti. "Chloe. Baby. Just—put me out of my misery."

She looked at him, finally, and he sucked in a breath. Couldn't help it. God, she was so beautiful. God, she made his head spin. She frowned slightly, shook her head, rolled her eyes. Then she said, "All right."

And kissed him.

He stumbled back into the wall, and she followed. Her hands

slid into his hair and her body pressed tight against his, but her lips were petal soft. Searching. Tentative. As if she wasn't sure how he'd react.

As it happened, he reacted like a starving animal.

He couldn't silence the groan her touch teased from him, couldn't stop himself from shaking, not when his blood surged with the knowledge that this was actually happening. His lips parted hers hungrily, and when she glided her tongue over his he gave a wounded, desperate growl that must've told her everything she could think to ask. *I need you. I'm desperate for you. I'm something without you, and I'll survive without you, but I don't fucking want to, so Jesus, please don't make me.*

He dropped the notebook. His hands went to her waist, then her hips, then the row of buttons sewn down the front of her jumper. Her hair next, smoothed-out ripples under his fingers, then the gentle curve of her throat, and then her face. Everywhere, he was everywhere. Wasn't enough.

She pulled back and panted, "I'm sorry."

Carefully, he took off her glasses. Now she was young and vulnerable, giving him that soft focus. "For what, love?"

"For letting you go, and for how long it took me to come here. I should've been braver. Like you."

"No," he said firmly, fiercely. "You're exactly as brave as you need to be. You're the one who makes me better. You're the bravest person I know."

She grabbed the front of his T-shirt, dragged him close, kissed him again.

It was slower, this time, not as urgent. Talking touches. The sweet pressure of her mouth on his: *I want you.* The way she smoothed her hands over his chest: *I missed you.* And when he laced their fingers together? Puzzle pieces slotted into place. *I'm yours.* His world was marshmallow pink, electric white, chocolate and earth and tropical ocean. His world was good.

She pulled back again, and everything seemed slightly paler. "We should talk properly."

Oh, yeah. Like rational, adult human beings. "Or we could kiss until we run out of oxygen."

She smiled and his heart broke and fixed itself.

"I mean it," he said. "If I die, I die."

She laughed and the air tasted different. Clean.

"Come on," she said, marching toward his studio, but she didn't let go of his hand. Not until she sat down, leaning against a rare part of the wall that didn't have supplies stacked against it.

Red sat opposite her and tried not to melt over the prim way she crossed her legs and arranged her skirt over her knees. But then his smile faded. "Chloe, I'm sorry. I freaked out, I took my own shit out on you, and I just—I shouldn't have. But you read the list, and you know I'm working on it, and I hope . . . Well, I hope that's enough."

Softly, she told him, "It is. Red—"

"Oh, wait. I forgot something." He found her hand again, held on tight. "I love you."

The corners of those lush lips tilted ever so slightly before she got them under control. He wondered how he'd ever thought of her as reserved—or, you know, up her own arse—when he could see every single emotion she tried to hide under that mask if he just looked hard enough. And right now, he realized with a grin, happiness was shining right through her severe facade. She might as well have shoved the sun under a pillow. He could see every last golden ray burning through.

But what she said was "We'll address that in a minute."

Red told himself this was too serious a moment to risk laughing.

"Right now," she said, "I need to apologize to you, too. I'm so fucking sorry, Red. I know everything about that situation triggered you. I knew it at the time. But I didn't know the right way to react, and I should've."

"No, Chlo," he said softly. "That's not on you."

"No, it's not," she agreed. "But remember what you told me once? About filling in people's gaps? You do things for me when I can't do them for myself. I want to support you in the same way. Can we work on that? Together?"

She was so fucking lovely. So lovely, and she wanted him. He closed his eyes and nodded slowly. His voice came out like gravel. "Yeah, love. We can do that."

"Good. Because you mean the world to me and I don't ever want you to struggle alone." Her words were a balm to everything in him that ached or stung or bled. Their fingers laced together so tightly he hoped they'd never come undone.

"You," he told her quietly, "are everything."

Dry as a bone, she murmured, "Flatterer."

He smiled and felt it down to his soul.

"That day," she said softly, and his smile faded. "That day, neither of us gave the other a chance. You reacted badly to an admittedly confusing situation, and then I reacted badly to you reacting badly. I wish I'd been more understanding. But I was trying to protect myself—trying to avoid taking a risk, because the truth is, you scare me. You're monumental. Avoiding everything between us seemed easier than facing pain. But I refuse to be afraid anymore, Red. You're more important than that."

Hope and relief and this impossible, incandescent happiness swirled in his chest, as if his emotions were mixing to create the perfect color for this moment. Something beautiful and brilliant and Chloe, like those cute blue glasses or warm brown eyes. "Maybe we should solemnly swear that in the future we'll both keep our heads out of our arses."

"Maybe we should," she said with a slow smile.

"All right. I swear."

"I swear."

She held out her little finger, and he grinned. "What am I supposed to do with that?"

"Give me yours," she said sternly. He did, and she hooked hers around his and said, "Now it's official. We pinkie-swore."

He snorted. Pulled her closer because he couldn't resist. Her breath hitched as she leaned forward, her cheek brushing his. Just that slight contact sent a shower of almost-unbearable pleasure through him. He whispered in her ear, "We okay?"

"We are," she said softly.

Something jagged and broken inside him smoothed out, slotting back into place so firmly that he felt like he should've heard the *click*. This was where and who and how he should be: with Chloe.

He stood, pulling her up with him. And then, because he was in that kind of mood, he picked her up. She gave a little squeak of surprise as he cradled her against his chest, squeezing her to him, breathing in flowers and vanilla. Everything wrong with his world righted itself. "Just so you know, you aren't ever getting rid of me. You're it, and I'm fucked. I'm completely fucked."

She laughed, running a hand through his hair. The action was unthinkingly possessive. He closed his eyes for a moment on a wave of satisfaction.

"That's good to know," she said. "Where are we going, by the way?"

"My room. Since we're officially okay, there's no reason why you can't sit somewhere comfortable instead of the floor."

"Fair enough. We'll just sit, though. That's all."

"Oh, yeah. That's all."

It was, too, at first. She asked him a thousand questions about his plans, and nodded approvingly at his answers. He showed her the social media accounts he'd set up, and she told him why all his captions sucked and how to find decent hashtags.

And that was absolutely all.

But then Chloe got tired, so they lay down. And then she kissed him, and his brain malfunctioned, and the next thing he knew he was on top of her, holding her hands and licking into her mouth while she moaned.

And then, in the middle of it all, she gasped, "Oh, I almost forgot! Our shelved topic."

"What?" he growled, dragging his lips down her throat.

"The fact that you love me."

He stilled.

"It's very sweet, of course," she said, in a voice so innocent he just *knew.*

"Chloe."

"And highly flattering, particularly coming from someone as wonderful as you—"

"*Chloe.*"

"What? It's rude to interrupt, you know."

He grinned down at her. "Stop torturing me. Just say it."

"Say what?"

"Woman—"

"I love you, Red. I love you, I love you, I—*mmpf!*" She broke off with a squeak when he kissed her, hard.

Those three little words sounded so fucking good, but they tasted even better on her lips.

EPILOGUE

One Year Later

Chloe, you awful cow, it's about time you—oh, hello there, Red." Eve, as always, was on her best behavior the moment she saw Red's face on her phone screen.

Chloe didn't bother to hide her eye roll. "Yes, hello, dearest sister. I thought I'd check in before we got on with our day."

"That's not true," Red said helpfully, raising his voice over the sounds of traffic and the clatter of hundreds of footsteps that were part and parcel of a busy New York street. "I made her do it."

Chloe trod on his foot. He gave her an unapologetic grin.

"Honestly, Red, thank God you're with her," Eve tutted. "I bet you've already called your mum today. Like a *good* child." She glared pointedly at Chloe, then turned away from the camera and hollered, "EVERYONE! CHLOE'S ON THE PHONE!"

And, wouldn't you know it, the entire family happened to be at home. Just Chloe's luck. Dani appeared first—shouldn't she

be in a library somewhere, starving in the name of academia?—
followed by Dad, who was still wearing his coat as always, like
he might fly off somewhere any minute. Then came Mum—oh,
no, that was Aunt Mary without makeup. Mum was next, her
smile uncharacteristically broad. She liked Red, thought he was
a *lovely boy,* which was code for "strong enough to protect my
darling daughter if she insists on gallivanting about the world."

Chloe did indeed insist.

And then, finally, Gigi appeared, shoving everyone else out of
the way until her face took up almost the entire screen. Gigi still
hadn't quite grasped the finer points of a video call, so she liked
to make absolutely certain that her brilliance could be seen. She
beamed and held up a wriggling, protesting Smudge.

Yes, they had Smudge. When Chloe and Red moved into a flat
that allowed pets, Annie had provided a most welcome house-
warming gift.

"Darling," Gigi purred, "are you having the *absolute* time of
your life?"

"Perhaps," Chloe said with a private smile.

Down where her family couldn't see, Red's gloved hand
squeezed hers.

"Smudge misses you awfully. Don't you, Smudge?"

Smudge looked, at best, apathetic.

"I miss him, too," Chloe said.

New York in winter was absolutely freezing. For that reason,
despite missing her family a little bit, Chloe hurried through
the call. She'd text them all later, she assured them, and yes, she
was feeling fine, and New York was indeed exciting, but no, she

wouldn't compare it to Kenya or Belgium or Cuba because they were all just so different and all equally amazing.

Which was a lie, of course. Cuba had been her favorite. But she and Red weren't done jet-setting.

Then, finally, the last of her relatives said good-bye, and she put the phone down and turned to Red. "Sorry. I should've known that would take forever."

"It's fine, Chlo."

"It's not. I was practically teasing you." She glanced at the glass entrance behind them to the Museum of Modern Art, then back at Red. He was almost bursting with excitement. The cold had turned the tip of his nose and his high cheekbones pale pink. His green eyes were bright, like a spark of midsummer in the middle of winter. He was so, so divine. She didn't know how he could be real. "I know you're dying to go in. Shall we?"

"Oh, yeah. But first . . ." He brought his hand to her cheek, and she didn't even mind that his glove was cold and a little wet from the softly falling snow. "Let me see if I can find anything to kiss under all these layers."

Maybe she'd gone slightly overboard with the scarves—two— and the hats—again, two—but it was *cold*.

"You want to kiss me now?" she squawked as he nudged aside the wool protecting her skin from the harsh wind. "At this very minute?"

"I want to kiss you every minute of the day," he murmured, his eyes suddenly serious. "And I want to kiss you in every city on earth." Then, as her heart overflowed with sickening amounts of love, his lips brushed hers. Quick, light, and still so wonderful that her knees felt the tiniest bit weak.

He pulled back and took his time nudging her scarves in place, even though they wouldn't be out here for much longer. Biting back a smile, she said, "Now, shall we go in?"

"Are you feeling okay? You're not tired from the walk, are you?"

"Not yet." Well, only a little bit.

He was practically vibrating with his eagerness to go inside, but still, he held off to check on her. "Buprenorphine still going strong?"

"I am high as a kite, my love." She tried not to use her opioid patches all the time, but a trip to New York definitely required them.

"Good," he said, clearly pleased to know his girlfriend was appropriately drugged. And then, after a long exhale, he grinned. "In we go, then."

"Full speed ahead. Try not to wet yourself with excitement, you big nerd."

He shot her a quelling look as they stepped into the museum. "Chloe. Please. This is a classy establishment."

"Sorry. I can't be tamed."

With a wry smile, he said seriously, "I know."

ABOUT THE AUTHOR

TALIA HIBBERT is a Black British author who lives in a bedroom full of books. Supposedly, there is a world beyond that room, but she has yet to drum up enough interest to investigate. She writes sexy, diverse romances because she believes that people of marginalized identities need honest and positive representation. Her interests include beauty, junk food, and unnecessary sarcasm.